GLAXSYA

By
P. D. York

For Lauren
The big sister I never had… but was glad to

And Ruth
My Key West Grandma

ISBN: 978-1-7348706-0-2 (E-Book)

ISBN: 978-1-7348706-1-9 (Paperback)

Front cover art by Tobias Phelps

Edited by Barbara York

Creative Notes by Jeffery Swope

DISCLAIMER: Glaxsya is a fictional story. All characters, names, likenesses and events that parallel real life persons and events is purely coincidental.

This story is told from the perspective of three different characters. They are indicated by the following (applies to color print only):

Nathan's perspective is this color

Donna's perspective is this color

Keller's perspective is this color

In the year 2219...

Chapter One: "Just Another Day"

(*Nathan*)"Nate. Get up, you're on next watch," I hear in a half dazed state almost as if it's coming from afar.

I realize quickly that I've been dreaming. Peering out of my rack I see my supervisor.

"Shit, did I sleep in again?" I ask.

My supervisor responds, "No, J'Bell contracted Low-Grav sickness, again. You'll have to take his watch for now, but I'll see to it you get cut from the work day."

Yep. Just another day aboard the Ex Dell Seven. My name is Nathan McNill. I'm one of five navigators aboard a mining freighter. I say five as my supervisor has had to fill other roles on board since we're shorthanded, and as one of the more junior crewmen of course I get to supplement anyone who can't stand their watch.

Being on a mining freighter isn't the most glamorous line of work and certainly wasn't my first choice in careers, but when your first choice doesn't quite work out, well... you take what you can.

I get out of my rack, still half asleep. Put on my somewhat dirty pants, a clean shirt and strap on my boots. Passing through the mess hall I try to get some coffee. After my cup fills about half way the coffee tank stops pouring. Empty. Go figure. Since I don't have the time to brew a fresh pot I just accept this minor setback and head toward the front of the ship where the bridge is located.

Upon my arrival, I'm greeted by my irritated co-worker, "Took you long enough."

"Dude... shut up," I reply, unable to formulate a better response. "What's going on?" I ask.

My co-worker begins, "We're slow cruising our way to grid 7XRG." He begins manipulating the holo-display which shows our ship's position and the target area as well as the projected course I'm expected to stay on; a specific track which transits along just outside the asteroid field itself.

My co-worker continues, "Captain thinks we'll find a more rich deposit of Osmium there. So keep the ship at a safe distance as we transit."

I nod in acknowledgement. My co-worker finishes, "If anything happens, bother someone else. I'm tired and had to stay up longer than I wanted to."

He leaves through the same door I came in. My co-worker, Nicklo Banner, irritates me most especially. I swear, only he can do right. If someone is so much as thirty seconds late, the entire universe is about to collapse.

Enough about him. I have the bridge all to myself for the next few hours. Even though I've been promised rack time after my shift, I doubt I'll get it. Hopefully there will be more coffee to get me through.

At this point, you're probably wondering more about who we are and where we're at. As I said, we're a mining freighter. We mine rocks for minerals, specifically Iridium and Osmium. As we process those minerals we determine whether we have enough in our hold to return to a processing center or if we can stay out and mine for more.

Most often, we end up staying out longer than we should. So many times the ship's cooks have had to bust out the ration paste, but they're both good people. They've been able to make the most shitty of meals seem like home cooking. The secret of course is in the spices they use. On a ship of about seventy, I'd say they do a pretty decent job of keeping us fed. I anticipate that this particular stretch will result in us staying out longer. You see, our Captain likes to overload our stores. The more we're able to bring in, though, the more we get paid so it's a double edged sword.

Double checking the attitude thruster, I realize there's a slight discrepancy in our auto-pilot.

I call back to the engine room using the direct-line COMM by pressing a button on the navigation console, "This is the bridge, Engineer, what's the status of our attitude thruster?"

"**Nathan?**" A voice I recognize asks, "**I didn't know you were on this watch.**"

Tim M'Nar. Maybe this watch won't be so bad after all.

I reply, "Yeah I'm surprised to be on this watch too. Tim, what's the deal with the attitude thruster?"

Tim replies, "**Nothing to worry about, buddy. She's just overdue for a tune-up. You'll have to keep an eye on our course, but she shouldn't drift off too much.**"

As I said, just another day. Captain often runs this ship into the ground every time we go out and as always takes the bare minimum amount of time in port to fix problems. Thankfully, Tim is a skilled mechanic. It's almost as if the man speaks to the ship. One of the things I admire about him is his simplistic nature. The entire vessel could be on fire and he'd still be happily doing his job.

I make the necessary adjustments to correct the discrepancy. Scrolling through the auto-pilot options, I come across something I haven't really seen or messed with: a variable course compensator. Scrolling through the options, I specifically come across "attitude thruster compensation."

I take note of our current course and after a couple of minutes I look again. We appear to be off by only a couple meters, specifically on the Z-Axis. In space you have three axis of navigation... well, some could argue nine, but the agreed standard is three: Y for forward and backward, X for port and starboard and Z for up and down.

Back in the auto-pilot compensator I enter "-2 Z". Maybe that'll fix the problem. Would have been nice to know, but God's gift to the Ex Del Seven Nicklo obviously told me all I needed to.

It's still an adjustment phase for me, even though it's been almost two years since my discharge. I originally enlisted in the Guardian Armada, one of the branches of the

United Constellation Republic's Stellar military forces. The Stellar Navy didn't appeal to me very much. Seemed rather large and that life didn't seem all that appealing. The Marines and Army also seemed like it would be much of the same: pretending to fight battles for an enemy that may exist or not.

Ever since humanity finally made it to space, we've mostly expanded our economy into the stars. As far as we know, no other known sentient species like us exist.

I almost went into the Stellar Exploration Division. Looking back I wish I had applied a second time instead of settling for the Armada. It didn't seem like settling at the time, but the whole life saving side of things isn't the main mission. At least it didn't feel as important as enforcement of Mining Guild Regulations and vessel safety standards. I suppose in the vacuum of space it's a lot harder to save people since you can't exactly free float in the Big Empty without a suit and at least a day's supply of oxygen. And decompression can be almost instantaneous.

As for my discharge, I would sum it up to a disagreement between myself and the military, but obviously it was more complicated than that. I'm sorry, but that subject leaves a sour taste in my mouth.

After checking my course once again, sure enough the compensator protocols worked. The autopilot managed to compensate for the attitude thruster.

There's some dispute as to historically what had happened. Some say we finally achieved space exploration when we started mining for minerals beyond Earth. Others argue that we achieved peace after some big war. A lot of the historical record of the mid twenty-first century was lost and what bits were recovered don't tell much except that humanity was more divided than ever. It's actually amazing that we got to the stars as quickly as we did since in 2115 our civilization was similar to a period known as the 1600s. Now in 2219 we're sailing the stars. It actually makes sense, the technology was already there, we just had to re-teach ourselves and once we agreed to come together and travel the stars, we finally had peace.

Peace… such a relative concept. You would think once we got passed all the religious extremism and greed, that everything was all fine; that if there's no opposing force, then why would we need a military? Unfortunately, stellar piracy is a thing. And as we very quickly branched out to colonize worlds beyond the Sol System, some planets had no interest in remaining in the Republic and wanted to remain independent. The corporations, of course, couldn't allow this and to keep everyone "united" they strong-armed use of the military to incentivize people to remain under one rule. At the time the solution made sense. However as anti-imperialism popularity grew, it gave rise to the current ruling party, the Unitians, who sought a more peaceful and less forceful resolution. Or so it seemed.

Yes, in a half awake, half-coffee-filled state, these are the things I think about.

The Traverse Drive changed everything. Even in its infancy we could reach worlds in mere weeks instead of decades. Our encouraged expansion brought about a wave of human fertility that we had never seen, but needed. Growing children in vats also encouraged people to reproduce with no hardship of pregnancy. Instead, people had the option to send in their samples and nine months later they welcomed their child. I, myself, was grown in a vat.

As my watch comes towards its final hour, the Captain comes in.

"Good morning," I say.

He looks over at me, half nods and grunts.

At his chair he looks over the night log which I updated with my correction to the autopilot system.

"Are we still on course?" he asks.

I nod and activate the holo-projector displaying our

ship on course.

"Haven't had to make an adjustment since I applied the compensation to the autopilot."

"What?" My captain asks, obviously having just awakened. The crusty old man is obviously used to more rudimentary systems. He's been a miner since the dawn of time, or so we and the crew often joke amongst us. My point being, it took some convincing to let him allow only one navigator on the bridge at a time. He was used to older systems that always failed despite being infallible.

I explained to him the adjustments I made and how the system works. Unsure if anything I said made sense I ask, "Do you understand?"

The captain nods, "Just keep an eye on it. I don't wanna drift into anything."

He then leaves the bridge.

Within the next hour, the bridge starts to come to life with the hustle and bustle of asteroid navigating. It's no simple task. Two people have to sit up in what we call the "eye" a small, transparent bubble just above the bridge that extends out a few meters to give full view of the ship. Basically all they do is keep a lookout for potential threats and with control of the ship's repulse array, they stave off any smaller objects that could potentially damage the ship as well as recommend course corrections to the navigator to avoid bigger objects the repulse array can't handle.

My supervisor, acting as the mining foreman, comes up to me.

"Yeah so about that sleep I promised you…" he begins

I reply with a disgruntled look.

He continues, "J'Bell is still under the weather and with Nicklo having taken the night shift, you're going to have to stay on as navigator until he gets up."

I nod, noticeably irritated. Lack of sleep on the job has never hindered my ability to do my job, however that doesn't mean I enjoy working under such conditions.

The captain comes in along with one of the other navigators, Slobin who sits down at the helm console. The two lookouts report they are ready to enter the asteroid field. My supervisor, the foreman, comes in and briefs the captain.

"Good morning, Captain," he begins, "our mining plan for today consists of entering the asteroid field here," he points on the holo-projection, "More detailed scans indicate we'll strike a rich deposit of Osmium within two hours. I recommend we maintain a safe distance while we drill until we hit the deposit. We'll have to remain at asteroid navigation stations for approximately four to five hours to extract the minerals."

The captain nods, "very well."

Thankfully I SHOULD only have to participate in part of this operation.

The captain orders, "Helm, take us in. Do not go above thruster level 4. Navigate around objects at your discretion and take recommendations from the Navigator. Foreman, advise me once we've started the drilling. I'll be in my room."

The captain gets up and leaves. In a series of organized chaos, the helmsman begins to state his actions to myself and the foreman. Standard protocol for the blackbox.

Over the ship's PA system the foreman announces, "Now on board Ex Del Seven, all hands set your mining stations. Drill team, stand by to receive drilling coordinates and advise when drill is hot. Extraction Claw team stand by for extraction of minerals. Let's dig up our paychecks, boys."

Bleh. I swear if I'm ever promoted to mining foreman I'll never end with some stupid remark. I put on my headset so I can hear if the lookouts spot anything large. As we enter the field towards our destination, chatter lights up the open COMM. The lookouts point out larger asteroids, but they don't appear to be of any threat to us. Finally one spots something.

"Helmsman," I say, "Lookouts sight a large object bearing 310 by 345 from the ship. Recommend we adjust course by 30XG +15Z."

That navigational jargon I just rattled off basically recommended the ship turn right thirty degrees and shift up fifteen meters.

"Noted, thank you," the helmsman replies.

This goes on for a good thirty minutes. We finally approach our destination and remain off station a good 5 kilometers. At this point our plan is to enter a geo-sync course to keep the drill pointed at our target as the asteroid continues its natural drift.

As soon as we set our course the helmsman notifies the Foreman who then goes over the PA, "Drilling team, lock target on the designated asteroid and commence drilling operations."

On a display monitor near my console, I watch as the laser fires off. The noise is a loud hum and rattles the ship. Continuing the operation requires us to maintain our navigation stations so as to keep accuracy of our drilling operations.

One of the cooks, Devon Michaelson comes in with food for the three of us.

"How's it goin, gentleman?" he asks in an upbeat tone.

"Same shit, Devon," I reply, "what's on the menu for today?"

Devon smiles and answers, "Turkey clubs. Figured I'd keep it simple since you're all still working on the bridge."

The Foreman reminds, "You know the Captain doesn't like food on the bridge."

Devon chuckles, "Well if there's an issue, have him

talk to me. Enjoy and don't work too hard."

After leaving a plate for everyone, Devon exits the bridge. Looking at the clock, I realize Nicklo should be up by now- hell should be relieving me.

"Supervisor," I say.

"What?" He responds.

"My relief should have been here by now. I've been up here since mid-morning after only sleeping a couple hours."

"Tired?" he asks.

"Very much so," I reply.

My supervisor nods, "He's probably eating in the mess hall, you know, where people are supposed to eat. I'm sure he'll be here soon."

Almost a half an hour later, Nicklo finally comes onto the bridge.

The lack of sleep gets the best of me, "Gee, took you long enough," I say reiterating his bullshit statement from earlier.

"I was up late. I get to sleep in late," he says.

"Dude, we're shorthanded on navigators," I begin, "I had to cover J'Bell's shift, I'm tired!"

Nicklo begins, "You're not the only one entitled to sleep on this ship. I'll show up when I feel like it. How about I-

Our Supervisor interrupts, "Hey! Knock that shit off, both of you. We're in the middle of mining operations."

I look over at my supervisor/foreman and then back at Nicklo. I give him a quick rundown of what's going on.

"Are we on autopilot?" he asks.

"No. Slobin has the helm," I answer.

"How long is this going to take?" he asks

"Ask the foreman," I answer, "now if you don't have any productive questions, I'll be leaving."

Nicklo begins, "Um, I'm not comfortable taking

over-"

"Hey," our supervisor interrupts again, "If you have any questions, ask me. He's fatigued and needs time off. Nate, take all these plates with you."

I gather up everyone's plates that Devon had brought up earlier and make my way back to the mess hall. After dropping off the plates I take note of the drill still humming loudly as I make my way back to my bunk. I can almost feel myself falling asleep as I walk along the decks of the ship.

Finally I get to my room, empty as all the rest of the crew is working. I remove my shirt and pants, climb into bed and sleep for what will hopefully be more than a couple hours...

...The crew quarters on this ship could have been placed in a better location. After only a few hours I awake to the loud clanking and crashing of the processing machinery. Go figure. Looking at the time, I choose to stumble out of my rack in the hopes of finding some grub in the mess hall. I put on the same shirt and pants from earlier.

This is the part of the job I was glad to sleep through. After the drilling was completed, a large claw was deployed to extract the minerals. But now the processing part has begun, where the processing crew sifts through the extracted chunk of rock for Osmium using smaller drills, crushers, hammers and anything else they can use to extract pieces of raw materials without damaging the desired metals.

Coming into the mess hall I see a bowl of corn dogs. I obviously just missed the full-on meal. Grabbing a couple deep fried sticks of goodness, I sit down to enjoy them. I can still hear the rattling and clanking from the processers. I'm obviously not going to get back to sleep any time soon and my watch is once again almost upon me.

After finishing my meal, I decide to go to the bridge to see our status.

"Nathan," Slobin says, "you're early."

I shrug my shoulders, "Processors woke me. Any plans for tomorrow?"

"We extracted a pretty big chunk," Slobin says, "They'll probably be processing for another couple hours before they stop for the evening."

I nod my head, "Just in time for me to start watch."

Out the main viewport I notice we've come out of the asteroid field. Makes sense. We're in the processing phase hence why we headed back out. We'll probably process for the next day or so before seeking another rock to pull from, or grab more from the same rock.

In the distance I notice something approaching.

"What is that?" I ask.

Slobin looks up. Then back at the Navigation Console, "I'm not picking anything up on... wait... scanners are detecting a mass, but no transponder signal."

We could be out of range. We don't always pick up transponder signals right away. As the object starts to get closer I begin to recognize the shape and profile.

I look over at Slobin, "Uh oh... Captain is not going to like this."

Slobin raises a brow.

Over the COMM we hear, "**Mining freighter Ex Del Seven, this is the Constellation Cutter Valkyrie on HAD channel, please respond.**"

Slobin sighs grabbing the COMM mic, "Constellation Cutter Vlakyrie, good evening. How can the Ex Del Seven assist you today?"

"**Ex Del Seven, Valkyrie, am I speaking to the Captain of the vessel?**" they ask.

Slobin replies, "Uh, negative. Captain has retired for the evening. Is there anything you need us to relay to him?"

The Valkyrie comes back, **"We'll need to speak with him directly. We have a series of standard questions that we need him to answer personally."**

I nod, knowing what Slobin is about to ask of me and proceed out of the bridge. Heading one deck below, I come up to the Captain's room and knock.

A few seconds roll by before he opens the door, "Yeah?"

"The Guardian Armada wants to speak with you."

His face becomes irritated as he slams the door shut.

Entering the bridge I say, "He's on his way up. Probably should let them know before they ask again."

Slobin relays to the Valkyrie that the captain is on his way up and they'll be waiting a few minutes.

In a couple minutes the Captain walks over to the navigation console, grabbing the mic from Slobin who steps away.

"What's the ship called?" the Captain asks.

"Valkyrie," I respond.

I myself had served on a Valkyrie Class Constellation Cutter during my time in. The Gondul to be exact. Valkyrie is the first of her class.

The captain says over the COMM, "Valkyrie, this is the Captain of the Mining Freighter Ex Del Seven."

After a couple seconds silence, **"Captain, good morning. Please send your authentication code."**

On the console, the Captain inputs some sort of verification and sends it over via radio-text.

"It's on its way," the Captain says.

After about a minute of silence, **"Verification complete. Alright, sir, first question: we're detecting a higher than normal output of Ion radiation emitting from your exhaust. Are you aware of that?"**

The Captain replies, "Uh, yes. The converter module malfunctioned during our trip. My engineers say it doesn't pose an imminent threat and we have it under control."

"**I see**," the COMM chatters back, "**As you understand this does pose cause for concern and we will have to conduct a standard safety boarding. Are you engaged in any mining at this time?**"

The Captain hesitates for a second, "If I say yes, will you still come on to my ship?"

"**We'll wait here as long as we have to, sir**," the Valkyrie says.

The Captain makes a big long sigh, "No we're not engaged in drilling. We are in the middle of initial processing."

The Valkyrie says, "**Very well. We'll still be able to conduct our boarding. Please prepare your starboard side airlock. Our boarding vessel will be along shortly.**"

The look on the Captain's face was indication enough that this had ruined his day. He had lied about the ion radiation. Instead of getting the converter module fixed during our last dockside, he chose instead to forego it so as not to pay for it later. Of course, more discrepancies are about to be discovered.

Out the viewport I watch as the Valkyrie's boarding craft begins to make its way to our ship. The Valkyrie… an impressive design to say the least. Hell all the ships in the Guardian Armada were well built, but this one resulted in the Guardian Armada being taken more seriously. Unlike the smaller class of ships, these ones were built to intimidate. They are large, almost 230 meters in length. It is like one of the older warships that were once built for sea, long before humanity began traversing the stars, except it was built for space.

It has one primary gun on its bow that rotates on a sphere so it can point in just about any direction. A second large gun is fitted on the top about 20 to 30 feet from the bow. The ship also has several smaller, energy based guns, but overall the ship's armaments were meant for defense, meaning no missiles, nor was it armed like a Destroyer.

Near the aft of the ship are two large wings near the aft of the main hull which extend at a downward diagonal. On the port side secondary hull sits the Traverse Drive Dish, a device which can generate a wormhole for which to travel through. The back half of the hull is a hangar. The Starboard side secondary hull is entirely a hanger.

Where the wings connect to the ship was also referred to as the "superstructure". Half way up to the top of the superstructure are the bridge wings, two wings with the purpose of holding one defense turret each to protect the bridge located at the top of the superstructure.

At the top of the bridge sits the main antenna array and various forms of sensors. Constantly rotating.

On the bottom of the ship, lining up at about the same area as the second main gun, known as the dorsal gun sits the secondary bridge. The purpose of this bridge, besides serving as a secondary should the main bridge become compromised, is also to help land the ship. Yes, these large vessels can actually land planet-side if necessary, provided there was an area large enough.

As I admire the ship, my supervisor taps my shoulder.

"Come with me," he says.

I follow him down the decks to the starboard airlock. Already there are crew clearing out the area. Normally we dock on our Port side, so the starboard airlock inadvertently became a storage closet for miscellaneous items: crew luggage, engineering equipment that's used maybe once in a while and even some burnt out laser drills that were intended to be refurbished.

We get the area clean just in time for the boarding craft to make a successful seal. The door opens and we're greeted by the squadron leader, dressed in tactical gear.

The intimidating armor of the boarding team consists of a dark blue, skin tight fluid metal. I never put one of these on myself during my time. My specific job didn't require it. The entire suit bonds to its user. It is like a metal onesie. Most of the member's armor seemed to be recently polished and buffed out and shined dark blue. Their helmets consist of a similar metal to allow for full movement and have a visor that could deploy if they are in an environment without oxygen.

They also have tactical vests which contain COMM units and their laser pistols. Some of them are armed with larger standard issue K-LL5 laser rifles with extendable butt stocks.

My foreman/supervisor begins, "Uh, welcome to the Ex Del Seven. To what do we owe the pleasure exactly?"

The squad leader replies, "Just a routine boarding. Are you the captain?"

The foreman shakes his head, "No. Captain is waiting on the bridge. I'm the acting Mining Foreman."

"Acting," The squad leader inquires, "where is the licensed foreman?"

My supervisor lies, "Um, he couldn't make this trip due to a family emergency. I'm staying in his stead until he gets back."

"Do you have papers?" the squad leader inquires.

"Er uh, yeah on the bridge I believe," another lie.

Our old foreman got into a disagreement in regards to compensation with the captain and was fired. Of course the effects of this and probably many more discrepancies were about to unravel.

The squad leader states, "It appears our discussion is better continued on the bridge, then. My men will begin their standard sweep. Understand this is a safety boarding and nothing more, however if my men find any other problems or issues, they will be noted. Your men are allowed to observe the inspection; however we ask that you stay clear of whatever my people are looking at. If they are asked to assist with something specific, we ask for full cooperation. Any questions?"

Totally wasn't scripted or something that he obviously hadn't repeated before. My supervisor asks, "Can you possibly say all that again on the ship's PA when we get to the bridge."

"Very well," The squad leader says, then turns to his men, "Secondary, wait here until I give the order to begin the sweep."

"Understood," the secondary squad leader acknowledges.

I follow the squad leader and one other member of the squad as my Supervisor leads them to the bridge.

Upon entering, the squad leader goes up to the captain, "Are you the Captain?" he asks.

The captain nods, "Yeah."

The squad lead offers his hand for a cordial shake. The captain shakes his hand.

The squad leader says, "I have a spiel I need to announce over the ship's PA, with your permission, sir."

The captain nods and points to the mic located at the Navigation console.

The squadron leader grabs the mic and begins, "Good morning crew of the Ex Del Seven. This is the squadron leader of the Guardian Armada boarding team..." He then reiterates almost word for word his initial statement and ends with, "we just ask for your total cooperation and this should be completed quickly and smoothly." He sets the mic back down.

Turning to the Captain he begins, "Captain, I'll need to see-" having already had it in hand the Captain hands his papers in the form of a digital pad, to the squad leader. The boarding officer grabs the pad and begins sifting through them, checking the license, ship registration and Mining Guild Endorsement.

The squad leader says, "Alright, everything appears

to be in order. Now I'll need to see the Foreman's license."

My supervisor goes over to the navigation console and starts looking through the computer.

"Um," he begins, "I can pull up the active one from our last mining foreman."

The other squad member looks over the last one.

The squad leader asks, "How long has your current foreman been away on emergency?"

The captain looks puzzled as my supervisor responds, "Um, he couldn't make this voyage so I've been acting since then."

The other squad member looks up at his squad leader. He moves over and whispers something in his ear.

The squad leader nods and then says, "According to your logs your last stop at a station was over thirty days ago."

"Okay?" the captain says.

The squad leader states, "Your acting foreman here is only valid as acting for thirty days. Does he have a temporary permit?"

My supervisor sifts through the console in vain, "I'm sure it's here somewhere…"

The Captain decides to confess, "He's not off board due to an emergency. We had a disagreement on our last port stop regarding a pay increase. I told him to piss off and he did. My acting foreman said that he would get a temporary permit until we could hire a new foreman."

The squad leader nods condescendingly, "Well… that's a few violations of Guild Law. The primary one being that you've been mining without a valid foreman. That can also constitute several safety violations."

The Captain becomes noticeably irritated. Another boarding squad member enters the bridge. The squad leader acknowledges his presence and then says, "If you'll excuse us for a second."

They both converse in a corner of the bridge out of

earshot of the rest of us. After about a minute or two, the squad leader walks back over to the Captain.

He begins, "Sir, between not having a valid foreman on board as well as an out-of-date engine coil calibrator, I am now authorized to terminate your voyage. I could continue the boarding, but seeing as it could run the risk of incurring more fees, I think we can agree that you need to return to port and fix these major discrepancies."

The captain replies, "We'll start heading to Keldon Colony as soon as we're finished with our processing."

"Sir, I don't think you understand," the squad leader reiterates, "these are serious violations. Not to mention the safety issues regarding your engines. We can either formally terminate your voyage or spare you the potential disavowment from the Mining Guild. Either way, we'll be escorting you to Keldon Station."

"That'll take us at least three weeks," the Captain states, "are you sure you want to follow us for that long?"

The squad leader replies, "I'm going to brief up this situation to our Commanding Officer. Most likely we'll be taking you to Keldon via traverse drive tunnel. Should take maybe half an hour."

The Captain reluctantly nods, "I understand... we'll cease operations for safety concerns."

The squad leader nods to his two team members and begins to speak through his COMM as they leave the bridge, "Boarding squad, this is team leader, cease the boarding and report back to the air..." I don't catch the rest of what he says as he proceeds down the passageway.

I turn to see the Captain glaring at my supervisor. He says, "You fucking told me you had a temporary permit."

My supervisor replies, "Well I uh, I found a solution that would save us some money-"

"Us?" the Captain interrupts, "you mean you! You told me you would pay for a temp permit on your own!"

My supervisor lacks a response as the Captain turns his focus to me, "And you," he begins, "come with me."

Unsure of what I did wrong, I'm obviously a little uneasy right now. As I enter his room he says, "Sit down!"

At his desk there is a comfortable, cushy chair and a not so nice, small folding one on the other side for me. I do as he says. He sits in his chair, noticeably annoyed.

He begins, "You mind telling me how I manage to get my voyage terminated when I have a former member of the Guardian Armada working on my ship?"

"I didn't know about Grael not purchasing a temp permit," I answer candidly referring to my supervisor.

"I meant the other shit. Are you so tunnel visioned that it didn't occur to you to point those things out? Maybe recommend they get fixed?" He inquires.

I can't quite tell if he's serious or looking for an excuse to shift blame. Maybe he's figuring out what to write in an appeal to the Mining Guild, should they find out about any of this. Whatever his reasons, I decide to tell the truth: "When I first showed up, I noticed some things that needed to be addressed. I spoke up about them to the people in charge. Very quickly, Grael told me to back off. He said that I was messing with other departments and getting involved with business that wasn't mine; that they were all capable of running their own shit. So yes, I've been forced into having tunnel vision because my supervisor told me to focus on my job and leave everyone else alone."

Yep. I just threw my supervisor under the bus, but rightly so. He's a shitty supervisor and a total ass kisser. Hmm… maybe that's why I didn't last too long in the Armada. Regardless my Captain believes what I said.

He begins, "When we get to Keldon Station, I want you to go through this ship, bow to stern. Make a list of all the-"

We're interrupted by his COMM system beeping.

"What," he answers after pressing a button on his desk.

From the speaker we hear, "**Um, the Valkyrie is wanting to know when we'll be ready to leave.**"

The Captain replies, "Now. Follow their lead and instructions. Unless you need me to be up there to do that."

"**Uh no sir,**" my Supervisor, Grael replies, "**I can handle it. However I need McNill back up here. He's on watch.**"

The Captain, annoyed, "No he's not. He's talking with me. Stand by for him." He presses the same button disconnecting the COMM.

Focusing his attention back on me, "As I was saying: I want you to make a list of discrepancies and get it back to me. I'll figure out how to fix them from there. As far as Grael is concerned, we'll need to have a conversation. Send him down once you're back up there."

My Captain nods, his way of finishing the conversation and turns to his computer terminal. I get up and leave.

Upon relieving Grael at the Navigation console, I say, "Captain wants to have a word with you."

"About what?" Grael asks.

"Everything," I say.

Grael hesitates for a second and then asks, "What did he say?"

I reply, "You do realize you're making him wait, right?"

He then turns and leaves the bridge. I realize I didn't get much of a passdown, but thankfully I know what's going on.

I grab the COMM mic, "Constellation Cutter Valkyrie this is the Ex Del Seven. We're ready to proceed to Keldon Station when you are."

They quickly reply, "**Understood Ex Del Seven. We're heading a few meters away from the asteroid** field. Go ahead and align yourself 50 meters off of our bow. Once in position we will begin initialization of our traverse drive. Continue forward at 20MPS as we generate and stabilize the wormhole. Once we give the order, increase speed to 70MPS until you hit the threshold. You'll feel the singularity start to pull you in. Once you do, cut power to your engines and let it take you. We'll be in behind you. The transition into the singularity is a little bumpy, and you'll experience the sensation of gravimetric rolls for the duration of the trip. Are you ready?"

I think to myself for a second. I'm obviously going to need control of the engines. I've never done this by myself before. I know the Captain authorized transit- well in a matter of words, but should I do this on my own? Fuck it.

I activate the ship's PA system, "Now on board Ex Del Seven, prepare to enter traverse tunnel. Uh, secure for turbulence. Engine room, transfer control of main engines to the Bridge. That is all."

Within seconds the direct COMM beeps.

"Navigator McNill," I say.

"Are you by yourself up there?" the Captain asks.

"Yes, Captain. It's open space navigation for the most part," I reply.

"I'm on my way up," he says before closing the COMM.

I head over to the helm console, sit down and prepare to drive the ship. The engine room has transferred control of the main engines. Noting Valkyrie's course, I begin to maneuver towards them. The entire ship at my fingertips. It's not often that we don't use the autopilot.

The Captain enters the bridge, "How close do we have to get?"

I reply, "50 meters off their bow."

"That's cutting it a little close on your own, don't

you think?" he rhetorically says. He grabs a mic attached to his chair and over the ship's PA, "This is the Captain. I need a navigator to come to the bridge."

Within a few minutes all the navigators including Grael arrive on the bridge. The Captain instructs Slobin in particular to assist me with Navigation while telling the rest to head below.

At this point I have our ship alongside Valkyrie's starboard over taking them. The Captain orders a continued course until we're 50 meters ahead.

"We're in position," Slobin says.

"Very well," the Captain replies then orders, "port thrusters until we're in front of them, then slow to their desired speed."

"Understood," I reply.

I activate the port thrusters drifting the ship in front of the Valkyrie, then I throttle the engines back to 20MPS.

Slobin says, "We are aligned."

A few minutes go by, when suddenly Slobin says, "Energy signature detected."

I state, "They're probably opening the singularity. Our sensors are gonna go nuts."

Out the main viewport probably, 1,000 meters or so off the bow, a small whitish orange light appears. It begins to expand and these sort of light tentacles; three of them emerge and begin to swirl. As the center of the singularity begins to expand, the tentacles extend out and continue to swirl as the opening expands, they come together forming the mouth of the tunnel.

I look up at the aft view camera and notice the traverse drive dish on Valkyrie emitting three much smaller light tentacles, mimicking the motion of the singularity as it stabilizes.

The opening stops growing.

"Ex Del Seven, this is the Valkyrie," We hear over the COMM, **"The singularity is stabilized. You can go on**

through."

I look back at the Captain who says, "Do it."

"Understood, Captain," I reply and say, "Increasing speed to 70MPS. Standing by to cut power to the engines once we hit the threshold."

After a few seconds, the ship rocks slightly. I immediately cut the engines and as instructed allow the ship to be taken in by the singularity. The wormhole has stabilized in a brilliant solid orange color with white streaks as it continues to swirl. Upon entering the wormhole, the ship begins to shake violently.

The bridge is rattling. I look around and yell, "Not to worry! It'll calm down in a couple minutes."

The shaking becomes more intense before relaxing a little into a rolling sensation. I glance at the camera and take note of the Valkyrie behind us.

The Captain asks, "How long is this transit going to take?"

"Uhhhhh..." Slobin replies.

I get up from my seat and head over to the Navigation Console, "Give me a second, Captain."

On the flat table touch screen panel, I press a button projecting the map in 3D. I zoom out until I find Keldon, and then level it with where we were using the maneuvering controls. Pressing the same button the holo-image recedes back into 2D on the table. I grab the stylus pin and draw a line from our previous position to our destination.

"Okay..." I begin mumbling to myself out loud, "we're at Transverse level 2-"

Slobin interrupts, "Couldn't we just ask them?"

I reply, "You're more than welcome to try but radio COMMS don't work in Traverse Tunnels."

I continue mumbling, "Traverse level 2, distance of about thirty-one hundred Astronomical Units or so, compensate for gravimetric distortion from any nearby stars," I grab the compass attachment and draw a circle from the star in the Keldon system. Then from other stars, one that intersects my line, "So roughly thirty minutes, Captain."

The Captain nods as he stands up, "you two remain here, please. Let me know if anything comes up. Mr. McNill, if you can think of any way to stabilize the ship better, please do so."

After about ten minutes of trying a few things I realize no matter what we do, we won't be able to stabilize our ride any better. No matter how I adjust the thrusters, whether or not we run the engines slightly or burn them out, we have no effect on our movement.

The singularity is what's moving us. Propelling us through the galaxy at what used to be impossible speeds, though it isn't so much speed as it is folding the space between our destination. I'm no engineer, but as a Navigator in the Armada I had to have a basic understanding of the physics of the Traverse Drive. As it folds the space, it moves us through with gravimetric propulsion generated by the Drive Dish and doesn't stop until we reach our destination... or the Graviton Generators fail forcing us to resurface into normal space... had that happen to me once when I was on a Constellation Cutter... not fun and I'd hate to find out what would happen to an object being moved in front of the ship generating the wormhole, or in this case, us.

"Call the Captain," I say to Slobin, "We're about five minutes from exit."

"K," Slobin acknowledges. He then carries out what I say.

In a couple minutes the Captain comes on the bridge and sits in his chair, "How long until we resurface?"

I reply, "Uh, any second now."

We all sit awkwardly and wait. Out the viewport and faster than I can actually say this, the ship "drops" out of the tunnel and back into normal space. We feel a sensation of simultaneously dropping and slowing down. Unsettling when you don't quite expect it.

The ship is quiet and no longer rattling from our journey through the singularity tunnel. In the rear camera, I see Valkyrie out, still the same distance they were when we entered.

Over the COMM we hear, "**Ex Del Seven, this is Valkyrie. Proceed towards Keldon Station and contact Docking Control.**"

Slobin replies on the COMM, "K."

As I throttle the ship forward up to a cruise speed of 100MPS, Slobin goes out on the COMM, "Docking control, this is the Mining Freighter Ex Del Seven requesting a docking port and docking instructions."

After a couple seconds we hear, "**Ex Del Seven this is Docking Control, change to Docking Channel Z-3-4.**"

As Slobin is changing the channel we hear, "**Docking Control this is Constellation Cutter Valkyrie-**" the transmission cuts as the channel is changed. Slobin says over the COMM, "Docking Control this is Ex Del Seven on Z-3-4."

Docking Control replies, "**Ex Del Seven, good afternoon. We don't have you on our schedule of arrivals today. State the purpose of your arrival please?**"

Slobin looks over at the Captain asking what to say with his facial expression.

The Captain answers, "Tell them unexpected maintenance."

Slobin begins, "Uh, Docking Control we have some unexpected maintenance that needs to be taken care of."

"**Stand by, we'll see if we can squeeze you in.**"

A notification appears on my console advising me to slow to 50MPS. It's a general message that's broadcast from the station when ships arrive to a certain distance, to slow down. I do as generally requested.

Through the viewport I see Valkrie overtake us. They're about 70 meters away from us also heading into the station.

"**Ex Del Seven, this is Docking Control.**" We hear over the COMM.

Slobin answers the call.

Docking Control says, "**Proceed to Docking bay Five. There's a smaller maintenance dock, B-20 that should be able to provide the services you need. Constellation Cutter Valkyrie is also proceeding to that dock. Follow them in, but maintain a safe distance of 40 meters. Welcome to Keldon Station.**"

I do as instructed. Paying attention to navigating safely, I maneuver the ship while also taking note of other vessels transiting in and out of the station.

Speaking of... the station. One of the newer models, it stands as a beacon to humanity's accomplishments. The center ring is large and holds a variety of shops and restaurants as well as living quarters for anyone who so desires to live in orbit of Keldon. The two smaller rings at the top and bottom of the station house the various equipment needed to keep the station in orbit, direct energy from the solar collectors to the power needs of the station, and overall are considered engineering rings.

The station's main hull is like an hour glass. In the center it is thin and as it expands outward to its ends. Holding the main ring are six struts that connect directly to the station's center and in between the rings are the various docking modules for ships to park.

On both ends of the station are large, defensive missile launchers and scattered along the station are its defensive laser cannons should someone be foolish enough to attack.

Approaching the large bay doors, I receive a message on my console to stop and await outgoing traffic.

Valkyrie has already been told they can enter and are doing so.

The Captain orders, "Navigator, inform the crew to set docking stations."

Slobin nods and says over the ship's PA, "Now on board Ex Del Seven, set docking stations, repeat, set docking stations."

Two of the crew acting as lookouts come up to the bridge and head up into the observation bubble, but don't extend it as they would for asteroid field navigation. The engineer reports they are ready for emergency take over if my console for whatever reason fails.

As a ship passes by us, on its way out, my console lights up green with the message to proceed in.

I say, "We're good to head in, Captain."

He replies, "Very well, proceed in no more than 30MPS."

I nod and slowly bring the ship up to speed. As we pass through the bay door, we cross an energy field, standard on all docking modules with a large inside bay. It's purpose is to keep the air in.

On the main viewport, a track has appeared, transmitted from Docking Control to indicate where we need to go. As I try to keep focus on steering, I can't help but take notice of all the various ships. Unlike a military station or space port on the ground of a planet, this place has a variety of ships: mining freighters of different classes, civilian deep space transports, personal ships and even a Constellation Explorer… where I should have gone.

Approaching the dock, I slow the ship down. Lining up with the dock, I ease her in slowly and then throttle to zero.

The mechanical, automated mooring arms magnetize to the ship, shaking us slightly.

"Moored safely, Captain," I announce.

"Well done, Helmsman," my Captain compliments,

"Navigator, call down to engineering and let them know I'm on the way to figure out what we need. As of now, this isn't a pleasure stop so if anyone asks, no they can't leave the ship or the immediate area and if they do, let me know so I can replace them before we leave."

Slobin makes the call on the internal COMM as I grab a nearby pad and begin taking notes. Figured I might as well get some work done while we're here and not moving.

Slobin heads below after making his call. I grab a nearby pad. Scrolling through it I see nothing super important; just random notes and what not. I start a new page and begin to take note of stuff on the bridge. Checking things like our Emergency Breathing Devices in the event of a decompression, I make sure that the control systems inspection is up to date and a whole bunch of stuff that I already know is good because that's one of my jobs.

Upon looking throughout the lower deck, I notice that the crew is running around, probably trying to figure out what needs to be fixed with the ship. I'll check that later so I go outside.

Previously mentioned, inside the docking module is breathable air. Someone has already extended our gang plank. I hit the "outside air" and it smells fresh. Considering the station's atmosphere is generated by an arboretum, it's no surprise to me that the air is the freshest thing to being planetside.

Heading towards the front to inspect our hull markings and insignia, I notice the emergency decompression station. It's a small post with a handrail, breathing masks, emergency harnesses to strap into and a comforting sign at the top that reads, "IN CASE OF DECOMPRESSION, STRAP IN AND HOLD ON TIGHTLY, AND BREATH NORMALLY." Before you ask, no they couldn't come up with a better system and enclosed docks can make loading and unloading equipment a bigger hassle. Plus, what are a few unfortunate losses, but a few bucks saved in construction?

I take note of our ship's name. It could use some touching up. The "Ex Del" logo could use a new paint job, but that's hardly to be of concern. More for style than it is for any practical purpose.

As I head towards the stern of the ship, I inspect our navigation lights. Still on as we're not intending to stay long, or at least the Captain isn't. They all seem to be burning brightly, but it might be worth replacing them before we leave. I observe them suddenly go dark.

Coming to the stern, I hear, "Nate!"

I turn and see Tim dressed in non-work clothes coming towards me from the plank.

Heading towards him I say, "What's up? Did you get fired?"

"Hehe," he chuckles, "naw man. The Captain just spoke with Station Engineering. They can't get anyone to work on the specific components we need to fix and since it's contracted through our parent company, we'll have to wait until they can, so Captain has authorized off time."

"Sweet," I reply, "Just let me go get changed out."

Hell yes! A much needed day off.

Chapter Two: "Light the candles, it's a party!"

(*Donna*)After organizing a few things on my pad and transferring accounting information to my computer for the day, I look up at the clock. 0656. Almost time to open.

Being a restaurant owner in orbit of Keldon Colony has been one of my greatest accomplishments in life. Whereas most would probably open a business and hire people to do the work for them, I prefer to be hands on with my employees. I try not to micromanage, but I also prefer to give them the reassurance that the owner is here working alongside them. I don't even see them as employees, they're my family.

One of my family members, Jarred, pokes his head into my office and asks, "Donna, we're set up out here, can we open?"

"Yeah, I'll be out there in a minute," I reply.

As a cook, I'd say I'm decent. No master chef, by any means, but I can't say the same for Jared. That man could have his own five star restaurant if he wanted to and the fact that I have his cousin Lynn working back there, too, makes this place a whole hell of a lot more than it should be.

Coming out into the main area I see our morning rush has arrived. They were probably eagerly waiting to feed themselves before starting with their various lives. On the station I have my regulars, but there's certainly no shortage of interesting people who come in these doors. Travelers sightseeing the nearby nebulas, military service members seeking a chill place to relax on a port call, scientists taking a break from their latest expedition. My restaurant even contains a piece of some of these guests' history which I proudly display on my walls. All these people with fascinating stories and they choose to grace my little orbital café. Wouldn't have it any other way.

I did my best to make this place different from the

average eatery. Most places just offer their business, a place to consume food and then try to get you out the door so they can bring in more people. Not here at Fed's. I specifically tell my customers they're welcome to stay as long as they like.

I nod to the bartender, Martin who's been with me since day one. Yes, in the early morning my bar is open. I'm still waiting on approval from Station Command to allow me to keep it open 24/7. My argument is that visitors might be arriving from different time zones and where it's morning to us, they could have been out working all day. It's been a couple months, but I'm sure they're considering it as well as all the other vendors who've put in their various requests.

As noon hits, the pace goes up a bit. I hate rushes. Not enough time to talk and get to know people. Maybe someone will stay, but if breakfast was any indication, it seems that this is one of those mundane days where people come in, eat and go about their day. No problem. We're here to serve.

After checking the numbers of today's customers so far, I venture out once again into the dining area. It's 1500. Besides one or two people who I tried to chat up earlier, this place is quiet. Then a couple people walk in. One seems like a gentleman in his early thirties. He looks a little rough, but judging by his cheery attitude he must be an engineer or something. His companion is younger. Seems to be keeping to himself.

I greet them, "Hello, welcome to Fed's. Sit anywhere you like."

"Thank you," the older one says. His friend just nods. They sit down at a booth a few tables up from the entrance.

"Can I get you gentlemen something to drink?" I ask.

The cheery one replies, "Got anything decently

strong on tap?"

"We've got a few, one I'd recommend after a long day is a local brew from the colony. It's a bit fruity, but it's not too sweet. One of my personal favorites," I state.

Smiling he replies, "I'll have that!"

"And for you," I ask his friend.

"Um," he says, "I'll just do a NuBud."

"Great," I say, "My name is Donna if you have any questions about the menu. I'll be right back with your drinks."

I proceed to the bar, tell Martin their order and he starts getting it ready. Martin and I sometimes play a little game to guess the customer's origin.

I ask Martin, "What do you think their story is?"

He answers as he pours the first beer, "Did you ask them yet?"

A few times we've played I already knew the answer, "No."

Martin finishes the first drink pour and then takes a few seconds to examine them, "The older guy is definitely an engineer. The other… he seems clean. What's his demeanor?"

"He seems a little reserved," I reply.

"Definitely on a ship," he says.

I sarcastically look at him, "Really? What gave that away?"

Martin shrugs his shoulders and says, "Could be miners."

He always had an ability to read people, although in his line of work he tends to hear more detailed stories.

"Do you know if any military ships came in today?" I ask.

Martin replies as he sets down the last of the order, "Not that I'm aware of. Though it has been a few days since a Navy ship or a Cutter came into port so maybe."

I grab the tray and head back to the table. After

setting the beers down and telling them which is which, I say, "Figured out what you would like to eat, yet?"

The younger one answers, "I'm not that hungry. We were just looking for a place to relax."

"Well you definitely came to the right place," I say, "At Fed's you're welcome to stay as long as you like. How about you?" I finish saying looking at the older one.

"Probably get an appetizer here in a bit," he says.

"Sounds good," I begin, "So what brings you to Keldon Station?"

"Engine trouble," the engineer says.

The other one smirks, "Among other things."

"Oh yeah?" I inquire, "So I take it you're either miners or military."

Delightfully curious the older one asks, "What makes you say that?"

"Well, you definitely look like an engineer," I state, "and you," I say looking at the other one, "Well… you're a little hard to place exactly."

The younger one nods, probably impressed, "In a way, both assumptions are correct?"

"Prior service?" I inquire further.

He raises a brow and asks, "How could you tell?"

"Guess you could say it takes one to know one. I served for ten years in the Stellar Marine Corps. You?" I finish asking.

"Guardian Armada. Three years," he states directly.

"Only three?" I wonder.

The engineer interrupts, "It's not a subject he likes to discuss. Not necessarily anything bad, but wasn't really good either."

"I understand," I say, "Sometimes military life just isn't meant to be. I got tired of simulated warfare so I got out and decided to start my own business. It was good while I was in, but I'm glad to be here now."

The younger one states, "I wish I had gone into

Exploration."

I nod, "I've had quite a few of them come through my doors. They definitely have some interesting stories to say the least. Though there was this one in here recently who kept to himself. Like I have no problem leaving people alone, but the Explorers are usually more talkative. They love talking about their discoveries and travels. This one made it seem like he wasn't allowed to talk about it. Seemed odd."

"Well to be fair," the young one begins, "sometimes their findings are withheld until it's determined that the public won't freak out. Sometimes they come across rogue asteroids or a potential supernova that could have lasting effects on a system. Black holes are also something they like to release carefully, but quickly for navigation safety. Don't take it personally, but sometimes their missions aren't declassified right away."

"I understand," I reply, "I never really had that issue with what I was doing. We were told to be ready to deal with pirates or separatists, but nothing came of it. Seems you guys have a lot of that under control," I say referring to the Guardian Armada.

The former Guardian shrugs and says nothing more.

The engineer asks, "So, ten years? What was your rank when you got out?"

" Lead Sergeant," I answer, "I didn't advance super quick because I liked working with my people. When my last promotion came around I knew it would be less hands on so I chose to get out and do something else. I finished up school and after a little while here I am, owner of my own restaurant."

"You're the owner and you wait tables," the former Guardian says condescendingly.

"Yes," I answer, "as I said, I like to be hands on. Maybe one day after I open up a couple more restaurants I'll assume the lavish CEO position, but right now I'm happy where I am."

The engineer reaches out his hand, "I'm Tim. Tim M'Nar, by the way."

I shake it then turn back to his friend, "And you are?"

"Nathan," he replies reluctantly offering his hand.

"I'm glad you guys stopped in. If you would like something, I'll be back to check on you in a second." I notice more customers coming through the door. Clean cut, short haircuts, I think I know who these guys are. Definitely military.

I greet them and they choose to sit at a table across from Tim and Nathan. I take their drink orders and head back to Martin

As I approach, he says, "Military."

"What," I say.

"Those guys who just came in, they're military." He clarifies.

"Oh, yeah I agree. Guess a ship just came in," I say and then give him their order, and then say, "The first two are an interesting group. They're miners. One of them used to be in the Armada."

"Interesting," Martin says.

I continue, "Yeah. The older one seems eager to get to know me. The younger one well… he seems he could care less. Kinda cute, though."

Martin smirks, "Maybe you should try showing a little more interest."

I laugh, "I did, but at the same time, you know my rule."

"No ship personnel," he scoffs, "I'm aware. But that doesn't mean you can't spend a little time with someone, Donna. Who knows, maybe he'll give up his life of free space living and find a job here," he finishes sarcastically.

I smile and glare simultaneously, "I highly doubt he'd change his life around just to see if there was something between us. Like I said, he's obviously not interested anyway."

I study the two groups of people. One of the military guys seems to be talking to Nathan. Guess he recognized him or something. Martin sets the last drink on the tray and I deliver it promptly.

As I approach, "Yeah our Captain isn't too happy about it, but I just work here. If anything you guys gave us some time off," Nathan finishes.

As I deliver the drinks I realize that Nathan and Tim must have been victims of a vessel termination, or at least their ship was. Not too uncommon. But I've also realized the four military guys are Guardian Armada.

The Guardians place an order for food. I give a couple recommendations and take their order to the kitchen.

Coming back out to the dining area, I ask if Nathan and Tim need anything.

"Well actually," Tim begins, "Nate here doesn't think I'll be able to walk out of here without your contact information."

Oh an admirer indeed. I've never thought of myself as attractive at least not as much as most, but it does happen.

I politely reply, "You're not the first one to ask, but I don't usually date miners or travelers. I tried it once, but my work is here so I try to stay local." I wasn't lying. I already had dated a mining foreman for a few months. When we were together things were okay, but being apart made it hard to concentrate on my work.

Tim says, "I get it. But we could at least go to dinner."

"Then stay here for dinner," I say.

"No I mean somewhere else when you're not working," he says.

"Somewhere else," I begin pretending to be

insulted, "You haven't even tried the food yet and already you want to go somewhere else?"

His face turning red, he tries to come up with a response, "I- uh, tell you what, I'll try an appetizer and if it's good, I'll take you to dinner here."

I reply, "Oh honey, I'm flattered, but most days I work open to close."

Nathan decides to jump in, "Really, because I've been here a couple times before and this is the first time I've seen you."

"Well maybe it just happens to have been on my days off," I postulate, "So what can I get you to eat, Tim?"

"I'll try the Keldon Fritters," he answers.

"Nate?" I ask.

He shakes his head. I check on the table of military members and they seem fine. I head to the kitchen and two of the four food orders are ready. I drop them off and ask if there's anything else I can get for them. They all seem content for now.

Walking back to the kitchen, something out the viewport catches my eye.

"Hey Martin," I say, "Were we expecting a fleet today?"

He looks out the viewport and then over at me and replies, "Do I look like I work at Traffic Control?"

Two of the Guardians get up from their seats and join me at the window.

One of them says, "Those don't look like Navy ships. At least, not ones I'm familiar with."

I, too, haven't seen anything like this. They appear to be large and most of them look like they have various, jagged prongs. In fact, they seem, dare I say… alien. We observe a beam of light emanate momentarily from one of them- BOOOOM! The station shakes!

One of the Guardians standing next to me quickly turns and says, "We gotta go!"

As the Guardians start to rush out the door, Nate and Tim get up to take a closer look. Jared comes out from the kitchen and asks, "What's going on?"

I observe a couple more beams of light followed by more shaking of the station. I then see smaller ships headed towards the station at a high rate of speed.

Turning to Jared I say, "We're under attack."

"What!?!" he gasps.

I turn to Nathan and Tim who are unsure what to do.

Nathan says, "We- we need to get back to the ship!"

"Wait!" I say, but it's too late. They're already headed towards the door. The station shakes, but this time the noise is almost as though something just rammed it. I chase after the miners, coming into the main walk-way they stop, stunned. Standing in front of them is a creature the likes of which no one has ever seen. It has two; I guess you could call them legs, except at where the knees are split off three smaller legs each. In-between its upper legs appear to be an abdomen or thorax. Where its chest would be looks like this thin connection to its upper body which connected its long, lanky arms and what appears to be its head. Where the legs and abdomen are connected are two long tentacles and at the end of these tentacles are mouths with teeth hissing at us loudly. It appears to be wearing some sort of armor. And the hands appear to be claws.

It's only been a couple seconds that we're all standing there.

Tim says, "Uh, Nathan…what the fuck was in that beer?"

Nathan says nothing. The creature appears to be evaluating us. It raises it's arm- "Look out!" I scream as it fires two laser bolts, one of them striking Tim in the right shoulder.

Nathan quickly grabs his friend and starts helping him back into the restaurant. I quickly draw my concealed pistol. Firing a couple shots, it seems unaffected. The alien begins to fire back, missing me as I move for cover. I take a couple shots at its abdomen which bursts. The creature screams out in pain as it falls over. I look and I see more creatures as they pour out from behind the corner.

Running into the restaurant, I hit a button sealing the door.

"Get him to the back," I instruct Nathan, "We need a med-pack out here!" I order. Looking at Martin I yell, "Light the candles, it's a party!"

Martin looks shocked for a second, but then scrams over to his register. Pressing a sequence of buttons, the back shelf of the bar retracts down revealing an arsenal of weapons.

I head over to a booth as Lynn comes out with the med-pack and starts attending to Tim's wound. He's been hit on the shoulder. Looking at the front door I see that a few more of the creatures are now attempting to shoot it down. It won't hold up for long.

Removing one of my trinkets on the wall, I reveal a touch-pad. After entering a sequence of numbers, a wall opens up revealing another hidden arsenal.

"Can you shoot?" I ask Nathan.

He replies, "Uh… yeah-"

I interrupt tossing him a rifle. "Lynn, take him into the kitchen," I order referring to Tim.

Speaking of, out of the kitchen comes Jared, strapped up with grenades, a shotgun and dual wielding pistols. Martin has grabbed the sub-rifle and is mounting it on a table pointing it toward the door. I throw a table over and point for Nathan to take cover. He does so.

"What's the plan?" Nathan asks.

"For now, we hold the restaurant until Lynn can get your friend able to move. From what I saw out there, these things appear to be storming the station. Our best bet would be to get to an escape pod and take this fight to the surface," I explain.

Nathan asks, "What about getting to our ship?"

"No offense, Nate," I begin, "But a mining freighter isn't exactly-"

I'm cut off as the door finally fails and the aliens start pouring in. The firefight ensues. Martin lets loose with the sub-laser gunning down the first wave. The second wave takes note and starts to fire on him. I see him hit the ground as I poke from behind cover and open fire. Nate's trying to fight back, but I can tell this is not his forte. It's hardly even mine. We trained for a possible alien attack, but we never knew what it would be like if it ever happened.

Through the chaos, I faintly hear Jared screaming, "Grenade out!"

A few seconds later, there's a small explosion near the entrance taking about five or six of them out. I gun down the last two.

I order Nathan, "Go check on Martin."

We seem to have a break in the fighting for now. Lynn and Tim come out from the kitchen. Tim is still injured, but he's at least attempting to hold a weapon. Lynn has her sniper rifle set to short range mode.

Nathan comes back to me and shakes his head. For a moment I feel sadness, but I quickly put it to the back of my mind. I'll mourn later.

From the right side of the entrance I see laser fire. The type of laser appears to be the same as a rifle from the security forces. Within seconds an entire team pours in.

The squad leader says, "Is everyone okay in here?"

I stand up and say, "We've got one down, most likely fatal. Another injured, hit to the shoulder."

The leader explains, "The escape pods are being intercepted. We're trying to fight them back, but they're overwhelming us. Our best chance, I believe, is to try getting to the hangars."

Nathan speaks up, "There's a Constellation Cutter parked in Bay 5. I think we should go there. They'll be able to cover our escape."

The squad leader nods, "I suggest you get moving. We have the area cleared for now, but they're most likely sending more boarding ships. We're looking for any survivors, so don't wait up for us."

I acknowledge the squad leader with a nod and then order, "Alright, you all heard the man: grab whatever guns you can and let's move. If we find people along the way, we'll add them to our little team. Let's roll!"

Nathan heads over to the arsenal behind the bar and starts grabbing any rifles he can. Tim tries to shoulder an extra rifle, but Lynn grabs it from him and shoulders it herself. Jared, though loaded down already, insists on trying to bring more. I grab an extra shotgun and even pack up my projectile weapons in case they prove to be more effective against the alien armor.

Leaving the restaurant, I look back one last time where Martin is laying and realize he would rather we try and escape so we do.

Nathan asks, "Why do you have so many guns in the restaurant. Not that I'm complaining."

I explain quickly, "The restaurant is also our home. The living quarters are right above it. I keep all these guns in case of pirates or some dumb shit decides to go on a homocidal suicide. I'll be happy to explain more later, but we need to stay focused."

Continuing down the main concourse, we encounter about ten more aliens. A firefight ensues and lasts only two minutes. Lynn, staying in the back of our misfit squad, is able to pick most of them off. I instruct her to aim for the lower abdomen which seems to be their most vulnerable spot. The station isn't shaking as heavily now. Guess they did all the damage they felt they needed to. I'm trying to figure out why they didn't just destroy us. Maybe they want to preserve it for some reason.

At the entrance to the walkway on the strut towards the center of the station, we encounter a group of aliens firing into one of the stores. Taking cover, I notice whoever is inside is firing back.

"Lynn, watch our backs," I yell, "everyone else, take em out!"

We ambush the attackers, almost taking them by surprise. Their laser bolts wiz past our ears. Nathan and Tim are trying their best to keep their courage, but this is obviously something they were never prepared for.

Four aliens lay dead and suddenly all is quiet. I get up and head towards the entrance of the shop.

A couple lasers fly out and I yell, "hold your fire, it's clear!"

They stop shooting and I enter the shop. Behind the shelves a couple heads poke out. I instantly recognize them as the group of Guardians who were in my restaurant earlier.

"Is everyone okay?" I ask.

One of them stands up and answers, "We were on our way back to our ship when we encountered these- these whatever they are. They immediately started shooting so we ran for cover. We discovered that our pistols are mostly ineffective unless we hit that dangly area between their legs."

"Their lower abdomen," I clarify, "Yes that seems to be their most vulnerable spot. Is anyone from your group missing?"

The Guardian shakes his head.

"Okay, we're trying to make our way to Bay Five," I inform, "we've got extra weapons. If we stick together we should be able to survive this."

"Alright, we'll take the lead," he says.

I reply, "No offense, kid, but I served ten years in the Corps and left as a Lead Sergeant. I trained for this type of scenario. I also know this station pretty well. I'm leading."

"Uh… okay," he says, "guys, the Calvary is here. Grab a weapon and let's keep making way to the ship."

I shout to my group, "It's clear, move up!"

As the other three Guardians come out from their cover, they arm themselves with weapons we provide.

The first Guardian says, "I'm Marcus Agsnon, by the way. That's Dutch, Al, and Jim."

"Sergeant Donna Kroeling," I reply.

I give the order to keep moving.

We enter the strut's concourse. It's not very wide and there are aliens in our path, but they haven't noticed us yet. There's no cover and I have no doubts about Lynn's ability to pick off long range targets, but it's too dangerous. I quickly think of a plan. It's crazy, but I think it'll work.

I begin, "Okay, here's what we are going to do: Tim, I need you to disable the nearby grav-generator. Once it's offline, everyone needs to get on the bulkhead and jump as hard as you can. Your momentum will carry you to the end. Hopefully the aliens will be disoriented long enough to take them out. Don't shoot them unless you're really close or they see you."

Lynn asks, "Why don't I just take them out?"

I answer, "Because as soon as you take out the first three or four, they'll lay down suppressive fire and have us trapped."

Dutch asks, "What about the station's tram?"

"Doesn't run when it's on lockdown," I say, "I'll go first, but I want at least two of you right behind me. Give each other a little space. As soon as we hit gravity on the other side, we'll drop to the deck and probably roll a little bit. Everyone ready?"

I receive a couple half assured nods and mild yes's. I nod at Tim and he begins to take the gravity for the strut offline. It's a long, narrow passage, but floating through it should shave off a little time... provided we hit all our targets.

I see one of the aliens start to float as well as some minor debris. They are obviously disoriented.

"Check your targets, and stay calm," I say, "And remember... push off as hard as you can. Your momentum will get you to the other side."

I "step" into the concourse and immediately start to float. Maneuvering toward the entrance bulkhead, I squat into a launch position. I gotta remember to push off hard, but I won't be able to tell without any inertia.

Marcus floats in and sets himself up much the same. I glance at him and then push off as hard as I can. I raise my rifle to a tactical position. I'm floating forward in a prone... never thought that would happen.

I see the first alien and take a couple shots. Nailed him on both of them. Marcus starts firing on another one floating a little further up. Hits it after about six shots, kills it on the eighth.

Glancing back for a second, I make sure everyone else is floating. Looks like they're spacing out like I told them.

ZZZHHHHHEEEEWWWWW!!!! A bolt barely misses my face. I turn facing front and start to open fire. At what, I don't know. It's more of a panic fire. I see my target and take a more concentrated shot. It's now dead.

I see a small group of about three. They are starting to become aware of what's going on and are trying to organize themselves.

"Heads up!" I yell.

Lasers begin to scream by. One of them hits "Dutch!!!" Marcus screams.

"Keep your focus," I say.

"They killed him!" he screeches.

"Focus, Guardian!" I order.

He looks down his sights and begins to lay down

fire on the group. Manages to get two of them and float past the third. Facing back we quickly realize that shooting at it could inadvertently hit one of our own people.

Keeping our focus forward, we pick off the last couple or so near the end of the concourse.

Approaching the end, I say, "Brace yourself!"

Marcus and I float into the main part of the station. Gravity instantly pulls us to the deck, but our continued momentum forces us to slide forward and into a roll. I quickly spring back up and attempt to gain my bearings. No aliens in the immediate hallway.

The other members of our team come through in a much less graceful fashion than we did. Dutch's body floats through and flops on the deck. The blast he took must have slowed him down. Marcus goes to roll him on his back and jerks suddenly at the sight of his dead comrade. His face is scorched black, unrecognizable.

Lynn, having taken point, shouts, "Incoming!"

We look for nearby cover, but there is hardly any. I order everyone to fall back. Down the other direction of the hall we see shadows illuminate the bulkhead. We're trapped.

"What do we do!?" Nathan panically asks.

I quickly look for a solution and see a door.

"Everyone into the elevator!" I order.

We all pile in. I press a button taking us to the docking bay deck.

Stepping out of shock for a brief moment, Marcus reacts, "Wait, during lockdown the trams don't work, but the elevators do?"

"Take it up with Station Operations," I say.

The ride towards the docking modules shakes a little. The station is still either being fired upon or more boarding craft are impacting into the hull. I take this time to assess my group.

"How's everyone doing?" I ask.

There's mostly silence. A lot of these people haven't known what to expect in a situation like this- hell not even I knew despite my training.

"Marcus," I say, "Are you going to be able to make it?"

Marcus is quiet. He's unsure how to respond and probably doesn't know how to cope with everything that's going on.

The door opens and I proceed out. It appears to be quiet. We start to make our way towards the hangar module. We encounter a couple more aliens here and there and dispatch them quickly. Everyone seems to still be shaken up, especially as the bodies seem to stack up the further along we move.

"Keep moving," I order, "the best thing we can do for these people now is to survive this."

We come to the opening of the hangar module. There I can see the large Constellation Cutter. Behind us, laser fire whizzes by. A larger group of aliens has come upon us.

"Keep moving towards the Cutter!" I scream.

Everyone else hurriedly starts to make way. A couple more, well armed Guardians appear on the walkway and begin to engage the aliens providing my group cover.

As I come to the dock where the ship is at, I overhear Nathan arguing with one of the Guardians, "but our stuff is on that ship!" he finishes.

The Guardian replies, "You're safer with us! Just get on board!"

I add, "Just do as he says, Nathan!"

Nathan and Tim reluctantly board the ship.

The Guardian asks Marcus, "Is there anyone else?"

"Dutch didn't make it," Marcus answers.

"Alright," the Guardian says, "that appears to be everyone. You guys were the last couple. We weren't going to wait much longer. Everyone else get on board!"

I run up the gangplank behind Lynn and Jared with a couple Guardians behind me. The last one gets on board, secures the door and I hear him say over the COMM, "That's everyone, Commander. We have full accountability. Recommend we detach and get out of here!"

"Acknowledged," a voice says back over the COMM.

"Come with me," one of the Guardians orders.

We follow him up a couple decks and into the crew mess area. A couple of nurses come out and escort Tim to sickbay. Marcus, Al and Jim head off to their assigned areas, I assume for combat leaving myself, Lynn, Jarred and Nathan. I motion for us to sit down at a table out of the way. In this moment things seem to become quiet. I look at the civilians in my group, unsure how to process the last-wow it's only been fifteen minutes. I also take note of the organized chaos as the ship scrambles to get underway. I can hear something over the ship's PA, but I don't pay attention to it. Now I am starting to try and figure out what's happened. What were those things? Why did they attack us? And above it all, I begin to feel the sadness start to set in from the loss of my friend Martin… Did the ship just shake? I guess it did. The crew mess falls quiet as the four of us just sit and try to process.

Chapter Three: "Free to engage, free to engage."

(*Keller*) **"That's everyone, Commander. We have full accountability. Recommend we detach and get out of here!"** one of my crewmen says over the COMM.

"Acknowledged," I reply and clip my personal COMM unit to my belt.

The bridge is complete chaos as we not only prepare to get the ship underway, but also man up Battlestations.

One of the Communications Operators, Crewman Mk II Graham, informs, "Commander, Sub-Commander Devlin reports Secondary Bridge is ready for operations."

"Very well," I say, "Helm, retract all moorings, back us off one nine and stand by to swing around."

Lead helmsman, Crewman Mk II Knoop replies, "Sir, I've been trying to interface with the station's moorings, but they aren't responding; we're magnetically sealed to the dock."

I unclip my personal COMM unit, press "PA" and announce the following, "All hands this is the Commander, brace for shock as we attempt breakaway from moorings."

Without having to actually give the order, Crewman Knoop and Crewman Mk I Hulx scramble to get us loose. The ship shakes in our attempt to pull away. Finally on the third attempt, the station's moorings give out and we're free, drifting towards the other dock.

"Helm, back us off two nines speed," I order, "Then swing us right and proceed towards the door. COMMS, contact control and have them release the lockdown."

Everyone acknowledges and carries out my orders. The ship begins to pull back from the dock and soon after we swing around proceeding towards the door. Simultaneously, the communications crewmen are attempting to reach Docking Control with no response.

As we approach the door, Crewman Knoop slows

the ship down. Standard procedure during an attack is for the hangars to be locked down. Were it pirates or rebels we'd be fine. But from what I've been told by some of the crew and what the Station Commander claims, we're up against a full-on fleet of unknown ships. Suffice it to say, the station already appears disabled and we need to get out there to face this enemy.

"Blow the door," I order.

First Lieutenant Kaight Esker replies, "Sir, if we do that, it will decompress the entire module!"

"I'm aware," I reply, "but unless you can provide me with an alternative, we need to get out there now, by any and all means. Blow the door."

She hesitates for a second and then says, "Understood, sir. Main Gun, prepare to fire."

The Gun Controlman, whose name escapes me at the moment, says, "Locking Main Gun on viable breach points; request four precision shots."

"Granted. Initiate firing sequence when able," I say.

Within a few seconds, the Gun Controlman says, "Firing sequence initiated."

The Main Gun Rattles off four shots, intensely vibrating the ship with each round. They strike the door from its top left corner in a line down to the lower right corner. The remaining pieces of the door are pulled into space along with the module's oxygen. We jerk forward momentarily, but begin to drift after decompression completes.

"Ahead one third, Harbor Speed" I order.

"Aye Commander," The Lead Helmsman acknowledges.

Clearing the door we finally get a good look at what we're up against. For the longest time we thought we were alone in the universe yet before us in all manner of hellfire and chaos sits proof to the contrary. Overwhelming, hostile proof.

These ships are nothing if not intimidating dark colored hulls with only the blue-green highlights on their ships and light from Keldon's star to show where they are. They seem to be made up of a couple massive Capital Ships, easily 950 meters or more. Considerably bigger than us. There are also a few smaller ships and from our current distance I can't determine their size due to the overshadowing of the larger ships, but roughly our size if not smaller. These ships appear to have sleek yet jagged hulls; their prongs are like a combat knife, smooth on the outside and serrated on the in.

The most noticeable feature of this fleet, the swarm of what I can only assume are fighters which of course are-

"Commander, I'm tracking several contacts on an intercept vector!" One of the crewman shouts.

I order, "Free to engage, free to engage."

Lieutenant Esker relays, "All batteries, free to engage! free to engage!"

The Gun Controlmen all erupt with acknowledgements of my orders relayed by Lieutenant Esker. As the small craft close in, they begin firing on us. In the midst of the initial barrage, I observe a bright orange beam emanate momentarily from one of the capital ships. BOOOOM!!! The sudden strike shakes the ship, throwing all of us on the bridge off our balance.

I order, "Bring us out of range of the larger ships. Evade and avoid as best you can."

Crewman Knoop begins to throttle back while Crewman Hulx fires the maneuvering thrusters tilting the ship in various directions in an attempt to evade attacks from the large ships. The Gun and Turret controllers do their best to compensate for the rolls and pitches while they target and defend against the attacking fighters.

From the surface arrives the Keldon Colony Defense Fighters. They seem to be trying to come to our aid, but are swarmed by several groups of attacking ships.

Another shot is fired from the capital ship, but misses… barely. It streaks just above the port side secondary hull module.

Lieutenant Esker reports, "Commander, the Keldon Defense Fighters are asking for any help we can give. Our defense fighters are standing by to launch at your command."

We can barely help ourselves, "No." I order, "Our pilots are good, but they've never trained for anything like this."

One of the Communications Crewman informs, "Sir, the Ex Del Seven is underway and attempting to flee. They are requesting our assistance."

I see them emerging from the station which is now off our left side. I look back at the Keldon Colony Fighters which seem to be holding out, however they're likely to be overrun shortly. And the cause of all this, the large hostile fleet in front of us.

"How long until the nearest Naval Fleet arrives?" I ask.

Lieutenant Esker answers, "Last report put them three hours out, sir."

The defense fighters are being forced to fall back. That civilian ship doesn't stand a chance without a Traverse Drive. This battle, if you could even call it that, was lost before it began, "Helm" I say, "Swing us toward the Ex Del Seven. This battle was over the moment the station was fired on."

"Desired speed, Commander?" Crewman Knoop asks.

"Your discretion," I answer, "Stand by to bring us into a broadside drift."

The fighters outside come around for another pass lighting up our hull. So far the armor is holding, even the transparent armor.

"Brace for impact!" Lieutenant Esker shouts.

We're hit again by one of the massive energy weapons.

I don't recognize who, but someone shouts, "Sir, one of the larger ships is headed for us!"

Another crewman shouts, "More fighters incoming on an intercept vector for the civilian ship!"

"Helm," I begin my order, "bring us hard to starboard into broadside position. Cut engines and drift. Make sure we don't hit the Ex Del Seven. Lieutenant Esker, focus the Main and Dorsal guns on the larger ship."

Damage Control Crewman Mk III Whitmore alerts, "Commander, the armor can't take much more of the larger hits."

"Noted," I acknowledge.

A COMMS crewman informs, "Sir, report from the Ex Del Seven: they're dead adrift and requesting assistance!"

"Commander, the fighters are breaking off and resuming their attack on-"

Crewman Whitmore interrupts, "With the combined firepower of-" he's cut off as we take another major hit on the starboard side just behind the Main Gun. This hit takes a chunk of hull, and as pieces fly off I notice a couple of particular objects flailing about: members of my crew.

I look over to my right at the Ex Del Seven off our starboard quarter as we drift past.

Lieutenant Esker reports, "Main Gun is offline!"

I quickly order, "Helm, Full Nine Standard Speed away from the hostile fleet." I look over to Delta Crewman Webb, one of the Bridge Control Traverse Drive Specialists, "Begin initialization of the Traverse Drive."

Both crewmen acknowledge my orders.

Lieutenant Esker informs, "Sir, the fighters are still-"

"Commander," she's interrupted by 3rd Lieutenant Jeff Hale, the Situational Officer, "they're concentrating their attack on the port module, specifically the Traverse Drive Dish!"

"How long until full initialization?" I ask.

"Fifteen seconds," Delta Webb answers.

I order, "Lieutenant Esker, concentrate your defense on the fighters. We lose that dish, we lose the ship."

"Aye, Commander," she acknowledges.

So begins the fifteen longest seconds of my life. We're still getting pounded by enemy weapon's fire. My combat officer is trying her best to counter-attack the Dish, our only means of escape, but it's not looking good.

Finally I hear the words I've been longing for, "Gravimetric Core initialized, Commander!"

"Spin it," I order.

Off the Port side secondary hull module I watch uncertainly as the light begins to glow from the Dish. In just a few more moments we'll have a singularity generated and-

"Gravimetric Core Emergency Shut-Down Activated. Traverse Drive Dish compromised." Is blasted through the Ship's Public Announcement system.

No... our only means of escape.

"Commander, the fighters are going for the engines!" someone shouts.

Lieutenant Esker asks, "Orders, Commander?"

I turn to face her and everyone I can see, "Keep fighting. If this is to be our end, let it be something these assholes never forget."

One of the COMMS crewmen informs, "Sir, Sub-Commander Devlin is requesting you on personal COMM!"

I nod. Activating my COMM unit, I say, "This is Keller."

"Jaysen!" Sub-Commander Devlin excitedly says, "We still have one last option, but it's desperate!"

"Just say it," I order.

"A propulsion blast!" he says.

He's right. That is desperate and with no guarantee of success. It could also leave us drifting at high speeds without engines.

"I'll give it some thought," I say and press a button switching from the call to PA mode, "This is Commander Keller, all hands prepare for propulsion blast. Engine Control, begin overcharging the engines."

Delta Whitmore warns, "Sir, doing so will leave us on-"

"If you have a better suggestion," I interrupt, "I need it about thirty seconds ago. They're trying to destroy our engines. Might as well do something unexpected and destroy them ourselves."

Delta Whitmore hesitates for a second and says, "Uh, aye, Commander."

Crewman Knoop reports, "Engine overcharge at seventy-five percent... eighty... ninety-five-"

"Blow the engines," I order.

Looking out the aft windows and gripping onto a nearby brace bar, I watch the explosion forced from the exhaust ports consume some of the fighters as we're hurdled far and fast away from them.

Lieutenant Hale informs, "They're trying to pursue... Looks like they're unable to keep up... we're pulling away, Commander."

Crewman Knoop reports, "Current speed calculations coming through... we're holding well passed nine, sir... holding at two-hundred eighty-eight million MPS."

Faster than our engines were even capable.

"COMMS," I begin, "Put me in touch with Stellar Command. Have the transmission routed to my quarters."

"Sir," the COMMS crewman replies, "Our communications system is down."

I walk over to Crewman Whitmore, "How long

until communications are back up?"

He replies, "I don't know, sir. I'm still trying to get a complete damage report."

I take a breath for a second, "Alright. Get that to me as soon as you can. COMMS, have Sub-Commander Devlin meet me in my quarters. As for the rest of you, well done. None of us were ever really prepared for anything like this, but we're still here and hopefully soon we'll be ready to get back into the fight alongside the Navy. Until then, Navigation, start looking for resources, asteroids, planets anything we can use to begin fabricating the materials we need to get back to one-hundred percent. Lieutenant Esker, remain on Alert Status for now. You have the bridge."

As I leave, I can sense that my words have lifted the spirits of my crew, rather I hope. Truthfully, I'm just as scared and uncertain, but they can never know.

Making my way down to level three, I realize I need to figure out how to make my ship ready for the next engagement. As I head down the passage way towards my quarters I am joined by Sub-Commander Devlin.

He begins, "All things considered, I'd say we're lucky."

"Luck had nothing to do with it, Sub-Commander," I reply, "We've got a capable crew, but we're not completely out of the woods. We're drifting at high speed without any engines, we've suffered casualties and are now at war with an unknown, hostile alien race."

We step into my room. I go behind my desk and sit down, continuing, "I need you to get me a full crew status. I know we lost a few, but I need to know the status of injuries as well."

"I'll get on it right away" he says turning to leave.

"Thank you, oh and Sub-Commander," he stops turning back to me, "Good job with that last ditch suggestion. After the Traverse Drive went down, I thought for sure that was it."

He nods and says, "The second that message played over the PA I knew you'd probably need an alternative. I'll get back to you with the crew status."

I turn to my computer console as he leaves the room. Accessing all of our sensor data such as gun cameras, eagle eye cameras, radar, sound detectors, energy signatures- basically every form and type of sensor we have. With all this information, I put it into a computer program which then turns it into a holographic reenactment of the battle.

This program was designed to help us find exploits in battles with pirates and rebels. Hopefully it will shed some light on this unknown enemy's weakness. Within minutes the program finishes compiling the data. I activate my holo display which shows a low quality projection of the ship in the dock, just before we got underway. Some of the missing pieces of the image are filled in with a grid estimating the shapes.

I fast forward the video file to just after we left through the remains of the docking module door. Playing at normal speed, I begin my analysis. My first realization is that they don't fire off their large energy weapons too frequently, possibly indicating they require a lot of time to charge. The next thing I observe is the fact they primarily attack with their fighters while the larger ships maintain distance. Now this could indicate a few things, either they're just carrier type vessels with minimal weapons except their primary large beams, they attack with fighters first, THEN can engage with the larger ships if necessary, or the larger ships are slower and can be out maneuvered. Either way, we'll need more info on their tactics, but this at least gives us something.

Based on this, I'm still mostly left with speculation until I can get ahold of the Navy's data after they engage them. I won't be able to come up with effective exploits, but then again, I'll want to review this with my Combat Officer, defense fighter pilots and weapons control crewmen.

The Stellar Navy will have teams of specialists looking at various engagement data as well figuring out tactics to pass to myself and the other starship commanders. However, I'm this crew's Commander. I know what they're capable of and what tactics will best work for my ship.

I must have lost track of the time. As I'm studying the battle data, my personal COMM goes off.

"Keller," I say.

Lieutenant Esker informs, "Commander, it's Kaight. We've found a nearby cluster of asteroids. Unsure of the minerals they might contain, but it looks like our best bet. Recommend we divert our course."

"Very well," I say, "Do you need me to come up there to coordinate the maneuver?"

There's a slight hesitation in her response, "Um, I think I can handle it, sir."

I add, "Remember, we're without main engines so you'll have to adjust our momentum with maneuvering thrusters. You'll need to push the entire ship to the desired heading."

"I understand, sir," she says, "If I run into trouble, I'll be sure to contact you right away."

"Please do," I say "And let me know once we're on our new course."

"Aye, Commander," she says, ending the conversation.

A few seconds after that call ends Crewman Whitmore knocks on my door frame. I swivel over in my chair while motioning with my hand for him to enter.

He begins, "Sir, let me just say outright; it's not pretty."

Perhaps cynicism isn't the best response right now, but I already started- "Oh? We were just in a battle with a hostile race of God only knows what, forced to destroy our own engines in order to get away- Crewman Whitmore, I'll be pleasantly surprised if this report isn't as bad as I'm already anticipating."

The look on his face indicates he's taken what I said a little too personally. Perhaps a little prompting is needed, "Well, go ahead, then."

"Uh, right, so um, Superior Delta Neuavos believes we can get at least one engine back up in several hours. Lieutenant Slaighter agrees. Thankfully Main Two wasn't compromised in the blast, at least not as bad as the other three."

"How many hours?" I ask.

He replies, "About twenty-four to forty-eight."

"And the other engines," I follow-up.

"Neither of them have an estimate yet, but it's bad," he answers, "Superior Delta Nuevos thinks it would be best if we could set down somewhere to effect better repairs. All the other Delta Ranked engineers are all in agreement."

"Very well," I say, "what about COMMS?"

He sighs, staring down at my desk, "All external communications are down, hard. We can get short range back up in a day, but long range well… options are being considered to cannibalize one of our short range orbital sensor satellites. The technicians are confident that they can reconfigure the parts to repair the long range systems. This would, however leave us with only one orbital sensor remaining."

"Do it," I say, "Communications are top priority."

"Aye Commander," he replies, "The COMMSTechs are also recommending we go planet side somewhere as there is extensive exterior work that needs to be done."

"I understand," I reply, "But have them work as best they can right now on getting communications restored. Anything else?"

"The main gun should be online in a matter of

hours. One of the power relays was taken out and started to surge prompting the gun to lock down: standard safety protocol to prevent the weapon from firing uncontrollably," he says.

"I'll need to review those safeties," I say.

He continues, "The Traverse Drive Dish will have to be inspected to learn the extent of the damage. The Gravimetric Core didn't seem to have been damaged, but the Drive Specialists are looking into it anyway. The hull was compromised on levels four and five on the starboard bow. Emergency doors have been sealed, no estimate on when or how that will be repaired."

"Let me guess," I speculate, "Planetside repairs would be best?"

"We'll also need to fabricate the hull and deck plating," he answers.

I nod, "Continue."

"One of our laser batteries was destroyed," he says, "But they're putting together a replacement and that concludes the report, sir."

"Very well, Crewman Whitmore. Good job and dismissed," I say.

He stands up and turns to leave the room. I turn my focus back to the holo reenactment. Analyzing the fighters a little more closely, I may have found another exploit.

My personal COMM goes off, "Keller," I say.

"Lieutenant Esker, sir. We're steady on our new vector. That took longer than I expected."

"It's not easy moving a starship without engines," I say swiveling in my chair. Pressing a button on my computer console, I pull up a screen that displays the ship's status and the course we're on.

"Everything looks good, Lieutenant. Any sign of enemy ships in the last hour?"

"None, sir," she replies.

"Very well," I say, "Go ahead and stand down to

Cruise Condition."

"Aye, Commander," she says ending the call.

Fifteen seconds later I hear over the ship's PA, "**Set Cruise Condition throughout the ship, say again, set Cruise Condition throughout the ship.**"

Sub-Commander Devlin walks in, "I have the crew manifest if you're ready."

"As I'll ever be," I say, swiveling to face him.

He takes a breath and begins, "Six confirmed dead at Keldon Station, seven critically injured currently in the infirmary. Sub-Commander Jackson is unsure about their survivability. Two were for sure killed during the battle and two are missing. The missing crewmen were believed to have been decompressed in the hull breach."

"Yeah I saw them. Their names?" I ask.

Sub-Commander Devlin concernedly asks, "Are you sure you want to do this right now?"

I nod.

He says, "Crewmen Estavas and Lietzell."

"Damn," I express, "Lietzell was a good kid too. Don't know much about Estavas, I think he was a recent transfer. The rest?"

"Doxell and Stromin were the two killed in battle. Hemmer, Johnson, Klayvir, Blette, Romo and Dutch were reported as killed at the station."

I nod slowly, "Hemmer just came out of Officer training, correct?"

"I believe so, sir," Sub-Commander confirms, "I think he was assigned to engineering."

"And Romo was on her twilight tour." I remark, "So much potential and experience gone just like that."

Sub-Commander states, "I fear this is only the beginning."

I bitterly nod, "Unfortunately I agree."

Sub-Commander Devlin informs in a lighter tone, "We did however pick up extra passengers."

I raise an eyebrow in response.

He continues, "I ran into them on the crew's mess. Three of them are refugees from the station: one in particular is a former Stellar Marine. She actually helped save some of our crew. The other two are from the Ex Del Seven. One of them claimed to be a Navigator and when he told me his name, I could have sworn I heard it before."

"And that would be?" I ask.

"Nathan McNill," he says.

"Wait, seriously?" I confirm, "As in Crewman Mk I McNill?"

He nods in confirmation.

"No shit..." I say and explain, "He was accused of espionage on my last ship, the Gondul."

"Right," Sub-Commander starts to remember, "You believed he was innocent."

I clarify, "I believed the evidence presented wasn't substantial enough to place him as the perpetrator. Of course his supervisors didn't agree and presented their case to Stellar Command. Without hearing my perspective, they deemed him a security risk and demanded he be discharged. I was able to convince them to allow it to be honorable, but that's all I was able to do. They still took away all his benefits and blacklisted him for any reentry into any branch of Stellar Service."

Sub-Commander says, "I thought they were able to trace the information trail."

I shake my head, "Hardly. Delta Wernival had drawn the conclusions based on where McNill went on his off time. His connection was purely speculation with no concrete proof of his actions. To this day I think Wernival was covering for himself or someone else in his shop. But the case was already decided and I lacked the so called 'counter-evidence' to support my stance."

"Why didn't you try to investigate locally?" he asks.

"I did," I reply, "but Delta Wernival alerted Command of my actions. I was quickly ordered by Sub-Admiral Yelkin to cease and desist."

"That's when you left, isn't it," he postulates.

I nod, "I submitted a resignation letter to Yelkin explaining that I was no longer the Commander of my ship. That I was being remotely manipulated by a Delta Crewman through him and that I either needed to resign or go elsewhere. Yelkin accepted my resignation, but his boss found out and denied my resignation offering a different Command."

"Valkyrie," Sub-Commander says.

"Yes," I say, "though interestingly enough it seems things have come full circle."

Sub-Commander assumes, "I take it this isn't a story we want people to find out about?"

"It's certainly not one I would ever like brought up in casual conversation," I say, "Though if he's here now… I need to meet with our new passengers. Make sure they get settled in. Tomorrow morning I want to sit down with all of them. They may be able to assist us."

"I'll see to it right away," Sub-Commander says.

"Also," I say, "Plan on a normal workday for tomorrow. I feel it best if the crew just focuses on their normal duties. Keep their minds off the war of which we know nothing about right now."

Sub-Commander nods in acknowledgement and leaves the room.

The rest of the day proceeds somberly. As I walk the passageway to the galley for some evening chow, I can sense the uneasiness of everyone. Unsure if we'll be attacked again or when and how we're going to war.

I choose to take my meal back to my quarters. I'm not ready to sit with my fellow officers just yet as I'm still trying to accept this situation.

Watching the holo reenactment, I don't find much

else to be of use. I'll need to review it with others.

I realize the crew needs their leader. I wish I could give them certainty, but hope will have to do for now.

I pick up my personal COMM, activating PA mode, I begin, "Good evening Valkyrie Crewmates, this is the Commander speaking... I know a lot of you are anxious, worried and unsure about the days to come. As soon as we get communications back up, we'll contact Stellar Command to find out what our orders are. Until then, plan on a normal work day for tomorrow. Reason being is for now I would like all of you to go on as though nothing has happened. Our focus needs to be on getting Valkyrie back to one-hundred percent, but we also need to maintain level heads and focus on the task at hand. Right now we're drifting at a high rate of speed towards an asteroid field to gather minerals for parts and hull fabrication. We'll be there in a couple days.

I would also just like to say how proud I am of each and every one of you. Today we faced something unexpected and you all performed your duties better than I expected. We lost a few crewmates, unfortunately. I'll read their names... Hemmer... Estevas... Leitzell... Johnson... Klayvir... Blette... Romo... Dutch... Doxell... and Stromin... in fact, please join me in a moment of silence for our fallen brothers and sisters..."

I wait about thirty seconds and continue, "My condolences to those of you who knew these people well. We will continue to live and fight on in their honor. Get some rest this evening. Keller out."

Chapter Four: "It is good to see you again..."

(*Nathan*) I awake to an almost naked woman coming towards me. Yep, I'm dead. She continues past where I lay. As I inadvertently turn my head, I notice others stealing glances. She hangs up her towel before heading into the shower compartment.

It's not that we don't have coed berthing on the mining freighter, it's that we just don't have very many women who opt for being underway on a dirty, cramped ship for weeks on end earning a meager salary. Hell most of us males don't even want to be there.

Since it's been a while, maybe I'll shower too. As I start climbing out of my rack, I look down only to notice my body's natural reaction in progress. Of course, I'm not as desensitized as I used to be. Probably best to shower later, then.

I grab a pair of generic slacks provided to us from the ship. They aren't uniform. They're just pants they have for prisoners, survivors, refugees and anyone who wants a free pair of generic, gray ,bland slacks. I decide to also change my shirt. They were kind enough to give us only the finest plain white t-shirts. In the process of donning my clothing, I notice one of the male crewmen peering out of his rack right at me. I pause for a second, then remember the sight I was graced with so I suppose fair is only fair.

I put on the final piece of clothing, which I actually like, a unit Sweatshirt. It has the Armada's logo on the left breast with a large picture art of the Valkyrie on the back. Underneath the picture is the ship's motto: All the Way or Not At All. Stupid. I always preferred the Gondul's motto: Anything and Everything for the Cause We Believe. Much more inspiring, wouldn't you agree?

Strapping up my boots, I leave the berthing area. Scratching my head I can't seem to figure out where the Crew's Mess is located. One of the other crew members stumbles out of the berthing about as half asleep as I. He's wearing his uniform pants along with the ship's unit sweater, except his is a zip-up. The uniform pants are a solid blue with an orange stripe running down the outside of the left leg.

"Are you going to the Crew's Mess?" I ask.

He sort of half nods and starts walking down the passageway. Keep in mind, it's been a while since I was on one of these things and I lived in a different section of the ship. Most people told me I should've gotten to know the ship from stem to stern, but I didn't care. Now I wish I had.

We're getting closer to the Crew's Mess as indicated by the presence of more crew and the smell of generic ship breakfast. Eyeballing the chow line, I really don't feel like standing in it. I decide to see what alternate options have been laid out on the salad bar. My choices are fruit, over sugared cereal and extra bland cereal. I shrug my shoulders, grab a bowl and fill it with both cereals as well as some fruit. I snag a seat at a mostly empty table near the end.

I'm not looking forward to today. My saving grace from yesterday's attack turned out to be my old Commanding Officer from the Gondul. And of course he wants to meet with me.

I'm distracted for a second. Sitting down in front of me is the woman from earlier.

"What?" She says.

I start to look away, "Oh uh, sorry, still waking up."

She glares at me for a second then says, "Aren't you the guy who used to be in the Armada?"

I reluctantly nod my head, "Yes that would be me."

"What did you do while you were in?" she asks.

I reply, "I was a navigator aboard a Constellation Cutter like this one."

She nods in acknowledgement

"What about you?" I ask, "What do you do on

board?"

"Engineering," she answers, "Specifically electrical," she finishes her response and takes a bite of her meal. She also decided to grab a mix of the cereals and fruit.

"My name is Nathan, by the way," I say.

She politely nods then focuses her attention on her fellow crewmates who just sat down. Understandable. I'm a stranger on this ship and wearing their team colors might be coming off as an insult.

Donna, having the patience for line standing and probably up earlier than I sets her tray and self down across from me.

"How'd you sleep?" She asks.

"Surprisingly well," I rep-lie. I'm not looking forward to seeing my old CO or ever again for that matter.

Donna interrogates, "Oh really? Because to me it looks like you need a few more cups of coffee."

How does she do that?

"I've met a lot of people," She inadvertently begins to answer, "I've seen patterns so I not only know when someone is tired but also when they're lying. I'm sure you have your reasons, Nate, but you shouldn't lie to your friends. And I'd like to think that after all we've been through recently we are friends."

I contemplate a response, "Well… it's not everyday you survive an alien attack so I guess that makes us more than acquaintances."

Donna concludes, "Lie to whoever else you want, but please don't lie to me."

"Or me," Tim says slamming his tray on the table. Sitting down next to me he says, "If it isn't the savior of Keldon Station."

Donna plants her left elbow on the table and her cheek into the corresponding palm all while condescendingly smiling at Tim's flattery, "How's the injury," she asks.

Rotating his right shoulder, Tim replies, "Doc says it'll heal just fine. Takes a lot more than a laser hit to bring me down."

Nodding, Donna says, "I'm sure it does."

I look to my left and notice the Valkyrie Crewmen's attention has been grabbed.

The female engineer asks Donna, "Excuse me, are you the one who saved our crewmates?"

Donna nods, "I certainly tried my best. Unfortunately one of them didn't make it."

A somber silence hits the table.

The engineer breaks it, "Still, you saved some of our people yesterday. Thank you."

The other Crewmen nod in agreement and appreciation.

Donna humbly replies, "I did what anyone else in my position would do."

"Still, it's appreciated. I'm Cassy, by the way," she says. Pointing to the other three Crewmen she introduces, "That's Phelps, Pore and Stienburg."

A couple of them half nod and/or wave.

Donna acknowledges, "Pleasure, though I'd rather we were meeting at my restaurant."

Cassy asks, "Oh which one was yours?"

"Fed's" Donna Answers.

Cassy explains, "I think we were going to go to that one, but we didn't get Freedom until like right before the attack. Life of an engineer, ya know?"

Donna slowly shakes her dead, "No I don't. I was infantry in the Stellar Marines."

Cassy's interest is piqued. I mean so is everyone else's but her's especially. Guess she plays for the other team. Not that it matters. Regardless, she's not interested in me. Maybe she hates Navigators. Maybe she does prefer women. I'm thinking in circles and have invested more time in this thought than I should have.

Disinterested as Donna explains her backstory, I happen to glance at a clock. 0835- oh shit! We're late!

"Sorry to interrupt, Donna, Tim, we're late for our meeting," I finish standing up.

Tim starts to reply, "I thought it was at oh eight forty-five…"

Donna starts to get up and explains, "Whenever someone sets up an appointment, they mean fifteen minutes earlier."

Tim protests, "But we're civilians-"

"Just trust us, please," Donna orders.

After dropping off my dishes at the washer station, I hear sarcastically, "Oh you're welcome."

I don't have time to deal with a lowly entitled Crewman. Donna and Tim drop theirs off and catch up to me assuming I know where I'm going. I hesitate for a second, then go to a nearby computer screen display.

Tim remarks, "You don't know where it is?"

"Some of the layouts can be a little different," I half lie.

In truth I get turned around on the Crew's Mess. But it is also good to double check. Seeing as we're two levels down and a few compartments ahead, I point the way and start walking fast. I catch a stairwell out of the corner of my eye and turn towards it.

Tim asks, "Nate, can't we just take the lift?"

"Too slow," Donna assumes.

We emerge at level three. Well, Donna and I emerge, I can hear Tim struggling to keep up. He's not fat or anything, he just only works out his liver. Continuing aft, I turn a corner into the Command Section which consists of a waiting room decorated with a clean carpet in the pattern of the Guardian Armada logo, "The Shield of the Republic" as it's sometimes referred to.

The walls are decorated with portraits of the Prime

Minister and the rest of the chain of command all the way down to Valkyrie's real commander, Sub-Admiral Daradds. Some personal accolades and items from different boardings and skirmishes with pirates and rebels are also on display. Unlike the rest of the ship which is very functional with it's plain white walls and metal floors, this section is very clean with a soft yellow glow and feels more inviting.

In front of us sits an oak desk and behind it two doors, one leading to the Sub-Commander's office and the other to the Commander's. Sitting at the desk in full uniform appears to be a Mk I Crewman as indicated by his rank insignia: a silver circle with a single arc underneath facing downward. The insignia sits on the left breast of the outer garment and under it his name plate which appears to read "Caephurt". Also to note about the uniform top, it also consists of an orange undershirt as well as an orange stripe lined on the left side with the stripe on the pants, runs on the inside left of the garment all the up to the arm and all along the outside of the left sleeve from the wrist all the way over the shoulder and to the neck where it wraps around the neck to the top of the right shoulder.

Crewman Caephurt asks, "Can I help you?"

"We have an appointment with the Commander," I say, "Sorry we're late."

"You're fine," he replies.

From around the corner, Tim finally arrives. Attempting to catch his breath, he says, "See… I… told you we'd be fine."

I roll my eyes as I sit down in one of the chairs. Tim and Donna do the same. I sit quietly and ponder how this meeting is going to go. I was hoping to never see Commander Keller again and almost wonder if dying on the station or Ex Del Seven would have been a preferred alternative.

"How long do we normally have to wait," Tim asks

breaking the silence.

Crewman Caephurt looks up, "The Commander will see you when he's ready."

It's rare that Tim actually pisses me off. He definitely deserved my glare for that stupid question. I know Tim is just a civilian, always has been, but you would think common sense would dictate showing a little respect and patience.

A few awkward moments of silence later the Commander's door opens. Keller stands there, also in full uniform. Only difference from Caephurt's is the rank insignia: four silver shields in a row. And his nameplate of course. He's gotta be in his late forties, early fifties by now, with head mostly gray hair combed mostly to the left. His moustache has aged better, still as black as I remember and mostly neatly trimmed. He stands at a towering six foot, three inches: a textbook, poster child Starship Commander.

Greeting us with a fake, cordial smile, he says, "Welcome, come in."

The three of us get up and proceed toward the door. Tim and Donna go in first.

"Hello, Nathan," the Commander says.

"Sir," I unenthusiastically reply heading in without so much as giving him the dignity of looking him in the eyes...

(*Keller*)...I guess I should expect as much. He probably blames me for his career coming to an end. I face my guests as I close the door and go to my desk to sit. "Please, sit" I offer trying to be as least aggressive as possible.

I don't consider myself aggressive unless the time calls for it, though being a Starship Commander comes with a default amount of intimidation even to civilians.

Sitting down at my desk I say, "Good morning. Thanks for taking the time to meet with me, Let's start with you," I say directing my attention towards the female, "I understand you used to be in the Stellar Marines."

She answeres, "Yes, sir."

"Name and rank, please," I say, preparing to write the information on my pad.

"Lead Sergeant Donna Kroeling," she replies.

I inquire, "And were you full-sep or standby reserve?"

"Second Tier, standby reserve, sir," she answers.

Second Tier. Basically they're only available if absolutely necessary. Most Marines often option for Second Tier because they get to keep their health plan, only have to train every six months and get full access to any military facility.

I sigh as I begin to say, "I'm sure you can guess what comes next..."

She nods and says, "I understand completely, sir. After what I saw at Keldon, I'm more than willing."

"Willing for what?" the older gentleman asks.

I pull up the script in my pad and begin, "Lead Sergeant Kroeling, effective immediately you are hereby restored to Active Service. The current situation requires that you be taken out of Second Tier as you are a necessary asset to deal with the current situation being that... uh... " I think for a second as this part is left blank, "we are at war with an unknown hostile alien race." I turn my attention back to her, "Our communications are currently down so we won't be able to make the official change, except in our local records for now. I'll need you to provide more info to Crewman Caephurt when this meeting concludes."

"What are your orders, sir?" She eagerly yet professionally asks.

I begin, "Since we're at war, best I can tell you're the most qualified to train my crew for close quarters combat. My crewmen are good at what they do, but they're not Marines."

"I understand, sir," she acknowledges.

I continue, "When you finish speaking to Crewman Caephurt, track down Delta Crewman Larrodo. He'll be expecting you."

I turn my attention to Nathan and the other male, "As for the both of you, I have an extra special assignment, but first I need to get acquainted with you," I finish focus on the male whose name I don't yet know.

"I'm Tim M'Nar. I'm an- well I guess I was an engineer aboard the Ex Del Seven for a few years. Before that I mostly worked as a mechanic on small craft," he tells me.

I inquire, "And what did you do on the mining freighter as an engineer?"

He excitedly answers, "Oh pretty much everything from the engines to the laser drill, processor, you name it I worked on it."

"And what about you, Mr. McNill?" I ask focusing my attention to Nathan.

"I was just a Navigator, sir." He answers.

"So you have experience navigating asteroid fields, then?" I clarify.

He nods, "Yes, but I advise against taking a ship this size into one… not that my opinion matters."

I glare at him for a second, taken slightly off guard. Indeed he's allowed to say what he wants to me. I reply, "As a matter of fact, it does. We have the capability to fabricate various parts on board as well as materials for the hull. Only problem is right now we're low on resources. My crew aren't experienced with mining. We've salvaged materials before, but we're going to need a lot to begin repairs."

Tim asks, "Do you have a processor on board?"

I answer, "Yes, but it's not industrial like you're probably used to. However it should suffice."

"I'll need to look at it," he says.

"Absolutely," I reply, "anything else you both need to make operations successful will be provided. We're on our way to a cluster of asteroids right now. We're still about seventeen hours out thus leaving time to prepare."

Nathan speaks up, "I'd like to see the charts to get a look at this field we're going to. If it's one we've mined before I can point out the rich deposits we didn't tap."

"Very well," I answer.

"Also," Nathan continues, "I'll need a list of required minerals. Various rocks offer different deposits."

I reply, "The Engineering Commander is getting a list put together. He and the other engineers are working down in the port module hangar."

Nathan and Tim nod in acknowledgement.

I say, "I know neither of you were expecting this- hell we certainly weren't. But we need your help in order to make Valkyrie battle ready. As soon as we get communications restored, we'll figure out what our orders are and see about letting you all off at the nearest station or colony world. Until then, we have a lot to do. Sergeant Kroeling, Mr. M'Nar, you're dismissed. Mr. McNill, please stay behind."

The Sergeant and the Engineer get up and leave. I notice Nathan appears to be staring straight ahead, not really looking at me.

After the door closes, I say, "It is good to see you again, despite the circumstances all around."

He's not looking directly at me, but I can see he's thinking of a response.

Finally he says, "You left me out to dry. I literally had no one and could trust no one."

"Nathan," I begin, "I tried to fight for you."

He shoots his gaze directly at me, "Then why did my career end?"

"I did everything I could," I answer.

He replies, "Which is why I'm sitting in your office

in civilian clothes..."

An awkward, uncomfortable silence takes the room. I don't have to explain myself, but in not doing so, I probably solidify his opinion on what transpired. Regardless, I have more pressing things I need to tend to.

Breaking the silence, "You have... obviously made up your mind about the entire incident."

He condescendingly nods.

I continue, "Look, I don't have time to debate what happened. I just need to know despite our past history you'll do everything you can to help my crew."

"That's a tall order, Commander," he says standing up, "But I want to survive just as much as you and your crew. I'll do what I can to the best of my abilities. If there's nothing further, I'd like to get started."

He turns and starts leaving. I can't order him to stay, or show respect not that I feel the need to, but to his credit he was polite in front of the others.

I stop him by saying, "I'll set aside time when I can to discuss the incident in more detail. Maybe give you my full perspective."

He turns for a few seconds and shrugs his shoulders...

(*Nathan*)"...Okay," I say and leave. So glad that's over. I notice Donna is still speaking with Crewman Caephurt. Tim is sitting in his seat, unsure of what to do.

"Everything okay?" he asks.

I respond, "I don't want to talk about it. You ready to head down to the Port Module?"

Tim shrugs and gets up. Inspecting another map of the ship, I make sure we know where we're going. I don't know what Keller expects. He did the bare minimum to save my job, my livelihood at the time. But what I do find more interesting is that he'd assume I wouldn't help out of spite. No one on this crew, as far as I know was there when that happened. They deserve to live through this just as much as I do… not that they're going to.

Tim interrupts my thoughts, "This is a nice ship."

I reply, "Compared to our freighter, this ship is a Cruise Liner."

"Food isn't too bad either," Tim states.

We arrive at the lift which leads down the strut into the Port Module Hangar.

"Oh thank God!" Tim expresses.

On the ride down, we stop a couple times picking up one or two crew each stop. Tim greets them and I just politely nod. Hopefully Keller will get the charts to me soon. I'm not sure what else I'll be doing in this project besides looking over them.

I nudge Tim and he turns around. The shaft opens up to the Port Hangar. As we ride down we can see various crew members getting things together: some working on setting up the processor, others conducting maintenance on several of the larger craft. I remember seeing these newer models on the Gondul. We only had a couple of test prototypes at the time. The ones we mainly used for boardings and such were much smaller. Only seated about six. These things look like they could seat an entire platoon. Well, that explains why so many came aboard the Ex Del Seven when we were boarded.

The lift comes to a stop on the deck and we exit. The crew members disperse into their routine. Tim and I look around trying to figure out where to go. A Mk II Crewman dressed in an orange jumpsuit with the standard uniform's corresponding stripe, only this time in blue, comes up to us. His rank is indicated by a dirty patch on his right arm: a dot with two upside-down arcs below it.

"Are you the civilian miners?" he asks.

Tim assumes, "You must be the Engineering Commander."

Annoyed, the crewman corrects, "Uh yeah, not

even. That would be First Lieutenant Slaeghter. He's right over here."

The Crewman leads us to the Engineering Commander who appears to be looking over something on a pad. Next to him is a burst laser-gun battery normally mounted on various parts of the ship and primarily used for combat. I can only assume he wants to try and use it for mining.

"Sir," the Crewman says, "These are the civilians the Commander mentioned."

"Cool man," the First Lieutenant acknowledges," Hey guys, Lieutenant Jeff Slaeghter. So I'll be honest, I don't know shit about mining."

The Lieutenant's demeanor fits his attire. He's not in full uniform like the other two ENGCOMs I've known. He's wearing an orange jumpsuit and like most of the rest of the crew's is rather dirty. One noticeable distinction is the lack of rank insignia which should be three silver bars.

Tim steps up, "What kinda laser is that you're trying to work with here?"

Lieutenant Slaeghter responds, "Standard TXL-25."

Tim further inquires, "What's the power output?"

"Eight-hundred seventy-five," the Lieutenant answers.

Tim exclaims, "Eight seventy-five!? Unless you plan on mining sand, that won't do. We need something that can output closer to nine fifty-five."

Tim looks more closely at the laser and notices something. He asks, "Is this a burst laser?"

The Lieutenant nods.

Tim sighs, "We can't mine with a burst laser. We'll need a sustained beam."

The Lieutenant and Tim begin to dive into details of how to go about mining. Seeing as I have nothing to contribute, I decide to give one of these larger craft a closer inspection.

As I approach, I realize it's a rugged yet a beautiful design in its own right. The main cockpit is small, but looks like it comfortably seats four people. The front of it has two small guns on each side with the nav lights above which are rectangular in shape. In between the lights is a compartment that opens up. What's inside, I haven't the slightest clue. Maybe the ship's main reactor. I start to walk towards the back. It widens out into a larger section becoming what I assume is the cargo hold. It also has a turret on top, probably controlled remotely from inside.

When I was on the Gondul we had one like it, but as I said it was a prototype and never used as far as I recall. This one looks like it's definitely clocked in some hours out in space. Maybe even on the surface of planets.

I approach the aft. The doors are open. There seems to be enough space for large cargo and/or large numbers of personnel. This would make an ideal vessel for small mining operations- actually, it's perfect.

I note the marking on one of the doors. "SLVRDO". I don't quite remember this acronym.

A female voice says, "Sub Light Voyage and Reconnaissance Deployment Outflyer."

Outflyer is the designation for all Guardian Armada small craft regardless of class. I turn to greet my informant. She's also wearing an orange jumpsuit, her insignia patch indicating she's a Mk II Crewman.

I say, "Finally got one that works, I see."

She chuckles, "We've had a few working for a couple years now. Are you one of the guys ENGCOM said we'd be working with?"

I step closer to her and extend my hand for a shake, "Nathan McNill."

She grasps my hand with a firm Engineer's handshake, "Devorah Belkrest… where have I heard your name before?"

"Served three years on the Gondul as a Navigator,"

I answer.

"Oh." She replies semi-excitedly, "My husband was on that ship. He was actually a Navigator too."

"Todd Belkrest," I clarify.

"Yep," she confirms, "he told me about what happened… that's very unfortunate."

I say, "That's one way to put it, I guess. Anyway, what can you tell me about this ship?"

She begins, "Well, she's capable of just about anything except Traverse Drive, obviously. Can stay underway for long periods of time and is able to hold her own in a fight."

"We might be looking to-" I stop and realize that Tim and Lieutenant Slaeghter are nearby taking a look at the ship. I nod at Crewman Belkrest to follow me.

"...We should be able to mount it on the module slot here," Lieutenant Slaeghter finishing his sentence.

Crewman Belkrest asks, "Mount what, sir?"

Lieutenant Slaeghter answers, "A mining laser that we still have to build. It'll need its own power source."

Crewman Belkrest ponders for a second. She looks under the ship, then pops back up, "If we remove the missile launcher, we should be able to put a special reactor in its place."

Lieutenant Slaeghter nods, "We're pretty much converting this thing into a mining vessel anyway. Dev, correct me if I'm wrong, but you're Engineer Lead for this particular one, correct?"

She nods, "Yes sir."

"Perfect." Lieutenant Slaeghter says. "You'll be working directly with these two. Assemble some of your fellow mechanics, get this thing up on gravs and start retrofitting immediately."

Crewman Belkrest nods and heads off to her task.

Tim says, "We'll also need a processing station."

Lieutenant Slaeghter acknowledges, "Delta

Crewman Nalo is working on that right now. He's the Fabricator Project Head."

"Where can I find him?" Tim asks.

"We'll find him later," Lieutenant Slaeghter says, "right now I need your help with Franken-laser."

They both walk off and I decide to get a closer look inside the cockpit of this little ship to get an idea of the controls. I've only had basic small craft pilot training, though I can't imagine it being much different from larger vessels.

The main control wheel is basic with only a couple of buttons. What I find interesting is the large control stick in the center console. It doesn't look like it's just a throttle. Looking at the symbols it appears to have about four, maybe five different engine functions. Looking at the gauges, my basic flight course is starting to come back to me: altimeter, speed, engine temperature, exhaust temps, all of it appears standard except for a couple I don't immediately recognize.

Looking around, something interesting catches my eyes: my current view. Soon this entire hangar will become a processing center fabricating metals into hull and other vital components for the ship. The best part? I'm a project lead. Circumstances aside, this should be fun.

Chapter Five: "Spoken like a true Marine."

(*Donna*)I notice Nate leaving Keller's office, but am too occupied with Crewman Caephurt to say anything, "HX-7115," I say to him giving my Service Identification.

"My mistake," he says and makes the correction in what I assume is my personal record for the ship. It's obviously not from the same form, but with communications down, they can't receive anything from the Galactic Network.

He asks, "And confirm rank, please."

"Lead Sergeant," I answer.

He presses a couple buttons on his console and says, "Alright. When we get Communications restored, I'll download the proper form and make sure it gets submitted to the Stellar Corps. Is there anything else I can help you with, Lead Sergeant?"

"Just Sergeant is fine," I reply, "I need to know where I can find Delta Crewman Larrodo."

Crewman Caephurt responds, "He's probably in the fitness facility."

I look at him with an indication of obviously not knowing where that is.

"Right," he says getting out of his chair. He walks over to a nearby map. I follow.

He begins to explain, "Okay so the ship is laid out quite simply, actually. Level three" he explains while pointing on the map, "where we are now is Senior Command offices and berthing. Level four is junior officer's deck as well as Officer Lounge and Officer Mess. Level five consists of all our amenities. It's sometimes referred to as 'Main Level' as it is the largest and is the location of the galley, Crew's Mess, Delta Lounge, the three crew's lounges, medical bay, onboard store and fitness facility. Level six is crew and Delta berthing. Everything below that is engineering. Should you ever need to go to either: starboard module is the main hangar. The port module houses the Traverse Drive and DIsh up forward and the secondary hangar in the aft. I believe that's where your friends are working."

I ask, "Where on level five is the fitness facility?"

"Oh right," he answers, "It's about mid ship. Your best bet would be to head aft until you see the lift. Ride it down to level five and proceed forward. It's rather large and takes up two levels so you shouldn't miss it."

"Thanks," I say and start to leave.

"Um, aft is the other direction," Caephurt informs.

I nod and change direction.

Upon arriving on level five, I find the ship feeling like a ghost town; I suppose because everyone is working and my impression is level five is the rec deck. I pass by a couple Crewmen dressed as chefs. They must be preparing for mid-day chow. I'd check to see what they're making if I wasn't already tasked.

At the end of the Crew's Mess passage way there is a bulkhead leaving the only options left or right. I go left which then turns right, taking me forward again. I can hear the thumping of a loud bass. I must be close. To my left I pass a door marked "storage closet" and a little further on my right is a door most likely leading into the large space next to me. The music is getting louder.

I enter the room. A lovely stench of sweaty men and women wafts over me. This is definitely the place. The facility is large, and as indicated takes up two levels. There's a ball court to my right: smaller than regulation league play, but that's to be expected. In front of me is a caged area with a few Crewmen throwing their weights down and screaming each time they do. Rather unnecessary if you ask me.

The entire facility seems to be divided into smaller sections. As I move into the next section, there's more weight lifting gear and equipment including treadmills and ellipticals for… less enthusiastic crew. There are only a few in here. I hear some loud chanting, coming from the last section. I enter it to find a couple Crewmen sparring on a set of mats. On a large set of stationary bikes next to them are thirty to forty Crewmen aggressively peddling away.

The guy on the lead bike out front of them and facing them yells, "PUSH PUSH PUSH!!!!"

Everyone else screams back, "ALL THE WAY OR NOT AT ALL!!!!"

I've experienced similar rally cries, but having been a while I did feel a chill or two.

I walk up to the stationary bike leader. He glares at me, but says nothing, sweat dripping off his head.

I ask, "I don't suppose you would know where I could find Delta Larrodo?"

"Hu?" He says, "Speak up, please!"

"DO YOU KNOW WHERE I CAN FIND DELTA LARRODO?" I ask audibly loudly.

He turns back forward, "You found him! You must be the Sergeant I was told about!"

"Correct!" I answer.

He pushes a button on his console and the music in this room stops.

"Alright boys and girls, call it in!" he shouts.

I notice the room gets even quieter as a previous noise of a bunch of stationary bikes suddenly stops. Delta Larrodo hops off his, wraps his towel around his shoulders and faces me. He stands, sweat dripping at only five foot five, I estimate. He's still an imposing bulk of human meat. Though height not threatening, I'm sure he could put a dent in a bulkhead.

He sticks out his hand, "Pleasure."

I shake it without hesitation, "I'm Sergeant Donna Kroeling. I've been ordered to teach your crew members to fight like Marines."

"So I'm told," he replies. He starts walking towards

his stateroom and continues, "I'm all for learning new combat tactics. But just a fair warning two el tee isn't too thrilled about this."

I reply, "I've dealt with egotistical officers before."

Delta Larrodo chuckles, "It's not so much his ego as it is his devotion to the Armada and its principles. We're Guardians not warriors."

I nod and say, "I understand that, Delta, but Marines aren't just mindless killing machines. We still have our humanity… granted it's buried under layers of apathy sometimes but we're still people. What I can teach you and your people could save your lives in a firefight against these aliens."

"You're preaching to the choir," he reaffirms proceeding down a stairwell, "I'm not the one you have to convince although I suppose since you're on orders from the Commander, you don't have to convince anyone."

We turn towards what I perceive to be forward and head down the passageway.

I reply, "Though I'd prefer everyone to be on board, I'm still willing to do whatever it takes to get the job done even if it means hurting feelings."

"Spoken like a true Marine," Delta Larrodo states.

We enter his stateroom. It's cozy with only four racks stacked like bunks. A female steps out of the head, walks to what I assume is her locker and starts getting dressed.

"Perfect timing, Lana," Delta Larrodo says.

The female, I presume to be Lana replies, "I was hoping to be gone before your stinky ass, but I guess you decided to quit early. Who's your friend?"

Delta Larrodo laughs, then answers, "This is Sergeant Kroeling of the Stellar Marines. We rescued her from Keldon."

Lana replies, "I heard she actually saved some of our people."

"Meh," Delta Larrodo says, "She saved our guys, we gave her a place to stay on the ship. By the way, where do they have you staying?" he finishes directing his attention towards me.

I answer, "Crew Berthing Two."

He ponders for a second, "What is your rank equivalent to?"

"I'm actually a Lead Sergeant," I clarify, "I believe that's the same as yours."

He nods, "Alright, we'll see about getting you assigned a more appropriate accommodation... actually we've got a spare. If that's okay with you, Lana."

Lana shrugs as she walks up to me, "I don't mind as long as I still get the shower before you, Danny."

Delta Larrodo glares, "Man, you wish you could smell this good after a work-out," he says while stripping out of his clothing.

Lana puts her hand out and says, "I'm Delta Lana Miranda, one of the lead Computer Technicians. You actually saved one of my crew members, Marcus Agsnon."

I reply, "Yes I remember him. He's actually a decent fighter."

Delta Miranda nods, "Yeah he likes to spend his free time in the range. Anyway, I'm glad I get to thank you in person. Seriously. We owe you big time."

I semi shake my head, "I would think that were the roles reversed he would've done the same.

"Still," she says, "Thank you. Oh and since we're going to be roommates please, just call me Lana. You already know Danny."

"It's just Dan!" Delta Larrodo screams from the head.

"Anyway," Lana says, "I need to be on my way. My shop is hard at work with the COMMSTechs trying to restore communications. So far it's proving more challenging than indicated." She finishes her statement as she walks out the door and into the passageway.

I begin to survey the room, scoping out where I might want to put my things, not that I have much. After a few minutes, Delta Larrodo comes out of the head, goes to his locker and starts getting dressed. I pay no attention, as he is entitled to some amount of privacy, or so I feel.

He says, "So... what exactly do you have in mind for training?"

I reply, focused still on the rack in front of me, "Delta Miranda mentioned something about a range on board?"

Delta Larrodo chuckles, "Come on, Donna. You can call her Lana. Same rank after all. We do have range facilities, but it's more like a simulator."

I inquire, "Like a target screen?"

He confirms, "That's exactly what it is. We also have a virtual combat setup."

"How many headsets," I ask.

He replies, "Ten. But three of them are broken."

I hear what sounds like a belt clicking together. Turning around I see he has his pants and undershirt on.

I state, "Seven virtual sets isn't going to be nearly enough."

Delta Larrodo asks, "Why not? We can train some on the headsets, some on the range and the rest hand to hand in the fitness facility."

I shake my head, "These aliens don't even come close to being humanoid. Letting alone the fact we don't know all of their vulnerabilities to be effective in hand to hand combat."

Delta Larrodo nods, "Well, we'll just have to train as many as we can with what we have."

I ask, "Do you have training rifles. Or can the standard issue weapons be equipped with training battery packs?"

He answers, "We have about twenty we can train

on. What did you have in mind?"

"Sweeping and clearing training for starters. Then progress into close quarters combat," I say.

He clarifies, "We already have training in that."

"Yes" I acknowledge, "But I'm talking more intense training. More thorough sweeps, proper advance and fall back maneuvers and quick draw of sidearms. I have ten years of Corps experience and in an effort to fulfill the Commander's orders, I intend to make use of all of it."

He says, "I mean I'm all for it, but I know for a fact Lieutenant Ephrryn isn't going to be on board with any of this. I'm sure your training will be beneficial-"

I hold out my hand and interrupt, "Then let's at least put together a training program first and present it to him."

"Worth a try, I suppose," Delta Larrodo unconfidently says.

We spend most of the morning working on a training plan, which is extensive and rigorous. Delta Larrodo insists the Second Lieutenant will outright reject it. We'll present it after Noon Chow.

As I stand in line waiting for my meal, I run through my head what to say to the Lieutenant. Not knowing who he is makes it difficult. I've dealt with unreasonable Officers before, but all I have is Delta Larrodo's description to go off of. This presents me with only his perspective and personal bias. It's better than nothing, but I have to remember to keep an open mind. Maybe Delta Larrodo has had some personal bad experiences with the Lieutenant that he has chosen to withhold from me. I'll have to make up my own mind about him when we meet.

I approach the food section of the Chow Line. To my surprise, I'm greeted by Lynn.

"Hey Donna!" She says excitedly, "So what they got you doin?"

I answer, pointing out the food items I want, "My

service status was reactivated. Now the Commander wants me to train everyone. Are you and Jared both working back there?" I finish, trying to find him.

She eagerly nods, "We can catch up about it later! Got lots to do after lunch."

I half smile and nod. I was hoping Commander Keller would leave my friends be. They haven't had time to process everything, including Martin's death. Hell come to think of it, neither have I. But work is a good distraction for me. Maybe it's good for them too.

I spot Nate and his buddy Tim. They seem to be joined by a female Crewman, Engineer by the looks of her. As I get closer, she seems to be genuinely interested in Nate. Too bad for her, he'll never realize.

Tim notices me and says, "Well if it isn't the brave Sergeant here to save the day!"

"Hey Tim, Nate," I say sitting down, "and you are?" I ask focusing on the mystery Crewman.

"Devorah Belkrest," she says, "You must be the Hero of Keldon Station."

I sigh, "Is that what they're calling me now?"

Tim smirks as Belkrest replies, "No. That's just something Tim came up with."

He's persistent. "So what is it you do Crewman Belkrest?" I ask.

She replies, "Please, call me Dev. Most everyone else does."

"Noted," I say, "So what do you do, Dev?"

"Small Craft Engineer," she happily answers, "Nate and I are actually working on converting one of them into a miner."

She seems genuinely cheery. Maybe I mistook her interaction with Nate. Then again they are on a first name basis. "And how's that going?" I ask, turning to Nate.

He replies, "Well if dipshit over here can get a laser working without killing everyone, we should be right on schedule."

Tim retorts, "Gee, you test fire a laser in the wrong direction one time-"

"You could've gotten us all killed!" Nate interrupts.

Tim notes, "So you've reminded me a hundred billion times."

Curiously, I ask, "What exactly happened…"

"Okay," Nate begins, "so we need a laser that fires a sustained beam. We can't just use burst bolts because we'll just shoot chunks out of rocks. Anyways, I know nothing about configuring that stuff… so there I am in the SLVRDO: that's the small craft we're working on, learning a couple things about the flight controls from Dev. I look up and dumbass over here has the thing pointed toward the back of the hangar."

"Okay…" I acknowledge.

Nate continues, "The back of the hangar is where the compartment for the Traverse Drive is located."

"Oh geeze…" I express.

"At first," Nate resumes, "I think maybe he's still working on it. No big deal. Then I hear a noise and sure enough I look up to see a laser beam being shot at a test plate with nothing else behind it except people and the bulkhead protecting the Gravimetric Core."

Tim points out, "It was on low power, it's not like it would have gone through."

Nate says, "The entire deck freaked out. Everyone, including us two started running towards him, yelling at him to turn it off. Thankfully, ENGCOM was near the power supply and shut it down."

"What happened after," I inquire for more.

Crewman Belkrest decides to respond for some reason, "Well, after ENGCOM finally calmed down and his vocabulary became coherent words and less swearing, he instructed Tim that future laser tests would be conducted with his approval only and Tim would be supervised when conducting work on the mining laser."

"Well done, Tim," I say. "Nate, was he prone to this kind of self-destructive behavior on your freighter?"

Nate replies, "I honestly couldn't tell you-"

Tim interrupts, "I mean considering most freighters don't have Traverse Drives..."

"Why is that?" I wonder.

Nate answers, "Too expensive."

I inquire further, "But wouldn't you be able to complete deliveries faster?"

"The cost doesn't justify the payout," Nate explains, "Believe me, I looked into it. A private Sector Traverse Drive Tech salary is half what the Master of the Vessel makes, if not more. You need at least two of those for even a Class One Drive which doesn't make that much of a speed difference over time."

Tim adds, "Throw in the cost of maintenance on top of that and you might as well buy an extra ship. It's practical for large passenger vessels and of course private transport, but not really for mining. Unless you're freelance and have a bigger ship."

I nod my head, "Interesting... so were you guys permanently berthed at Keldon?"

"No," Nate says shaking his head, "The Guild has these large transport vessels for moving miners long distance. You can request a transport to a different system and if enough ships want to go to that same system, the captains can agree to split the cost."

Tim says, "However, you gotta plan on being in a system for a while and sometimes at the last minute changing systems if there happens to be a transport in your area offering rides to other systems. We actually got a free ride to Keldon cause a transport was making the stop on its way to pick up a group out in Grebnar."

I clarify, "So you guys had just recently gotten there?"

Nate answers, "Yeah. We'd been mining for about a month."

There's a silence for a moment until Crewman Belkrest breaks it, "So Sergeant, any good stories to tell?"

"A few," I answer, "But they'll have to wait. I have an important meeting with Lieutenant Ephrryn."

Crewman Belkrest suddenly becomes less cheerful, "Oh… good luck with that."

I ask, "Everyone seems to have a sour taste about him."

Belkrest replies, "Let's just say I'm glad he's not in my department."

There's got to be a story behind that. I ask, "What happened?"

Belkrest explains, "One of my fellow mechanics was late for muster during port call duty. He was out late the night before, but hadn't been consuming. Actually he was trying to look after another Crewman who went a little too hard. Personal shit."

I nod.

She continues, "Ephrryn didn't buy it and had him tested. He came back clear, but it didn't end there. Ephrryn demanded the name of the Crewman he was supposedly looking after. Of course he refused. That Crewman out of guilt ended up coming forward, but Ephrryn still had him punished for refusing to cooperate."

I've had similar experiences in the Corps, but what Belkrest isn't grasping is Lieutenant Ephrryn, though a dick, still followed policy.

I say, "That's unfortunate, I've heard worse."

I get up and take my dishes to the drop off area. The dishwashers spout off some sarcastic remark, but I care to pay no attention to it. I make my way back down into Delta Larrodo's room, which I guess will be my room as well. I sit down with pad in hand and begin going over the presentation.

Delta Larrodo walks in, "I didn't see you in the Delta Mess for lunch."

I look up, "I was dining with the crew. A couple of my friends eat there and I wanted to see how they were doing."

"You can always invite them in," he states.

I shrug my shoulders.

He sits down at the desk next to me and says, "Uh… As I've been saying expect a lot of pushback from the el tee. As in like total pushback."

I glance over at him, "I understand, believe me, I'm ready." I look up at the clock and say, "We should get going."

Delta Larrodo nods in agreement. I follow him down the passageway as I still don't know where I'm going. We head up two flights of ladder-stairs to level four and forward a little ways to what I assume to be Lieutenant Ephrryn's stateroom.

Delta Larrodo knocks.

A male voice says, "Enter."

Larrodo opens the door and enters the room. It's small, a two man berthing, one bed all the way to the right of the room up against the bulkhead, the other on the left. There's a door at the end of the room which I assume leads to their personal head. Both beds have L-shaped desks attached to the end and sitting at the desk to my left is a younger man, possibly mid-twenties. He's in full uniform. I notice the two silver bars indicating his rank of Second Lieutenant. His facial expression is a stone cold, stern stare directly at me.

"Please, sit," he instructs pointing his knife hand, which consists of all fingers and thumbs extended, at the empty seats in front of his desk. As we're sitting down, he moves his hand, reaching out for a shake.

As I move my corresponding hand to shake his, he retracts a little and says, "No, the pad," softly yet stern.

Alright. That's how you want to play. I hand him the pad and finish my sit. He begins sifting through it. I doubt he's actually reading anything.

I say, "If you want I can-" I'm interrupted by a very asinine gesture: his index finger pointing up while he still focuses on the pad.

I look over at Larrodo who's rolling his eyes and ask, "Do you treat everyone this way sir," I turn my head back to the LT, "or just me?"

Without looking up he says, "I'll get to you when I'm ready, Sergeant."

"Lead Sergeant, sir," I correct, "If we're gonna play 'respect the rank' it goes both ways."

I catch a glimpse of Larrodo's eyes widening.

He replies, "Very well."

Ephrryn scrolls for about a minute or so. Finally he turns his attention back to us, well mostly me, "Sergeant-excuse me, Lead Sergeant, before we go over this, I want to make very clear to you that these are my Crewman. I've instilled the pride of being Guardians within them and I will not allow you to turn them into mindless killing machines, robbing them of their humanity. Is that understood?"

I reply, "Sir, I'm-"

"Yes or no, Lead Sergeant," he contemptly interrupts.

I express, "I don't know how things are run in the Armada, but in my service low ranking officers usually respect those who have more experience."

Ephrryn replies, "I'm aware of the tradition and I don't care for it. Policy is very clear that I outrank you."

I stand up, "Then I will put this in a language you understand: I am on orders to train this crew to become war fighters. Orders directly given to me by your Commander. If needs be, we can continue this discussion and all future discussions in his presence, but I'd like to think that we can discuss and work on this project without his mediation as people and not just mere ranks. How do you want to proceed... sir?"

Ephrryn swallows his throat for a second and ponders a response.

Finally he utters, "That... won't be necessary, Lead Sergeant. Understand that I will be watching you and your training program closely and I will not hesitate to express any and all concerns to Commander Keller."

"I understand, sir," I acknowledge, sitting down, "but I'd rather you express concerns to me first to facilitate an immediate and efficient adjustment to training. This will go over better if we work together."

"We'll just see how this goes, then," he retreats.

Two long and somewhat arduous hours pass as we discuss my proposed training program. I explain everything in detail as well as the importance of our battle stances and tactics during a firefight and how to properly sweep and clear. Ephrryn and Delta Larrodo inform me how they and their boarding crewmen were taught.

Towards the end, things smooth out, however I can tell the LT is going to complain to Commander Keller at least once a day. He doesn't like that I'll be retraining his Crewmen on everything they've been taught. I don't care. I follow my orders and do what needs to be done even if that means stepping on a lowbie Officer's toes.

Delta Larrodo and I arrive back in our stateroom. I sit down and let out a huge sigh.

Larrodo smirks, "I will hand it to you, not many have shut down Ephrryn like that and lived to tell about it. You also managed to effect cooperation and at the very least we seemed to be in agreement at the end."

I say, "I'm not one to abuse my position when I've got a Commanding Officer backing my stance except when necessary. I just hope I'm not too presumptuous when it comes to him having my back."

"He will," Larrodo affirms, "He knows how Ephrryn is and has tried to influence him to be more human. It lasts maybe a day or two."

"Ironic," I point out, "he thinks I'm the one who tossed away their humanity."

Larrodo states, "Ephrryn doesn't actually care about the whole Warriors Guardians thing. For him it's all ego. Someone else is training the Crew to be better fighters and he doesn't like that. The thing I said to you this morning about being Guardians and not Marines was said similarly by him to Keller last night. He doesn't actually mean it, but when I said it, I did."

My eyes widen, "What exactly are you getting at?"

Larrodo sits down in the other chair, "I meant what I said about learning new things and bettering ourselves, but I don't want to see my guys lose the part of them that makes them human."

I reply very clear and directly, "They won't."

Larrodo half smiles and nods. We discuss a little more in detail about when and how training should begin. We agree the sooner the better and the first group to train will be mostly his fellow Boarding Crewman, as they have actual experience with tense situations.

The announcement for evening chow goes off and suddenly I realize I'm hungry. Making my way up towards the galley, I'm greeted by an almost familiar smell. Could it be? Sure enough Lynn somehow threw together crème chicken pasta.

As I present my tray, Lynn says, "It's not exactly what we made in the restaurant, but it's damn close."

I smile, "I'm just happy to taste home."

I get a serving along with some Eggplant Salad.

Behind me, Larrodo says, "Hey come join us in the Mess."

I reply, "I'd like to check on my friends, actually. See how they're doing."

Larrodo understandingly nods. I make my way through a crowded Crew's Mess and spot Nate, Tim and of course Crewman Belkrest. There also doesn't seem to be much room near them. Perhaps I will eat in the mess after all.

I'm greeted by Larrodo who introduces me to all the other Deltas, most of whom I won't remember except Lana. We chat mostly about our various jobs and the silly stories about our respective subordinates. It even comes up about the meal being from my restaurant. I guess one of the Deltas was a customer once. I wish I had remembered, but part of meeting new people daily is that you forget faces unless they leave a lasting impression.

After the meal, I decide to take a little down time and relax in the Delta Lounge. A couple of other Delta ranked Crewmen happen to be watching Star Treader Three. Never much cared for that series... until now.

One of the Deltas, name I'm remembering not, says, "Why couldn't we have met peaceful aliens like the Glorkaans?"

"Yeah no shit." Says the other Delta, Bendon I believe, "First alien contact we have and they try to kill us. At least we're not stuck using primitive technology."

Damn... suddenly this unrealistic science fiction universe sounds like a better place to exist in than our reality.

The other Delta breaks my thought, remarking, "Oh yeah like that old classic from the late 20th century?"

"You know they made a sequel to that?" Bendon says, "Wasn't as good, but I like it. 3D is a little primitive, but still... both are classics. What about you, Sergeant, you got a favorite Sci-Fi?"

I shake my head, "Never much cared for that genre."

Both of their heads jolt back. Bendon says, "Wait... you're a Space Marine and you don't like Sci-Fi? It's practically our lives!"

"Nope," I explain, "I like ancient war movies and shows; more realistic than made-up hyperlanes, Quantonium Canons, aliens- well... that last one not so much anymore."

They both laugh a little.

"Alright, to each their own, I suppose," Benden says turning his attention back to the movie.

"I will say this," I remark, "Considering our current situation, this movie does seem favorable."

The other Delta chimes in, "You should see the show. It's more diplomatic and less pew pew, but man... when I was a kid I dreamed of meeting a Glorkaan. Instead I got shot at."

I ask, "You were in a firefight?"

Bendon pauses the movie.

The other Delta continues, "More like a slaughter. Watched my friend, Delta Romo fall in front of me as we ran for the ship... she was shot in the back."

"I'm sorry," I say, "I can, unfortunately relate."

Benden grabs a bottle of Scotch, judging by the smell and pours three glasses. He hands one to myself and the other Delta.

He raises his glass and says, "To Hal."

I add, "To Martin, my bartender."

We clink, touch the table and shoot. Bitterness, thy name is pain.

There's a silence among us for a moment.

The nameless Delta looks at me and asks, "How many of those mother fuckers did you waste?"

I take a breath and think for a moment, "Well... I wasn't really keeping score. Survival was my priority. But definitely more than ten."

He follows up, "Are you gonna train us how to kill them?"

Obviously I'll do my best to prepare the crew. The

look on his face, however solicited this answer, "Absolutely."

Nodding slightly he says, "I never used a laser after basic. Never needed to. I will be at your training tomorrow. I got a score to settle."

I nod, "Me too."

He's got a heart of vengeance right now. Under normal circumstances not the best mindset to learn to pick up a weapon. But these circumstances are far from normal. I'll train everyone, especially the ones eager to learn.

We have a couple more drinks throughout the movie. I guess when a character says their signature line we're supposed to take a shot or a swig. I catch the time on the clock. It'll be a long day tomorrow starting the program. I should try and get some rest.

Chapter Six: "I should've anticipated this."

(*Keller*)"Fire braking thrusters along with applying the gravity brake this time," I order

Lead helmsman Branson replies, "Will do sir, but the Grav-brake is having little effect on our momentum. We fired thrusters simultaneously during the initial attempted slow down, but our speed was only brought down by ten million MPS"

I should've anticipated this. We're going faster than our own engines could have ever possibly taken us. Problem is if we don't slow down soon, we'll miss our intended target area. I pick up my personal COMM and dial up the ENGCOM.

Lieutenant Slaighter answers, "Engineering Control, ENGCOM speaking."

"Lieutenant Slaighter," I say, "I need options here."

He replies, "Well, we got one good engine, but it won't be enough to slow us down even if we turn the ship around. In our current state, we're still looking at at least three to four weeks to repair the other engines unless we can set down somewhere and hopefully salvage metals for parts fabrication."

The asteroids we're heading for are supposedly rich with the minerals we need. Our Grav-brake is rated for slowing us down if we were going two-hundred sixty million MPS and we're cruising passed two-hundred seventy million.

I ask, "Would it be possible if we turn around, full blast the one engine to get us on or under Full Nine?"

ENGCOM replies, "Honestly, Commander I don't know. The speed we're traveling now wasn't even possible. The MaxNine engines are the fastest ones built because we don't need to go faster than two-hundred fifty million MPS."

I note, "Since we discovered Traverse Drive there's

been no need. A lot of good that's doing us now…"

I ponder for a minute. If we try and slow down the ship and we're successful we'll be able to mine resources for parts fabrication. But, we'll be stuck limping with one engine for up to four weeks, leaving us essentially stranded at Four Nines, which only comes out to fifty thousand MPS. If we try to slow down and we're unsuccessful, we're still drifting, but at a lower speed, meaning if we wanted to drift to a nearby moon or planet, it would take longer and we wouldn't have metals for fabrication. In fact, it would take so long that we would run out of supplies LONG before making it to the edge of anything.

ENGCOM breaks my thoughts, "Commander, should I fire up the engine?"

"No," I say, "Stand by for now," I end the call.

Sub-Commander Devlin walks up to me, "What's ENGCOM saying?"

I explain to him the conversation and we discuss my previously mentioned thoughts.

Sub-Commander sighs, "Now I'm even wondering if suggesting the propulsion blast was a good idea…"

I point out, "It gave us a fighting chance. Now we have to figure out our next step. It's certainly a more favorable position to be in than the alternative." I look over at the navigation table, "Navigator, start looking for nearby planets. Lieutenant Jefferson, send someone to wake up Mr. McNill. Helmsman Branson, how long until we arrive at our destination?"

The Navigator and Bridge Watch Officer acknowledge my commands.

Crewman Branson replies, "At present speed…" he takes a second to verify his display, "About two hours, sir."

I look over at Sub-Commander Devlin, "We have less than two hours to come up with a new plan."

Sub-Commander asks, "What do you have in mind?"

"As we discussed," I begin, "Trying to mine the asteroids puts us at significant risk. Our best bet is to locate a planet, use its gravity to slow down and then land. Hopefully we can find one with enough available mineral deposits to get the engines repaired."

Sub-Commander nods, "That sounds like a good plan. Can we talk for a minute?"

I nod and walk over to the forward port corner of the bridge with Sub-Commander hopefully out of earshot. I look at him indicating I'm listening.

He begins, "I'm concerned about allowing Mr. McNill on the bridge. I think he presents a security risk."

"How so, Mike?" I ask.

"I know you think he's innocent," he continues, "But he was officially kicked out because of espionage. True or not that does present a potential liability."

"His record says he was kicked out due to a conflict of interest," I clarify, "but let's say you're correct and he really was a spy. What's he going to do? Communications are down. He can't contact anyone."

Sub-Commander counters, "I understand, sir. My job however is to look after the safety of this ship and that includes potential security risks. He should be supervised at all times."

"Absolutely not," I say, "I trust Nate. I believe he was innocent and he will not be treated as a prisoner aboard my ship. We need his help and expertise on mining. Your concerns are noted."

The Sub-Commander says nothing more. I notice Nathan stumbling up to the bridge and walk over to greet him.

"Morning Mr. McNill," I say, "I know you weren't expecting to be up so soon, but we've run into a problem."

Nathan says nothing. He's probably waiting for further explanation. I start moving towards the Navigation table, "We've realized we might not be able to slow down so we're looking for nearby systems, hopefully one of them has a planet with resources we can use. That's why I had you come up here."

Nathan nods and steps over to the Navigator console, "May I?" he asks.

I nod at the Navigator and she steps aside. Nathan begins looking at nearby systems from our current position.

"What's our current speed?" he asks.

I answer, "About two-hundred seventy-four million MPS."

"Well passed Nine?" he clarifies, raising a brow.

I nod. He begins to manipulate the controls on the holographic map, he cycles through examining a couple systems.

Finally he speaks, "There's a Class Thirteen Bee planet about two weeks away, but it's mostly trees. Other natural resources are unknown. Without a complete survey crew, the only resource I can tell you for sure there is water. Maybe some vegetation, but as far as what we're looking for, I recommend the Seventeen Eff world. It's almost three weeks away, but it has the minerals we want as well as two moons we can mine."

Sub-Commander asks, "You're sure of this?"

Nathan nods, "Yes. My old Captain on the Ex Del Seven was considering an extended excavation there. We'll have to use environmental suits, it's pretty barren with little oxygen, but it's worth setting down there to mine the surface and the moons, assuming we have the food and water resources to make it."

I nod unenthusiastically, "We're gonna have to go on water rations as well as fire up the recycle plant… Do you remember how to send coordinates to the helm console?"

Nathan nods.

I order, "Do it. Helm, stand by to receive a new course, Lieutenant Jefferson, let me know once we're steady up on it. I'll be in my quarters…"

…(*Nathan*)Keller exits the bridge. As I'm setting up to punch over the coordinates to the Helmsman, the Sub-Commander comes up to me.

He begins, "I know you're a guest on this ship. However you are prior service so maybe show a little respect to the Commander of this ship, okay?" he finishes in a stern tone as if he's barking an order at me. I'm not really sure what I did. Or maybe it's what I didn't do.

I reply, "Okay."

"What!?" he asks sternly.

I think for a second, "…Aye… Sub-Commander."

"That's right." He says, "When you're done sending the coordinates, leave the bridge. You're only allowed up here if I or the Commander allow it and either of us is up here, understood?"

"Yes, Sub-Commander," I timidly acknowledge as an awkward silence takes the bridge.

Just what I needed. It isn't bad enough my entire life has been turned upside down and that I was dragged aboard the last ship I ever wanted to be on, but Sub-Commander Dick Waffle wants me to act as though I was reinstated under restrictive circumstances. Now I feel rough… like I'm a prisoner on this ship.

After leaving the bridge, I decide to head down to the Crew's Mess. Morning Chow will be starting soon. Might as well eat since I'm already up. I pour myself a cup of coffee and sit down. I take a sip. Bitter and gross. Just like my life. I notice a few other Crewmen scattered about at other tables, probably waiting for food as well, or so I assume.

Donna enters the Crew's Mess, grabs herself some coffee and sits down across from me.

"Good morning, Sergeant," I say.

Shocked, she asks, "Were you reinstated?"

"No," I shake my head, "I got yelled at by the Sub-Commander because apparently I wasn't giving Keller his due respect."

"What?" she says, "You're a civilian. You aren't obligated to respect anyone if you don't want." She takes a sip of her coffee and produces a disgusted look almost immediately, "Has it always tasted this bad?"

I nod, "Yeah. When it tastes good that's how you know something is wrong. Anyway, apparently cause I'm prior service I am supposed to act as though I was restored to Active." I explain further, "But here's the kicker, I don't even know what I did that wasn't respectful."

"That's bullshit," Donna says, "Maybe you should mention something to Commander Keller."

I shake my head, "He wouldn't care. If anything he probably told his Sub-Commander to put me in my place."

Donna raises an eyebrow, "You really think he's out to get you?"

I reply, "He didn't bother saving my career; wouldn't surprise me if he'd go so far to save his ego…"

…(*Donna*)Commander Keller is anything but egotistical. If Nate would share his past with me maybe I could understand his disdain.

Changing the subject I ask, "Are you all set to start mining today?"

He informs, "Nope. There's been a change in plans. They'll probably announce it shortly."

"Oh?" I inquire.

He nods, "Yep. Apparently we couldn't slow down so instead we're going to a desert world that's about three weeks away."

One of the other Crewman nearby asks, "What?"

Nate reiterates what he told me and explains he was just on the bridge helping set the new course. The Crewman thanks him and turns back to his cup of shitty coffee. I swear, it's worse today than it's been other days.

Nate turns back to me. I ask, "So what does your day look like, then?"

He answers, "I guess tweaking the new mining vessel."

"Well if you have time," I suggest, "you should come get some combat training."

Nate gives me a smirk, "Yeah, I'm not planning to fight in your war."

I clarify, "It's not necessarily offensive training. But if something happens to the ship, you'll be better prepared to protect yourself."

Nate informs, "Donna, here's how things are going to go: we're going to get communications restored and ordered to the nearest port away from any enemy incursions. Soon after, we'll Traverse there, whereupon I'll be getting off this ship cause I sure as shit ain't staying here or going to the front lines. I'll get my insurance claim from the Guild processed and then I'm off to a far away colony world away from the fighting to continue on with my life. This is just a minor blip in my story, but it doesn't continue on this ship."

I nod and ask, "And what if the fighting comes to you? What if where you think you go isn't far enough away, then what? Or better yet, what if there is no running from this enemy? What if no matter where you go, they find you?"

"Then at that point I'll fight them if I have to," he replies, "I did alright on Keldon Station."

There's a silence as I try to put this nicely, yet convey my point, "Um… you did okay, sure, but I highly suggest you come to training, as you could benefit from some improvement."

"I'll think about it," he says.

The Galley opens. Nate and I get our meals along with other Crew who were waiting. Prefab scrambled eggs and spam... great, I hope this doesn't mean the food stores have already run out. Nate heads back to his seat. I decide to head for the Delta Mess.

Besides a couple "Good mornings," the other Deltas mostly concentrate on their food.

Our attention is suddenly grabbed by the ship's PA system, **"Good morning Valkyrie Crewmates, this is the Commander. As most of you were expecting in about an hour we were supposed to arrive at an asteroid field to commence mining. Unfortunately we were unable to slow down. Instead we're going to try for a planet that is three weeks away. I know this means stretching supplies. As of now water rations are in effect. And the recycling plant will be brought online. We are not intending to use recycled water, however should it become necessary, we will make sure Re-Meds are distributed to everyone. With that in mind we'll also plan on normal work days for the next couple.**

I would like to inform you that one of our guests, Lead Sergeant Donna Kroeling of the Stellar Marines will be conducting training for enhanced combat. Boarding personnel are required to attend; however I would encourage the rest of you to attend if possible. I'd rather we be combat ready as a whole crew should the ship come under attack and be boarded. Otherwise, keep up the good work at restoring our other systems. We'll keep you advised should anything change. Keller out."

I ask, "What exactly does he mean? Like shower water?"

Most of the other Deltas grin while one shakes her head and explains, "The Recycler is a sewage treatment plant. It extracts water from the waste container. That's why you need to take Re-Meds to prevent getting sick in-case a little fecal matter ends up in your coffee."

The look on my face gives way to roars of laughter

from everyone else.

I sort of half smile and say, "Oh this is a joke, right?"

All of them confidently shake their heads. Great. Not only do I have to train over three-hundred people with no gear, but now I might be drinking poop water in a couple weeks.

Somehow I was able to make it work. We ran drills at least twice a day. I developed a system that put two teams together. Crew Members would swap out and train when called up to do so. This allowed them to tend to their other duties. Nate even showed up a few times and as I expected he's improved. Lieutenant Ephryn gives push back just about every day. Even Delta Larrodo agreed that I was training a little too hard. When I explained my reasoning to Commander Keller, he agreed that rigorous training was necessary...

...(*Nathan*)I spent the last two weeks converting two more SLVRDOs into mini miners. Keller decided to have more converted so we can scout and gather more resources. The extra time has proven a blessing in disguise. As much as I hate showering with only a sponge, we did in fact need more time to complete the conversions. I also decided to take Donna's advice and train. I think she had me set up on a special program or maybe I'm really not as good a combatant as I thought.

I tried to set up a simulator to practice mining, but the parameters were all combat based. Didn't make a whole lot of sense to go after a rock that's also shooting at you. So instead I logged some combat time. I really hope I don't have to take a SLVRDO into a fight. That thing flies rough. But I don't think they'll give me the keys to a CMRO...

...(*Keller*)The weeks go productively. Sergeant

Kroeling's training program is tough, but it's for the best. I need my crew to be combat ready should my ship come under attack. I also asked Mr. McNill and Mr. M'Nar to convert another ship along with the other two already converted. The more mining vessels we have, the faster we can gather minerals for fabrication. Though Nathan insists he'll have to train pilots as well, I'm confident my Crew Members will do an adequate job.

We also made a minor adjustment to our plan. Mr. McNill pointed out that we might bounce off the planet's gravity since we're going so fast. We're going to use the systems star to slow down. It'll add a few more hours to our trip, but it's necessary. Smart kid. I wish I could do more for him. He didn't deserve what happened.

On approach to the star, I'm sitting in my Command Chair located just behind the Lead Helm's chair.

"How long until we reach the star?" I ask.

Crewman Knoop replies, "About ten minutes, Commander."

I can see it in the distance. Hopefully it'll slow us down enough as we deflect off. The plan here is to approach the star, then bounce off towards the planet, using the star's gravity to slow us down in the process. Only problem is at our current speed if we don't turn in time we could either be thrown off course or, well, burned up faster than anyone hopefully realizes.

I order, "Swing us about one eight zero."

I pick up my personal COMM device and call engineering.

"Crewman Whitmore," a familiar voice answers.

I say, "Crewman, it's the Commander. Fire up engine two and transfer control to the Helm."

"Aye," he says and ends the call.

I order, "Navigator, activate the shades."

"Aye, Commander," Crewman Marriah Lopez

acknowledges.

A layer inside the transparent armor extends up. It is heavily tinted and makes everything except the star we're approaching, which is currently sitting on our rear, barely visible. Actually, it pretty much drowns out all other visible stars.

Crewman Knoop reports, "Commander, Main Engine Two is online. I have control."

I swivel around in my chair to face aft. I activate my holo display showing our current trajectory and distance to the star. The bridge starts to get brighter despite having the light screen up.

"Helm... " I order, "Full throttle."

"Aye," he says and engages the engine. Within a few seconds he reports, "Engine is at full, Commander."

"Shut it down and swing us about one eight zero," I command.

As we turn back to face our original heading, I follow the sun until it's back on our port bow.

"How is the armor holding?" I ask.

The situational officer answers, "Good, heat is within tolerance."

"Very well," I acknowledge. I notice our speed: two hundred sixty million MPS. I made the right call to not slow down at the asteroid field. Basically we would've been traveling to this system over another month or two if not more at our new current speed.

"Okay, people, now comes the fun part," I begin to say, "Helm, try to angle us as best you can to deflect off the star's gravity. Try to get us to come down under two hundred sixty million MPS."

"Uh, Aye, Commander," Crewman Knoop acknowledges, hesitating a little. He continues saying for the ship's record, "Coming up on Star XF-Thretta in the Thretta system. Current speed, two-hundred sixty-five. Angling ship with thrusters for gravitational deflection.

The secondary Helmsman, Liz Roy says, "speed is slowly increasing from Star's gravitational pull."

"Understood," Crewman Knoop says, "Firing starboard thrusters on full... turning ship to starboard, standby Engine Two... now!"

"Firing," Crewman Roy says.

We start to turn away from the star.

Crewman Roy says, "Speed reducing... two sixty-four... two sixty... two fifty... two twenty... "

Crewman Knoop interrupts, "Full turn away from the star."

After a couple of minutes the Helm stabilizes our course for Thretta V.

Crewman Roy says, "Stable speed... holding at eight point seven Nines, two-hundred two million MPS."

"Dammit!" Crewman Knoop expresses.

I lean in and say, "It's alright, Crewman Knoop. It just means a few extra hours on our trip. Our Gravity Brake can now slow us down effectively. Let me know what our new ETA is once the Navigator calculates it."

"Aye Commander," Crewman Knoop acknowledges.

I ponder for a second and realize that at this speed we can run some much needed combat drills for our small craft.

Crewman Knoop informs, "Commander, our new ee tee a to Thretta V is now thirty-seven hours."

"Very well," I say. I activate the ship's PA on my personal COMM. "Good afternoon Valkyrie Crewmates, this is the Commander. Our star brake was a success. We've slowed down to a safer speed which our Gravity Brake and thrusters can compensate for. It'll be another day before we arrive at Thretta V. For now I would like all CMRO pilots, co-pilots and trainees to suit up and stand by in the mission brief room. Flight Commanders meet in my office in ten minutes to discuss a training scenario. Keller

Out."

I get out of my chair and as I leave the bridge I say, "Lieutenant Esker, you have the bridge."

"Aye Commander, my bridge," she says.

I walk into the waiting area outside my office and am greeted by First Lieutenant Chet Lester and Second Lieutenant Malcolm Ruiz. They are dressed in their dark blue flight suits which consist of attachments for their cockpits. They snap to attention.

"At ease," I say, continuing into my office. They follow me in. "Please be seated," I say going to my chair and sitting down. I pull up the holo reenactment; specifically the sequence involving the fighters.

"I know last time we looked at this you said you would start simulator training based on combating these ships," I say pointing to the enemy ships on display. Continuing, "now we need to go live. I want you to conduct drills for the next few hours. We're moving at eight point five Nines so stay with the ship. We still only have one good engine. If we have to slow down, it'll be quite the setback."

Lieutenant Lester says, "We'll be sure to stay close, sir. I think we'll be able to train as though some of us are the enemy."

"Good," I say, "throw together a training plan and let me review it before you start."

Both LTs acknowledge, "Aye Commander."

"Dismissed," I say turning my focus to the holo recording for the thousandth time.

The Combat Mission Ready Outflyer is a small fighter specifically designed for the Armada. It seats two people; a pilot and a co-pilot, side by side. It is armed with three TXRL-44 Laser Cannons, two in the front and one in the back, as well as a large complement of micro missiles, small projectiles that could fit in the palm of your hand. Don't be fooled by their size, however. They pack quite a punch.

A consistency that was noticed by one of the gun control crewmen the last time I looked at this footage was that the projectile weapons were almost completely useless against the enemy's shields. The lasers on the other hand are not. The strategy is simple: use lasers to take down shields then hit them with the missiles. The other advantage to the micro missile is that the small size makes it almost impossible to shoot down.

My personal COMM goes off, "Keller."

Lieutenant Lester says, "Sir, we've got a drill plan put together. I've sent it to your console for review.

"Very well," I say, "Set Battle Stations for the Starboard Hanger," I end the call.

After reviewing and approving the flight plan I head to the bridge.

A COMMS Crewman states upon my arrival, "Commander, requesting permission to conduct Dogfight Drill, request approval for launch of all twenty-two CMROs."

I reply, "Permission granted. Launch all fighters from both hangars."

The COMMS Crewman relays the order. Within a few moments, the Outflyers pour out of the hangar; eleven from the front and eleven from the back.

I overhear on one of the speakers, "**Remember guys, the ship is moving at eight point seven Nines. Maintain a safe distance, but keep note of her course.**"

I hear most if not all of the pilots acknowledge Lieutenant Ruiz's transmission. I watch out the viewport as the fighters conduct their drill. They execute various maneuvers for defensive and offensive flying, attempting to outflank each other. It's a standard eleven vs. eleven simulated death match, so when someone is declared defeated, they leave the fight area and take station behind Valkyrie. There is no actual laser fire. Everything is simulated through their heads up displays.

In our current state, a significant challenge is presented to the pilots to focus on fighting, but also keep up with the ship. They're doing a good job of both.

They conclude their exercise just in time for Evening Chow. As I'm waiting for my meal, I take note how the crew appears to be in good spirits for the most part. It seems that our time spent adrift has been good. But soon we'll have the COMM array fixed as well as our engines and then it'll be time for war.

In the early morning, with coffee in hand I head up to the main bridge. We're just hours away from attempting to land the ship on one engine. Slightly nerve wracking.

"Commander on deck!" Lieutenant Esker shouts. Seems she's always on watch.

I nod my head, "My bridge. Is the planet within scanning range yet?"

"Yes, sir," Lieutenant Esker replies walking over to the Navigator's table, "We've got a couple of good spots so far. We've drafted initial approach vectors for them," she finishes, handing me a pad.

I scroll through them. They'll obviously need adjusting, "Which of these are closest to the resources?"

The Navigator begins looking at the information both on the charts and from our scans.

Finally Lieutenant Esker breaks the silence, "We'll have to look a little more closely and get back to you, sir."

"Very well," I say, "You have the bridge," I finish as a leave.

Lieutenant Esker replies, "Aye Commander, my bridge."

I head to the Port Hangar. The plan is to start mining operations as soon as we're landed. The elevator opens up to the hangar. I notice Mr. McNill hop into one of the newly converted SLVRDO miners. I walk towards him.

I take a sip of coffee then make my presence known

by asking, "You all set to start as soon as we're planet side?"

Nathan stops what he's adjusting and looks up, "Actually, sir, I wanted to talk to you about that. Tim and I were talking, and we think more rich deposits of minerals can be found on the moons."

"Okay," I acknowledge.

Nate continues, "So I'm thinking if you want us to get started right away, why not have us launch before you go on final?"

I nod and ponder his suggestion. It's a good one. I inquire, "Would mining the moons be easier than mining the surface?"

"Considerably," he nods, "the lower gravity makes extraction a lot easier and it would be safer to train your crew the essentials of mining."

"Alright," I say, "We'll probably change it up for the briefing, then."

My personal COMM goes off," Keller," I say.

"Commander, it's Kaight. We finished our scan of the planet. There's a spot we could squeeze into, but it's tight. However it's near what we believe to be a good source of raw materials."

I reply, "There's been a change in plan. Find a spot that's more open and safe. Draft up an approach vector and have it sent to my console in my room. Anything else?"

"No, sir," Lieutenant Esker says.

I close the COMM line.

By the time I arrive at my desk in my office an approach and landing vector has been sent to my console. After looking it over, I call up the bridge.

"Bridge, First Lieutenant Esker," Kaight says.

I begin, "Everything looks good. Before Final, I need you to add a point where we'll deploy the orbital sensor satellite and before that, another point where we'll launch the Outminers. They're going to commence operations on the orbiting moons before we land."

"Aye," she acknowledges, "Do you want that added to the brief?"

"Yes" I say, "Make sure you notify everyone involved."

"Will do, sir," she says, "we're about two hours from the final approach point. When shall we have the brief?"

"Probably in the next fifteen to twenty minutes," I suggest and close the line.

I'm not looking forward to this. Haven't been since we decided to skip the asteroid field and go right into a landing. Single engine planetary approach on a ship this size runs a higher risk of collision with the ground. Not only is it not advised, well... it's against Command Policy because it's so dangerous.

I hear the announcement for the updated brief time and start making my way to the mission brief room.

As I enter, Devlin says, "Commander on Deck" and everyone snaps up to attention.

"Be seated," I order approaching the front of the room. I say to Lieutenant Ephryn, "I would like to say something before we start."

He nods and steps aside.

I begin, "What we're about to do is not only dangerous, but it's against Stellar Command policy. Single engine landing on a ship larger than one hundred meters is forbidden. So if anyone would like, we can draw straws to see who gets a seat on the last two SLVRDOs that haven't been converted for mining."

The room is silent.

I continue, "Okay. Under any other circumstance I would not allow this, but we're left with little choice. I know briefs are boring, I've sat through a couple in my career-" a couple of the crew chuckle, I continue, "But I need you to pay extra attention to your roles in this one.

Lieutenant Ephryn, you may begin."

Lieutenant Ephryn goes over all the steps that I've already mentioned. The crew seems rather confident with what we're about to try and pull off which helps to boost my own. Some of them express their concerns for safety and others offer work arounds for those concerns.

Lieutenant Ephryn finishes the brief, "Alright stand by for notification. Until then secure for landing operations. Brief concluded."

I head down to my room to contemplate what we're about to do. I look at the bottom of my coffee, only a few cold sips left. This is not going to be fun. I hear the announcement over the PA for everyone to prepare for landing operations.

Stepping onto the secondary bridge, Lieutenant Ephryn announces my presence.

I nod, "My bridge."

"Aye, Commander, your bridge," he says.

The Secondary Bridge, located on the ship's underbelly, serves not only as a secondary command center for the ship should the main Bridge become compromised, but also as our landing bridge, as it offers a better view for touching down. It's significantly more cozy than the Main Bridge, has only one helm seat, a smaller Navigator's table, two COMM's consoles and only one weapon's control console. There's also only one chair for myself and the Sub-Commander.

Lieutenant Ephryn reports, "Sir, Sub-Commander reports Main Bridge ready for landing operations and ENGCOM says Engineering is ready as well."

The Navigator informs, "Two minutes to, uh, the launch point for the fighters- er I mean mining ships."

"Very Well," I say, "COMMs, inform the Main Bridge to launch Outminers once we're at the launch point."

"Aye, sir," the COMMS Crewman acknowledges.

Two minutes later the COMMs Crewman informs, "Outminers away."

"Aye," Lieutenant Ephryn acknowledges.

The Navigator informs, "Four minutes until, uh, Satellite Drop point."

"Very well," I acknowledge.

At one minute the Navigator starts counting down, "Sixty seconds to drop... " and so on until he says, "We're at drop!"

"Deploy Satellite," I order.

Within a few seconds the COMMs Crewman informs, "We have a good connection with Satellite, assuming standard orbit over Thretta."

"Very well," Lieutenant Ephryn acknowledges.

The Navigator nervously informs, "One minute to Final."

"Very well," I say, "Helm, align the ship for Final Approach.

"Aye, Commander, aligning for Final," Crewman Knoop acknowledges and rolls the ship left until the planet is below us.

"Slow us down to One Nine," I say.

Crewman Knoop Acknowledges, "Slowing to One Nine, Aye... the planet's gravity is starting to take us in."

"Take the Gravimetric Core offline and fire initial braking thruster," I order.

There is a loud rattling as the thruster fires off. It's close by the Secondary Bridge. Crewman Knoop holds the burst for about seven seconds. After he releases it's quiet for a moment before the viewport is engulfed in flames and the entire ship starts shaking violently.

"We've hit atmosphere!" Crewman Knoop shouts.

As our descent intensifies so too does the rattling of the ship. We're picking up speed.

"Fire second thruster!" I order, "Hold to prevent us from going into freefall!"

If we hit freefall, we lose the ship. Crewman Knoop holds the thruster longer than the first. It's barely noticeable as we continue piercing through the atmosphere. Finally we break through. The shaking continues, but not as violently. Only problem now is we're starting to fall faster than we're moving forward.

"Commander, we're off course!" Crewman Knoop shouts.

"Take whatever measures you need to get us safely on the ground, helm!" I order.

There's a reason Charlie is our go-to helmsman. He quickly brings the ship's speed back up to get us back on course. Using only one engine he fires the landing thrusters early to help maintain our altitude.

"Commander, I need more power from thrusters!" he informs.

I activate the ship's PA system, "Engineering divert power from generators to thrusters! Helm, don't burn them out!"

"Aye," he acknowledges and focuses on flying the ship. I notice through all the chaos what the surface reveals. It's mostly canyons and large rock formations leaving me a bit uneasy as this does not look like anything we could safely set down on.

Crewman Knoop informs, "We're back on course! I have the landing zone in sight!"

I look ahead and sure enough is a nice, open and mostly even area for us to set down on.

"Extend landing struts!" I order.

"Aye, extending landing struts," Lieutenant Ephryn acknowledges.

In front of us, a long, lanky strut folds out three times, partially obstructing our view. Smaller struts, rather pads, also extend on the front and back sections of both modules.

Lieutenant Ephryn informes, "Landing struts

extended and locked!"

Crewman Knoop says, "Coming over landing site! Slowing our approach! Setting engine to landing mode!"

The shaking continues as we come into a vertical landing, but we're starting to gracefully descend.

ENGCOM screams into the COMM, "Thrusters are approaching critical levels!"

"Crewman Knoop!" I shout.

He looks back at me with an irritated look and shakes his head. I realize there isn't much he can do. He then throttles back a little causing us to fall a little faster. We then abruptly shake hard one last time.

Crewman Knoop informs, "We're landed. Cutting thrusters, emergency shutdown of the engines initiated."

I sigh a relief, "Well done, Crewman Knoop. And well done all crew. Let's get everything settled and begin work to repair the ship."

Could that have gone better? Sure. We could also have had more engines and not be at war with aliens. Such is life for us now.

Chapter Seven: "This Was a Stupid Idea"

(*Nathan*)"**Mining vessels, you have permission to launch,**" I hear over the COMM.

Sitting next to me in the co-pilot seat, Tim picks up the mic unit and says, "This is Miner One, thanks. We're uh, launching now I guess."

I can't blame him for not knowing proper radio speak. He's an engineer, but I should probably handle communications from now on.

Anyway, with the craft powered up, I lift off from the deck and proceed out the port hangar door. My instruments indicate that the other three retrofitted mining vessels are following. With us is Crewman Belkrest and Crewman Mk II Lede Kamerov, a Navigator and certified SLVRDO pilot. Why isn't he flying? Because I'm actually teaching them how to mine and I got my basic small craft certification as well as some simulator time during our long transit. Kamerov observed my results and felt comfortable leaving me behind the stick with Tim in the co-pilot seat.

I note, "This thing is a lot easier to fly than I thought."

Kamerov replies, "Oh yeah, even Dev could fly one," referring to Crewman Belkrest.

Dev replies, "Oh fuck off, Lede."

"I'd rather fuck on," he retorts.

"I've already got a pinky for that, thanks," Dev burns.

Tim audibles what I'm thinking with an "Oooohhhh!"

Of course Lede and Dev are good friends so it's all in good fun.

I turn the ship towards Thretta V's moons. As we turn left and pitch up slightly, we can see Valkyrie going on final. I'm so glad to not be on that thing right now. I always hated landing even though it was a rarity. I never saw any practical value to it until now.

Our COMMS are configured with two radios; one for contact with the ship and the other for communications with the other mining vessels.

I grab the second mic unit and begin, "This is Miner One to all craft, acknowledge."

I hear over the COMM, "Miner Two here... Miner Three, here... Miner four, here."

I continue, "Alright, so mining isn't too hard, especially since we're using smaller ships. The technique is what's important. We mine in a cone pattern which we'll demonstrate once we arrive at the moon. It's simple to do, but execution takes time.

Once you cut out the piece of rock, turn your ship around, have your grappling crew grab the rock with the grapple gun and bring it into your makeshift cargo bay. Once you have your rock, return to Valkyrie, drop it off and then come back up for more."

Everyone acknowledges my transmission.

I finish, "You can mine the same spot a couple of times, probably more since we're using small craft. Just keep an eye on your sensors to determine if a spot is worth continued mining or not."

I then position the ship over the spot I intend to start drilling.

Tim says, "Ready when you are."

I nod, "Fire."

Tim presses a button on the control pad he rigged up for the laser. From the bow of our little ship emits a steady pinkish red laser beam.

Tim monitors its progress as it penetrates further into the moon's surface. Since it's a laser, it can also relay telemetry data.

"Can you bring us in a little closer?" Tim asks.

If I bring the ship in too close, the thrusters won't be able to compensate for the moon's gravity and I'll have to turn around. I slowly throttle forward while keeping an eye on our distance as well as the gravimetric intensity sensor.

Dev speaks up, "Nate, the thrusters aren't supposed to be sustained for long periods of time as is. I don't recommend going in any closer."

Tim acknowledges, "Alright, in that case, Nate, tilt the ship. We'll just have to get smaller pieces."

Nodding in agreement, I stop the ship where it is and tilt down.

Close to half an hour later, we've finished our cut. Tim powers off the drill and I swing the ship around while Dev gets up and goes into the cargo hold. After securing access to the cockpit, she opens the bay doors.

We wait a few seconds until she says over the COMM, "**I've got it hooked, but it's not coming loose.**"

I reply, "Lock in the cable, I'll try pulling it loose with the ship."

"**Okay…**" she says, "**cable is locked.**"

I throttle forward slowly until I feel the resistance of the tension. I have to be careful on how much I pull or I could potentially dislodge the hook and put Dev in danger.

The tension suddenly disappears, "Dev, talk to me," I say.

She replies, "**The rock is loose, reeling it in now.**"

"Awesome," I say.

I continue moving forward slowly in case the rock's momentum overtakes ours.

"**It's in,**" Dev says, "**sealing the doors now.**"

Less than a minute later, the cargo hold repressurizes and Dev re enters the cockpit.

She removes her helmet and says, "That wasn't so bad."

"Well done," I say. I grab the COMM unit for the mining frequency, "Just like that everyone. Take your time and be safe. We'll be back up in a bit."

The other mining vessels acknowledge my transmission. Tim punches up Valkyrie's coordinates into the computer and then contacts them on the COMM to announce we're on our way back. We get through the atmosphere with no issues. As we close in on our mother ship, I notice some of the Crewmen in environmental suits setting up atmospheric containment generators under the ship's hull. In dire circumstances, of which we are in, the ship can land and the hull section containing the engines can be lowered offering a larger and more open work area for extensive repairs. The engines can also be changed out for a new set in a shipyard, but unfortunately we are the shipyard and our replacements parts are sitting in their base form in the back of our Outminer.

We... I'd almost forgotten, I'm not a part of this crew. The sooner they get themselves fixed, the sooner I can be off at the next port and on with my life. Hopefully I can get my losses recouped in the form of credits and figure out my next chapter.

After receiving clearance for landing, I bring the ship back into the port hangar and set it down facing out the hangar door opening. The four of us get out and start unloading our haul. I look around as the crew is cleaning up from the landing. Guess not everything was secure.

The ENGCOM walks up to Tim, "Hey man, we may need you to oversee the processing and fabrication."

Tim replies, "Sure. Hey Nate, you're gonna have to take charge of things up there."

I shrug my shoulders, "Kay."

Dev starts extending the bed of the SLVRDO as the Processing Team arrives with a large, flat cart to carry it over to the Processor.

After it's unloaded, Dev starts retracting the bed. I stop and look out the hangar door opening for a bit. It always amazes me how the generators simply hold the oxygen in by attracting the atoms with an atomic field set to eight instead of some silly force field thing. Of course if it fails the oxygen will immediately disperse hence why they are hooked into the ship's power source and not used on field operations.

Lede breaks my distraction and asks, "You mind if I fly this one?"

"Not at all," I say and head to the co-pilot's seat.

Dev joins us from the back after securing the doors, "Gotta sit alone, eh?"

I remark, "Unfortunately, Tim is too cool for the rest of us." Grabbing the COMM unit mic for the radio set to Valkyrie I say, "This is Miner One requesting permission to depart."

A voice says back a few seconds later, "**Miner One, this is Valkyrie Control, permission granted. Be advised, Miner Three is inbound with cargo.**"

"Understand all, Val-Con," I reply, "We're standing by on Working Frequency Seven."

Lede gracefully takes off. As we climb, I locate Miner Three on sensors and point them out by highlighting them with a friendly target indicator on the HUD so Lede is aware.

The rest of our day goes productively and without incident. Some of the rocks we pull offer sufficient resources while others, well... we had to dig a little deeper in some spots. Lede and I traded off frequently and Dev even did a couple of runs while I worked the grapple hook to haul in the rocks.

With dinner time approaching, we decided to call this our last run for the day. While Lede is piloting, I, working the laser controls in the co-pilot seat, notice an energy signature pop up on one of our sensors.

"I'm stopping the drill," I indicate and power it off.

Lede asks, "What is it?"

Grabbing the radio set to Working Seven, I say, "Valkyrie Control, this is Miner One. We've detected an unknown energy signature and it appears to be headed towards the planet. I'm connecting with the orbiting satellite to send along our sensor data. I'll have it to you shortly."

They reply, "**Understand, Miner One. We're standing by.**"

As I'm working on the computer, Dev asks, "What do you think it is?"

"It's more what I hope it isn't," I answer.

Lede asks, "Should we bring weapons online?"

I ponder out loud, "Unknown energy signature, we're on the run from hostile aliens…"

Lede thinks for a second and then nods in agreement. He begins powering up the two forward laser cannons while Dev powers up the turret.

Over the COMM we hear, "**All ships, the is Valkyrie Control, be advised, the energy signature picked up by Miner One has a close match to the hostile ships that attacked Keldon. Take defensive measures and return to the ship immediately!**"

"Valkyrie this is Miner One," I say into the COMM, "I recommend broadcasting subsonic interference on all sub-band frequencies. It's a tactic I've used against pirates to disrupt their long range communications. Even though our long range COMMS are down, we can still create localized interference to the edge of the system."

They respond, "**Noted, Miner One.**"

I continue, "I also suggest we try and intercept this vessel. If it is a scout they could still get a signal out by other means we aren't familiar with."

"**Also noted,**" they say.

Dev says, "I wonder how long it will take for them to make a decision…"

"Too long," I say, "give me helm control."

Lede asks, "Why?"

"I'm just going to follow them for now," I explain,

"Plus, if I act before getting orders you won't get in trouble."

Lede throttles the ship and starts heading for the enemy contact. He must know it's the right thing.

"That works too," I say.

He keeps a reasonable distance. Hopefully it hasn't detected us, but there's no way to know.

Lede says, "It's heading into the atmosphere."

We observe a small burst of flame above the planet as the ship enters it. We're still far enough back that we can't see the ship itself yet-

"I've got visual," Dev states.

My assumption is she can see the ship on the turret camera.

We hear over the radio, "**Miner One, this is Valkyrie. Free to engage free to engage.**"

"Understood, Valkyrie, free to engage," I reply back into the COMM.

Lede orders, "Dev, try to keep eyes on him as we hit atmosphere."

I note, "I've plotted an estimated trajectory based on their movements. I don't think we've been detected."

Lede says, "I'm gonna go in a little hot. The sooner we get through, the quicker we can get back on them."

Before I can say anything, a transmission comes over the COMM, "**Miner One, this is... we've... radi...**" the communication cuts out as fire engulfs all around us. We transition much rougher than we have all day. Lede is trying to break through as fast as possible. The COMM unit mics rattle off their hooks. Our sensors give impossible readings. I hope Lede is aware the faster you go into an atmosphere, the longer you burn.

I feel for a second the planet's gravity followed by a dropping sensation as we tilt down towards the ground. We had better not be in a fucking free fall.

"We're through," Lede notes, "but we're in free

fall."

Fuckin idiot. A huge problem that can occur when entering a planet's atmosphere is that if you go too fast you'll burn up or worse, the planet's gravity pulls you into terminal velocity while speeding in and brings you into free fall. It's not impossible to get out of, but it's damn sure nerve racking. Lede punches the throttle to maximum while tilting the ship straight back up to counter the fall. For a good ten seconds we're ground bound until finally the engines overcome and our descent slows. Finally we regain control of our altitude and Lede levels out the ship.

He chuckles, "Well that was close."

I reply, "What the fuck, dude!?"

"Excuse me?" he says.

"That wasn't necessary," I begin, "you should have slowed down! The extra time we've spent having to brake-"

He interrupts, "I know full well what I'm doing! I've been flying-"

"Guys," Dev tries to say.

By this time we're engaged in incomprehensible arguing until finally Dev yells, "SHUT THE HELL UP!!!!"

We both look back at her surprised at the rather intimidating scream such a typically sweet young woman just belted out.

She states, "Lede, I trust your piloting skills and have known you for a while now, but he doesn't know you and has every right to fear for his life. However, Nate-" there's always a but, "we're trying to track down a hostile vessel. We will discuss this incident AFTER we've taken care of the alien threat."

Lede and I look at each other for a second then look down, well I do anyway. Then I turn back to my console analyzing the enemy ship's projected course.

I say, "Recommend you proceed at two eight seven degrees true to local planet's navigation."

Lede throttles the ship while Dev, I assume, scans around with the turret.

I grab the COMM unit mic and say, "Valkyrie, this is Miner One. Were you trying to reach us earlier?"

A few seconds pass and they say, "**Miner One, affirmative. Be advised we've set battlestations and the Dorsal Gun is armed. We've set a danger radius of 500 meters. If that ship enters our zone, steer clear.**"

"Understand all," I say in response and set the mic back on its hook.

I verify my assumed trajectory and for a second marvel in amazement at our technology. Any time we approach a planet we're unfamiliar with, that's unmapped, our orbital satellite is able to create navigational grids after one sweep. We try to keep it as close to Earth's as possible, but each planet has varying differences. Some planet's maps will go as high as 75 even 80 degrees North and South and 240 degrees East and West. It does this by identifying the magnetic poles, analyzing the angle of the planet towards its star and confirming where the most heat constantly hits the planet to determine its equator.

Lede asks, "Anything?"

I shake my head, "Go to plus ten Z."

"Increasing altitude," Lede confirms.

I watch our sensors closely. Inside the planet's atmosphere sensors are significantly more degraded than when using them in open space. Especially this desert rock. They could easily disappear in a dust storm or if they get close to a mineral deposit our scans could be disrupted by magnetic interference.

Along with other objects on the planet's surface, finding something, even just the energy signature, is becoming more difficult.

It's quiet for a few minutes. Lede breaks the silence, "Nothing?"

I shake my head while keeping focus on the screen.

Something blips for a second. I watch for a few more seconds... noth- wait there it is again. Watching the XY axis screen I check the YZ axis to determine if the object I'm seeing has an altitude. Sure enough it's constantly popping up.

"I think I have something," I say, "It's just off our starboard bow... at about four thousand meters and just slightly below us."

Devorah asks, "Can you give me the technical coordinates relative to spatial navigation?"

I reply, "3776Y25GX-12Z."

After a few seconds, Dev says, "I have visual! Their current reported distance puts them out of weapon's range. I'll hold them on view while you drop fourteen meters"

"Can you lock target?" Lede asks.

Dev replies, "I can, but if they detect the tracking laser they might become aware of us if they haven't already."

I note, "Nothing in their pattern indicates they are aware of our presence. If they are, they don't seem to see us as a threat."

Lede retorts, "They are an alien civilization, possibly more advanced than we are. If they have detected us and don't see us as a threat... then they probably think they can take us in a fight."

I ponder for a second, then suggests, "Maybe we should wait for backup."

Lede shakes his head, "There's one thing we can do. Devorah, lock weapons. Let's see how they react."

Our viewport HUD pops up with a target lock indicator showing the ship in the distance. Suddenly their movement becomes erratic.

"Looks like we spooked them," Dev states.

I also lock target with the ship's sensors. The enemy vessel dives towards the surface. Lede follows. As we follow, the ship does barrel rolls and corkscrews to shake us. Lede does his best to keep up, but our ship is considerably less maneuverable. Finally we get within weapon's range.

"Engaging!" Dev says as she lets off her first volley.

At this distance, Lede and I can see the ship. It may be much bigger than we initially thought. As the laser battery makes impact the entire vessel appears to light up.

"Did you get it?" Lede asks Dev.

"No," I say as the light dissipates and reveals an undamaged ship. I speculate, "They appear to have some sort of shielding."

We level off. The alien vessel looks like it's heading towards a canyon of rock formations. As we've gotten closer this ship looks to be about eight times our size yet it somehow can out maneuver us.

Over the COMM we hear, "**Miner One, what is your status?**"

Grabbing the mic I say, "We've located and engaged the hostile ship. They are trying to lose us in a rock formation canyon."

"**Miner… can't… again.**" they answer very broken.

I attempt to repeat what I just said. This time there is no response.

Suddenly our ship shakes.

"Ah hell!" Lede screams.

I realize quickly that the enemy vessel has out flanked us and we're being fired upon.

"Dev, shoot-" he's interrupted as Dev rattles more shots off.

With a more sustained burst, the hostile ship lights up considerably brighter. We sustain another hit. Unsure exactly where. Suddenly the enemy ship's bright light disappears and as Dev continues to pound them with lasers, they veer off.

Dev and I cheer for a second at this minor victory. Lede isn't as excited. I notice that we're tilting left and he's trying to stabilize.

Lede explains, "I'm not getting a response from the port attitude thrusters."

I run a diagnostics check and sure enough, "Yeah they're offline."

"Put Valkyrie's position in the HUD," Lede orders.

I do so. Lede turns towards her and starts to climb as high as he can.

I grab the COMM mic and say, "Valkyrie, this is Miner One, come in!"

"Miner one this is Valkyrie, what is your status?" they answer.

I reply, "Inflight emergency! We've taken two hits, one knocked out our port attitude thruster. We're attempting to return to you now!"

They ask, **"Miner One, what is your position?"**

"Sending it-" wait, the subsonic interference, dumb ass. It blocks data transmission frequencies. "One second!" I say. Pulling up our track history I determine our estimated position.

I say into the COMM, "Estimated position is two four one eight south. One one three... five six west."

"How many hits did you say?" they ask.

"Two," I answer.

We're hit again.

"Make that three," I correct.

Lede screams, "I've lost Engines! We're going down!"

"Starship down! Starship down!" I scream into the COMM saying our position over and over.

Lede starts to fire descent thrusters to prevent us from entering freefall again. Dev maintains her calm, trying to target the enemy ship. As I'm screaming into the COMM, I notice the enemy ship try to straiff our port side.

Dev plugs them full of energy as they come across to our bow. Without thinking, I slam the fire control for the drill. The solid beam hits their ship and begins to do noticeable damage to their hull. Dev hits them some more and they begin to fall out of the sky. We got em.

But celebration will have to wait as we're still falling too. I set the COMM down after reporting that we somehow managed to take out the enemy ship. I then try to track it as long as I can. We may end up a smoldering heap, but maybe Valkyrie can salvage our records.

Dev reports, "Enemy ship is out of weapon's range."

"Good," Lede expresses.

He reaches up and pulls down a lever located in the overhead.

"Emergency chute deployed," he says.

"Wait, what?" I ask.

Puzzled, Lede inquires, "You didn't-" he's interrupted as our vessel's momentum abruptly slows upon what I assume is this emergency chute being completely unfurled and the wind catching it.

"As I was saying," Lede continues, "you didn't know we had that?"

I shake my head, "The concept was still, well, just a concept. The Armada didn't see the practicality of storing one since we mostly operate in space."

Dev clarifies, "Well, that all changed when two of them went down during a planetary mission killing everyone including my husband."

"...what!?" I shockingly ask.

She asks, "You didn't hear about that?"

I answer, "No. After I was kicked out, I never really kept in contact with anyone. I'm so sorry... why didn't you mention it earlier?"

Dev answers, "I was about to, but we were interrupted... It didn't come up again and it's not something I like to bring up often."

"I understand," I say, "Damn… I really liked Todd, too…"

"The feeling was mutual," Dev says, "From what he said about you-"

"Guys!" Lede interrupts, "I'm not liking the looks of this!"

I look out my right viewport and sure enough we're headed for steep slopes and what looks like concentrated, violent wind storms. Ideal for landing… into our deaths.

Lede states, "I'm going to try to push us into a better spot with the last functioning thrusters."

After scanning with the sensors and visually, I suggest, "If you can, try heading for 50Y RX12."

"Easier said than done," Lede remarks.

He tries to manipulate the thrusters towards that location.

Over the COMM we hear, **"Miner One, what's your status?"**

I reply into the Mic, "Uh… we deployed the emergency chute, but we are descending into an unfavorable landing zone."

Valkyrie replies, **"We've got your last position. Try to give… update… we…"** they cut completely. We've descended out of communications range.

Lede tries his best to move us to a better landing zone, but is unsuccessful as the wind keeps tugging on the chute and pulling us back. A gust kicks up sending us further away from where we want to go and almost into a large, thin, towering rock obelisk.

Dev remarks, "That was a little close for comfort."

Examining the surface, it seems conditions are as favorable as they are going to get.

Lede asks, "What's the distance to the surface?"

I look at the computer for a couple of seconds and say, "About twenty meters."

"Brace yourselves," Lede orders. He twists the lever and pushes it forward.

I hear the cables release followed by a falling sensation for an uneasy 3-6 seconds and the anticipated crash as we hit the ground. Then comes the grinding as we slide towards what appears to be a wind storm. We pick up speed, hit a rock and are now facing up towards the obelisk, sliding backwards. We're consumed by the sandstorm, hit another object, spin again and end up wedged as we stop moving. The three of us sigh relief despite the sand and dirt pelting our hull. Then the ship starts to creak as we tilt forward slightly.

"Get out," Lede says lifting up the center console. Dev has already opened the cargo bay access and is ripping out the environment suits for Lede and I. The ship continues to creak and slide forward over what must be a cliff. Dev puts on her helmet and tries to help me put on my suit.

Lede orders, "Dev, get the emergency kits and rifles ready."

Dev pulls up one of the cargo bay panels and pulls up another panel underneath that. She starts pulling out rifles and emergency kits while I scramble to get my gloves on. Outside, the wind has picked up and continues to push us over the unseeable edge. Lede and I fasten our helmets, pick up our rifles and grab a set of gear each. Dev pulls the emergency release on the bay door, bypassing the decompression sequence blowing the doors open. They sort of blow back closed and the entire ship fills with dust and whatever is in the air.

Lede says, "**COMMS check.**"

Dev and I both reply slightly staggered, "Loud and clear!"

"**Let's move,**" Lede orders.

We emerge from the vessel, making sure we've got everything.

Lede says, "**Stay here. I forgot to make sure the beacon was transmitting.**"

"Leave it!" I yell.

He disregards common sense and heads back into the ship. It starts to slide more and more.

"Dammit, Lede!" I express.

Dev and I anxiously wait. The storm has picked up or so it seems making it harder to see. Lede's lights from his environment suit finally appear as he approaches the back of the vessel, it begins to go over. He runs as quickly as he can, but he and the ship disappear into the thickness of the storm.

Dev and I approach cautiously to see if he made it. I look around and finally see orange lights indicating the back of his suit. He starts to get up and I reach down to help him.

Letting out a big sigh he says, "**That was close. Hopefully the signal goes out.**"

"Assuming there's anything left of the ship," I note, "we should try for higher ground to make contact with Valkyrie."

"**We should stay here and wait for a pick-up,**" Lede says.

I state, "We can't sit here in this storm. We don't even know if the beacon is transmitting. If we can make contact, it will better our chances."

Dev speaks up, "**What about the crashed alien ship? We're the only ones who saw roughly where it went down.**"

Lede ponders for a second, "**That's assuming we could even find our way to it. For all we know, it'll be caught up in this storm. I think we should stay. The storm could let up here.**"

I unsling my rifle, power it up and say, "Wait here if you want. I'm going to try and make contact higher up."

As I start to leave, Dev says, "**I'm with Nate on**

this one."

Dev and I begin to make our way up the slope.

Over the COMM, Lede says, **"Fine. We'll do it your way."**

We slowly hike up. But the storm's intensity is unchanged or it's getting worse, but conditions are not improving. We get brief periods of better visibility, but it's not helping much. All I know is up is the direction we want.

Gusts continue to kick up every so often making it hard to determine if conditions are improving. Then suddenly the strangest thing happens: we completely step out of the storm and into complete clear and calm. We can see everything, including a rock slope leading up to one of the towering obelisks and other nearby, similar rock formations.

The three of us look back in amazement. The storm is still blowing below where we were, yet where we stand it's calm and clear.

Lede expresses, **"Wow... that's not something I've seen before..."**

"Me neither," I say.

I start looking around for signs of the crashed alien ship. So far all I see are more obelisk rock formations atop rock slopes similar to the one we're on. From what I can tell by other ones not as badly obstructed by these strange wind storms, they seem to drop off into vast canyons through which these storms are gusting.

I walk over to Dev who has been scanning the storm we emerged from.

She says, **"I think I can map these currents. But my specialty is mechanics, not meteorology."**

I nod and say, "I can't find any initial indications of the crashed alien ship."

"Try using your DigiNocs," Dev suggests.

Lede joins us, **"I've sampled the air. It's mostly**

Nitrogen and CO2. But there's almost five percent oxygen. We should scoop some while the air is clear."

Even though our tanks are mostly full, he's right. One of the first things they teach in planetary survival is always keep your tanks as full as possible. Underneath the left wrist on our suits is a small scoop device which absorbs outside air, filters the oxygen and adds it to our tanks. On my inside forearm I activate the device using a small control panel.

"VuapVuapVuapVuapVuap," the device sounds as we begin collecting air.

We walk in separate directions swinging our arms left and right for about five minutes until our tanks report full.

After securing the devices, we hike further along the rock slope. Lede tries to contact Valkyrie with no luck. We come around the ridge and stop. On my left wrist are the controls for my DigiNocs: a zoom display on my helmet's viewport. I pop the protective cap off the controller, which is attached to the suit so it doesn't get lost. I manipulate a small camera mounted on the top of my helmet and I zoom in and start scanning the horizon. Dev starts to do the same, starting and scanning in a different area. I catch what appears to be pinkish smoke. Zooming in some more, it appears to be behind another sloped hill out in the distance.

"I think I found the crash," I announce.

I assume Dev scans over to where I'm looking.

"I see it too," she confirms.

Lede also adds, **"Yep, I think that's it. Question is, how do we get there?"**

I suddenly remember that the environment suit is also equipped with a mapping tool. On my right forearm is a controller for it and a small map that can be projected in my helmet's Heads Up Display. I press the "scan" button and from the exact top of my helmet emerges a small scanning laser. It quickly sweeps the area with about a ten thousand meter range and up to about two hundred meters high from where I'm standing… If I'm remembering the specifications correctly. It maps the terrain as far as it can reach giving us a better idea of which path to take.

I point my hand in a direction that seems best to get where we want. It takes us further along the side of the slope we're on. We begin making our way.

As we're walking, I say to Dev, "I'm sorry to hear about your husband. I can't believe what happened…"

"Sometimes I can't either." she replies, **"I specifically chose the assignment on Valkyrie to help me move on. Maybe it would just feel like I was away on a deployment."**

"Does that actually help?" I inquire.

She answers, **"Some days are better than others. I took some time to myself and started to realize he'd rather I continue on with my life… as hard as it is."**

"Absolutely," I add.

She continues, **"I dated a couple of guys here and there only to realize I was trying to find Todd in all of them… but they weren't him. I'm kind of in a thing with this guy on Douger Colony right now."**

"Kind of?" I speculate, "Like friends with benefits?"

She clarifies, **"I mean he's not ready for commitment until I'm ready to see him as him and not Todd. But we've spent time together and what not. It's hard to describe what exactly we are."**

I say, "Together, but not together?"

"Yeah…" She says.

We're silent as we trudge along the side of the slope. I look to our right where it slopes down and observe the continued wind patterns. How they seem to just sit at the lower elevations is truly a wonder of what you'll find out here. Had I been on an Explorer, maybe I would've catalogued and observed this phenomenon more intensely. Maybe I would have been on the ground team that studies it up close kind of like we are now. Instead I just ended up as a navigator and a victim of someone else's screw up.

We stop at the slope which appears to descend gracefully into the stormy valley. However the wind patterns seem to veer off forming other wind tunnels. And coming from the left seems to be another wind sand storm tunnel going off in another direction. Before us looks calm as it goes into a maze of rock formations, I can see the pinkish smoke emanating from what we believe to be the crash site. It seems steady enough that it's not down in one of the wind tunnels. Yet we may have to pass through some to get there as the cliff in front of us is too steep and too smooth to climb.

Dev steps up and starts scanning the various wind tunnels and currents while I update the map.

Dev says, "**I'm picking up wind currents of up to three hundred kilometers per hour in there. Nothing sustained, just appears to be gusts every now and then.**"

I also note, "The laser is having trouble with mapping the valley. Probably due to the dirt being moved around. I'll have to switch to constant scanning."

Lede, skeptically asks, "**Are we sure we want to go in there?**"

Dev says, "**If I track the wind patterns long enough, we should be able to determine a separate pattern in the gusts and if we all three switch to constant map, we should be able to find a way through.**"

Lede ponders for a second, then says, "**We should attach life lines then. Dev should take point and I'll bring up the rear.**"

Dev and I nod in agreement. On the front of my suit, around the belt area is a small, rather tough tether coiled into a small compartment. It stretches out about five to seven meters. I attach my end onto a small hook-ring on the back of Dev's suit. Lede does the same hooking into mine.

We start our descent into the opening. As we come eye level with both wind tunnels howling on our left and our right, I'm mesmerized by the sight. Where we're standing is calm, yet near us the winds rage on in their various patterns. We stop once we're on level ground.

Lede suggests, "**We should refill our tanks before going in.**"

I disconnect from Dev and Lede from me. We all three activate our collectors and start walking and swinging our arms as we did before. Upon our tanks reading "full" once again we re-tether ourselves and prepare to go back into the wind tunnel.

Dev asks, "**Ready, guys?**"

"**...Yeah.**" Lede replies.

"As ever," I say after hitting a couple of buttons on my map controller.

Dev steps into the tunnel and almost instantly disappears. I look over at Lede who is clearly unsure if this is a good idea, then look back into the storm as I step through. The lifeline starts to gain tension.

I say into the COMM, "Dev, slow down a bit."

She does so as Lede steps in... I assume.

The wind begins to pick up, roughly seventy to eighty kilometers per hour. It's becoming a struggle to walk, but it's manageable.

Dev orders, "**Activate GripS!**"

On my suit's left thigh is a button which activates small Grip Spikes to help keep our footing in the ground. We trudge along, only able to see maybe ten meters ahead intermittently. The dirt pounds our environment suits, but thankfully isn't doing any noticeable damage. The mapping tool, however, has become completely useless. It can't rectify the dirt moving through the wind tunnel. If we could find a wall- suddenly a large gust kicks up knocking me off balance and I assume the others as well.

"**Is everyone alright!?**" Dev asks.

Lede responds, "**We need to go back!**"

"**Calm down, Lede!**" Dev snaps, "**I think I see a clearing! Just keep your head level!**"

Lede reluctantly says, "**...fine!**"

As we get up another gust blows through. This one considerably bigger and more powerful than the last as it throws all of us forward about a hundred meters or more. I roll momentarily before stopping. The wind continues, sustained around eighty kilometers.

Lede screams, "**We should've stayed near the beacon!**"

"Well... we are near the beacon..." I say softly yet audible enough to still be heard.

Lede says, "**What do you mean!?**"

I answer, "What's left of it just landed in front of me."

Yes, before me are the remains of Miner One, only five meters from my face. It must have been kicked up and moved by even stronger gusts.

"Dev," I say, "Dev respond..."

I get up and detach the lifeline which is crushed under the debris. I try to assess the premise, but it appears the worst has happened.

Lede stumbles up, "**Holy shit! She wasn't... was she?**"

"Devorah!" I say, "Devorah please respond!"

No response, nor are we picking up her transponder. It shouldn't take a genius to figure out that Dev was in fact crushed.

"**This was a stupid idea,**" Lede expresses.

"We gotta press on," I say, "our best bet is to follow the currents, find that crashed ship and try to contact Valkyrie."

Lede nods and we continue, with intermittent gusts

and visibility. Another large one kicks up sending us flying about two hundred meters. As I recover, there's a mild break within the storm long enough for me to look up and see Miner One's remains tumbling towards me. For once I agree with Lede: this was a stupid idea.

Chapter Eight: "Two Birds"

(*Donna*)Sitting in a briefing, I can't help but wonder if Nate is still alive. The ship he was in was shot down and best the satellite imaging can tell, it was over an area not ideal for landing, let alone of the crashing variety. Their emergency beacon was also last reported moving before it went silent.

But that part of the briefing was for the Rescue Team. I'm on the Scout and Recon Team. Our mission is to infiltrate the crashed enemy vessel. I was charged with picking my team. Most of these guys have the same training, except Agsnon. He has computer tech expertise that I feel would be valuable for this mission.

Crewman Dayson and Crewman Putvel have proven themselves capable fighters and nothing personal against Valkyire's Crew, but I'm bringing Lynn for long range.

Lieutenant Ephryn finishes, "...so those are the Rescue Team's objectives. If there are no questions, I'll turn it over to Sergeant Kroeling for the tactical portion of this brief."

I get up and face everyone, grabbing the pad from him.

"Thank you, sir. Commander Keller, fellow crewmates, this is the Scout and Recon plan for this mission." I begin manipulating the large map projected behind me to display what I am discussing. "As the Lieutenant mentioned, the satellite has observed these strange weather patterns all around this valley. The crash site itself is on this rock slope, but there are low speed wind storms surrounding it and best we can tell, part of the ship is sitting in one. I want to use these for cover as we approach seeing as we know very little about our enemy with the exception that they are hostile."

I pause for a second to make sure everyone is still with me.

Continuing, "After we do our initial sweep for Miner One, we'll remain low as we approach this rock slope adjacent to the one the crash is sitting on. We'll drop off out of view, make our way along the side and find a place to plant our overwatch. Then the rest of us will proceed into the wind current, use it as cover for when we come upon the crash site."

I stop and notice Sub-Commander Devlin has his hand up.

"Yes, sir, question?" I say.

He asks, "What are the wind velocities in the area you intend to cross? From what I've seen it's been as high as ninety kilometers per hour with occasional stronger gusts."

I answer, "The strongest observed has been up to sixty kay pee aitch, but also consistent. Visibility, however will be low, but I feel it is the most discreet approach. Any other questions?"

No one says anything. Commander Keller gets up and stands next to me in front of the screen.

He says, "I want to assure everyone that this is the best plan we could come up with. Finding our people is one of our top priorities, however we have a rare opportunity to possibly learn who our enemy is. I'm confident that under Sergeant Kroeling's direction this will be a successful mission and we'll bring everyone home safely. Dismissed."

As I leave, Commander Keller gives me a nod of confidence. I'll do my best to ensure there are no casualties. I just hope he understands there's a good chance not everyone will come back home.

In the Armory we get ready for our mission. We don what's known as the Tactical Environmental Armor or TEA for short. It's a skin tight, partially fluidic metal suit. The helmet is much smaller than the standard environment suit, which means a smaller HUD, but wider field of view. I clip the belt on which has extra mag pouches, a lifeline and triage kit. Finally, a vest with a couple more pouches, secondary air tanks and a grapple harness should we need to repel anywhere. We also decide to put on standard environment boots in case we need to use the GripS.

I walk into the storage area where we had to turn over our rifles that we brought aboard at Keldon. The Crewman in charge of small arms, a Weapons Specialist, I believe they're called, attempts to hand me one of their standard issue 100-M60s.

He says, "Are you sure I can't interest you in some real firepower?"

I roll my eyes brushing passed him to where mine and Lynn's rifles are stored

"Listen kid," I say opening the case and grabbing my guns, "I was still in active service when we switched to that underpowered peashooter and I gotta tell ya," I pause to admire my rifle, "I'll trust my personal rifle over that thing any day."

The Crewman retorts, "Yeah, but you're limiting yourself to the civilian version."

I counter, shaking my head, "Not even. This is the 10-400M, Full Mil-spec. And my friend's weapon is the 10-40MX with adjustable settings. Ten years of honorable service allows for a lot of options when it comes to personal gun ownership."

I leave, handing Lynn her rifle. She checks that it's fully charged. I do the same.

We step off the lift into the port hangar. Tim walks up to me as I walk towards the drop ship being loaded up.

He says, "Do you think he survived?"

I assume he's referring to Nate.

"I don't know, Tim," I reply, "but my tasking is to investigate the alien ship."

He's quiet.

I stop and face him, "Look, these guys are good at that they do. And Nate is resilient. Were the situation different and you were the one lost, would you want us to worry?"

He shakes his head slightly, says nothing and returns to his work.

As I board the drop ship through the back, I notice an open seat, only to be informed by Agsnon, "We have a spot up here for ya, Sarge."

I look back at Lynn who nods. I head into the cozy cockpit, taking a seat on the port side.

"Have we got everyone?" The Crewman in front of me asks.

I answer, "My team is accounted for," I finish, situating my rifle.

The other Crewman in front of Agsnon grabs what I believe to be a handset for the COMM unit.

He says into it, "Valkyrie Control, this is Rescue One. We are loaded up and ready to fly, requesting departure authorization."

"**Departure authorized,**" a voice says back, "**no known traffic interference on your intended route, good hunting, Rescue One.**"

The pilots gracefully take off, turn towards the opening in the hangar and we're off. The ground below passes in a blur as we head for Nate's last reported position. We come up on it, slowing down and descending rapidly. I observe some debris on the slope leading into one of the wind tunnels. We move along the tunnel, following it to the last reported position sent from the beacon.

One of the Crewman reports into the COMM, "Valkyrie Control, this is Rescue One, initial sweep complete, only spotted some traces of debris, no signs of life. We're heading to the drop point for the Recon Team."

A voice replies back, "**Understood Rescue One.**"

You may think it's cold, but I'm putting speculation

of Nate's fate out of my mind. I've been tasked to investigate the bastards who shot him down.

We approach our drop point. In front of us is one of the tall, thin rock tower formations which is based into a more reasonable landing area. Surrounding this large slope are the wind tunnels. If currents hold, we should be able to use them for cover.

We approach low and set down out of sight from the crashed, alien ship. I head out the back of the cockpit with Agsnon. Two of the other crew, a part of the Rescue Team take our seats in the cockpit and seal it off so we can safely decompress the drop bay.

"Helmets," I order.

Everyone quickly snaps on their small Tactical Environment Helmets. The bay decompresses and once all the breathable air is pulled into the storage tanks, the doors open. My team and I leave the ship.

"Agsnon," I say, "tell them we're clear."

He nods and says into the COMM, "Rescue One, we're clear of the ship. Valkyrie, we've disembarked Rescue One. Proceeding on foot towards crash site."

As Agsnon finishes his transmission, Rescue One departs.

We hear back through the COMM, "**Understood, Recon Team. Proceed at Sergeant Kroeling's discretion.**"

I wave my hand to move forward along the south side of the rock base. The reason he's doing all the talking is because he's been designated as the Primary Communicator. He carries a small-ish piece of gear which helps boost transmissions to Valkyrie. It also helps to prevent my squad's local chatter from being transmitted and clogging up the frequency. I can however speak to Valkyrie if I ask to be patched in.

Lynn says, "**Donna, I think I should check out the base of the obelisk. I'm not seeing many other options**

- 150 -

for cover."

I visually scan around. She's right.

I reply, "Very well, break off. Also call me Sergeant while we're on mission."

"**You got it,**" she says and takes off for the base of the obelisk.

I suppose technically we're walking along the base, but what she's referring to is where the narrow tower portion meets the base. And I don't like having my friends call me by rank, however we're conducting an operation and I need uniformity... as well as emotional detachment.

We move along the base towards the side, scanning for hostile targets. We can see some of the ship on the adjacent rock base. Below and in front of us is the wind tunnel we'll use for cover.

Lynn reports, "**Sergeant, I'm in position, but I don't have a lot of cover. If something happens, I'll probably get three or four shots before I'm exposed.**"

"Just keep an eye out for now and hold fire," I order.

We make our way towards the area connecting both rock bases.

Putvel, looking at his arm display says, "**Wind speeds are at fifty kay pee aitch, Sergeant. I think that's as good as it's gonna get.**"

I acknowledge, "Very well. Overwatch, we're moving in."

"**Understood, Sergeant,**" Lynn says, "**No movement that I can see.**"

I head right into the wind tunnel. My squad follows and we're immediately pelted with dirt tinking our armor loudly as well as cutting down our visibility.

Dayson expresses, "**I can't see anything! And I'm pretty sure our surprise is gone by the lovely music being created on our armor.**"

"Just keep moving!" I order, "Activate GRIPS if

need be."

"**I'm through the clearing!**" Agsnon announces.

Guess he moved a little faster than me. I emerge to see the crash site on my left. Part of it is sitting inside the wind tunnel further down from where we entered. Dayson and Putvel come out of the storm. We immediately start scanning the area for hostiles.

The ship itself is rather large. Maybe 70 meters. Most of it seems intact. From the description I got of the ships that attacked Keldon, this one doesn't look anything like that. It's actually a light brown color and very smooth.

Dayson reports, "**I think there's an entrance up near the front.**"

"Let's head towards it," I order.

Still sweeping the area, we make our way to the opening. It looks as though there's supposed to be another door, like an airlock. Upon a closer look, I can see another door behind the other. A three door airlock system or so it would seem.

"Agsnon," I order, "see what you can do about the door." I then inform Lynn, "Overwatch, we're proceeding into the ship. Voice check COMMS once inside."

"**Understood, Sergeant,**" She acknowledges.

I hear some strange beeping, then turn to see the door opening.

"That was fast," I note.

Agsnon explains, "**I just hit this button.**"

The four of us pile in. It's rather cozy. Agsnon hits the corresponding button, but nothing happens. He ponders for a second.

He then says, "**Dayson, try hitting the button on your door.**"

As soon as Dayson does a strange alarm goes off. The door we came through closes, but only seconds later, the other door opens. We eagerly get out and clear the room. It's got three hallways decorated in a smooth brown with purple highlights and teal colored lighting. Immediately after clearing the area, Putvel starts scanning the atmosphere.

He reports, "**Rich CO2, some nitrogen, very little oxygen.**"

I check my HUD and note that we have three hours of air left.

"We need to find a computer terminal," I say, "We've only got so much time to learn all we can and then call for an extrac-" I'm interrupted by a notification from a nearby environment suit, "Is anyone else seeing this?"

"**Yes,**" everyone just about simultaneously answers.

"**Should we split up?**" Dayson suggests.

"Negative," I say, "this just became a rescue op. We need to find whoever this is, we'll secure a terminal after we've saved our crewman. Based off the transponder's location, we should go down this passage to our left."

I take point. Though against regulation for any squad leader to do so, I always felt it was my responsibility to lead the way.

I say into my COMM, "Overwatch this is TEAMLEAD, how do you read?"

Only static returns in my COMM.

I order, "Agsnon, attempt a comms check with Overwatch."

He does so, "**Overwatch this is TEAMCOMMS, come in.**"

I only hear static.

Agsnon reports, "**I have decent communications with Overwatch, but we'll have to exfiltrate the ship in order to talk to Valkyrie.**"

"Understood," I acknowledge.

As we continue to sweep and clear, I notice the various textures on the walls and ceiling. They're quite soothing along with the overall feel of this ship. Had I not known anything else about these aliens, I'd assume they were peaceful.

I turn a corner to see one of them standing as it turns its, I guess, head, I take no hesitation in firing a couple shots. The creature cries out from its snake mouths as it falls to the deck.

I sweep the immediate area along with the rest of my squad.

"**Clear!**" Dayson shouts.

Putvel adds, "**Clear.**"

Agsnon mutters, "**Clear.**"

We gather around the downed foe.

"Strange," I say, "This one isn't wearing the same armor as the ones that attacked Keldon."

Dayson postulates, "**Maybe this one is just wearing standard environment gear.**"

Putvel notes, "**If by standard, you mean none at all.**"

He's right. This one appears to be dressed in clothes, I assume. But I know nothing of their anatomy to determine for sure what they need to cover. Another disturbing fact is that since this one isn't wearing armor, it also doesn't have the same arm cannons as the others and therefore I may have killed an unarmed alien.

"Let's keep moving," I order and then continue down the passage way towards the transponder.

No other aliens come upon us as we make our way through. We enter what appears to be a facility where they conduct experiments and observations. There are tables and shelves with various equipment similar to what someone would expect to find in a human science lab.

Agsnon says, "**It should be in here.**"

We look around. Spotting movement out of the corner of my eye, I raise my rifle and realize suddenly that it's a human hand. I scan up to see their face; it's Crewman Belkrest. She has some kind of breathing apparatus, but the look in her eyes, one of sadness and sorrow. She's fading. I come over to the table she's propped up and strapped to, completely declothed.

"Good, god!" I express, "Someone find her suit, now!" I order. "It's gonna be okay, Devorah," I say, "Just remain calm, we'll get you back into your suit."

She slowly nods in acknowledgement.

"I can't imagine what these savages have done to you," I say.

Agsnon says, "**Sergeant! I know we've got a MEDEVAC situation, but I found a computer terminal.**"

"Two birds," I say, "go ahead and hook up. Start learning what you can, we'll take care of Crewman Belkrest."

As I start to undo some of the restraints holding Crewman Belkrest, Dayson and Putvel come up with her suit.

"Help me get her back into it," I order.

Belkrest slowly moves into the suit and we try to help her in.

Putvel informs, "**There's a bit of a problem, Sergeant. They cut her out of it. We can seal the air into the helmet, but the suit won't protect her against the environment.**"

"Use the emergency adhesive," I suggest.

"**Can't,**" Putvel further explains, "**they cut down her back and legs. Even if we combined our emergency patching, there won't be enough.**"

- 155 -

"Look around the lab," I order, "There's something in this lab that will work as a temporary seal."

Putvel nods and begins looking around while Dayson assists me into getting Belkrest into her suit. We get her upper piece as secured as we can and configure the helmet connection.

I look at Dayson who has her helmet in hand and nod. I look at Belkrest as I grab the apparatus attached to her mouth, "are you ready?"

She nods. I pull the apparatus and to my expectation, some tubes come out with it. Finally the ends emerge and she starts coughing. Dayson quickly moves to get her helmet securely on and once it does, air floods into it. Belkrest coughs a little more, but starts to breathe normally.

After a few seconds she calms down and says, **"Much better, thank you."**

Putvel walks up with a can, **"I think this will work."**

I nod and he starts attempting to mend the suit together with some sort of gel.

I turn my attention back to Crewman Belkrest, "What happened?"

She thinks for a second and then explains, **"I was with Nate and Lede making our way through the wind tunnels. We had lifelines but a gust kicked up. I'm not sure how high or how far I went. All I remember is when I woke up, I was being dragged through this ship."**

I acknowledge with a nod and ask, "What about Nate and Lede?"

"I don't know," she says, **"as far as I could tell it was just me that they found."**

I dreadingly ask, "What did they do to you?"

"**Thankfully, not a whole lot,**" she replies, "**I was mostly out of it because whatever they had shoved down my throat had very little oxygen. They told me to take everything off, but I couldn't because I needed my suit to breathe. So they cut me out of it as well as all my other garments down to my skin and gave me the tubes. After that, they began conducting scans, but then left... that's when you guys showed up... I think... I might have blacked out.**"

"Wait," I say, "You talked to them?"

She nods, "**They know our language.**"

"**Uh, sort of,**" Agsnon pipes up, "**From what I can tell they have a translator algorithm.**"

We all start moving towards the console Agsnon is at.

I notice Putvel has finished patching up Belkrest's suit, "Watch the door," I order.

"**Looks like they've been observing us for quite some time,**" Agsnon notes, scrolling through clips of various human entertainment shows and news clips.

A tense, uneasy feeling envelopes us all. How long have they been watching us? It certainly puts us at a greater disadvantage knowing nothing about them. Sans their hospitality.

I ask, "Can we use their computer retroactively?"

Agsnon hesitantly replies, "**Theoretically yes, but I don't know what language this system speaks. If it's mathematical, I should be able to learn it after a few days of study, but if it's in their spoken language then it'll be nearly impossible without a professional linguist.**"

"Do we have one on board?" I inquire.

Agsnon answers, "**Well, considering that the study of alien languages was science fiction until a couple weeks ago, no. Language experts are typically assigned to exploration vessels.**"

Putvel informs, "**Sergeant, we got incoming!**"

"Everyone take cover!" I order.

I hand Belkrest my sidearm as most of us get behind the equipment in the center of the lab. I listen closely through my enviro-suit's audio receiver. From the footsteps it sounds like there're twelve of them. Only two of them enter the room and I remember they are hex-peds, a fact I'm not yet used to.

They begin looking around their lab, hissing loudly from their snake-mouths. One of them notices Agsnon's computer crudely hooked up to the terminal. As it moves towards the computer, I rise from my position, rifle poised at its head.

"Stop," I command.

The creature turns, hissing aggressively.

I begin, "I know you can understand me," pointing my gun quickly at the computer I say, "now make it so I can understand you."

Out of the corner of my eye I see Putvel and Dayson holding the other alien at gunpoint.

The one I'm holding appears to cooperate, slowly moving towards the computer console. It presses a few buttons then looks back at me… I think. It starts hissing again, but audible, computerized English emits from the ship's PA system, "*You swine! How dare thy disgrace our holy vessel!*"

I respond, "Pretty sure it was already unclean when you brought the other human on board."

The alien says, "*I speak not of thy hideous presence, but of that which they slain. You deprived a noble servant of the* Gkkkssskk *Sanctum*."

"The what?" I ask.

"*The* Gekrsslassk *Sanctum*." It tries to say again.

It repeats the phrase a couple times before finally the translator spits out, "*Gerlak Sanctum*."

Their use of the word "Sanctum" implies that their civilization is theocratic and if they have a superiority complex, this is going to go over oh so well… meaning it's not.

I explain, "My interaction with your species has consisted of hostile actions against my fellow humans and nothing more as far as we understand."

"*That includes if we unarmed*" the gerlak asks.

I continue to explain, "I didn't know and couldn't take that risk so I shot it- them."

The gerlak diatribes "*Ye race is a blight upon galaxy. In years to come we will extinguish ye aggressive and savage swine. Ye kills innocence out of fear. Ye will be easy prey*."

I sigh, "I can tell this is going to be a productive relationship. How do I reverse engineer your translation program?"

"*Ye is an inconvenience upon universe. Thy will be cleansed*," it says.

"Yeah yeah, I get it," I say, "just tell me how we can reverse engineer your translator so we can steal your database and learn all there is about the Gerlak Sanctum."

The gerlak responds, "*All ye needs to know is thy will be purged by Thee*."

Some static comes over the COMM.

I hear Agsnon reply, "**How many… very well, Sergeant! Six more have just entered the ship! Overwatch is asking for instructions.**"

"Tell her to try and slow them down," I order then focus my attention back to the alien, "You clever mother fucker."

The gerlak replies, "*I still meant every word.*" It continues, "*Your race is hideous, especially compared to some of the others we've wiped out.*"

I clarify, "So you're not just a religious cult?"

The gerlak explains, "*I am a scientist, but I am also a patriot. We are the Supreme Race divinely blessed to purge swine such as yourself from the universe.*"

"You sound awfully sure of yourselves," I note.

It replies, "*If it weren't true, how come we've never been beaten? How come every other scum we've conquered and eradicated hasn't been able to prevent their extinction?*"

I answer, aiming my rifle at what I hope to be its face, "For everything, there is a first time," and I pull the trigger.

It screams loudly and falls over dead.

Dayson asks the other gerlak, "Are you going to help us?"

It replies, "*Why? So you can shoot me too? You can't risk keeping me alive. You are scared, little swine!*"

I shoot the second one and remark, "He wasn't entirely wrong."

Putvel notes, "**Sarge, you just killed two unarmed aliens who weren't an immediate threat to us.**"

I contend, "Weren't a threat? I'd say intending to wipe out our entire race is pretty fucking threatening as well as stalling for armed backup to arrive. Speaking of, we don't have time for a moral dilemma. Agsnon, start grabbing information from their computers, anything you can at this point. Putvel, cover Agsnon. Belkrest, stay here with them. Dayson, you're with me."

There's a long static over the COMM. I look at Agsnon presuming the static to be Lynn reaching out.

Agsnon acknowledges, "**Very well, Overwatch. I'll let her know. Sergeant, Overwatch reports that she was able to take out a couple of them, but she has to reposition for an ambush. She couldn't stay.**"

I nod, "Tell her she has full discretion to do what she needs to stay alive."

He nods and relays my order. Dayson and I head into the passage way. My plan is to buy Agsnon time to steal all the information he can. I also realize that we need to disable the communications array... whatever that looks like.

We turn a corner and are greeted by gerlak with laser fire. Dayson and I find cover wherever we can and down one or two enemies. I motion for Dayson to fall back, in the hopes we can draw them away from the lab, but not into a corner. We slowly continually fall back from opening to opening along the passage. I can't tell how many there are. Dayson checks our back to discover one of them trying to get us from behind and quickly takes it out.

Rounding a corner, I notice there are no places for cover in our immediate area.

"Double time!" I order.

We make it to the corner at the end just as the gerlak come around. We engage them.

There's static over the COMM, but it starts to become audible. It's Lynn's voice, "**I'm pinned just over the base of the obelisk! Just get em off me and I'll cover you!"

"What?" I ask, "Lynn, we're still in the ship!"

She replies, "**Then… who's engaging the hostiles!?**"

Could it be? No, it's obvious.

I ask, "Did the rescue ship come back already?"

Lynn answers, "**No! I thought that was you guys chasing them through the storm.**"

"Well, figure out who it is and get them on our frequency," I order, "But don't put yourself at unnecessary risk!"

"**Will do!**" She acknowledges.

I motion for Dayson to fall back. If I'm understanding the ship's layout, we should be able to round back to the lab, but from the other passage. We turn right again and run towards an opening. Sure enough we round back into the lab.

Putvel lowers his rifle in relief as soon as he realizes who we are. I notice a few more dead gerlak have decorated the floor.

I ask, "What's everyone's status?"

"**Breathing,**" Putvel answers.

"What's the status of data transfer?" I inquire.

Agsnon responds, "**It's going good so far, but the memory drives are almost full. And I have no idea what information we've acquired so far. I could have anything ranging from tactical data to Gerlak home and gardening.**"

We hear the stomping of gerlak nearby quickly getting louder.

"Take cover," I order.

We all hunker down behind lab tables and whatever we can find to hide behind. We wait quietly as the gerlak enter the lab. They begin scanning the area for us. I engage them downing one, but taking a couple hits myself and stumbling to the deck. Dayson and Putvel finish off the remaining four.

"**Sarge!**" Dayson yells.

"I'm fine," I say, "My armor is holding. Wouldn't be a very good leader if I didn't come away with a few dents."

There's static over the COMM.

I look over at Agsnon who answers, "**Understand all, Overwatch. Sergeant, Overwatch reports that Crewman Lede and Civilian McNill were the ones who engaged the other gerlak outside.**"

I nod, "Tell her we're on our way out, and to try and radio the rescue ship. Maybe it's close by. If not, we'll have you establish contact once we're out there. Ask them to secure the entrance for us as well."

Agsnon nods, relays my orders and then begins packing up his equipment with the assistance of Putvel who shoulders the computer equipment as soon as it's packed.

Making our way back to the entrance, we encounter no hostiles. We emerge back outside and Agsnon immediately calls for the rescue ship to come pick us up. I sigh relief and partially smile seeing Nate mostly unharmed.

"Glad you guys are safe," I say.

Nate starts to reply, "**Yeah, well-**" he stops, noting Crewman Belkrest emerging from the airlock, "**Dev!**" he expresses, "**We thought you were dead!**"

As they start reacquainting I turn to Agsnon and order, "Patch me in to home base."

He does so and says, **"You're on."**

"Valkyrie, this is Sergeant Kroeling," I say, "We've gathered all the information we can and the crash survivors all ended up here as well. Requesting extraction from the crash site."

There's a momentary pause... then Valkyrie replies, **"Understand all, Sergeant. Stand-by, the Commander is on his way to the bridge to speak with you."**

As we wait, I order everyone, two at a time to restock air.

As I'm mid sweep, Commander Keller comes over the COMM, **"Sergeant, Kroeling, this is the Commander, what's your status?"**

I reply, "Everyone's alive, sir. Encountered several hostiles, but didn't take any casualties."

"And these are confirmed to be the same aliens that attacked Keldon?" he asks.

I confirm, "Yes sir... we actually managed to communicate with a couple of them before the firefight began."

He answers, **"What did they say?"**

I answer, "I can provide the full recording, but we're basically dealing with overzealous racists who believe humanity needs to be cleansed from the galaxy."

There's silence as we await a response.

Finally, Commander Keller says, **"What all were you able to find?"**

I explain, "Crewman Agsnon is unsure of what we pulled from their computers. What they did tell us is, they call themselves the "Gerlak Sanctum" and they believe wholeheartedly to be the dominant race in the universe."

There's more silence before Keller orders, **"Sergeant, I need to be sure that ship isn't transmitting**

- 164 -

a distress signal. **Once Crewman Agsnon and the survivors are loaded up, make sure your oxygen is full, then head back into the ship. We'll get a relief team out as soon as we can, but right now I need you back inside, making sure our presence isn't being transmitted to the enemy.**"

"Just so I understand, sir," I say, "you want me to seize control of this vessel and eliminate all remaining hostiles."

"**Yes,**" Keller replies, "**It seems these Gerlak are aggressive and intent on our destruction. If any of them surrender, take them into custody. Otherwise, eliminate them.**"

"Understood, sir," I say.

Keller says nothing else. I assume we're done talking. The drop ship arrives and two of the survivors immediately hop on. Crewman Agsnon trades the enhanced transmitter gear for the computer system with Putvel and then gets in.

I look at Nate, "I guess I'll see you back at the ship later," and turn back for the Gerlak ship.

I notice Nate following me, stop and turn, "What are you doing?" I ask.

He replies, "**I wanna stay and help.**"

I shake my head, "You're not suited up proper for this. Go back to Valkyrie and get tactical armor then come back with the relief team," I order.

"**Donna,**" he explains, "**my whole life I wanted to be an explorer. That didn't end up happening. But now I have a chance to explore an alien ship. Please, Donna, I can help you figure out how it works.**"

I ponder for a second. Nate probably has knowledge of various ships that could be valuable here in determining what we need to find.

"Okay," I reconsider, "but you stay close to me the entire time."

Nate eagerly nods and double checks his rifle.

I order, "Putvel, contact Valkyrie and let them know Mr. McNill is staying behind. Lynn," I turn my focus, "are you sure you're good to stay out?"

She nods and sets her rifle back to short range mode.

I wave to Agsnon who nods and closes the door to the drop ship.

"Let's head back in," I order.

The drop ship takes off as we make our way back to the Gerlak vessel. After getting through the airlock, I notice a laser scanning the immediate area. I look over to see a small scanner atop of Nate's helmet.

He says, "**I'm uploading a small map to everyone's HUD. This will help give us a layout of the ship.**"

And to think I wanted him to come back with tactical gear. I inform, "Back that way is the lab where we found Crewman Belkrest. I'd like to check forward for the bridge."

"**It could also be even further aft,**" Nate supposes.

I reply, "I got pretty far back there earlier. Didn't see any indication it's there."

Nate adds, "**We'll want to get a look at their engine room as well. We should figure out what makes this thing fly, especially figure out what their version of Traverse Drive is.**"

"No one on this team is an engineer," I point out, "I'd like to check forward first."

Nate contests, **"I mean there are more of us. We could split into teams-"**

I interrupt, "This is the way we're doing it, Nate!"

Nate nods understandingly. We head towards what we believe to be the front of the ship. We encounter no hostiles as we move up the passageway. All we find are four small rooms which contain these suspended cocoon-like chairs and a computer console. We see several of these as we approach the front, but the passage way starts to curve and head back down the other side.

In the center, we finally see a door leading toward the middle.

"This must be the bridge," I suspect.

Nope. Upon entering the space, it's mostly tables and what I guess are chairs.

"Fan out," I order, "but remain on guard."

Lynn and Dayson head off to my left. Putvel starts looking around to my right. Nate, however is looking up with his hand pointed at the overhead where a large, coil-like object sits suspended in the bulkhead.

"This is interesting," he says, **"judging by the amount of electromagnetic radiation coming from that thing, this might be what powers their energy shield."**

I inquire, "It's based on electromagnetism?"

He nods and explains, **"The basic principles of an energy shield are, in theory, generating an electromagnetic field around the ship and then polarizing it."**

"Polarizing it with what?" I ask.

- 167 -

He answers, "**With another type of energy. Humanity hasn't figured it out, but it seems the Gerlak have. The question is, what energy source?**"

"Get all the information you can," I order, "the engineers might be able to figure it out."

Nate nods in acknowledgement.

Lynn informs, "**Sergeant, I think this might be where they prepare food… it's not like anything we would eat, but it looks like they have perishables and dry goods similar to us.**"

"Hold on," I take a second to evaluate where we are, "Let's make sure we understand this… the same place they eat is also where the shield generator is located?"

There's a brief silence.

Nate supposes, "**Maybe it doubles as mood lighting.**" Looking around, he changes, "**Actually, I think it IS the primary source of lighting for this room… rather functional…**"

I ponder for a second then a laser wizzes passed Nate.

"Cover!" I order.

I kick one of their tables over and begin laying down fire. This seems familiar.

Lynn says over the COMM, "**Sergeant, if you and the miner can keep them distracted, I'll pick them off!**"

"Agreed!" I say, "Nate! Spray down fire when you can! Dayson, Putvel, same thing! Lynn will focus on taking them out!"

Everyone acknowledges my order. After a few seconds, the firing stops from the enemy's direction.

"**Clear!**" Lynn announces, "**Counted and downed five.**"

That's upwards of almost thirty total. How did they fit that many in this small ship?

I order, "Putvel, get on the door while we investigate the rest of this compartment."

"**Aye, Sergeant.**" he says and posts on the door.

We finish searching the room with nothing more to note. We proceed down the passageway towards another opening which goes towards the front of the ship. Finally, this must be the bridge.

Rounding the corner, we discover it's not. Rather it's a room that explains how so many gerlak are able to fit in the ship.

Putvel asks, "What… is this?"

There are empty vats, probably twenty to thirty, all along the front bulkhead. They're filled with a blue-ish green liquid and contain some kind of apparatus in each of them. If I had to guess I would say these are for extended periods of hibernation.

"**Sleeping pods?**" Nate puts my thoughts into words.

"But why?" I ask, "Humanity only used such devices back before Traverse Drive was discovered. Is it possible the Gerlak don't have a faster than light mode of travel?"

Nate shakes his head, "**If that was the case we would have detected them long before they entered orbit of the planet. Their energy signature just showed up meaning they most likely popped into the system.**"

Putvel asks, "Then why would they have these pods?"

Everyone thinks for a second.

Finally, Nate says, "**Crew rotations. And maybe even for extra crew in case something happens. Think** about it, the ship can probably be run by five or ten gerlak, but if they enter battle or have a situation where they need to repair the ship, everyone else can be woken up and put to work."

I note, "Okay, but humans take several hours to come out of hibernation."

Nate nods, "**Indeed, but maybe gerlak don't…**"

"Let's move on," I order, "We need to find the bridge. We can study this more in depth later."

We head down the passage on the other side of the ship, the port side, back towards the lab. Maybe their bridge is offset from the center. As we work our way back, we mainly find more small rooms each with a console and cocoon chair. We turn down the passage towards the lab, located middle-aft of the ship. This so far seems to be the most functional to give us answers.

"Okay," I begin, "we know this ship is more or less purposed for scientific endeavors."

Nate adds, "**Agreed. Compared to the ships at Keldon, this wasn't armed as heavily.**"

Putvel asks, "**But where's the bridge?**"

We all stop and think for a second.

Then it hits me, "Maybe there isn't one."

Everyone looks at me confused.

I explain, "Consider that in each of the small rooms there was a console. A rather large console at that. What if their bridge operates like we are now?"

"**What?**" Putvel asks.

I continue, "What if there is no bridge at all. What if they all have assigned roles that they can do from each console?"

Nate asks, "**You think their bridge is just a network?**"

Dayson, watching the door says, "**That would make sense. Instead of having everyone in a central location, keep everyone spread out, but still able to function like they are all on a bridge. I mean isn't that how our bridge simulators work?**"

"So if that's the case," I say, "then we could access all their systems and determine if they have sent a distress signal."

Nate shakes his head, "**Unfortunately, we can't get into their systems until the Computer Techs figure out if they can interface. I suggest we learn everything else we can until then. I'd like to head back to the galley and study that shield generator some more.**"

"Agreed," I say, "Putvel, you're with him. Dayson and Lynn with me. We're going to contact Valkyrie and update them on our situation then we'll meet you there. By my count all the gerlak are dead, but stay sharp just in case."

Chapter Nine: "Incident?"

(*Keller*)I sit as patiently as possible on the bridge awaiting an update from the recon team. Their last update had them entering the ship for a second time. Under normal circumstances, we'd have constant communications, even video. Unfortunately, being planet-side and relying on our orbital satellite leaves us with limitations.

While we wait, I decided to resume mining operations and with Sub-Commander's recommendation, dispatched patrols to escort them and alert us if Gerlak reinforcements arrive.

Speaking of, Sub-Commander Devlin shouts across the bridge, "Commander, they're radioing in!"

I jump out of my chair and move over to the Intel and Communications Crater located on the starboard side of the bridge. Stepping into the crater, I nod at the Communications Crewman.

She nods, "Go ahead Sergeant."

Sergeant Kroeling comes in over the COMM, "Commander, we've finished our sweep. We encountered a few more hostiles and neutralized them. No casualties to report at this time. We've been able to observe as much as we can. We located what we believe to be the source of their energy shielding. Nate suspects it's electromagnetically based and I suggest sending some engineers out here to take a look."

"Very good," I acknowledge, "what else?"

"Without being able to access their computers," she says, "there isn't much more we can do here."

I ask, "Are they transmitting a distress call?"

"I don't know, sir," she replies, "As I said, we need to access their computers. We think their bridge is actually a network. We found several small rooms each with a very sophisticated looking computer setup. But again, it's just a theory until we can get access."

"I understand Sergeant," I acknowledge, "Stand by."

I step out of the Crater, pull out my personal COMM device and call up the COMMSTECH Shop.

A female voice answers, "Delta Miranda."

I ask, "Delta, what's the status of analyzing the alien computer data?"

She replies, "Commander, we have good news: their systems seem to be mathematically based like ours. Crewman Agsnon thinks he can reverse engineer the translation algorithm within a couple hours."

"Can he take his work back to the Gerlak ship?" I ask.

She hesitates a reply for a second, "Uh, I guess with the right equipment."

"Have him suit up," I order, "Make sure he's able to take everything and anyone he needs and have them loaded up in the relief drop ship in the port hangar."

"Aye, Commander," she acknowledges, "Is there anything else?"

"Yes," I inquire, "what's the status of Communications?"

There's an even longer hesitation, "Yeah… that's not such good news, sir. The proposed retrofit of the satellite isn't going as well as we had hoped."

"Elaborate," I say.

She explains, "The satellite capacitors aren't as compatible with the ship's long range capacitor. We've only been able to use some of the pieces to rebuild the long range capacitor. Other parts have to be completely rebuilt and require fabricated components. I've already put in the order to Lieutenant Slaighter. He says he'll get it done when he can."

I say, "Tell him your project is now top priority, then give me an updated estimated time of repair. We need long range communications before we can do anything else." I finish closing the COMM line.

Sub-Commander walks up to me, "What are you thinking?"

I answer, "Wait about two minutes and contact Slaighter. Have him pick three engineers who might be able to study that shield generator. Maybe even extract it."

"We're stealing their technology?" he questions.

I explain, "Any advantage we can give ourselves over the enemy we must take. We'll figure out how to integrate their systems into our own, and if we can't, we'll at least learn something about them."

Sub-Commander nods, "Makes sense. I concur. I'll have them gather for a mission brief."

I ask, "If you don't mind handling this one on your own, I'd appreciate it."

Sub-Commander half smiles, nods and leaves the bridge. I head back into the Crater, "put me through," I order.

The Crewman nods and establishes communications with Sergeant Kroeling.

I say, "Sergeant, good work so far. Crewman Agsnon is heading back out with a team to begin assessing the computers. I'm also sending an engineering team to look into extracting the energy shield."

"Understood, sir," she acknowledges.

I continue, "Also make sure Mr. McNill gets on the transport. I understand his desire to stay out and explore the ship, but we need his expertise leading our mining operations. We may be on borrowed time here.

She acknowledges once again, "Understood, sir."

"Finally, how are you holding up?" I ask.

"I can stay out as long as needed, sir," she answers.

"Very good," I say, "If anything comes up, let me know right away. Keller out."

I nod to the Crewman and return to my chair. Uncertainty is the enemy of patience. On normal missions, such as interdicting pirates or responding to a distress call, I would wait in my room, planning our mission. In this instance, there is too much uncertainty for me to be absent from the bridge. There is no book for this one. We have no communications and a hostile force could show up at any minute.

Awaiting the next update on the field operation or ship repair, one of the Navigators comes up to me and asks, "Commander, would you like me to bring up a plate from the galley?"

I look over and nod, "Yes, thank you."

He returns the nod and leaves.

This planet is quite fascinating. An exploration vessel designated it "open" for extensive study, meaning any other ship that happens to be in the area could come by and conduct a more detailed survey. We would be doing exactly that were our reasoning for being here better than what it is. I find it odd that an exploration vessel didn't do the survey themselves. The wind patterns alone are different from anything I've seen on any other world.

I hear some radio chatter from the COMMS, but it sounds like it's just the miners.

I pull up my desk attachment from the side of my chair and put it in table position. The Crewman from earlier arrives and drops my food off to me.

"Thank you," I say and continue waiting for the next event as I eat.

Fish n chips. Simple, but filling enough. I specifically asked the cooks to mix up meals with emergency rations and to vacuum seal and freeze regular food to make it last. There's no knowing how long it will be before our next provisioning.

Some years ago when I was a Second Lieutenant aboard a smaller Constellation Cutter, we were forced to stay out on a deployment well passed our needed time to re-provision. For almost three weeks we got to eat emergency ration packs and paste and had to go down to eating twice a day. I promised never to let anyone under my command suffer through that same fate again. Instead we'll mix up the rations with "the good stuff" hopefully stretching our food supplies out evenly.

I finish my last bite as Sub-Commander Devlin walks up to me, "The relief drop ship is underway."

I nod in acknowledgement. I also hear the chatter over the COMM. There isn't a need to exchange words.

At this point, we're just waiting again. I can't recall the last time I got some sleep. Suffice it to say, the dusk isn't helping so I decide to head below for a bit.

"Call me if anything important comes up," I order.

Lieutenant Jefferson acknowledges, "Aye Commander."

I make my way down the ladder-well towards my quarters. The lights flicker on as I enter the opening towards my and Sub-Commander's respective offices. I enter my office door and then head into my cabin door located on the right bulkhead. It's a rather large, royal accommodation that wraps around my office in an upside down "L" shape. Like a small, modular apartment, it has a kitchenette, dining area and even a separate living room space complete with a Master Suite and personal restroom facilities. Sub-Commander's cabin is mirrored out the same.

I retire to the back compartment where the bed is located. Should I bother changing out? No. If I'm lucky, I'll get a light nap at best. I'm not even completely tired. I guess I just wanted to lay down. I begin to think back to that particular assignment on the smaller Constellation Cutter, the Azure Dragon Xin, a Mansion Class with only a crew of 65. The Commanding Officer was a First Lieutenant; someone at the time I felt took unnecessary risks... but now might be better suited for my current mission.

Our assignment had minimal intel. A pirate group was anticipating a resupply from a colony that had defected from the Republic. It was on the outlying border. A larger Cutter should have been provided, but the Valkyrie Class was still under construction and the other larger ships that have long since been decommissioned were patrolling for rebels during what was known as the Three War; a war between the United Constellation Republic, a group of rebels known as the "Righteous Resistance," another, larger group calling themselves the "People's Kingdom", and the aforementioned pirates, "Anarch".

The Anarch supply ship was anticipated to pass through an unpatrolled section of space that was a four-day tunneling from the nearest supply station. The mission was purely optional and of course my over ambitious CO chomped at the bit, but he wasn't alone. We were all fairly young, even the Delta Crewman, therefore it didn't take much convincing for the crew to dive right into such a risky mission. Overall it was a total bust. We spent days trying to position ourselves for an interdiction only to come up with an empty cargo vessel claiming to be lost... they were actually most likely keeping us distracted while the actual ships made the rendevouz with the pirates.

I finally had to convince him that we needed to resupply. At first he didn't want to. But finally he agreed. By the time we got back to the nearest station, he asked for new orders and insisted that our ship was too small to be out that far... I had never seen him so defeated.

His strongest quality was inspiring the crew. Getting everyone excited for missions even if they were just routine inspections. I've tried to utilize that trait for myself, but I don't feel I quite get the... um... uhhhh...

...I awake to my COMM going off, "Keller," I say.

"Sir, it's Lieutenant Jefferson," a male voice says, "Delta Miranda says we should test long range COMMS."

I hurriedly jump out of my bed, "I'm on my way up."

Probably because I'm half tired, my transit to the bridge passes in a blur. Lieutenant Jefferson announces my presence and I nod and take the bridge.

I descend into the Crater and order, "Bring long range communications online. Mega-band, open frequency."

"Aye, Commander," the COMMS Crewman acknowledges as she activates the long range transmitter.

She says into the mic, "To any vessel or listening outpost, this is Constellation Cutter Valkyrie, please acknowledge."

She waits about five seconds with no response and tries again… and again…

Sub-Commander, having joined us orders, "keep trying."

I activate my personal COMM and contact Delta Miranda.

She answers, "Delta Miranda."

"Delta," I begin, "it's the Commander. We're trying to establish communication on open Mega-Band but have had no response. Any suggestions?"

She ponders for a second, "Try having them direct the signal to the Phelpsryn Colony on Narrow Ultra-band. There should be a listening post that will automatically relay our signal to a Net Control Center. But keep in mind, the planet's rotation could make directing a signal tricky."

"Noted," I say and look at the COMMS Crewman who nods and anticipates my next order by carrying out the Delta's suggestion.

She presses a few buttons and then tries calling out again. Still no response. We wait a few minutes until finally there is some static that might be someone calling us back. The COMMS Crewman makes an adjustment, probably to the modulator and tries again.

This time, over the COMM we hear, "**Unit claiming… Valk.. Mod… twenty-one… xitt…**"

The COMMS Crewman makes another adjustment and says, "Station calling, this is Valkyrie, say again."

Extremely garbled, but audible, we hear, "**Unit claiming to be Constellation Cutter Valkyrie, adjust your modulation to twenty-one point seven seven five.**"

She fine tunes the adjustment then says, "Unit calling this is Valkyrie please identify."

They respond, "**Unit claiming to be Valkyrie, this is Net Control Center Seventeen Zero One. Transmit identification matrix.**"

She looks at me and I nod. She pulls up a special panel that transmits various tones over the current frequency. Each ship in the Armada and Navy is given a specific sequence of tones to enter. If a unit attempting to fake the challenge doesn't have the exact gear to receive the tones, they'll only hear static.

The COMMS Crewman says, "Commander, they're requesting your personal tone."

I walk over to her console and put in my tones holding down a couple of the keys longer than the others.

A voice comes back over the COMM, "**Commander Keller, forgive the suspicion, but we heard you were destroyed during the Keldon Incident.**"

"Incident?" I say, "It was an act of war! I need to speak with Constellation Command right away."

"**Of course, sir,**" they say, "**It'll take us a little while to get ahold of them. We'll work with your communicators to establish a better connection.**"

"Very well," I say and I leave the Crater stepping back up into the rest of the bridge.

Sub-Commander, following me says, "Incident? They're referring to the slaughter as a mere incident?"

I ponder for a second, "Maybe the Navy showed up and wiped them out."

Sub-Commander considers, "I don't know… unless all the fleets in the area all at once… no it just doesn't-" I stop him by holding my hand up. He notices me looking over at the uneasy Crewman over-hearing our conversation. I have no issue with them being informed, but adding to their own uncertainty is the last thing we need right now.

"Let's continue this conversation in my office," I say and start heading for the ladder.

"Aye," Sub Commander acknowledges following me down.

We exchange silence as we descend the steps into Level Three and heading into my office.

After Sub-Commander closes the door behind us, I turn to him, "This is damn peculiar."

Sub-Commander nods in agreement, "Maybe they agreed to a cease fire and began appropriate first contact."

I activate my holo-map and pull up the data just before we docked at Keldon Station. I look up some specific data pertaining to the Stellar Navy and run a quick calculation.

"According to our latest intel feed," I begin, "the nearest Naval Fleet was two hours away and only had a single deck carrier, three destroyers and a cruiser. Maybe if they had a battleship or two they could have stopped, but even then I'm still skeptical."

Sub-Commander notes, "We do also have limited data on our enemies, Jaysen."

"True," I acknowledge, "which, considering our experience, makes this whole situation seem more odd."

Sub-Commander nods in agreement. Silence takes my office momentarily.

My COMM goes off, "Keller," I say.

A female voice says, "Sir, it's Crewman Wersman, I have Sub-Admiral Yelkin on visual. He's asked to speak to you privately."

"Patch him in," I order.

I sit down at my desk and press a button turning my holo map into a two dimensional display. Within seconds, the Admiral's image appears.

He orders, "Isolate this transmission."

I hesitate for a second and reply, "Aye, Admiral."

With the press of a button, our communication is isolated to only us and can't be recorded.

"It's just us," I say.

"Is the room clear?" He asks.

I lie, "As I just said, Admiral, it's just us."

"Very well," the Admiral says, "I see reports of your destruction were greatly exaggerated."

"Yes," I confirm, "I'll have our battle logs sent for analysis. We're conducting repairs on our Traverse Drive and engines, but we will be able to support whichever fleet needs us."

"Needs you for what?" the Admiral raises a brow.

I respond obviously, "The war, Admiral."

The Admiral explains, "There isn't a war, Keller. The incident on Keldon was a misunderstanding."

"A what!?" I question, "Begging your pardon, Admiral, but that's one hell of a misunderstanding."

The Admiral forms a response, "I understand how that sounds. Just get your ship repaired. Actually, transmit your location so I can get a ship out to you to assist."

"I appreciate that," I say, "but what do I tell my crew regarding there being no justice for Keldon?"

The Admiral is silent for a second. He suggests, "Do you need to tell them anything? Just tell them you'll get new orders once the ship is repaired."

I reiterate, "Admiral, I lost crewmen at Keldon. Telling them to wait isn't going to go over well."

The Admiral insists, "All you have to say is that new orders will be given once your ship is repaired. Let them think what they want until then."

"Alright," I say, "but I would at least like to know what's going on. I myself was looking forward to some payback".

The Admiral sighs, "Very well, Keller, just for you. The Prime Minister is working towards a plan for peace with the Gerlak. Suffice to say it is a rigorous process and requires great sacrifice. Right now the rest of the Republic only knows that contact with Keldon was lost. Details are remaining under wraps as we go through this extremely delicate process. Keep your ship disconnected from the Galnet for now until the Prime Minister is ready to make the peace talks public. We don't need speculation being generated right now."

"Speculation regarding what?" I inquire.

The Admiral clarifies, "Officially, your ship is missing in action. Officially it will stay that way until the peace talks are made public. Is that understood?"

"Yes, Admiral," I say.

"Transmit your location," the Admiral orders, "Yelkin out."

His image buzzes out and seconds later my two dimensional screen returns to my map.

I look up at Sub-Commander, "Well… this is an unexpected turn of events."

"Peace? Misunderstanding?" Sub-Commander states, "I…" he struggles to find words. I struggle to find thoughts.

Finally he says, "I don't know, Jaysen. Maybe we got them all wrong…"

"No," I say, "They definitely fired first and continued coming at us guns blazing. They're an aggressive species, BUT attempting to pursue peace isn't out of character for the Prime Minister. She did campaign on the promise of unity during the Three War."

Sub-Commander scoffs, "Ha! Peaceful..."

Indeed our final resolutions with the Righteous Resistance and The People's Kingdom were anything but. Of course it didn't matter what was really going on. As far as the general public knew, Prime Minister Valyree Jackson had successfully reunited the United Constellation Republic peacefully.

But, "This is not the time to get into that," I say, "I need to think of what I'm going to tell the crew."

"The truth never seemed to fail you," Sub-Commander points out.

I nod, pulling out my COMM unit. I contact the bridge.

"Lieutenant Esker," a female voice answers.

I say, "Kaight, it's the Commander, I need you to build a patch that connects me through the whole ship, the Outminers, and our salvage teams at the crashed, enemy ship."

She clarifies, "Uh, okay, sir it'll take a couple of minutes, but just to clarify, the Outminers haven't gone out yet. It's 0500, they have yet to start their day."

I seem to have lost track of time, "Very well," I say and close the COMM line.

Looking up at Sub-Commander I say, "Mike, if you don't mind, I'd like to be alone with my thoughts."

He nods and exits my office. I swivel in my chair and contemplate my speech. On our normal missions, I've always been upfront with my crew. Now I'm hesitant. We're not warriors, but some of them lost good friends; brothers and sisters who they would gladly go to war for. Now we've not only been told not to fight... but to stand down and make peace with these aggressors over a so-called 'misunderstanding'. I have no words for this, but I'll find them anyway.

Lieutenant Esker informs me she has the patch ready. Here I go.

"Good morning, Valkyrie crewmates, this is the Commander... I know some of you have yet to get up for the day so I'll wait a few seconds for you to come back to reality..." I'm quiet a few seconds before continuing, "A quick shout out to Delta Miranda and her team restoring communications. We were able to get ahold of Stellar Command and receive new orders." I pause for a second. I have to be careful or what I could say might start a mutiny.

"I know all of you were expecting to go to war. I know a select few of you were hoping for a chance at vengeance, but the Prime Minister has chosen to try and make peace with our perceived enemy."

I can almost feel some of the crew's outrage. Continuing, "I'm going to have to ask that you let go of those feelings. For now repairs will continue as they have been, after which we will be given our new orders. Some of you might have grievances. Sub-Commander and I will be willing to listen to them. Continue the hard work you've all been doing. Keller out."

A few seconds pass and there's a knock at my door. "Yes," I say.

Sub-Commander enters, "That was well done. I'll try to field most of the complaints."

"I appreciate that," I say, "but some might not be satisfied just speaking to you. I'm sure you'll give good explanations, however-"

"You're the Commander," Sub-Commander finishes, "I understand, sir. What should we do about our salvage team? Being in that alien vessel is violating the Admiral's orders."

"Is it?" I ask.

Sub-Commander raises a brow.

I postulate, "They did shoot down our Outminer."

"Maybe they felt threatened," Sub-Commander suggests.

"Maybe," I say, "The only other conclusion I can think of is that they didn't get the memo about peace with humanity… or… and just maybe, they aren't peaceful at all."

Sub-Commander asks, "Do you think they're lying?"

"Possibly," I clarify, "but what strikes me as odd is the Admiral said the attack on Keldon was a mere misunderstanding. What we saw and experienced was much more than that."

"What are you suggesting?" Sub-Commander asks.

I pause for a second, "I am not entirely sure… maybe something in their computers can explain in detail their motives."

"You still want to salvage it?" Sub-Commander confirms.

"Yes," I explain, "we're conducting an investigation into why they shot down our craft and why they fired on our people. Doesn't seem peaceful to me."

Sub-Commander adds, "And what about stealing their tech?"

I ponder for a second, "Indeed… I guess we'll have to tell our salvage teams to stop… at the same time, what kind of friends would our new allies be if they didn't share their stuff?"

Sub-Commander half smirks, "If I may suggest, let's just figure out how it works instead of physically removing it?"

I nod in agreement, "I suppose. Go up to the bridge and make it happen. But get some breakfast first and if by the time you get to the bridge and they've removed anything, don't make them put it back."

Sub-Commander nods and exits. I get up and head for my cabin. Hopefully I can get some sleep before the assisting ship arrives. I lay in my bed...

...and once again am awoken by the sound of my COMM unit, "Keller," I say.

"Commander," a male voice says, "One of our patrols is reporting the arrival of a Gerlak fleet!"

"Okay," I say, "Tell them to attempt to establish communications. I'll be up in a minute."

Guess it's time to meet our new friends. I quickly make my way back up to the bridge.

My presence is announced and I acknowledge, "My bridge."

Sub-Commander informs, "Sir, the Gerlak attacked our patrols. I ordered them to retreat along with our Outminers."

I'm quiet longer than I should be, "Did, did they respond to communications?"

Sub-Commander nods, "Yes, they opened fire."

A Communications Specialist shouts, "Uh, I've lost connection to the Net Control Center!" followed by more panicked and indistinct chatter.

I ponder for a second, take a breath and order, "Battle Stations."

Sub-Commander acknowledges loudly, "Aye Commander, Battle Stations!"

I add, "And get the ship ready for launch."

Over the public announcement system an alarm goes off indicating to the crew to set Battle Stations. After about five or so seconds one of the Navigator Crewman says into the PA, "Battle Stations, Battle Stations set Battle Stations throughout the ship. Hostile fleet reported in orbit. All hands make preparations for take-off."

Within seconds, the bridge comes alive with crewman coming up to man their posts, prepare for battle and get the ship ready to lift off.

I walk up to the Navigator's Table and ask, "How many ships?"

The Crewman answers, "Looks like two, maybe three of their ships comparable to our own. They appear to be deploying fighter craft!"

Lieutenant Jefferson informs, "Commander, it's going to take at least ten to fifteen minutes to retract the engineering compartment."

"We don't have that long," I say, pulling out my personal COMM.

I contact Main Engineering.

"Slaighter." ENGCOM answers.

"Jeff," I say, "we need to get off the ground, now."

"I understand, sir," ENGCOM says, "I can route the Fusion Generator exhaust into the boosters. That should at least get us started. We can retract the engines while climbing."

This is a very risky call, but I really have no choice.

Someone shouts something about our fighters as I reply, "Make it happen, Lieutenant," and I close the line.

Lieutenant Esker informs, "Sir, most stations are reporting ready, but a lot of the crew are asking what's going on."

I noddingly acknowledge and hit the "PA" button on my personal COMM. I begin mitigating confusion, "Attention Valkyrie Crewmates, this is the Commander. I realize I mentioned something about peace with the Gerlak a little while ago, but unfortunately a fleet of their ships arrived in orbit and started attacking our fighters. I've decided to take defensive measures and get underway. Let's get to it, Valkyrie! Keller out."

Lieutenant Esker informs, "Sub-Commander reports Secondary Bridge ready to fly."

"Very well," I say, "What's the status of the Port Hangar?"

"I believe they're still getting secured," she answers.

The Navigator informs, "Multiple ships entering the atmosphere and headed our way!"

I say, "Helm, status?"

"Just got the green light from engineering," Crewman Truman informs.

"Up and out," I order, somewhat anxious.

There's a slight hesitation before both helmsman acknowledge, "Aye Commander, beginning launch sequence."

Within seconds the ship begins to rattle.

Lieutenant Ephryn informs, "Commander, Outfighters report ready for launch."

I acknowledge and order, "Launch fighters and order them into defensive formation."

Helm informs, "Beginning lift off!"

The ship begins to shake more violently than it should, the result of the Fusion Generators being routed into the thruster exhaust. I notice the CMROs pouring out of the starboard hangar. They form up behind us and out both sides.

Slowly making our way up, the ship rattles and shakes worse than when we landed. The fusion exhaust wasn't meant to be used as a take-off thruster. Thankfully someone thought it should be a feature.

A distressing report comes over the radio, **"Valkyrie, this is Oscar Seven! A crewman just fell out of the engine compartment! We're breaking formation to try and catch them!"**

We're not even five-hundred feet up unless they're able to do the impossible-

"Valkyrie this is Oscar Seven... unable to recover... and they just impacted on the surface. Returning to formation." We hear over the COMM.

Lieutenant Ephryn is about to inform me, but I hold up my hand to stop him and say, "Everyone remain focused. Survive now so we can mourn later."

Most everyone acknowledges my order. I ask, "Status of salvage teams?"

"I'll find out," a Crewman answers.

"And what about the enemy ships?" I inquire.

The Navigator answers, "Some of the smaller ships are chasing our two Outfighters that were on patrol. The rest are heading right for us."

"From what direction?" I add.

"Uh..." the Crewman studies their sensors, "It seems the smaller craft are all coming into the planet. One of the larger vessels is entering orbit. Unsure about the other."

"Find out," I order. "What's the status of engines?" I ask directing my question at the Operational Status console.

The Crewman replies, "The engine compartment is almost completely retracted and sealed."

"Bring them online," I order.

The Crewman hesitates a reply, "Uh, aye, Commander."

I add, "Bring the Traverse Drive online as well. I want to tunnel out of here as soon as we clear the planet."

Lieutenant Esker acknowledges, "Aye, Commander."

I watch one of the monitors as the enemy fighters close in on our position.

I order the Flight Control Commander, "Tell the Outfighters to break off, but remain in defensive patterns. Only attack if their ships get into range of OUR weapons."

The Flight Control Commander acknowledges.

"What's the status of our patrol ships?" I ask.

One of the COMMS Crewman responds, "One of them was destroyed. The other regrouped with our salvage teams and one of the Outminers in orbit. They're getting ready to recover the orbital satellite."

"Who told them to do that?" I ask.

Lieutenant Ephryn pipes up, "I did, sir it seemed-"

I cut him off, "Well done, Lieutenant. That was quick and prudent thinking."

The Crewman at Operational Status reports, "Main Engineering compartment has been retracted and secured. Switching to Main Propulsion."

Lieutenant Esker informs, "Sir, the Grav-Specialists insist against using the Traverse Drive. They weren't able to successfully test the dish before launch."

"Noted," I say, "tell them to turn in on anyway."

Someone shouts, "Enemy fighters are closing into weapon's range!"

I turn around and approach the back viewport, "Free to engage, free to engage," I preemptively order.

"Aye, Commander, free to engage," most everyone acknowledges.

Still off in the distance, I see the enemy ships making their approach. Then our aft laser batteries on the port and starboard modules light up sending energy bolts streaking at them. I also notice the Outfighters beginning their assault. It's hard to tell what exactly is going on. All I can see now is the light pink colors from our ships and the blue-green lasers of our enemies.

The helm informs, "Clearing the upper atmosphere. Switching on gravity plating."

There's a slight jolt, hardly noticeable due to the ship shaking as much as it is, but I know my ship.

Lieutenant Esker asks, "Commander, how do we want to recover our-" she's cut off as we take a hit to our port side.

I immediately look over and one of the larger ships has made their way over to us by staying in orbit.

"Engage that enemy vessel!" I order. "Navigator, where is the other large ship?"

The Crewman responds, "It, it followed the fighter craft into the atmosphere after us. I was tracking that other one until our satellite went offline."

"Very well," I say, "Lieutenant Esker, destroy that ship. Lieutenant Ephryn, have the salvage teams recover in the starboard hanger-" I'm cut off as the ship shakes loudly from the main and dorsal guns firing six shots each. I continue, "Then I want the fighters to begin their recovery."

"Aye Commander," Lieutenant Ephryn acknowledges.

I walk over to the port side of the bridge and watch as the laser batteries on the forward part of the port module and the port bridge wing spray energy, lighting up the Gerlak ship.

We sustain another hit.

"Lieutenant Esker, before they destroy us, please," I order.

Lieutenant Esker Orders the Fire Control, "Main and Dorsal guns, ten round salvo each!"

Within seconds, twenty shots are fired concurrently. At about the sixth or seventh shot the Gerlak energy shield fails and the remaining rounds rip them apart. The crew cheers as the enemy smolders briefly before the vacuum of space extinguishes the flames.

"Is the Traverse Drive ready?" I ask.

The co-Helm answers, "Yes, Commander."

"Spin it," I order, "And tell our fighters to recover."

Lieutenant Ephryn acknowledges, "Aye Commander, but we still have enemy fighters swarming them."

"Lieutenant Esker," I order, "Keep the Gerlak fighters off the dish this time."

"I'll do my best," she nervously acknowledges.

In the chaos, I must remain calm and level headed. Lieutenant Ephryn scrambles to organize a recovery plan for the Outfighters. The enemy fighters begin to close in, but don't seem to have noticed our Traverse Drive spinning up a tunnel. We might actually make it this time.

Helm informs, "Traverse Tunnel stabilized!"

"What's the status of our fighters?" I ask.

A Crewman shouts, "All fighters recovered!"

"Let's go!" I say as the helmsman full throttles into the singularity.

The fighters attempt to close around us, but break off as soon as we enter. The ship begins to rattle and sway as it normally does when traversing. We wait a few minutes to make sure we're stable.

Lieutenant Esker informs, "Traverse Tunnel is holding, Commander. Recommend we stand down Battle Stations."

"Concur." I say.

One of the crewmen announces our standing down from Battle Stations over the PA.

I walk over to the Navigator's table.

"I know I didn't get a chance to order a course," I begin, "but I assume you picked something good."

"Yes, Commander," the Navigator replies manipulating his holo map, he explains, "I picked the Sol System, but instead of going directly there, I figured along this track would be best. We can resurface to normal space near these systems along the way."

I ask, "Do any of them have resources?"

He answers honestly, "I'd have to look at the survey data more closely, but I assume so... hence the course I put in."

"Pull it up, let's take a look," I say.

The crewman acknowledges and starts looking into the survey data.

Someone screams sternly at me, "COMMANDER!!!"

I look over and see a very disgruntled Delta Benden storming his way towards me.

"His blood is on your hands!" he screams, "You killed him you son of a bitch!"

Some of the other bridge crew move to stand in front of him, Lieutenant Ephryn rushes up and grabs ahold of him from behind.

Delta Benden continues, "I don't care if you demote me or-"

I interrupt him by holding one finger up and calmly yet sternly say, "My office." I nod at Lieutenant Ephryn to let him go and I proceed towards the ladder to descend down.

The Delta says nothing.

We happen to run into Sub-Commander, "What's going on?"

"My office," I reply.

We all walk in. I sit behind my desk while Delta Benden and Sub-Commander remain standing.

I take a large breath, "I'm aware I stated many times that if any crew members had problems with any of my orders they could voice those concerns directly to me or Sub-Commander. I was also clear that doing so," my voice inadvertently starts to raise, "would also be done professionally in front of other crewman or privately otherwise."

I pause for a second. Continuing, "I'm aware you care about your crewmates, but don't assume for a second that I don't."

Sub-Commander interrupts, "I'm sorry, sir, what is this about?"

I order Delta Benden, "Tell him."

Angrily fighting back tears he informs Sub-Commander, "If we had stayed on the ground, Crewman Farhad would still be with us."

Sub-Commander asks, "How was he killed? When we got hit?"

"No!" Delta Benden responds, "He fell out of the engine compartment during lift-off. If we had waited-"

"We would have died," Sub-Commander finishes.

There is momentary silence.

Sub-Commander asks, "Was he wearing his life-line?"

Delta Benden thinks for a second, "It... uh...I don't know."

Both of them are thrown off balance for a second as we take a gravimetric roll, tilting the ship starboard. The gravity plating compensates and we feel the sensation as though the ship were righting itself in an ocean.

I say, "Circumstances considered, I'm not going to demote you. But I do expect a formal and public apology within the next two days. Until then, you're relieved for the next twelve hours to think and rationalize our situation. Dismissed."

The Delta sniffles and says, "Aye, Commander," and leaves.

Sub-Commander states, "I hope he's the only outburst, but I doubt it. In the meantime, where are we going?"

"Sol System," I reply, "but I have a feeling-" sure enough, I'm interrupted by my COMM going off.

"Keller," I say.

"Commander," Kaight says, "It's Lieutenant Esker. The Grav-Commander is recommending we resurface immediately. Apparently some of the traverse stabilizers are causing variances that could become quantum distortions."

"Could or will?" I clarify.

"Sir?" she asks.

"Call them back," I explain, "and verify what EXACTLY they are saying. If the variances cause a QD then let me know, but I'm not resurfacing unless there is a sure danger to the ship.

"I understand, sir," she acknowledges.

I add, "And get ahold of Nate McNill. Have him meet me here in my office."

"Will do, sir," she says and I close the line.

I look up at Sub-Commander, "I'm pretty sure we're going to be resurfacing much sooner than Sol."

He nods in agreement, "But the real problem we need to address is why our new friends attacked us. I mean maybe someone forgot to tell them."

I stand up, shaking my head, "I don't know what, but something isn't right. Attacking Keldon, attacking us… again."

"They must not be sincere about peace," Sub-Commander speculates.

I agree, "That much is certain… we'll need to resurface at one of these upcoming planets, establish communications and update Stellar Command. We also need to see what's in that computer… as well as debrief with Sergeant Kroeling."

"I'll sit down with the Sergeant," Sub-Commander says, "You should figure out where we're going. I'll have Delta Miranda start looking at the data we've recovered."

I nod and then sit quietly.

Sub-Commander notes, "What's on your mind?"

I shake my head, "This whole situation… so much of it just seems wrong."

"I agree," Sub-Commander nods, "Perhaps we should discuss it once we figure out what we're doing."

I sigh deeply, "I guess that would be the Commanderly thing to do-" My personal COMM goes off, "Keller," I say.

A male voice identifies, "Sir, it's Lieutenant Jerak. I asked Esker to forward me to you so we could speak directly."

"I assume this is about quantum distortions," I say.

He affirms, "Yes, Commander. At present time, there is only the potential for them to form, but if we keep running the core at high variance- if we keep tunneling for too long, that potential is going to transform into actuality. I cannot stress this enough, we need to resurface."

"I understand," I acknowledge, "and I have no intention of pushing that far, but I need to know how long you can give me."

The Gravimetric Commander ponders for a second, "I'd say anything longer than an hour and those variances will begin to cascade at which point we'll start over-polarization of the singularity tunnel. The rest is up for speculation as to what could happen, but certainly nothing good."

"Very well," I say, "We'll resurface in an hour. If anything changes, let me know right away. Permission granted for the time being to contact me directly."

"Understood, Commander," and he closes the line.

I say, "Alright, it just keeps getting better."

Chapter Ten: "We're snagged!"

(*Nathan*)I make my way up to the galley sort of fumbling, as I do, from the gravimetric rolls. Evading gerlak and fearing for my life has left me famished. The galley has yet to open and it smells as though we're getting synthetic BLT sandwiches. Gross. I instead settle for some dried mangos and leftover cold egg whites.

I sit down and begin eating my food. What a day it's been. Or maybe it's two days now. Yes, it's two days: yesterday I explored the Gerlak ship then was recalled to supervise a job that the rest of the crew was doing just fine without me.

The COMM unit mounted to a nearby bulkhead goes off and a passing Crewman answers.

"Yeah I think that's him," she says, "I'll let him know," and she puts the hand unit back into the wall.

The crewman walks up to me and confirms, "Hey you're that civilian miner guy, right?"

"One of them," I clarify.

She informs, "The Commander has requested you in his office as soon as you can go."

I angrily sigh, "Of course he has."

My appetite has been curbed. Keller probably wants to yell at me for staying on that ship. I pick up my dishes and leave them in the dish washing station. I mean, I'm grateful to be alive I guess. But this feels like prison. I don't get to do what I want- nope I got kicked out and became a miner, now only to be exploited for whatever Keller wants. Tim could have just as easily run operations. I don't even know as much as he does about actual mining, I just flew the ship. I can't wait to get off this hell hull.

The ship creaks and howls, a side effect of tunneling through space. An eerie change from the subtle hum and silence.

Finally I arrive at the door to Keller's office and knock.

"Come in," he orders.

I open the door and walk in, "You were looking for me, sir?"

"Yes," he confirms, "I need your expertise once again. We're probably going to have to resurface soon, but I'd rather it be somewhere near more minerals. You can probably guess we didn't get enough to begin with and need more after our rather eventful escape."

I nod and start to sit down. He interrupts, "Actually come over here, you can use the controls."

As I round the desk he explains, "Our options are limited to this system: Melyar. I can try to push the Traverse Drive longer if there's nothing of value, but I'm hoping you'll see something I didn't."

I scroll through each planet and moon's survey data. There isn't much except frozen worlds out really far, or hot worlds too close to the sun. No happy in-betweens, but some of the moons yield promise.

I say, "Melyar Six has three moons. One of them was classed Ex Seven, potential for very rich minerals. Only problem is Melyar Six itself is a frozen world. We could potentially harvest the ice for water, but I do not recommend setting the ship down there."

Keller nods, rather annoyed. He notes, "This would slow down operations considerably."

We're silent for a minute. I propose, "I think the most efficient way we can do this is to load the harvested minerals in bulk."

"How do you mean?" Keller asks.

I explain, "We'd have to spread out the Outminers around the moon. Everyone would have to try to mine at the same speed, then travel back to Valkyrie together. Once they arrive at the hangar, the hanger personnel could evacuate, decompress the hangar, let us in to drop off the haul, the Outminers leave, operations resume."

Keller says, "We'll start decompression when you start coming back to the ship. Otherwise, that's a good plan," he finishes pulling out his personal COMM. He contacts the bridge and orders them to resurface as close to Melyar Six as possible.

As I stand up, "Well, sir if there's nothing-"

I'm interrupted by Sub-Commander Devlin bursting in from his door that's connected directly to Keller's office, "Commander, sorry to interrupt, but Crewman Agsnon has discovered the crashed Gerlak ship to not have been transmitting any sort of distress call."

"What?" Keller gasps.

Agsnon enters from behind Devlin and explains, "I was able to translate most of their ship functions. There was no indication they transmitted a call for help."

"That doesn't make any sense," Keller notes, "why wouldn't they ask for help after being shot down?"

Everyone ponders for a second and then I explain, "Uh, Commander, we discovered a room that seemed to house more gerlak than could function normally on that ship."

Devlin speculates, "What were they? Hibernating soldiers?"

Agsnon has a moment of clarity as he starts, "Kind of…" he formulates thoughts into words, "I did come across something that controlled the tanks. From what the computers could translate, they seemed to have designations and functions, but one command was activated: Repair All Crew."

Keller affirms, "Which could mean they were all woken up to repair the ship... still, double check everything," he orders, "at least see if any kind of transmission was sent. At the very least they could have informed other gerlak they had crashed, but were going to repair themselves."

Agsnon nods and leaves the room.

Devlin notes, "This changes things a bit."

Keller shakes his head, "I'd rather not speculate until he's studied that database some more. In the meanwhile, we're going to resurface at Melyar Six, or at least close to it," he finishes pointing at the map. Keller continues, "Mr. McNill believes that will be a suitable source of minerals. And we might be able to replenish our water tanks. When's your debrief with Sergeant Kroeling?"

Devlin answers, "She's putting her suit and armor back in the armory then she'll be up."

"Good," Keller nods, "We'll debrief in here."

I pipe up, "If there's nothing else, sir, I'd like to be dismissed."

Keller raises a brow, "You were in the ship for a bit, weren't you?"

I reluctantly nod.

Keller says, "We'll sit down with you both, then."

I noddingly acknowledge and move to sit on the other side of his desk.

Devlin asks, "What was it like?"

I describe, "It was surprisingly peaceful. Light levels were low, but the interior of the ship was actually rather nice and clean. I guess I expected something worse, based on preconceptions."

Keller asks, "Understandable. Did you see any of their assault ships?"

I shake my head, "No, sir."

Keller reacts how I didn't expect: he scoffs slightly and smirks, "You do know you've been out for almost two years now. I appreciate the show of respect, but you don't have to call me 'sir'."

I, puzzled, looked over at Devlin who is looking away from both of us, "Oh, I... uh..." then I realize Devlin was presumptuous in his order towards me. At least for respecting Keller, "Is there something you'd rather I call you?" I ask.

Keller stops whatever he's doing on the console and looks directly at me, "Nate, I know you have your side of things regarding what happened. When we have a moment, I'd like to discuss your perspective. The short version: I tried my best to fight for you, but apparently Wernival or whoever else was in your division had connections and abused them. You're a civilian and a guest on my ship. You don't need permission, but I'll give it anyway: call me Jaysen."

"Okay..." I reply, "That may take a little getting used to..."

"I'm sure it will," Keller finishes returning to his console. A few seconds pass and he pulls up an image of one of the gerlak attack ships.

I nod, "Yeah, the ship we explored did not look like that."

We hear what sounds like a knock on Devlin's door. He returns to his office, answers it and leads Donna into Keller's office.

Devlin notes, "We're gonna debrief in here with the Commander."

Donna enters and partially smiles after noticing me.

She hands a small memory stick to Keller, "I was told to bring this to you."

Keller nods, "Yes, take a seat."

She does, next to me. Devlin takes the last seat next to her.

Keller begins, "We're going to watch this from the moment you deployed from the drop ship. If at any point there is something you would like to explain more on, we'll stop and discuss it. If Sub-Commander or I have questions, we'll pause and ask. Is there anything you want to say before we begin?"

Donna ponders for a second. She takes a breath and says, "At one point, I took down an unarmed gerlak. My reasoning for this was because prior to this encounter, I had only known them to be hostile. I lost a friend at Keldon, but I was fearing for the safety of my team at that moment and not for my chance to fulfill a personal vendetta."

Keller nods, "I understand. Anything else?"

Donna sighs concern, "We encountered and talked to two more… They also appeared to be unarmed, but I'm pretty sure they had their wrist weapons- I can't recall for sure. I held them at gunpoint while we talked, but once I realized they were using stalling tactics until backup arrived, I had to take them out to prepare for an ambush."

"Okay," Keller says, "right now I don't think there's any cause for an investigation. We'll review your footage and if needs be I'll review the footage from the other members of your team."

With the press of a few buttons, the holo-display projects an image to my right and large enough for everyone to view comfortably. We watch as she leaves the ship and her team begins to fan out. The first fifteen or so minutes are extremely mundane. It is interesting for me to see what was going on while I was still stumbling around in the wind tunnel that I eventually emerged from.

Speaking of, the moment Donna and her team start to enter it, a bit of uneasy tension creeps upon me. I won't lie, it was a struggle for Lede and I to get through it especially thinking Devorah had been killed. But then I recall the outcome and remember things turned out surprisingly well.

Snapping back to the moment, I notice Donna has entered the ship. Donna has been explaining some of the other details not noticeable on camera.

We get to the part where Donna guns down the unarmed alien. Keller pauses the playback.

He asks, "Sub-Commander, your thoughts?"

Devlin shrugs, "I think I would have done the same given the circumstances."

"Concur" Keller says and he resumes the recording.

After a couple minutes, Donna says, "Sir, can we pause it?"

Keller does so.

Donna explains, "This is the part where we located Crewman Belkrest. She was completely… exposed."

"Okay?" Keller acknowledges.

Donna tries to express, "Sir, if that were you up on display and this was being reviewed by your Commanding Officer and others- I mean, would you want to be seen like that? Because I know I wouldn't."

Keller nods slowly and ponders.

Devlin notes, "We still have to verify the authenticity of your report, though."

Keller points out, "Not exactly, Sub-Commander. We're not conducting an investigation at this time. We'll let it play however, we'll all look away, except for you, Sergeant. Since you've already seen what happened, I trust you… not that you can delete anything from the footage anyway."

Donna nods, "I'll let you know exactly when you can turn your head back, sir."

Keller resumes playback. This room I hadn't seen. It's definitely not as serene as the rest of the ship was.

Donna says, "Alright if you all don't mind looking elsewhere."

I shift to my left to prevent any unintentional viewing. As much as I would like to see Devorah without her clothes on, in this instance I quickly whip my natural desires back with the reminder that she might have been tortured at this point.

"Pause it, sir?" Donna asks.

Without looking at the projection, Keller reaches over and pauses.

"If you want to look real quick," she explains, "I happened to get a close look at her face."

We all look over and are jolted by the perspective.

"Holy shit," Devlin expresses, "What did they do to her!?"

"Thankfully, not much," Donna answers, "This was a crude breathing apparatus they rigged into her throat. It supplied very little oxygen, hence why she seems so out of it. If you don't mind turning back and resuming, I'll let you know when it's okay to watch again."

Keller half nods and we all turn away. Only about a minute passes before Donna gives us the all clear. We all cringe as Donna, in the recording, pulls out the breathing

thing the gerlak had rigged up. This is causing a bit of tension for me. Obviously there was nothing I could do. She somehow got separated and ended up further along in the wind tunnel, but seeing this just ignites a fire. I've gotten to know Dev over the last few weeks or so and yes I kind of like her. To see what these bastards may have subjected her too… it's almost too much.

I jolt back into the moment as the playback reaches the part where Donna talks with the aliens. It's almost surreal watching as she communicated with them. Their motives were certainly clear enough: wipe us out.

Donna asks, "Sir, can you pause it?"

Keller nods and hits a button.

Donna explains, "At this point I had figured out they were mostly stalling for back-up. Once I knew what was happening, I realized our lives were in danger. Somehow they had alerted the other gerlak to our presence. Without knowing whether or not they had access to weapons we didn't know about or if they were already armed, I decided to take them out. I can say with absolute certainty that they had no intention of surrendering."

Devlin asks, "Why didn't you apprehend and hold them?"

"The number of incoming would have overwhelmed us," Donna explains, "I'm not sure if they themselves were armed, but as I said, they were not interested in being prisoners."

Devlin nods, "I see… we can resume."

Keller pushes a button and the playback resumes. We take another gravimetric roll and as the ship tires to "right itself" we continue to feel the effects; as though we're spinning. A couple of items on Keller's desk begin to slide off and I start to brace in an attempt to hold myself in my chair as does Donna. Devlin stumbles and props up against a cabinet. Keller grabs his desk to stop from rolling back into the bulkhead.

Outside, the howling starts to get louder and more consistent. My arms are starting to give. I quickly twist around, loop my arms around the chair armrests and hold on tight.

A COMM chirping goes off. I hear, "Keller! What in the hell is going on!?!"

"Sir!" the person on the other end struggles, "We're snagged! Request to... rrrr! Take the grav plating offline to effect repairs!"

I've never been in a snag this bad. Sometimes, if our tunneling isn't properly stabilized the ship will snag on a gravity well from a near-by star. This forces the ship into a continuous roll which can potentially rip us into pieces as we're forced to resurface.

"Wait for my signal!" Keller orders. He struggles to hit a button, at least that's what it sounds like. Donna and I are gripping our chairs like they'll somehow save us. I mean right now they're stopping us from flying into the bulkhead.

I start to hear loud creaking. The hull is under serious stress.

Keller screams into his COMM, "All hands, this is the Commander! We've hit a snag! On my order, the gravity plating will be taken offline, at which point I need you to find something to hold on to while the grav specialists prepare to take the Traverse Drive offline. On their order, grav plating will come back on and we will attempt to resurface. Bridge, stand by to bring gravity plating down in ten... nine... eight... seven... six... five... four... three... two... one... now!"

The howling and creaking continues as the rolling sensation vanishes and suddenly my body begins to float.

"Back here against the bulkhead," Keller orders.

Donna and I float our way to the bulkhead behind Keller's desk. Keller floats the chair towards Devlin who floats it into his office and secures the door.

Over the PA we hear, "All hands, stand-by for gravity plate activation followed shortly by forced resurfacing."

My nerves are complete haywire in anticipation. We could easily die a horrible death in the next few seconds. We try to stay as close to the deck before- WAM! The gravity kicks back in and we're pulled to the bulkhead. The ship immediately shakes violently as a loud, intermittent screeching noise is heard. This lasts for about six to seven seconds before things finally calm down.

As we start to get up, Keller says, "Dismissed. I'm needed on the bridge."

He starts to leave and then I suggest, "Sir, I think I can help determine where we are and maybe help figure out how to get to our destination."

"Yes," Keller says, "Come with us. Sergeant Kroeling, we'll try to finish this at a later time."

I follow Devlin and Keller out of the Commander's office. Making our way towards the bridge we come across a crewman stumbling along the passageway. Devlin breaks off to assist him as he appears to have suffered a head injury. Some of the lights in the passage are also flickering, indicating that the power supply lines have suffered damage. We ascend the ladder up to the bridge with haste. Keller stops suddenly and almost loses his balance. He slowly takes the last three steps and as I come up behind him I can see why: we're spinning out of control. We're pretty much in an offset barrel roll.

"What's going on?" Keller asks, "Why are we spinning?"

Lieutenant Esker answers, "We resurfaced into a roll, but the stabilization thrusters aren't responding, at least not all of them. Helm tried to stabilize and that's what offset us even more. We're drifting at about four nines, but we don't know where we are."

Keller continues talking to Esker as I head over to the Navigator's Table. Three of the Navigators are trying to figure out where we are. Since we're spinning so fast, the navigation system can't get a lock on any of the constellations to determine our position.

One of them notes, "I can't get a fix for shit!"

I squeeze in and say, "Mind if I take a look?"

"Psh," one of them smirks, "Sure why not."

I pull up the map and activate the intended course layer and ask, "How long had we tunneled for?"

The other female Navigator looks at another screen and says, "About… an hour."

"Can I get the exact minute, please?" I ask.

"Oh, yes, um, fifty six minutes," she answers.

Our intended course was supposed to last about five hours. I estimate a quick spot on the map and then something catches my eye: a possible black hole.

"What is this?" I ask, pointing to the chart.

The other navigators crowd around and study what I'm pointing at.

"Oh no…" one of the Navigator's says… "How did I miss that!?"

I've mentioned before that gravitational pulls from nearby stars can have effects on traverse tunneling. Black holes have considerably less effect… unless you tunnel too close which is what we did. Long technojargon short, if you plot a course too close to a black hole, it will pull the ship to the edge of the tunnel causing it to snag; basically tangling the ship in its own tunnel. When tunneling passed a star, the pull is more spread out and so the effects aren't as dangerous, but a black hole pulls in a more focused direction hence why we were snagged, traveling so close by.

Commander Keller walks up, "Did we figure out where we are?"

I answer, "I have a rough estimation calculated, but we'll need more time to get a more accurate position."

Keller informs, "Please do. We're not sure how long we're going to be spinning out."

I look over at the erroristic Navigator who sheepishly says, "Uh, Commander, there's no easy way to admit this, but… I didn't account for a black hole along our trajectory…"

Keller takes a breath and slowly turns to face him, "Excuse me?"

"I…" he tries to explain, "I must have overlooked it in all the chaos-"

The Commander interrupts holding up a finger, "Crewman Todkins, correct?"

He replies with a slow nod.

Commander Keller orders, "You're relieved for the next twelve hours."

"Commander, I-"

Keller interrupts again, "I said you're relieved."

"Aye… Commander…" he says as he walks off.

The rest of us stand quietly for a minute. Then I decide to resume calculations and the other navigators do the same. Keller heads over to his chair and Sub-Commander joins him. It's hard to say what fate awaits Crewman Todkins. He must have felt pressured to get a course going, but he could have checked his work once we were stabilized to make sure there were no obstructions. Looking at the chart, we would have been ripped to pieces were we just a single kilometer closer. An overlook like that would have gotten all of us killed. So on the other hand, Keller should have checked the course before authorizing it. I'll have to find out what happens to him. Maybe Keller will accept his responsibility in the matter. And if so, well...

One of the Navigators says, "I think I've got a fix on our location. What do you think?"

I answer, "Did you account for the Flaxin Star?"

She nods.

Looking over her calculation I say, "Good job, uh, Crewman..."

She says, "Zantfa"

As I start moving away from the chart table, I stop myself and say, "You should go tell the Commander."

She acknowledges and heads over to him.

After about 20 seconds the Commander comes back to the Navigation table.

He asks, "Are you able to determine our heading?"

Everyone sheepishly looks around and Zantfa notes, "I mean we're good, sir, but that is impossible."

Keller nods, "I understand. We'll have to wait for the engineers to get us stabilized. Good work. Start figuring out a course for when we finally do stabilize. Make sure you check it three times before submitting it to me. Oversights like this one will get us killed."

Everyone says, "Aye, Commander."

Okay, let's see if I can help these guys not get us all killed. I have to be careful not to look up too often. The stars spinning out of control is really throwing me off. I also notice some other crew members having trouble walking in a straight line as well.

One of the Crewman asks, "How do we plan a course without knowing where exactly we are?"

I ponder for a second and then zoom the chart out so it contains our destination.

"Crewman…"

"Knoop," he answers.

"First name?" I ask.

He says, "Dale."

"Dale," I say, "Nathan, good to meet you. So what I'm thinking is, we have a rough idea of where we came out. We can at least plan a couple of courses starting at the destination and working our way back."

Dale nods in agreement as the other Navigators crowd around to start making a couple of different tracks.

After about five to ten minutes of working, I overhear some of the bridge chatter, "ENGCOM says we're ready to test thrusters."

"Finally," a female Lieutenant says, "Helm, bring us to a stop."

"Aye, ma'am" the helmsman acknowledges.

We begin to slow down. I watch as our erratic spinning finally comes to a halt and I can stand to look out the viewports again. While the LT gets ahold of Keller, who left the bridge momentarily, I begin manipulating the sensors to determine where we are.

"I've got a fix on our location," I say.

Dale notes, "Looks like my track was the closest one. Can you give me half of the table? I'm going to check for gravitational interference along my projected route while you fine tune the course."

I nod in agreement and activate the split function, giving us separate sections of the table to work on. I bend the projected course to our current position. Oh, you thought we could only tunnel in straight lines? It is the most efficient way to travel, but we can bend our lines to avoid obstacles as necessary.

I almost have the course ready when Keller's presence is announced. He quickly comes over to the table.

"Have we got a safe path to travel?" He asks.

Dale answers, "Fine tuning it and doing initial check for obstacles, Commander."

Keller looks at his personal COMM unit and then orders, "I want a course reviewed and checked three times by all of you in the next thirty minutes. By then the Gravimetric Core should be ready for us to tunnel. Get to it."

Everyone but me says. "Aye Commander"...

(*Keller*)...I nod and then head over towards the Crater.

"Have we established communications?" I ask.

Crewman Marfett answers, "I've called out to the Net Control Center, sir, but have not heard anything yet. I'm shifting through bands, but so far- hold on I've got something."

He focuses on his work and fine tunes the signal.

Confused, he looks over and says, "Admiral Yelkin is ordering to speak to you securely."

I acknowledge with a nod and as I head for the bridge ladder, I nod at Sub-Commander to follow me.

Descending the ladder, he says, "It's almost like they were waiting for our communication. Did we get a distress call out?"

"No," I remind, "The Gerlak were jamming our communications when they entered the system."

"That's something else we need to talk about," Devlin brings up, "What is their mode of travel. We can't detect them when they just show up so we know they don't tunnel or at least how we do."

"Hopefully we'll find out from the Admiral," I say as we round the corner and proceed into my office.

I round my desk and activate my communication screen which buzzes in the Admiral on 2D form.

"Greetings, Admiral," I say.

Angrily he says, "What the fuck, Keller!? We are trying to forge a peace and you destroy one of their ships!?!"

Taken back for a second, I respond, "Uh, begging your pardon, we were fired upon by them."

The Admiral says, "They felt threatened when your patrol craft surrounded them! What exactly did you expect!?"

I respond, "I expected them to accept our greeting with a less hostile response. I ordered my ships to greet them at which point they were immediately fired on. I ordered their retreat and our immediate departure. In the process, one patrol ship was destroyed. I ordered the remaining fighters to launch and take defensive posture. The Gerlak sent fighters after us and immediately engaged mine. Once their larger ship got in range, they fired on us."

"They claimed you were acting hostile," the Admiral says, "they also claim you slaughtered their crew on their exploration vessel."

I nod, "We investigated the ship, yes, but were met with hostilities. They took one of my crewmembers and prepped her for some sort of experimentation. Luckily the rescue team was able to get to her before anything bad had happened. During the rescue the Gerlak spoke of-"

The Admiral holds up his hand, "Just send your reports along… it seems there are some inconsistencies that can't be ignored. We're going to need your ship's records to confirm your story. And your location."

"We're in dead space, Admiral," I say, "We were heading to a planet with resources to repair our ship further until we hit a snag and were forced to resurface."

The Admiral nods, "I see… what's your status?"

I explain, "We're waiting for the core to cool down. The Grav Specialists are also inspecting the dish since they didn't get to before we left Thretta. After that we'll be heading to Melyar Six for resources."

"Very well," The Admiral acknowledges, "What about heading to Telo colony?"

I explain, "I can check, but Lieutenant Jerak wants to take the entire Drive offline and do a full inspection. He believes we'll make it safely to Melyar, but any longer and we could obliterate."

The Admiral says, "I understand. We'll get a ship there to meet you while this investigation proceeds. I'm sorry, but once your ship is in custody, you'll have to stand down until we can clear you of any wrongdoing."

I begrudgingly agree, "I will cooperate of course, but I have to insist that only a Republic vessel is sent to avoid another misunderstanding."

The Admiral says, "I will get another Cutter out to meet you. The Prime Minister thought as a show of good faith the Gerlak could escort you back, but perhaps that was a mistake considering you were in the dark since fleeing Keldon."

I nod heavily, "Yes it was. I'll debrief with the patrol flight crew that survived and look over their logs while preparing to send them-"

The Admiral interrupts, "I need the records now. Send your report from your pilots when it's ready, but we need to make sure the ship sensor logs aren't tampered."

"Okay..." I say, "And I'd like to allow my crew to access the net. Reach out to their families and let them know they are okay."

The Admiral takes a deep breath, "I understand that you care about your Crew's well-being. But for now I have to deny your request. I need you to trust us to keep control of what's going on. Until you're safely back in a port, I have to ask you remain dark."

"Alright..." I say, "I'll let you know when we're ready to get under way. Keller out."

The image dissipates and returns to the projection of Sergeant Kroeling's recording. Sub-Commander and I try to figure out where to even begin.

"Where do we even begin?" Sub-Commander coincidently says.

I shake my head, "I don't know. But I am getting damn tired of these "mis-understandings" and forcing the crew to remain in the dark."

"They definitely aren't telling us everything," he says.

I retort, "That much is clear."

He extrapolates, "I mean there seems to be a break in consistency. Like the Admiral has told us one thing and the Prime Minister or the War Noble is commanding something else. Should we contact the Council of Nobles directly?" Sub-Commander proposes, "I think we can reasonably invoke directive seventeen."

I shake my head, "Directive sixteen, maybe… but even then…"

I ponder for a moment. There's really not much we can do here.

I say, "For now we'll remain with our current plan."

Sub-Commander acknowledges with a nod. He then points out, "We're gonna need to sit down with Sergeant Kroeling and figure out how to go about explaining some of her actions in the alien ship. If this whole thing since Keldon has been a misunderstanding that could put her in a precarious position along with you."

I look down at my desk momentarily. So much about all of this is wrong. But I guess that's the price we paid for not having communications. Maybe all of this is a misunderstanding. Maybe we are the aggressors here-

"Jaysen…" Sub-Commander interrupts my thought.

I look up at him, "Mike… We need to reevaluate our situation before we go any further."

He raises a brow, "How do you mean?"

I explain, "We need to go over everything that's happened. Evaluate everything we have done up until this point to make sure that we've been doing everything right so far."

"I'd say we hav-"

I interrupt, "Let's make absolutely certain. Once we know where we stand, once we've confirmed everything that's happened and that we have done the right thing, then we can continue."

Sub-Commander confirms, "You want us to investigate ourselves?"

"Yes," I say, "we will compose an extensive report, attach evidence to support what's happened and then conclude with our statements."

"For what purpose," he asks, "at least right now."

I explain, "This situation is now causing me to doubt myself. I'm starting to second guess decisions and talking about them on the side isn't going to be enough. I may look over this report and consider invoking Directive Seventeen as you suggested. But before we talk to the Council of Nobles directly, we need to make sure our foundation is solid."

Directive Seventeen is a provision within the Articles of Governance and Freedom that allows ship Captains and Commanders to seek a meeting directly with the Prime Minister's Council of Nobles, in the event that they feel a situation isn't being represented properly. It's a check and balance to help ensure integrity within the government.

Reluctantly nodding, Sub-Commander says, "Okay... let's start with Keldon."

Chapter Eleven: "This thing has too many damn safety features!"

(*Nathan*)The howling and creaking through the ship wakes me momentarily. Seems like we're finally moving again. Dinner seemed rather lackluster and I guess I wasn't as hungry at the time. Now, as I roll back and forth in my rack with the rolling of the ship, I start to feel hunger setting in. I've probably got a few hours before I'm obligated to resume mining operations, so maybe there's some alternate snacks I can find.

The lights have been turned down in the halls, indicating evening/night hours. I'm not sure how long I must have been asleep. It's possible we've been tunneling for a while.

I make my way to the snack foods drawer. Looks like some oatmeal packs are all that's available right now. I shouldn't be surprised. We're probably running out of food.

Pulling the bowl out of the microwave, I place it down momentarily as it's hot. I pull out my sleeves and carry it towards the table. As I get ready to sit down, I notice Dev sitting by herself.

Placing my bowl down, I ask, "Can I join you?"

She looks up and smiles softly, "Yes, please do."

I notice a mug in front of her. If it's coffee, she might be getting ready for watch.

"About to start the rounds?" I ask.

She shakes her head slowly, "No it's tea. I have always had trouble sleeping whenever we tunnel."

I nod, "I usually sleep through it. But I was so tired at dinner that I skipped it. Now I'm hungry in the middle of the night. Go figure."

"You missed nothing," she informs, "Tasted like rubber."

I note, "The synthetic pork. Yum."

"Yeah..." she says, "rumor has it that we'll be out of food in the next week. I mean, we'll probably be down to emergency ration packs twice a day for three more weeks, and then we'll starve."

I finish swallowing a gob of oatmeal and say, "delightful." I take a sip of coffee... something seems off about it. I ask, "Did we switch over to recycled water?"

Dev sort of sheepishly answers, "We're not supposed to say... but our freshwater is low to the point where we are mixing both tanks to stretch the supply. The mixture is about one quarter recycled, three quarters fresh water. Apparently that is a safe enough ration that it doesn't require re-meds... yet."

I ponder my mug for a second and try not to think about the fact that I am drinking someone's bodily fluid... or rather it was.

There's some silence for the moment. As I get ready to say something to change the subject, I'm interrupted by a large roll. For a second my stomach drops. I'm thinking we've snagged again. Nope. We're starting to right. Sometimes the interference causes slower rolls which can last longer.

"Well... that was a big one," I state.

Dev just nods.

I ask, "So about how long have we been tunneling?"

She answers. "I think almost four hours now."

"Oh..." I say getting up, "I'm gonna need some more coffee."

"Why?" she asks.

I explain, "Well in an hour we're gonna resurface and then soon after I figure they'll want us out there mining... again."

"Ah," she acknowledges and hands me her cup, "do you mind getting me some?"

I say, taking her cup, "Not at all.... would be nice if there was a cleaner alternative."

I walk over to the large vat that automatically makes coffee every eight hours or when it runs out. The screen indicates the last batch was made over six hours ago. I position Dev's mug under the spicket. While filling her cup, I inadvertently look back to where she's seated. She's watching me intently... probably to make sure I don't mess up her coffee.

"Cream? Sugar?" I ask.

She shakes her head. She likes it straight black. Like I do. I begin pouring mine and look back over. She half smiles. I look back finishing my fill and pause momentarily... uh oh... feelings.

I bring both mugs over almost losing my step. A couple of drops fly out over the sides of both mugs. I plant the cups on the table followed quickly by planting myself on the seat.

"That was close," I note.

She chuckles a little and takes a sip.

"Mmm..." she insincerely indicates.

I take a sip and nod, "Yep... perfect."

Actually it's terrible. To prevent burning, the warmer kicks off after about four or five hours leaving us a lukewarm, bitter liquid. I, in fact, do like it this way, but it is undeniably awful, especially since the water supply is tainted.

Dev notes, "Well… at least we'll have coffee with our ration packs."

"Indeed," I agree, "I guess poop coffee is better than no coffee…"

We listen to the howling for a minute as I try to think of something.

"So…" I try to begin.

She gives me the "yes?" look.

"I… uh…" I stutter, "I was thinking about Thretta."

She nods slowly, "Yeah I think about it too."

"We, uh… should've listened to Lede." I say.

"Yep," She agrees, "thankfully I wasn't too traumatized, but next time we crash, we wait."

"Yes," I say… "Dev, I… after that large gust kicked up… I guess something must have parted our lifeline cause when we landed I thought you were dead… There was a large piece of debris where I thought you might have ended up."

Dev explains, "Wow… yeah I flew for a good distance and landed hard on my leg. When I sat up, I stumbled around a bit more, not sure where I was. Then I bumped into one of the aliens thinking it was you. Of course it wasn't… any number of things could have happened. Thankfully your friend showed up in time."

In agreement I nod, "She's good at that…." I trail my thoughts and think of what to say… "I mean along with learning what NOT to do in case there is a next time, I guess you never really know how much you care about someone until… um. I guess until you think you lost them."

Dev nods, "Oh yeah… I am aware."

More awkward silence. My strategy of making noise around the bush seems to be failing. Perhaps I should just plow right through.

I look into my empty cup, "Welp, unless we wanna do another round, I say we head on down to the Port Hangar and start prepping."

Dev agrees and we both get up.

Maybe she is aware of what I am trying to say and it's still too soon. I don't know. Do I even know how I really feel? Or have I just been alone for so long that the first full time contact I have with a female is just triggering my natural desires. I mean, I don't even know that much about her.

We fumble our way to the lift and proceed down to the Port Hangar. Only a few other crewmembers are about performing routine checks on the Outminers and fabrication equipment.

Dev walks up to Crewman, "Conwell. Do you know anything about our planned mining operations?"

He shrugs, "I know there is a plan to resume at some point, but last I heard the work day wasn't starting until the afternoon. I guess the Commander wanted to give the crew a little extra rest."

"Okay, thanks," She says.

I sigh.

She says, "Yeah I know... would have been nice to know BEFORE we had coffee."

I suggest, "We could still ask to go out. I mean it would be smart to sample the moons."

"Yes," she says, "I'll get the request started. Go start prep on Miner Three."

"Aye, Crewman Belkrest," I semi-sarcastically say as we part ways.

I inspect the ship's back doors. Seal looks good. I check in the compartment to make sure there are at least two emergency suits. I pull out the rifles making sure they

- 224 -

are charged. Then I head into the cockpit and begin checking thruster control, making sure the shifter works. There's proper power to the turret, the weapons power up- man if someone wanted to do some serious damage to Valkyrie from the inside it would be really easy.

Startling me, Dev pops her head into the cockpit from the back, "How are we looking?"

"Good so far," I say.

"You okay?" she chuckles.

"Yes," I say, "Just deeply concentrated on what I'm doing. Are we good to go?"

She informs, "ENGCOM is asking the Sub-Commander now. He approved so I would think we'll be good. Anything I should grab in case we crash again?"

"Isn't it bad luck to joke about that?" I inquire.

She responds, "Who the hell cares. But seriously, what will we need?"

"Melyar is a frozen world," I inform, "So maybe some blankets and some extra heaters."

"Standard sub-zero emergency kit," she confirms, "I'll be back."

I quickly make sure all the computer self-diagnostics come back green then sit in the pilot's seat and await Dev's return. She seems like a good person. And I mean, nothing brings people together quite like trauma… or in my case, brings me closer to her anyway. It's hard to believe the last time I was romantically involved with someone was almost five years ago. Of course the distance thing didn't work out, and before her was my minor school girlfriend… well she was more like a crush who had a boyfriend. And I was never really one for port call romances except once, and let's just say I have no interest in spending that much ever again.

Who knows, maybe Dev- I hear her this time climbing in. I turn my head back and see her lifting one of the compartments in the deck of the Outminer and placing the sub-zero kit into it.

I say, "I assume we're good to go?"

She nods, "Yes. Sub-Commander apparently wanted a full crew, but ENGCOM convinced him since we're just doing a survey mission that would be unnecessary."

"Cool," I say.

Dev enters the main cockpit and hands me a to-go cup, "Fresher coffee," she informs. "And I may have gotten the water directly from the fresh tank."

"Thank you so much," I say, taking it.

"We should be surfacing soon" she says, "and then they'll clear the hangar and get us out there. I guess Commander wants mining operations to resume within the next three hours."

I nod, "Awesome. Hey, I don't suppose you have heard anything regarding the salvaged shield generator have you?"

Dev shakes her head, "No. I know a friend of mine is working on studying it, but he hasn't learned anything worth passing on... I assume anyway."

"That would be quite the game changer," I point out.

Dev nods, "Especially if we can get that tech on these things."

Oh look, more partially awkward silence.

The COMM goes off ending it, "**Miner Three, this is Val-Con. Begin prepping for launch. The Port Hangar is evacuating and preparing for decompression.**"

Dev grabs the COMM handset, "Understood, Control."

She nods and heads to the back to make sure the ship is securely closed up. I double check my door and then begin activating the engines. It smoothly chugs to life.

Dev comes back up and gets situated in the co-pilot's seat and grabs the COMM handset, "Control, this is Miner Three, we are ready to fly."

The COMM answers back, "**Understood, Miner Three. Bay doors are opening now. Stand by for launch.**"

I gracefully lift the ship off the deck and angle it towards the door. It completes opening and we wait for the order to go.

Finally, the COMM says, "**Miner Three, you are clear for launch. Take off to your starboard and hold course until you clear Valkyrie air space then proceed to mission. Check ins every hour.**"

Dev replies into the handset, "Uniform Alpha."

I fly the ship forward and out into space. Gravity quickly shifts from the Valkyrie's, which is Earth standard, to ours, which is hardly anything. I turn right about 90 degrees and then proceed straight heading towards Melyar VI, a bluish white ice world with several observable large electrical storms taking place.

For scale, it's about three Earths, yet has a gravity field only 78% of Earth's. The entire surface is snow and ice with actual ground about four thousand kilometers underneath. What is interesting is despite the lower surface gravity, the planet's mass has a higher gravimetric pull, as indicated on my sensors.

Behind us is the Melyar Star, burning faintly as it's far, but also compared to Sol, it's about a third smaller, at least according to the chart. Speaking of, I look where we need to be going. Based off Valkyrie's sensor data and the information on the chart, the first moon we're going to examine is just up and to our left or in special navigational terms, 550Y, 30XR, +80Z.

Upon getting the ship on course, Dev asks, "How long?"

I look at the instruments, "About sixteen minutes. Initial scans look like some potential for light iron ore, but not much else."

"We could at least fabricate parts with that," Dev says.

I add, "And repair interior bulkheads. Hopefully we can see some denser carbon deposits and osmium."

I pass the time scrolling through the map information, specifically the last scans of the moons that were taken by an exploration vessel. Dev appears to just monitor the engines, but I could swear a couple of times I catch her looking at me.

We make our approach and I slow the ship down.

Dev pulls the controls out for the laser and asks, "So is it the same setting as before?"

I shake my head, "No, you're gonna set to a lower intensity. On a mining vessel we have several scanning lasers that penetrate a rock's surface to see if it's worth mining. We can typically scan through five to eight at a time. For this, we've only got one laser and all we want to do is mine until we get a rich enough sample to indicate a strong deposit."

"Okay," she acknowledges, "would one twenty be good?"

"Um…" I begin, "Sure… this is Tim's expertise, but he was asleep. Let's try it and see if it yields results."

Dev nods, sets the power level and says, "Ready."

"Fire," I say.

She hits the button and we wait. I watch the information coming in on the sensor data. Mostly useless rock.

"We'll mine for fifteen minutes then see what we have," I say.

"Alright," Dev says.

I let a few awkward moments of silence go by and then say, "So... um... are you uh... with anyone?"

"What?" Dev asks looking up. She was clearly focused on something.

"Oh," I say, "sorry were you focused on something?"

She nods, "Yeah, I'm monitoring heat levels if you don't mind."

"Not at all," I say, wondering if she actually heard me or- for fucks sake why does this shit still have to be awkward? I'm almost thirty and still nervous about talking to girls? Then again, Dev isn't a girl. She's a woman. A hardworking, dedicated, experienced strong woman. Yeah. I like women.

After a couple of minutes of silence and humming of the engine and laser, Dev says, "We're looking good here, what were you asking?"

"I uh..." struggling for words, "I was just wondering about you and things you do."

"And people that I'm seeing?" Dev calls me out, "Not officially with anyone, remember?"

I think for a second, "Oh yeah... the other guy you're with, but not with."

Dev confirmingly nods.

"Yeah…" I say, "I was seeing somebody before I shipped out to Keldon… well it was more like a friend thing… well I mean we hung out as friends and didn't do much else… I mean she also had a boyfriend."

"Oh," Dev chuckles, "So you weren't seeing anyone, then."

I ponder momentarily, "No… I guess not. I guess it's been a while."

Dev shuts the laser off, "It's done."

I look over the displays and interpret the results.

"Yep," I inform, "Mostly iron ore. Mostly spread out too thin. Mostly useless. Plotting course for our next moon. ETA, thirty minutes."

Dev nods, "Cool."

Some time goes by. I mostly monitor our speed and make sure we aren't drifting off course.

Dev breaks the silence, "So how did you end up in mining? That seems a little odd for an Intel Navigator to go into that field."

I take a deep breath, "Yeah, even though I didn't technically get a dishonorable discharge there was a partial media interest."

"What?" Dev asks.

I confirm with a large nod, "Yep. Every place I applied for where my Intel training would have earned me money almost instantly turned me down. So I looked at applying with cruise liners… same shit. Some of them said they would overlook it if I had any training on the Traverse Drive… since my helm was basic and not full on like your late husband, well… yeah. So I ended up applying for Ex Del Corp and they took me almost immediately… well my Captain took me almost immediately. Guess he thought having me on board would somehow deter us from being boarded by the Armada."

Dev chuckles, "Well thankfully that wasn't the case."

"Yeah-" I interrupt myself… "Huh…"

"What is it?" Dev asks.

"I… I guess it kind of hit me," I explain, "I could be dead right now."

"How do you figure?" Dev inquires, "Wasn't it because of us you ended up on Keldon?"

I nod, "Yes, but we were three to four weeks from Keldon at sub-light. Would have been a matter of time before we were found."

"Your ship didn't have Traverse Drive?" Dev raises a brow.

I explain, "No. Most mining vessels don't. Requires too much money to have maintainers on board and takes up space for a grav-core."

"Then how did you get out there?" Dev asks, "Earth to Keldon even cruising at Full Nine would take almost what? Twenty years?"

I nod, "Correct. We use specialized carriers provided and controlled by the guild. They take mining vessels out to the different colonies and from there we go to our intended mining location."

"And then almost a month out to your mining area?" Dev asks.

"Sometimes a month," I say, "Sometimes just a few weeks. Depends on what we prepared for and how far we want to go out. We were out almost six months once… we lived on ration packs during the voyage back which wasn't super lucrative."

"Wow..." Dev expresses... "Do you even bother having a home?"

I shake my head, "I moved all my valuables into my mom's house on Mars. I send her a check for keeping my shit safe. My plan was to work this for five years then head back to Sol and start a business. Mining doesn't pay very well to start, but after two years you can expect a raise, especially if you take on other responsibilities. Fuck..."

"What is it now?" she asks.

"Guess I'm having an existential morning... once I get off this ship I'm gonna have to start over," I realize...

Dev is silent for a moment, then speculates, "I bet you can't wait to get off the ship."

I nod slowly, "Being here, especially with Keller, has brought back sour memories. Memories I don't typically like to discuss."

"I understand," Dev says, "My husband is a tough subject... for different reasons, obviously."

"I was accused of espionage as you know," I begin, "We had an extended inport at Telo Colony. Almost three weeks. It was our mid-deployment. I had decided to spend a majority of the time off the ship when I wasn't on stand-by crew. So I got myself a loft at an extended stay hotel."

"Big spender," Dev notes.

I continue, "I had some extra money. The benefit of being focused on work and not making time for a companion. I actually spent most of my time there. Only went out a few times, but each time I did I ran into a few of the guys from my division."

"You never hung out with them intentionally?" She asks.

I shake my head, "I was never more than acquaintances with them. They were basically their own club. As I tried to get to know them and become friends, that's when they turned on me. All of a sudden I was accused of betraying the Republic and giving information to pirates. But I suspect who it actually was…"

"Oh?" She says.

I inquire, "Did Todd ever mention Crewman Fenz?"

Dev answers, "Yes… I had heard some things about him. Mostly unflattering."

I nod in confirmation, "I had seen him with a woman each time I was out. They were rather… friendly and comfortable."

"Wasn't he married?" She asks, "And didn't he have kids?"

I explain, "Wouldn't have known that seeing him with this woman. Anyway, a pirate crew was interdicted during the last leg of our patrol. We found intel on board that pertained to where we were going and when. Stellar Investigations was handed the case and determined that the information came from our ship… by that time, Wernival, Fenz and everyone in the division had their story airtight. Wernival tried to get me to "confess" and said things would go over better if I did. I immediately pushed back and stood my ground. In the end, I still lost.``

Dev shakes her head, "No. Had you confessed you would have been imprisoned. Or worse. I'm not saying you got off any better, obviously you still claim your innocence and if you're innocent, you still got screwed. Did you mention your theory to Ess I?"

"I did," I say. "I talked with them directly and articulated my side of the story and who I suspected the real leaker was. They concluded that I was just trying to deflect. The fact that I had spent so much time by myself didn't help my story at all and Wernival knew what was coming. He had things set up long in advance to make me the fall guy."

"Why?" Dev asks.

I shrug, "I honestly can only speculate. Wernival must have had contacts in high places and because that group were such good friends, I was the outsider, so it didn't matter that I went down for something I didn't do. I even went to Keller directly, pleaded with him to help me. I ended up being shipped off at Telo then escorted back to Earth and while awaiting a General Courts Martial, ended up being handed discharge papers and told I could go."

"And now you're here," Dev notes.

"Yep," I say.

Dev shares, "Todd had maintained your innocence, but after you left the ship, he told me if he was caught discussing it that he would be disciplined even though he wasn't involved. Soon after that, Keller transferred, but no one knows directly why. Honestly, it sounds like a cover-up for something bigger, but the question is, what."

"Who knows," I say, "I've been too busy trying to move on."

I slow the ship down as we approach the second moon. Like a well-oiled machine, Dev and I quickly get set up and get the laser cutting.

What Dev has brought up has me thinking. What were they trying to hide? Who were they trying to cover for and why? Well I know they were covering for Fenz, but why was Wernival so adamant about it? Damn… now I'm thinking of things I have tried to put behind me.

"Another fifteen minutes?" Dev asks.

"Hmm," I acknowledge coming back to the moment, "Oh, uh let's go for twenty. This moon is a little bigger."

Dev nods. The display starts to catch my attention almost immediately.

"Dense carbon," I say, "That's good, that indicates other possible minerals may be further in."

Dev notes, "Well that's good to hear."

I concur, "Yes, it is."

This time I keep my focus on the different readouts. There's even potential for some precious metals and crystals.

"I think we found a Chest," I say.

Dev asks, "A what?"

I explain, "In the industry we refer to a "Chest" as a rock or moon that contains more than just industrial metals, but also gold, silver, diamond- this one seems to have it all."

"Wow," Dev expresses, "Is that what we have here?"

"It's looking like it," I say.

I keep focus on the information and log the results as it comes in. This will definitely be a primary mining location.

Dev asks, "So what do you do with the precious metals when you find them?"

"We sell them and then distribute the bonus amongst the crew," I say.

"Oh…" Dev says, "I wonder how we'll do that…"

I speculate, "I think Tim and I will just take the haul and sell it ourselves."

"You would like that wouldn't you," Dev smirks.

I partially chuckle, "Yes, but seriously since you guys are a military entity you can't give everyone a bonus from engaging in commercial enterprise."

"Right," Dev points out, "But we aren't mining commercially."

There's that awkward silence again.

I try to end it, "I guess the Commander will have to decide."

"Maybe" Dev eggs on, "Or maybe I want a new diamond."

"Well, I know Tim and I would like to get paid for our services," I say, "And gold and diamonds from this rock split between the two of us would actually allow us to retire for ten or more years. But don't worry. I'll sneak in a diamond or two to you."

"Will it come on one knee and a proposal?" Dev teases.

I inadvertently blush, "We- uh… I- sure if that's what you want…"

Dev laughs, "No the diamond by itself will do just fine."

She calms down as I sit in silence, unsure of what to say.

A couple of minutes go by and Dev shuts off the laser, "That's twenty minutes," she informs.

"Well," I begin, "This one will be the priority moon. We almost don't need to bother checking the others, at least not now."

Dev asks, "How far is the next one?"

I answer, "It'll take us about an hour."

"I mean unless you're ready to go back…" Dev starts.

I ponder for a minute, "No not really. We probably won't be able to survey all the moons before heading back, but I'm down to at least get one more."

"Good," Dev states.

I figure out a course for the next moon and we start heading that way. I plug the course into the autopilot and let the ship take control.

"I'm hungry," I state, "I'm gonna grab a lunch pack, you want anything?"

"I'll come get it," Dev says.

I press the button and release the console, sliding it forward and up so we can get out of our seats. I head out and hear Dev follow behind me.

We get into the cargo area and I feel my hand suddenly grabbed. I turn around and am met with Dev thrusting herself into me as well as her lips into mine. The sensation is unexpected, yet pleasant... it has been a while.

She stops and steps back.

I say, "Uh... was it something I said?"

Dev laughs cutely, "I mean, I thought part of this trip was to spend some time alone..."

"I uh..." hadn't thought of that, but I did only realize my feelings for Dev just this morning. I mean they were there, but- I need to focus, "I mean, I guess I've been developing an attraction..."

"Wow..." she says, "You have such a beautiful way with words."

"Okay," I say, "I mean, you could try saying something romantic too. I didn't know you felt that way..."

"I mean I kind of knew I started to when we began working together," she explains, "It's silly, but I found the whole mystery behind your discharge rather interesting. But after going through near death on Thretta, that sealed it."

"Really?" I suspect, "You preferred me over Lede?"

Sarcastically, Dev says, "Oh the lack of confidence coupled with comparing yourself to another man is soooo hot."

"Well- it's just- I" oh screw words. I grab her and start kissing her back intensely. She moans slightly and I begin to slowly unzip her suit. She doesn't stop me so I assume we're doing this. Yes, she starts unzipping me. This is happening. I hope I still remember what to do.

I get her jumpsuit down to her waist and immediately remove her shirt. I stop momentarily and find myself lost in her hazel eyes- there's a loud beeping coming from the cockpit. We both cease passion and look over.

I say, "Proximity. Might be some large debris ahead."

Hurrying back into the pilot seat, I check the sensors.

Dev, looking over my shoulder asks, "What is it?"

No. It can't be… "Oh shit…" I look out the viewport, but see empty space ahead. I double check the sensors and can't form words or thoughts cause I'm running on auto pilot to- gotts uh er figure- fuck, "It's the Gerlak…" I say, "They're here."

The horror on Dev's face as she stands frozen behind me burns into my mind. She then springs back into her seat and jumps on the radio as I try to figure out where exactly they are.

"Valkyrie! Valkyrie Control, this is Miner Three! Come in!" Dev screams into the COMM as she pulls her jumpsuit back on.

As I'm trying to figure out just how far away they are, Dev is only met with static. It sounds like electronic noise. I can't pinpoint the Gerlak as we only picked up their energy signature nearby. I have a general direction, but so far no sign.

Dev cycles through the alternate frequencies and is met with the same electronic noise. Dev tries to call out with no success.

"Nate, I think we're being jammed," she says.

"Jump on the turret," I order, "I'm having trouble locating them."

Dev nods and hops over the console and into the chair behind me and starts scanning, I assume. I begin trying to locate them on sensors almost to no- wait... I think I've, "Got em," Dev says.

"Same," I say, "how many do you have."

"Lots," she says, "Upwards of twenty or more, mostly small craft. Can't tell if they have bigger ships, but they are headed right at us!"

My sensors confirm the same thing. Lots of unknown blobs coming for us. I take the autopilot offline, turn the ship around and start hauling ass for where Valkyrie last was.

"I'm powering up the turret," Dev informs, "Nate, they are gaining on us quick."

I try to think. We aren't gonna make it back to Valkyrie and their ships are more maneuverable than we are- well in atmosphere. I look towards the moon we surveyed. Perhaps I can give us an advantage. Use it for cover and knock out some of the pursuing ships. The odds are very low we will survive this, but I can't think about that right now, even though it's hard not to... dammit! I'm no combat pilot! As much as I wish-

"Engaging!" Dev informs loudly, snapping me out of my nervous break.

"I'm gonna try and use the second moon for cover," I inform.

I try not to let myself become distracted by the enemy laser fire wizzing past our ship. We get hit a couple times. I shift the ship into Overdrive which diverts all power to the engines.

Dev says, "Nate, I won't be able to do much against their energy shields if you use all the power."

"I know," I explain, "I'm trying to get to the second moon."

Dev reminds, "Okay, but be careful not to Over-Kill the engines. If they get too hot, they'll force shut-down and initiate an all stop."

"Really?" I ask.

Dev confirms, "Yes, it's a safety feature to prevent blowing out the engines."

"A safety feature," I nervously chuckle, "That'll get us killed."

"Uhh…" Dev struggles for a response, "It… uh, yes I suppose in this instance that is the case."

"At what temperature will the engines shut down?" I ask.

Dev answers, "Sixteen-hundred, forty degrees. Don't ask why it's that specific. Just don't go above that number."

"Understood," I acknowledge and try to keep an eye on the engine temperature reading. Then I cut the engines entirely.

"What are you doing?" Dev asks.

"Drifting," I say, "I'm gonna let the moon's gravity pull us closer, then try to use thrusters to orbit and slingshot off the moon towards Valkyrie's last known position using momentum."

Dev asks, "And then put all the power into the turret?"

"Not just yet," I say, "I want to try to boost power to the COMMs and try to alert Valkyrie of what's happening."

"Concur," Dev says and hops back into the co-pilot seat.

She quickly diverts as much power as she can to boost our COMM system and tries to contact Valkyrie. We can still hear the electronic interference, but something tries to respond, or so we assume.

Dev says into the COMM, "Valkyrie, if you can hear this, we've come under attack from the Gerlak! I say again, we are under attack by Gerlak ships! Mostly small craft, unknown if bigger vessels are in the system! We're trying to make our way back to your last known position, but are unsure-"

I interrupt, "They're starting to gain on us!"

Dev finishes, "We'll do our best to make it back, but just know the Gerlak are in the system and attacking us. Miner Three out!"

Dev jumps back to the turret control seat and immediately starts firing off more shots. Enemy laser fire blazes past and strikes us a couple more times as I fire thrusters and attempt to enter orbit. I miss-calculate and end up in a decaying orbit.

"Hang on!" I say, firing up the engines. I try to push us back into a stable orbit and then begin the slingshot maneuver, increasing orbital speed with thrusters. We start to come around, increasing speed. I realize I've got ships following us so I "raise" our elevation towards the moon's North Pole.

"Dev," I say, "I'm rolling the ship. We're gonna have Gerlak in front of us momentarily!"

"Okay," she nervously acknowledges.

Sure enough, above us as we complete one rotation there are several fighters. Some of them appear to break off, but we're going too fast to notice. Dev already starts firing at them. We go about another quarter of a rotation and I fire up the engines to push off. Our speed is almost three nines, faster than what this ship is capable of. Only thing to figure out now is where Valkyrie is.

Dev informs, "Nate, they're gaining on us!"

This is bad. I don't know what else to do and we need more speed. Over-Driving the engines won't do us any good- "Is this thing capable of a propulsion blast?" I ask.

"Yes, but it requires Command Override," Dev answers.

"What's the Command Override?" I ask.

She responds, "No it requires Command Override from the Commander. He has to send special authorization to the ship."

I state, "This thing has too many damn safety features! I'm gonna shift our momentum towards the planet. Maybe we can use it to get away."

"Okay," Dev says, "Um, they aren't gaining very quickly, by the way. Like it's a gradual closing between us and them."

"Oh," I acknowledge, "How soon before they hit weapons range?"

Dev studies her computers for a second, then says, "Probably five to ten minutes."

I nod for some reason, "Alright that gives me time to locate Valkyrie's transponder…" I should be able to pick

- 242 -

them up on sensors. Perhaps the communications interference is blocking us from picking it up… or worse.

"I'm taking us into the planet," I say.

Dev reacts, "What!?! Why?"

I explain, "I can't find Valkyrie on sensors. The Gerlak may have destroyed them or forced them to the surface."

"Or they are behind the planet," Dev points out and extrapolates further, "Also, the Gerlak ships are more maneuverable in the atmosphere than we are."

She's right. Still, I move the ship towards the planet.

"Nate!" She shrieks.

"I'm gonna drop into orbit," I say, "We'll look to see if Valkyrie went down, was destroyed or who knows what. Hopefully we can gain enough orbital momentum to stay ahead of the fighters."

"Then what?" Dev asks.

"Uh…" I try to think, "If we don't find Valkyrie or if she was destroyed then we'll head into the planet and find a place to- wait-" I'm interrupted by Valkyrie's locator beacon popping up momentarily. "There she is!" I express, "She's just on the other side of the plane-"

Dev interrupts, "Fighters in weapons range! Engaging!"

"I'm gonna turn the ship around!" I say.

Using thrusters I turn the ship one eighty degrees. I grab the mining laser controls and press the "fire" button, maneuvering the ship to hit any fighter I can with the sustained beam. The energy shields quickly dissipate and Dev finishes them off with the turret as I point the ship towards each incoming target.

We destroy three of them and then I watch as they seem to fall back momentarily.

"They're grouping up," I note.

They've slowed down to allow other ships to catch up. It appears they want to overrun us with numbers. About ten fighters group up before they begin their advance. We both sit in silence as I try to figure out how to survive this. Of course!

"I'm diverting all power to the turret," I say, "I'm gonna use the laser and move the ship in rapid sweeping motions across them. Try to shift your fire often. Maybe we can scramble their targeting and come out of this-"

I'm interrupted as enemy laser fire lights up my entire view. I fire the mining laser while Dev opens up on the turret. I try moving sporadically, but am forced to turn the ship around as the transparent armor quickly takes too much damage. Scorch marks inhibit my view as I struggle to figure out where we're going. My navigational screen is also offline. We're also getting pounded with lasers. The cargo bay breaches, but the cockpit door seals automatically before we decompress. This is it for us. Then the lasers stop momentarily.

Dev sighs heavily, "They're falling back... That was a good call diverting power to the turret."

We drift closer to the planet. I attempt to fire thrusters. They barely respond. I attempt to divert power to the engines.

"Engines offline" the computer says.

Dev peers out from behind my seat and notices Melyar VI getting closer.

"They didn't pull back because of me, did they..." Dev realizes.

I shake my head and then frantically try to get the thrusters to push the ship out of decaying orbit.

Dev tries to keep herself calm but is noticeably disturbed, "Here we go again."

Vainly smashing the controls, I start to accept the inevitable: we're going to crash... or burn up.

I look up at Dev, "You should get strapped in..."

I lift up the console and she gets back into the co-pilot seat, and straps in as do I. We grasp hands tightly, ready for the rough descent or as ready as we'll ever be. I try to maneuver the ship upwards or at least as upwards as possible. Hopefully we won't hit terminal velocity when we punch through the atmosphere and can safely release the chute. I look into Dev's eyes and she into mine. I feel as though we're now pondering what could have been between us. All I know is in this moment, I love her.

Suddenly we're engulfed by- a hangar? A stronger gravity pull kicks in and we sort of slam on the deck. The bay doors start to close. Dev and I sigh a massive relief.

Chapter Twelve: "Power up and prepare for combat."

(*Keller*)"We got em, Commander! Securing the Port Hangar now!" ENGCOM informs over the internal COMM.

"Very well," I acknowledge, "Helm, come right ninety degrees and proceed ahead at full Nine."

"Aye Commander," Crewman Knoop acknowledges and begins to turn the ship quickly before slamming the throttle forward.

Zooming out of the system we seem to be keeping ahead of the Gerlak.

"Status of the carrier vessels?" I ask.

Lieutenant Esker informs, "They seem to be remaining back. Looks like they wanted to snuff out Miner Three and then overwhelm us with fighters. Now they're regrouping and trying to pursue. We'll know in a couple minutes if they can even keep up."

"Good," I say.

"Commander, if I may ask," Lieutenant Esker inquires, "What exactly is our plan?"

I ponder for a second as I'm not sure, but, "We try to see if we can outrun them at sub-light since the Grav-Core is cooling down. If they catch up and we're forced to fight, I'll Command Override the Core and hope we don't explode."

I catch Kaight's expressionless face as she and the rest of the crew contemplate whether or not I was serious.

I look around at the total silence and break it, "I'm serious, people. We're outgunned again. The best chance for all of us to make it is to risk over killing the Grav-Core. Or do any of you want me to order our Outfighter pilots to their death?"

I'm met with more silence.

"That's what I thought," I say, "Everyone stay alert."

"Aye Commander," everyone says.

I'm done sugar coating reality and trying to maintain rationality. Someone in Stellar Command is betraying us. And this whole peace crap? Either someone is trying to undermine it or it isn't peace- I don't know what to think any more. All I have are theories right now. I need a second opinion from an outsider, but I need to contact them without anyone in Stellar Command knowing.

"Lieutenant Esker," I say, motioning for her to come over to me.

She walks up, "Yes, Commander?"

I order, "Find Crewman Agsnon. Have him come up here, I need to speak to him."

She acknowledges with a nod and directs another Crewman to carry out the task.

I head back to my chair and sit in it. Using my personal COMM I contact Sub-Commander who is manning the Secondary Bridge.

"Sub-Commander Devlin," he answers.

"Mike," I begin, "Looks like we're pulling away. Once again we find our position compromised."

"Yeah," he seems to agree, "I mean we can continue our internal investigation, but I think it seems clear there is a breakdown in the higher levels of Command."

"Yes," I say, "but we need to be sure of ourselves. I want you to finish the final report. I am gonna try to contact Mattie and arrange a meet up."

"Alright," he asks, "how do you plan to do that?"

I state, "The less you know right now, the better. I'm gonna have to ask that for now; you just trust me."

There is a hesitant silence before he acknowledges, "I will, Jaysen. Just don't leave me in the dark for too long."

I close the line and get out of the chair.

Catching the helmsman looking at me, I order, "Mind your helm, Crewman."

He snaps his head forward and back to the controls.

Walking towards the ladder-stairs I say, "Lieutenant Esker, once Crewman Agsnon gets up here, send him below to my office. For now, you have the bridge."

"Aye Commander," she acknowledges.

I stop at the bottom and wait for Crewman Agsnon. He quickly rounds the corner and I order him to follow me.

"Is uh, everything okay, sir?" He sheepishly asks.

I answer, "We'll talk in the Officer's Mess."

He's quiet and I can feel he is nervous. Understandable, but necessary.

We enter the Officer's Mess and I close the door.

"Sit," I order and take a chair myself at the other end of the table. Breaking silence, I say, "You're not in trouble."

Agsnon visibly sighs relief.

"I need to get a message out to a friend," I explain, "But it needs to be undetected and you can't speak to anyone about this assignment. Am I understood?"

Agsnon nods, "Yes, Commander, but if we're going through a Net Control Center, that will be almost impossible."

"Explain," I say.

He does so, "The NCCs give us the frequencies to sustain a connection to the Gal-Net based on our position and potential electronic, magnetic and gravimetric interference. Without those frequency modulations, I can't even get in."

I nod in disappointment. Then I ask, "What about going through a free net station?"

"I, uh," he fumbles for words, "I've heard of how to do that. Would certainly be more doable, but again we have to contact them. And I'll have to set up a specialized server that doesn't use our military identifiers on the Gal-Net."

"Are you able to do this from my office?" I ask.

Agsnon confidently nods.

"Get to it," I order.

He explains as he gets up, "I'll get started on the server, but at some point we'll need to reach out to Lantic Station to request frequencies."

Looking up at him, brow raised, "What makes you think that's who I'm going to connect to?"

Agsnon is quiet for a second, "Let's just say I am the right man for this job, sir. Now I can try to encrypt and send the messages in text from, but it would be easier if-"

"I'll reach out to the station," I say.

He nods and heads out. Is it suspicious that he knows about free nets and how to access them? Only a little. There are several outspoken people in the various military branches who want free nets, but of course such activity is attributed to piracy and right now I have more pressing matters.

Over the PA I hear, "Commander Keller to the-" she's interrupted as we take a hit and I'm nearly thrown out of my chair. Son of a bitch!

I immediately race out the door, passed Agsnon and through the decks to the bridge. We take another hit as I come onto the bridge and stumble a bit.

"What the hell?" I inquire.

Esker informs, "Two of their ships, sir. It's like they came out of nowhere!"

"Well did they or not?" I ask confirmingly.

Ephrryn informs, "Sensors picked up their energy signature for a moment, but it was moving so fast we weren't sure what it was. Then they ended up ahead of us and started shooting."

Esker adds, "We changed course, but they're still in range. Return fire?"

I order, "Maintain trajectory and swing us around."

We take another hit. We swing around to face our enemy. Esker orders five shots from each gun and they seem to slow their approach momentarily.

I head over to the Crater, but don't step into it, "Ephrryn," I say, "What did you mean by picking up their energy momentarily?"

He explains, "It was almost as if they were flying passed at a high rate of speed. Like they blasted themselves out ahead of us and waited for us when they slowed down."

I nod, "Interesting... I wonder if that is their mode of eff tee el travel..."

Ephrryn adds, "I was thinking the same thing, sir. We can't detect them whenever they enter a system. We only detected them this time because they were so close to us. Every other time they show up, we don't know they are there until they get close enough to be detected."

I rub my chin inadvertently, "It's like they catapult themselves to wherever they go…"

"But sir," Kaight interjects, "how would that be possible-"

The bridge lights up from a nearby streaking laser bolt of enemy fire.

"Let's get clear of them before we discuss," I order.

The Bridge focuses on making yet another escape. Curious that they didn't do this when running us out of Keldon. Maybe they were ordered to stand down?

Kaight informs, "Sir, we're out of weapon's range."

I noddingly acknowledge, "Now let's discuss the enemy's Faster Than Light travel."

Kaight suggests, "They must utilize their energy shield to prevent themselves from flying apart."

I, "Concur. They're able to avoid relying on some form of tunneling like us because they don't outrun their existence in what we perceive as normal space. But how would a catapult type system work?"

We both ponder for a minute.

Crewman Conroy walks up and adds, "Commander, I couldn't help but overhearing."

I nod, "What do you suppose, Crewman?"

He says, "Maybe their engines are designed to explode them forward. Kind of like a propulsion blast, but on purpose."

Kaight corrects, "Propulsion blasts are on purpose."

"Right," Conroy explains, "I mean like it's supposed to do that regularly."

"That means they don't have any other means of moving," I say, "all we have to do is take out their engines and they're dead in space. This gives us a considerable advantage."

Another crewman reports, "Commander! I just observed the enemy energy signature streak passed momentarily!"

"Helm," I order, "Come right one hundred degrees and pitch down forty-five." Focusing on the Operational Status Station, I order, "Delta Tennison, stand by to initiate Blackout Protocol Three on my command."

"Uh I uh," Delta Tennison fumbles around looking for the script to utter the appropriate reply for the ship's record. He finds it and confirms, "Understand the Commander has ordered Blackout Three, total and complete shutdown of all systems. Confirm command?"

"Command confirmed," I confirm.

Delta Tennison brings the PA online and announces, "Attention all Valkyrie Crewmates, Commander has ordered Blackout Protocol Three, stand by for complete shutdown of all systems."

Expectedly, Sub-Commander contacts my personal COMM.

"Yeah," I answer.

Sub-Commander asks, "Alright what's the plan here?"

I explain how we think their ships move through space faster than light, and finish with, "They're getting out ahead of us, I assume, by tracking our energy output or our engine exhaust, so we're going dead ship adrift to throw them off."

"I hope it works," he says.

I take a breath, "Yeah," and close the line. "Helm," I order, "Come to all stop."

"Aye, Commander," they acknowledge.

I wait a few seconds as they attempt to slow us down all the way then I look over at Delta Tennison, "Shut it down!" I order.

Lead Helm informs, "Commander we haven't stopped-" he's interrupted by all of the light going out as the computers and low level bridge lighting shuts off.

I make my way over to the Operational Status Station, brushing past a Crewman as I do, startling them a little. I peer over at the Delta who is startled momentarily as I'm lit up by the faint glow of his monitor.

He informs, "We are completely dark, Commander."

"Not completely," I note, "Modify Blackout to allow non emissions sensors. When you do, power down your monitor."

"Aye, Commander," He acknowledges.

I make my way over to the Crater, feel my way down into it and say, "I have ordered non emissions sensors back online. I want only one of you to observe and make sure your monitor is on the lowest light level."

Someone acknowledges my order.

I proceed back out and loudly order, "Remain battle ready. If the Gerlak are unable to detect us as they scream passed, this will give us a considerable tactical edge."

We all sit in darkness and silence waiting for something: anything to set off our sensors. The quiet ensues only broken by the occasional clearing of throat or cough from a Crewmate. Everyone seems to be awaiting in anticipation. A large and long flatulence breaks the silence followed by snickers and attempts to hold back laughter.

"It's okay to laugh," I permit, "But from now on, try to keep it quiet."

Everyone takes a second to appreciate and acknowledge the moment and then silence returns. We sit anxiously-

"Should we sing a song?" A Crewman asks.

"No!" I sharply shoot down, "We need to be on alert for if and when we pick up their energy signature. I know it is tense and boring, but we need to remain quiet. It is not an exaggeration to say our lives are at stake here."

Most everyone acknowledges at a low volume, "aye, commander…"

The silence continues for a moment. Then a Crewmen makes a noise almost as if to say a word, but doesn't.

"What is it?" I ask.

The Crewman responds, "I, uh, I thought I saw something, but it was just a momentary blip. I'm not sure if it was anything."

I note, "If they were moving faster than light while we're drifting slowly, it would probably only appear as a momentary blip."

Kaight asks, "But if that's the case how would we even pick anything up at all?"

I postulate, "An excellent question. It is possible that when traveling at those speeds, they give off a larger energy signature, but since it's moving so fast we only detect it momentarily and minutely. We'll have to log it for study later."

The silence reclaims the bridge. Time passes. Maybe an hour if not more. A quick shine of light sweeps across the ceiling in the port forward corner of the bridge.

"Did someone just activate their flashlight?" I ask sharply.

There's a hesitant response before a Crewman says, "Uh, no."

I hurriedly move over to that side of the bridge, brushing passed a couple of Crewman as I do. I arrive at the port window and look around. Looking down relative to me, I catch a faint beam of light searching the area. It appears to be rather far out in the distance.

I loudly ask, "Any energy signatures detected in the vicinity of 100R, negative 20 to 40 degrees?"

I wait a few seconds before someone answers, "No, sir!"

One of the other Crewman walks up to the window and looks out.

She asks, "Um… shouldn't we detect them if we can see their light?"

"Yes," I say, "unless they're running on low power…" I walk towards the center of the bridge and order, "Power up and prepare for combat."

My order is acknowledged and as I make my way to the Crater, all the computer systems come back on as the bridge comes back to life.

"Lieutenant Ephryn," I order, "Prepare to launch fighters. Disabling attack only."

"Aye Commander," he acknowledges.

I walk back towards my chair, "Helm, get us in close once you have their position locked in. They have more fighters than we do so we need to get our laser batteries in close so our fighters aren't on their own."

"Aye, Commander," Crewman Knoop acknowledges, "but, um according to the sensor data, it's a really small ship."

"What?" I ask indicating I want further explanation.

He says, "Yes. If the sensor information is accurate, it might be a fighter."

I ask, "What information are you receiving?"

He answers, "RADAR, energy, sound- everything, sir."

"Lieutenant Esker, confirm that helm's sensors are functioning," I order.

"Aye Commander," she says and orders crewman in the Crater to confirm sensor functions.

Crewman McSee informs, "I have the same reading, Commander."

I walk over to the Navigation Table and sure enough on display he has whatever is looking for us as a small target.

Lieutenant Esker walks up to me, "Sensors are functioning normally, sir."

"…very well," I say and move back to my chair. Sitting down I ponder a second and then order, "Emit sub-sonic interference on all frequencies until that fighter is confirmed disabled."

Someone acknowledges, "Aye, Commander."

Helm informs, "Sir, the target appears to be moving away."

"Keep up with it," I order.

We begin a pursuit. This makes more sense. They must have dispersed their fighters to seek us out. But that also means the carrier vessel could be nearby.

"Navigation," I begin, "Keep an eye out for larger targets. This single fighter isn't going to be far from its mother ship." At least I don't think it is. Maybe they're willing to risk their fighters to go out longer than we would risk our ships.

I inquire, "Delta Tennison, what's the status of the Gravimetric Core?"

He takes a couple of seconds to reply, "Still coming back online, but it has cooled down. We can have a singularity spinning in ten minutes."

"Very well." I acknowledge.

Lieutenant Ephryn loudly informs, "All fighters have launched and are moving to intercept target!"

"Very well." I say.

We wait as we close the distance to the fleeing Gerlak- "We did confirm this ship has the same energy signature as the Gerlak ships?" I make sure.

Lieutenant Esker confirms, "Yes, Commander."

We close the distance to the fleeing Gerlak fighter and wait for our Outfighters to intercept.

I hear over the COMM, "**ValCon this is Oscar Three. In weapons range and engaging.**"

I see out ahead of us the light of the fighter's weapons and the even brighter light of the Gerlak shield almost right away.

"**This is Oscar Four, moving out forward, we'll swing up and cut them off,**" over the COMM.

I pull up a display connected to my chair and watch the battle on a screen, being fed from a special camera mounted above the main gun on the bow.

We hear over the COMM, "**Shielding appears to be down. Firing disabling missile.**"

A few seconds later, "**Ineffective, firing two more.**"

And a few seconds more, "**Hit em with one more.**"

Finally what we've been wanting to hear, "**They're drifting out of control and are on low power. Prepare magnetic grapplers.**"

There's some cheering on the bridge that lasts under four seconds.

"Lieutenant Esker," I order, "Inform Delta Larrodo we are bringing the enemy ship on board and have him get a security team armed and down in the starboard hangar in ten minutes."

"Aye, Commander," She acknowledges.

I get out of my chair and start leaving the bridge. I pull out my personal COMM and call, "Sub-Commander Devlin."

I inform, "I'm heading to the starboard hangar to observe the fighter we're bringing on board. I need you to take the bridge."

"All due respect, Jaysen," Sub-Commander protests, "I should be the one doing that while you hold the bridge."

I respond with silence and an audible sigh and indicator that I'm not having this debate.

"Okay… I'll be up there," he acknowledges my order and I close the line.

I make my way down to the starboard hangar. Those disabling missiles really are quite a device. Not actual exploding ordnance, just devices that release a powerful electromagnetic pulse. Extremely effective for disabling ships.

Instead of riding the lift to the hangar floor, I get off at the upper enclosed catwalk which leads to an observation tower within the hangar.

The Crewman assigned to monitor the hangar operations snaps up, "I uh, Commander I didn't know-"

I raise my hand hoping he shuts up, "I'm here to observe the Gerlak fighter being brought in."

"Uh, of course, sir," he says and more or less stays out of the way.

A few minutes later, Delta Larrodo and his team including Sergeant Kroeling walk in fully strapped up in TEA and rifles.

"Delta," I greet.

"Commander," he acknowledges, "got here as soon as we could."

"I appreciate that," I state, "what is your plan?"

Delta Larrodo walks over to the viewport and ponders a second then explains, "I would like to keep the fighters out except those bringing the vessel in. I don't know what to expect. This thing could explode and if that happens could damage the other fighters."

A Crewman nervously expresses, "Wh- wait, explode?"

Delta Larrodo looks back, "You trained in EOD, didn't you?"

"Well, I mean," the Crewman fumbles for words.

I nod, "If it's all the same, Sergeant Kroeling, I'd like you to remain up here. You're our most qualified combat team leader, I don't need to lose you like that."

"I understand sir," she acknowledges, "but if that thing has hostile Gerlak on board then I need to be able to respond right away."

Delta Larrodo suggests, "What if she stays on the lift? Then she's still protected, but can respond if hositles come out of that thing shooting."

I consider that option for a second and then nod, "Very well. So the ship is brought into the hangar, then what?"

Larrodo explains, "Then I look for a hatch or some kind of door that leads into it. I will take point the entire time. Once we secure the ship, I'll ask for Agsnon to come down and help figure out the computers and we can start learning what we need to."

"Alright," I say, "I'll have Agsnon join me here. Be as careful as you can and you have permission to fire on contact."

"What if they surrender?" Larrodo asks.

I affirm, "Fire on contact. So far there has been no indication that they are at all interested in diplomacy, at least not with us."

A Crewman up on the bridge calls down, **"Starboard hangar are you ready to receive?"**

The Crewman on hangar control duty scrambles to their console, "Uh, I, yes. What side are they coming in from?"

"Forward," they respond.

"Uh, okay," the crewman acknowledges, "Closing the aft doors now."

Over the COMM comes another voice, **"HanCon this is Oscar Three, preparing to enter the hangar, confirm the gravity is off."**

"Co-confirmed," the Crewman acknowledges.

"This is Oscar Three, entering hangar now," over the COMM.

I look to my left out the window as they come in slowly. There are two of the Outfighters bringing the Gerlak ship in, about middle front of the hangar, stop, and maneuver towards the deck as best as they can.

"**Turn on gravity, slowly,**" Oscar Three asks.

The Crewman touches a toggle switch and slowly moves it all the way to maximum. As he does so, the captured vessel gracefully sets down. The Outfighters detach their cables and then start to land.

I pull out my personal COMM unit and tap into the Outfighter frequency then say, "Oscar Three, this is the Commander, depart the hangar. The security team wants the hangar clear until the ship is secured."

"**Understood, sir. Departing now.**" He acknowledges.

Both fighters leave. Once they clear, the Crewman announces, "Closing forward door, now."

We wait about forty seconds and then he announces, "Repressurising hangar."

"Alright, let's roll," Larrodo commands his team.

Within a couple of minutes, Larrodo reports over the COMM, "**Everyone but Sergeant Kroeling is exiting the lift. Turning on mission cam now.**"

"Crewman…" I await an answer.

"Gon," the nervous Crewman answers.

"Crewman Gon," I order, "can you set this monitor to Delta Larrodo's mission cam?"

He eagerly nods, "Y-yes Commander."

Within a few seconds the image on the screen shifts to Delta Larrodo's live feed. I watch it mostly, but also look down at them as they approach the ship.

Larrodo informs, "**Approaching the fighter...
looking for any indication of a veiw port... everyone
fan out around the ship.**"

They approach the side. Delta Larrodo and his
team appear to search closely for any crease or crevasse
which could indicate a point of entry.

One of his team members shouts something, but is
mostly inaudible.

Larrodo informs, "**Dayson thinks he found
something.**"

He hurries over to the other side of the ship. I
apologize, but I'm not sure which is the front just yet so I
can't exactly tell you anything more specific than that.

On the video I observe one of the Crewman saying,
"**This looks like one of the buttons on the hatch to the
scout vessel back on Thretta. Should I see if it works?**"

"Yes," Larrodo orders.

He pushes it and nothing happens. He pushes it
again and still nothing.

Larrodo suggests, "Try holding it down."

The Crewman does so and after a couple of
seconds a beeping is heard as the button lights up. The
door unpressurizes and Larrodo raises his rifle as it opens
at a split. Inside the ship appears to be in total darkness.
Larrodo activates his light and slowly enters the ship.

Crewman Agsnon walks into the hangar tower and
stands next to me watching the monitor.

"You called for me, sir," he says.

I explain, "Yes. As soon as the ship is secure, I
want you to go down there and get their computers back
up and running. Learn whatever you can."

He nods, "Okay, sir. It may take a minute to get
something configured."

"I understand," I say. We watch the screen. They look at what appears to be the pilot, but he seems to be emitting smoke as though he was roasted.

Larrodo says, "**The pilot looks to be dead. Cooked from the inside. No indication of a co-pilot. Looks like they fly their fighters solo.**"

I order the Hangar controller, "Give us the room."

"Uh, aye, Commander," he nervously says and leaves the room.

I ask Agsnon, "I assume you weren't able to carry out my other request?"

"I'm afraid the blackout complicated things," he explains, "but I could ask Miun to set it up for you. He's familiar with FreeNet systems."

"Very well," I say, "contact him and tell him to work on it right away."

"Aye, Commander," he says and he walks over to the control console to use the local COMM unit.

I turn my attention back to Delta Larrodo's actions displayed on the monitor. He and his team appear to be removing the Gerlak pilot from the fighter.

Larrodo asks, "**Can we get Sub-Commander Jackson down here?**"

I tap into the communications frequency, "Is the fighter secure?"

"**Almost, sir,**" Delta Larrodo answers, "**It looks like the entire ship has been fried. I don't see any indication of danger.**"

"Very well," I acknowledge, "I'm sending Crewman Agsnon down to start working on the computer systems. Bridge, get a couple of engineers down here to get power back to the ship."

Sergeant Kroeling chimes in, **"Commander, I would like to stay in the hangar on the off chance the gerlak is still alive."**

"Concur," I say and store my COMM unit back on my belt.

Agsnon walks up to me, "Miun is on his way to your office,"

"And he knows to keep it on the down low?" I confirm.

Agsnon nods, "He does, sir."

I nod and he proceeds out of the room. As the nervous Crewman comes back in to assume his post, I pull out my personal COMM and contact Sub-Commander.

"Sub-Commander Devlin," he answers.

I ask, "Is the Grav-Core ready?"

"Yes,' he answers, "I have a couple of locations planned out, but I think we should go to Earth."

"No..." I order, "get a course plotted for Lantic Station."

"Uh... okay..." he acknowledges, "Does this have to do with trusting you."

"Implicitly," I answer, "I'll bring you in the loop soon."

As I turn to leave the room I catch the young Crewman staring at me, "What?" I ask.

"Uh- nothing, sir," he says looking back out the viewport.

I leave the room heading for my office. Was I too harsh on the Crewman? I already know that what I say won't stop him from spreading rumors on the lower decks. I anticipate hearing them by chow tomorrow if not sooner.

I stop by the mess hall and fill up a small bowl with some dried pineapple. Not my favorite snack, but it'll do for now. I don't like keeping my second in command out of the loop, but for now it is necessary to give him plausible deniability. I will have to bring him into my plans soon.

I round the corner into my office area which is low lit. My personal COMM goes off. I set my bowl down on the desk outside my office and answer, "Keller."

"Jaysen its Mike. Can we stand down to Alert Status? We haven't detected any enemy ships and the crew is getting hungry."

Of course, we're still at Battle Stations. Everyone is standing by for a fight. "Affirmative," I say, "but we aren't going to Cruise Condition any time soon."

"Concur," He says and closes the line.

I grab my snacks and enter my office and yet another nervous Crewmember stands to greet me.

"H- hello, Commander." He says.

I ask, "Why is everyone on edge today? I mean I get it we're running from aliens trying to kill us, but is there something about my presence that has people scared of me?"

"Well," he begins, "I can't speak for everyone, but I myself have never worked for a flag officer directly before, and we haven't really met aside from my check-in."

I say, "First off, I'm not a flag officer, I am a Commanding Officer of a single ship. You have my rank confused with Commodore and above."

"Uh, right of course, sir," he acknowledges.

"Secondly, I understand it seems daunting to work for me directly, but I assure you I am not going to be breathing down your neck the whole time." I explain.

He says, "Well, um… I just… it's that you are trying to use your personal line to get on a Free Net circuit."

"Yeah, and?" I inquire.

He fumbles for words, "It's just… I mean… didn't you once try to exonerate someone who was guilty of espionage?"

My tone changes quickly to calm, sharp and harsh, "I once tried to exonerate someone who was innocent and wrongly accused. I don't know what version of things you heard, but I will give you the quick facts: Nathan McNill was innocent and I will stand by that until my lifeless body is launched into space. Now if you're uncomfortable doing a task that your Commander has asked, then find someone who is."

"Well it's, I mean" he tries to respond, "I just want to know what exactly I'm doing. Free Net access can get you into a lot of trouble and I just want to know whether or not I'm going to, uh, get in trouble."

"I'll make this easier for you," I explain, "get connected to the Free Net on my isolated frequency and I will take care of everything else. In the next couple of days you'll probably find out what's going on, but for now, you have to trust me."

"Okay, sir," he acknowledges and sits back down on the computer and continues to work to get me connected to the Free Net.

I sit down in one of my guest chairs while he works, focusing on my dried pineapple snack, thinking about how I'm going to reach out to Mattie. What am I going to say? It's been a while since we talked…

Crewman Miun informs, "I've got you connected, sir."

"Well done," I commend, "Please keep this between us for now," I order.

"I will, sir," he assures and leaves the room.

I sit down at my desk and pull up my personal electronic mailing system. My personal COMM goes off, "Keller," I answer.

"We've got gerlak on the incoming," Sub-Commander informs.

"Alright Battlestations and start spinning up a tunnel," I order.

He asks, "Are you coming to the bridge?"

"I'll relieve you when I relieve you," I say and I close the COMM.

I quickly think of something that Mattie will know indicating that it's me and that I am serious about needing to meet up at Lantic Station but without drawing attention. The order to set Battlestations comes over the PA as well as the notification that we're about to tunnel. As I type my message frantically I'm having a hard time even trying to believe myself. Is someone seriously out to destroy me and my crew? Is there really some kind of conspiracy against us? *I don't know for certain, but I intend to find out with your help.* I finish the message and send it. Hopefully it goes through.

I get up and quickly head for the bridge. I arrive and Sub-Commander announces my presence.

"My bridge," I say.

I sit in my chair waiting for the phrase I want to hear. The Gerlak ships appear to be closing in, fighters and the two carrier vessels. It's gonna be close.

Lieutenant Esker asks, "Sir, it appears the Gerlak will reach us before we have singularity stabilization. What are your orders?"

I look directly at her, "Defend the ship."

"Aye Commander," she acknowledges and then orders, "Helm, tilt 20R on the Port Module's axis. Main and dorsal guns lock target and energy batteries fire at will."

Several different stations acknowledge Kaight's orders. The ship then tilts twenty degrees left on the Port Module's axis, maintaining the position of the singularity as it's spun. The Main and Dorsal guns swing to the left and pitch up slightly to lock target. I get out of my chair and walk over to the port side of the bridge to watch as the enemy approaches. Maybe we should have just made way for Lantic Station THEN I could have sent out my message. Now I'll be waiting there hoping Mattie shows up... assuming we tunnel out of here in time.

The laser batteries begin firing at the approaching fighters. The bridge rattles from an initial six round salvo meant to disrupt their approach. The shells explode before impacting any specific target, lighting up some of the energy shielding from some of the ships. I see a bright orange beam appear momentarily as we take a hit to the Port Module. I am suddenly overwhelmed with panic as I frantically stumble to look out the port side at the potential damage.

Crewman Webb announces, "Singularity stabilized, Commander!"

I scream at the helmsman, "Go!"

Crewman Knoop slams the throttle forward and we enter the tunnel. The ship shakes a bit and then we settle into the expected gravimetric rolls.

Helm reports, "Tunnel is holding. ee tee a to Lantic Station: twenty hours."

"Set Cruise Condition," I order. I walk over to Lieutenant Esker, "Before you set the watch, I want you to have the Command Staff assemble in the Officer's Mess in ten minutes."

"Aye, Commander," she acknowledges.

I leave the bridge and decide to head straight to the Officer's Mess. I sit in silence contemplating our next move and what to say to the Command Staff.

Sub-Commander walks in, "Are you finally going to tell me what's going on?"

I look up at him and say, "Once everyone else is here."

Within a few minutes, Lieutenants Slaighter, Esker and Ephryn arrive along with Superior Delta Gabanyic, our ship's food procurement specialist. Lieutenant Jarek enters and takes a seat followed soon after by the Flight Commander, Lieutenant Lester.

I begin, "As some of you know, we're making way for Lantic Station. For those who didn't, now you do. There's no easy way to put this, but I have lost all trust in Stellar Command. Every time we reached out to them or informed them of our intentions, it seems the Gerlak conveniently knew where and how to find us."

Lieutenant Jarek asks, "What exactly are you suggesting?"

"Exactly what it sounds like," I affirm, "someone inside Stellar Command is trying to get us all killed."

Lieutenant Esker asks, rather confused, "But... why?"

"I don't know," I say, "But every conversation I have had with Admiral Yelkin has been extremely hostile: accusing us of being the aggressors in every encounter with the Gerlak. Claiming that we are disrupting the Prime Minister's plan for a peaceful resolution."

Most everyone reacts with surprised shock.

I continue, "I have each of our conversations recorded and will share them all with you soon, but first this is my immediate plan: I have reached out to an old friend that I will be meeting with to discuss everything that has happened to us since Keldon. I know you all can attest to the events that have taken place since, but I feel it would be wise to consult with an outside source who I can trust. However, while I am doing that, I would like to reprovision our supplies as well as give the crew a port call. They deserve it after all we have been through."

I receive a few nods of agreement.

"Superior Gabanyc," I begin, "will you be able to arrange for some food stores?"

He contemplates for a second then answers, "I should be able to negotiate a payment plan. Hopefully they won't charge right away, because if what you suspect is true, then chances are ship's funds have been frozen."

I nod, "At the very least try and get us some water. I'm tired of drinking recycled piss and showers as I'm sure all of you are."

Everyone nods in agreement.

ENGCOM adds, "I'll try to see about getting some supplies we need to continue repairs, but yeah, same as Superior, we won't be able to if our accounts are blocked."

I nod, "I want food and water to be our priority. We can more or less make our own parts and if needs be, we'll mine more supplies after we leave Lantic Station. Ensure that each of your departments is given the vague, simple version of what I have told you for now. Emphasize the fact they are getting a port call."

Lieutenant Ephryn asks, "What about communicating with loved ones?"

"We'll be on a station with Free Net access," I note, "they can contact whoever they want- in fact I want everyone to reach out to their families as long as they don't disclose our location."

Sub-Commander notes, "That would really stir the pot, assuming there is, in fact, a conspiracy against us."

"Exactly," I say, "Now we've got less than twenty hours to get this figured out. I want a security plan on my desk two hours before arrival. Dismissed."

Everyone but Sub-Commander leaves the room.

I say, "There's nothing else to be said. I told them everything I have planned."

Sub-Commander nods, "I guess we just wait and see how this plays out."

I nod, "Hopefully Crew Members contacting their families to help shed light on this situation will get us answers. Once people know we're alive, that should help to make sure we stay that way."

Chapter Thirteen: "United by force."

(*Nathan*)Packing up the rest of my things, I realize I don't have much except the clothes I came on board with and the stuff the ship gave me. I'll have to replace some of the things I lost on the Ex Del Seven. Unfortunately a couple of my shirts were irreplaceable.

Keller wasn't too happy about my decision to leave. He tried to convince me to stay on to help with mining and wasn't too specific, but it sounded like he believes someone is out to get him. Now he knows how it feels.

Dev walks up to me as I finish pulling the sheets off my rack.

She asks, "Are you ready?"

"Yep," I answer, "I don't have much, but I figured I'd keep the clothes since I don't know how long it will take me to get back to Sol. Got everything you need for the next couple days?"

Dev smiles, "Yes. Is there anything in particular I should have packed for?"

I shrug my shoulders as we start to leave the crew quarters, "Lantic Station is like any other station except it's in orbit of a Neutron Dwarf Star instead of a planet and since it's a free port, gambling is legal. In fact our hotel accommodations include a casino."

We continue down the passage way towards the laundry room.

She asks, "Are you interested in checking out the arboretum? Apparently they have some unique plant life that you can't see anywhere else: I guess everything is pink because of the sunlight."

I step into the room, leaving my sheets in the drop off as I answer, "Yeah I think tomorrow would be good for that."

We continue towards the airlock. It'll be nice to finally get off this ship. I'm grateful to be alive and all, but I've spent more time here than I wanted to, though it has given me an idea to maybe start my own mining business using smaller ships. If I had my own mother ship with a Traverse Drive, I could go anywhere I wanted including distant, remote systems like Melyar-

"Nate!" Donna interrupts my thoughts.

We turn around as she approaches and says, "I heard you're leaving?"

I answer, "Yep."

"And you were just gonna take off without saying anything?" she asks.

I explain, "Oh I'm planning on hanging out for a couple days before figuring out a transport back to Mars. I figured I'd probably see you out on the station."

Donna states, "It's a big station. Where are you headed?"

Dev answers, "We've got a room at the Blue Starblazer. I think tonight we'll probably just hang out at their casino."

Donna nods, "I see... I'm not sure what I'm doing just yet. What's Tim doing?"

"Apparently Keller convinced him to stay on board for a while longer." I say.

There's an awkward silence.

I say, "Well, you know where to find us, Donna. I'm ready to get off this thing, but please come on by later. I would like a proper farewell, I mean you did save my life."

She nods understandingly and Dev and I turn and continue on our way.

Once we're out of earshot, Dev says, "What was her issue?"

I speculate, "She's got some sense of duty I guess. If she wants to see things through, that's her call."

Dev points out, "It's not like she can go back home. And if she did leave the ship, she would probably be expected to return to the Marines since she was reactivated."

"True," I say, "but I was kicked out. I want nothing to do with this life anymore- hell I didn't even WANT to be a miner, but we've discussed that already. Can we just relax and think of other things?"

Dev nods, "Absolutely."

Stepping out of the brow and into the station, we are greeted by one of the better free ports. Lantic Station is large and looks nothing like a conventional Republic Station. The best way to describe it is as if they took city blocks and condensed them into a tubular looking cube with the casinos and hotels attached to them as large, independent modules. On one end is the shipyard with the docks entirely enclosed, leaving the ships exposed to open space. The center is made up of the upper market and medium to upper class hotels. It's very clean and always pristine. The lower market is a giant warehouse-like area where larger goods are traded, with steam vents, dirt and grime all over. It's meant to be functional, not presentable. At the bottom is the large arboretum which supplies the station's oxygen. It's staggered in a way, like stadium seating or Chinese rice fields. And attached on the end opposite of the shipyard is the solar farm that powers everything.

Lantic Station sits on the edge of Republic Space, but it's near the middle. It's also close to the other regions that are in a reunification process since the end of the Three-War. Thus the free trade has allowed for a cleaner station than some of the other free ports I have seen or heard of.

What kind of trade? Goods and services traded outside the Republic's taxes and tariffs and trade regulations. Even some mining vessels trade their minerals without having to go through guild regulations. Of course, if they're caught without permits mining in Republic Space, well... you know.

We get out of the shipyard and are almost immediately where we need to be. The upper market is where the smaller sized goods such as gems and precious metals as well as expensive gadgets are traded. It is also where most of the hotels are located. Ours is on the other side near the solar farm and it's one of the lower end ones by comparison with only twenty rooms and a smaller casino. Dev picked it because she wanted a quieter place to relax and I agreed. Especially since she was buying. Of course that means drinks and food are on me for the evening.

We get checked in, drop off our belongings and decide to check out the casino. After playing a couple of digital slots and losing, we agree to sit down at one of the bars.

After sipping my drink Dev asks, "Wanna try mine?"

I shake my head.

She follows up, "So... you excited to get back home?"

I nod, "Yeah, it'll be nice to be away from all this. If I was still in I would probably be more eager to fight in the war, but... I'm not. I have nothing to do with any of this."

"I understand," she says, "I'm almost tempted to go with you, but desertion at a time of war is death, so either way I guess I'm dead."

"Oh come on, don't talk like that," I say.

"Nate," she says, "Let's be real. A Constellation Cutter isn't a war ship. As much as we think it can be, it's not. We don't have missiles and our cannons are for defensive purposes."

"Yeah, but," I point out, "you may be the first ship to get energy shielding."

Dev smirks, "Great! Then we can delay the inevitable... Look, I'm just seeing it for how it is. I'm surprised we actually got away that last time. I honestly thought we were gonna freeze to death holding each other in that ice."

I say, "Well, we didn't and instead, we get to hold each other in a nice warm bed."

Dev giggles slightly, "Yes, yes we do," and she raises her glass. I clink it with mine and we sip.

Someone sits down next to me. I look over and sure enough, "Donna, you made it!"

"Mm hm," she hums and tries to get the bartender's attention.

My initial sense is that she's irritated. Great. I get to have a repeat of the Keller conversation.

She gets her drink and takes a sip. She turns my way and gets ready to say something.

I interrupt, "Look, before you start, I've already made up my mind. Keller tried hard to convince me to stay and it didn't work. Can we just enjoy the evening with some drinks and laughs before we part ways?"

"Nate," she says, "I think you at least owe me your ears for a bit. Keller may have let you stay on his ship, but I was the one who got you there."

I reluctantly nod.

She continues, "After everything you have seen and been a part of you're just gonna turn tail and run home? Your Republic needs you."

I chuckle, "Seriously? Did you like, memorize recruiter phrases?"

Donna, noticeably irritated says, "I understand you feel burned by the Armada, but this is bigger than any of your personal grievances. We're fighting a hostile alien race that wants to kill us. But it could even be worse than that. There could be high ranking members in the Republic working with them to destroy us."

I partially spit up my drink, "Fucking what?"

She speculates, "You haven't once found it strange how the Gerlak have been able to show up everywhere we've gone?"

I shrug my shoulders, "Maybe they're just really good at tracking us."

"And what about Tim," Donna asks, "Are you really just gonna leave your best friend behind?"

I clear up, "Tim is more like a really good acquaintance. He was my only friend on the Ex Del Seven, but he was friends with everyone."

"He's a friendly guy," she notes, "but are you sure he feels the same way towards you?"

I more or less nod.

She reveals, "He actually cares about you more than you know. When I was leaving on the Rescue and Recon mission on Thretta, he walked up to me distraught wondering if you were even still alive. Does he know you're leaving?"

I reply with silent shame.

"Wow…" Donna expresses.

"Look," I try to explain, "I think it's easier if I just leave quietly; no long goodbyes-"

"Except with Crewman Belkrest?" she interrupts.

"What, are you jealous?" I ask.

Donna responds with a glare, then says, "The ship needs you more than you realize. You bring a valuable skill to the crew more than you know. And not to mention people care about you; me, Tim, Crewman Belkrest-"

"You know, she has a normal people name," I remind.

"Devorah," she continues. "Speaking of, don't you have anything to say in this?"

I turn my attention to Dev who thinks for a second.

She says, "Uh, not really. I care about Nate, which is why I support him doing what he feels he's gotta do."

I turn back to Donna who says, "Well, if that's your decision. But at the very least I'm gonna reach out to Tim and have him join us so you can say a proper goodbye. You may not think it, but people do care about you."

I shrug and resume my drink. The three of us discuss other non-Armada related things like favorite music and stories. Tim arrives as we order some food to snack on. And predictably, Donna attempts to make use of the opportunity to once again control my life.

She says, "Tim, did you know Nate is leaving?"

Tim having smiled after telling a funny story says, "What do you mean?"

Donna explains, "He's leaving. He's not coming with us when we leave Lantic Station. He didn't tell you."

Tim looks at me, rather disappointed, "Um… were you just gonna take off? After all we've been through?"

I roll my eyes, "Oh geez not you too-"

"Yeah I only care about you," he says, "but fuck me, I guess."

"Tim it wasn't, I just-" damn I'm off guard caught, "Look man, I'm glad to be alive, but I hate being on that thing. I've almost been killed three times now. I left that life never wanting to have to look back and now I've been exploited for my new talents while treated like a prisoner by Sub-Commander Dick Ass. I'm over this shit. Why are you sticking around? Why don't you come with me?"

Tim explains, "Keller offered to work out payment to stay on. He claimed-"

I finish his sentence, "High civilian rank with time and half. Yes I had the same bullshit offer."

"Why do you think it's bullshit?" he asks.

I explain, "Cause it is. Once we get let off all they will do is make some claim about how there was a misunderstanding, or our pay sheets will be lost, or whatever. They'll give us some stupid ass medal and say that "service to the Armada and Republic should be payment enough" or some shit."

"Nate, that's slavery," Donna points out.

"Yep," I say directing my attention back to Tim, "Why don't you come with me. We'll get back to Mars and start our own business."

"Doing what?" Tim asks.

I explain, "What we've been doing. Think about it. We get a bunch of small mining vessels with a mother ship that can fabricate parts n shit. We can mine wherever we want whenever we want and go trade with whoever. Hell we could even trade here at this station!"

"Nate, that goes against Guild Law," Tim points out, "And do you have any idea how expensive a Traverse Specialist is? There's a reason we have to ride on tee dee transports."

"Yeah, but think of it," I insist, "we could find someone to do it for cheaper. Especially since we know where to find a rich, untouched deposit."

Tim asks, "We do?"

I nod, "Yeah. One of the moons at Melyar was a Treasure Chest. And we didn't get to survey the rest. Based on the findings at just that one moon we could pay off the ships and crew for a few months. We just gotta make it happen!"

Tim, concerned, asks, "Uhh... how much have you had?"

"That's not irrelevant," I say-

He cuts in, "I agree it isn't."

I pause for a second and realize maybe I have had a couple too many. I finish by saying, "Look you guys are still here for a few days, think about it."

"I have," he says, "We could make more money doing what we're doing now and then look into getting our own ship after."

"Ships," I correct.

"Right, ships," he says, "we would need a down payment for a mother ship anyway especially if we're not going to register through the guild... assuming we even do that, which we most certainly won't."

"You really want to pay 30%?" I confirm.

Tim points out, "Better than getting arrested."

I shake my head, "Look, we'll figure that out later. In the meantime, why do you want to remain on the ship? You can't collect any money if you end up dead."

"We're away from the war," Tim says, "I'll just be helping them mine."

I inform, "Donna thinks the Gerlak are following you. She pointed out that at every system we've gone to, they've shown up."

"Okay," Tim acknowledges, "but with how far we just traveled, they would HAVE to go way around or cut through Republic Space. Unless we go to the front lines, we'll be fine. Keller said he'd make sure I was off the ship if that happened."

I shrug, "Okay. Well if you survive, I'll bring you on as Chief Engineer."

This perks Tim's ears momentarily, "Chief Engineer? Well..."

I nod slowly, "That's what you want isn't it? You'll also be First Mate."

"Oh and I suppose you're the Captain?" Tim says cynically.

"Uh... yes," I say.

"I'll think about it." He says, "In the meantime..." He raises his glass and we all continue to drink.

The night continues on a lighter note. We laugh and discuss less serious things. We even get to a point where some of us decide to go blow some more money gambling. Tim walks out with a couple of wins on the slots, Donna loses a little at craps and I... end up more in the hole than I wanted, trying to bluff the dealer on Hold Em. Dev seems to decide to be sensible and just watches.

We return to the bar for some more food. Tim graciously buys. We catch the latest feed of ZeroG-Ball, an exciting game where each player gets a single shot laser that stuns the other player, but the shot takes almost thirty seconds to recharge. If you get hit, you're stunned for fifteen seconds, just floating until your suit unlocks. The goal is like any of the other old ball games that are no longer played: get it to the goal zone.

We decide it's time to call it after the game ends. As we get ready to leave, Donna pulls Dev aside, leaving Tim and I to finish our drinks out of earshot...

(*Donna*)...I make sure Nate can't quite hear us and then I ask Dev, "Do you love him?"

She half smirks then answers, "I mean, I care about him, but I wouldn't say I'm super attached. He's gotta go his way and I gotta go mine."

I rephrase, "Well okay, but don't you want to see what a future with him would be like? I've seen the way you get along: how often you hang out. Wouldn't you rather he be around to see where it goes?"

"I mean, we're friends," she explains, "but anything more is either going to happen or it isn't. And if he wants to leave then I have to respect his choice. Would it be a healthy relationship if I tried to control his decisions?"

I consider what she has said. She makes a good point and, "I can't disagree with that. But I will point out that I've seen what you two have so far and it doesn't always just happen so easily. I'd say don't necessarily push the issue, but maybe talk with him about it before we leave."

"Okay," she says as she starts to walk back to Tim and Nate. I follow...

(*Nathan*)…Donna and Dev come back to Tim and I. Dev asks, "You ready?"

I nod, "Yes."

We get up and say our goodbyes to Tim and Donna, who leave together.

Dev and I stumble down the walkway and then enter our room. I turn on one of the desk lamps, turn around and gaze at her as she gazes back at me and smiles. She giggles slightly as we close the distance to each other and embrace. We kiss. I begin removing her shirt and we pick up where we left off on the Outminer in the Melyar system…

(*Keller*)…"Trouble with your drink, sir?" a voice says.

I look up, "Hm? Oh. No it's fine. Just a lot on my mind."

He nods and leaves me be. I can't seem to figure out what I want to say. Maybe because I am having a hard time accepting it. My own government colluding to destroy me and my crew. But why? Then again maybe I need to consider the fact that our government is made up of many entities and it's not necessarily EVERYONE trying to get us.

Even still, this type of stuff isn't supposed to happen. This is the kind of thing that goes on in a Vlad Narkovski novel or mid-21st century screen entertainment programs. At the same time, conspiracy or not, I need to think of the safety of my crew and that's why I have arranged this meeting.

Someone sits down next to me and says, "Bourbon? Well this really must be serious."

I look over to see a woman dressed in a leather jacket, grey shirt and jeans. I crack a smile, "Actually it's just whiskey. It's good to see you Mattie."

She partially smirks and replies, "You too, Jay."

"Ha," I express, "you know, no one except you has been brazen enough to call me that. Devlin tried it once."

"Let me guess," she says, "You stared him down and slowly shook your head?"

"Sometimes I feel you know me too well." I say.

She states, "You're not as complicated as you'd like to be," turning her attention, "Bar keep, Gin n tonic."

I raise a brow.

She looks at me and explains, "I've cut back. Considerably."

"You've changed," I say.

"And you haven't," she retorts.

She gets her drink and we head to one of the secluded booths to talk more discreetly.

She begins, "Alright, Jay, you didn't drag me all this way just to share a drink. What's going on?"

I pull out a data stick and say, "This contains all of our logs, sensor data as well as an internal investigation conducted by Sub-Commander and myself of everything that has happened to us since the attack on Keldon."

"You were at Keldon?" She clarifies.

I nod, "We were on an unplanned port call after terminating a Mining Vessel and escorting them to the station. I was looking over the final mission report when the station came under fire and made the decision to get under way. What were you told?"

She says, "Just that we had lost contact with the colony, but it was being handled. People have been trying to get ahold of family members, but all ships have been ordered away from Keldon as well as Trista and Alpha Minor. Only special envoys have been going to those worlds, but all other information has been kept under wraps."

This is troubling news. But at the same time it confirms what Yelkin was saying about a plan for peace.

"I don't know what rumors you have been told," I begin, "but Keldon was attacked- rather invaded by and alien force called the Gerlak."

Mattie looks at me like I'm hopped up on drugs.

I pull out a small holo projector and place it on the table.

"Yeah I know how this sounds, but bear with me. This was taken during a scout and recon mission on Thretta Five."

I play a segment from Sergeant Kroeling's recording. Mattie's expression changes quickly as the Gerlak reveal themselves.

She looks up clearly horrified, "Holy shit... first contact."

"Yeah it didn't go quite as I would have liked," I say, "they are hostile, and every encounter we have been involved with has been hostile. Yet Admiral Yelkin has claimed that the Prime Minister is working on some sort of peace plan."

She nods, "Yes... the Envoys make more sense now. But I didn't think it was actually aliens. Honestly I thought it was a coordinated uprising."

I point out, "You and I both know that Prime Minister Jackson would have glassed those worlds and launched a smear campaign condoning the fire-bombing and how it resulted in a peaceful resolution. You know what they say about her party: 'United by force'."

She sighs monetarily, then says, "I'm gonna need another round or seven. How about you?"

I reluctantly nod, "Yeah, we haven't even really gotten into the meat of this thing."

She ponders for a second, "Were you planning on staying aboard your ship this evening?"

"If you're asking whether or not I got a room," I say, "I did. It would be a better place to continue this conversation."

"Is that all?" she asks.

"We'll see," I say, "Just get me a bottle of Amberglash and yourself whatever you want and close me out if you don't mind."

She smiles and nods.

I watch her now, and again as she gets the bottles. I do miss her. But we had our own aspirations. For a Captain of a Naval Destroyer and a Commander of a Constellation Cutter well… a marriage is an unnecessary burden. Then again, maybe it's Command that's the burden. She starts to return with the whiskey and I get up and lead the way.

We walk towards the room and she asks, "On a less serious note, how have you been otherwise?"

"Up until Keldon, I suppose things were fine. Depending on how things go, I think I'm going to extend."

"Really?" she says, "So I left the Navy for eight years for nothing?"

I sigh as I enter the passcode to my room, "No, Matilda, you didn't."

The door closes after we walk into the room.

She begins, "We talked about this. We agreed that because it was your dream to be Admiral that I would separate to raise our son until he was of an understanding age."

"Yes," I acknowledge, "And by now I would have been a Commodore. But over three years ago, something happened that changed everything…"

"The McNill incident?" She guesses.

I turn to face her, nodding as I do, "Yeah. What happened to that kid it was… it was wrong. And there was nothing I could do to help him. The politics of my organization killed an aspiring young man's career and unless I want to be a part of that, well…"

She says, "Over one person's career you stagnated your own?"

"I did," I say, "They offered me a promotion for cooperating. But I told them I'd rather quit. Instead they offered me another ship."

She clarifies, "I thought you asked for a transfer because Wernival was undermining your Command."

"That was a large part of it," I say, "but my original plan was to quit. I didn't tell you right away because I knew you would be upset."

"So why tell me now?" She asks.

I say, "Well… in a way he's come back to haunt me. McNill was on the mining vessel we terminated. And after the attack on Keldon, he ended up on my ship."

"Seriously?" She says, "Wow…"

"Yes," I say, "and now he's leaving." I take a breath and ponder what to say, "I know if I raised Jeff, you probably would be an Admiral by now, and I probably would have had nothing to do with Nathan McNill. But now something more serious is going on and I don't know who else to trust, which is why I called you out here."

"So there's more to the aliens?" she asks.

I explain, "I have reason to believe that someone within the higher levels of government is actively working to eliminate me and my crew."

"Why?" she asks.

"Well," I begin, "we have imagery and sensor data that could sway public opinion on these so called peace talks. We have a perspective that can change the narrative they want to control. Basically, we're a liability."

She nods, "I can understand… so you're hoping to invoke Directive Sixteen?"

"I think this warrants Directive Seventeen… but I need to be sure," I say.

"You need me to review your data," she correctly speculates.

I nod.

"Okay," she says, "give me the room. I think it's best I look this over and ask you questions after. I'll come find you at the bar when I'm done."

I leave the holo-device and then head out of the room. My fate and the fate of my ship rests in her hands now. What she chooses will decide whether or not we go directly to the Council. I have faith she will make the right choice.

I sit back down at the bar and the bartender comes up and says, "Back again so soon? And without the lady? Uh-oh…"

I chuckle slightly, "Oh I wish the problem was something as simple as what you're thinking."

"Well I hear a lot of things," he says, "but I'm never one to pry."

"Smart man," I say and he leaves me be.

I pull out my electronic pad and fold it open. I connect into the Free Net to catch up on news I have missed over the past month or so. Most of the official sources are very speculative of what's happening on the colonies. I decide to check some of the more opinion based sites and sure enough there's crazy speculation about alien invasions.

I chuckle to myself. I used to laugh at these people and now I have confirmation that they are actually right… for once.

My personal COMM goes off and I answer, "Keller," I say.

"**Commander**," a male voice says, "**It's Lieutenant Jefferson. I have unfortunate news regarding the Traverse Drive.**"

I sigh, "Go ahead with it."

He informs, "**That last hit we took before tunneling away from Melyar, well it looks like something shifted after we resurfaced and compromised the Grav-Core. We're not exactly sure what, but the Grav-Specialists have been recalled to investigate. I will contact you if we need to purchase parts.**"

"Negative," I say, "you have authorization to purchase any and all parts needed to get it functioning again."

"**Aye, Commander,**" he says, "**I'll keep you updated.**"

"Thanks," I say and I close the line.

The bartender approaches and fills my glass with more Amberglash.

"Thanks," I say.

He says, "You looked like you needed it. Wanna talk?"

I shake my head and return to reading articles.

Some of these are rather ridiculous. Now some people think the aliens have infiltrated the Republic. Some even accuse the Prime Minister of being an alien in disguise. Wouldn't that be an easy explanation.

I finish my drink and wave off the bartender as he approaches with the bottle. Mattie must really be getting into the reports. Who knows how long it's going to take her. Of course she could be alerting Stellar Command. She could be turning me in right now and is just making me wait until they show up to arrest me... of course they don't technically have jurisdiction here, but if we really are that much of a threat to Prime Minister Jackson's agenda, then I doubt that would stop them. At the same time, such an action would fracture her reintegration treaty with the other two factions and could have repercussions in Congress. I guess I could live here at the station as a refugee for ten years before reintegration completes and all free space becomes outlaw space.

This thought has influenced my decision to reconsider another round.

"You want me to just leave the bottle?" he asks.

I reply with a question, "If I bring back my other bottle unopened, would you be able to remove the charge?"

"I'd rather not," he says, "but yes I can if needs be."

I take a sip and then feel a tapping on my shoulder. I turn around and it's Mattie. She seems conflicted. I get up and we walk back to the room exchanging silence.

As I secure the door, she beings, "So... I had to reexamine some of this and... it's a lot to take in. I think you have a case to invoke Directive Seventeen. I sure as hell want to know what's going on."

"Okay," I acknowledge, "how are we going to go about doing this?"

She suggests, "As soon as you're ready, we should regroup with Sixth Fleet. Commodore Aiden is a good friend of mine. We should show him your evidence and then see how he wants to go about it?"

"What?" I protest, "As Commanding Officers, we have the authority to enact Directive Seventeen."

"Technically, yes," she acknowledges, "However it will be recognized more seriously if a Flag Officer initiates it."

I raise a brow, "It's my understanding that any of the directives are supposed to be recognized regardless of the rank initiating them."

"Indeed it's supposed to be," she says, "but it's not how it works. The Admirals don't recognize accountability from us."

I'm quiet for a second... I shouldn't be surprised, but that defeats the entire purpose of the policy. It's borderline tyranny.

I clarify, "So you believe with the Commodore's help we can make a compelling case for Directive Seventeen?"

"It's almost unbelievable," she says, "but there are a lot of problems that need to be answered. We should not, however be quick to accuse anyone of conspiracy. At least not right away."

"Why?" I ask, "Why not get it all out in the open?"

Mattie takes a breath and explains, "Even with a Commodore's endorsement, Conspiracy is never taken seriously. We'll need to see how they answer our questions and then slowly walk them towards a possible conspiracy."

I sigh irritably, "I've already been through this shit with Yelkin. He accuses me of being the aggressor, I explain how we're not, then the Gerlak show up and try to kill us. It happened on Thretta, it happened again right after we arrived at Melyar and I just have this strange feeling it will happen again if we try to get anyone else involved. I came to you for your help with a serious, life threatening issue and instead you want to go play politics! So forgive me if I'm not exactly on board with gambling the lives of my crew just so we can be taken seriously by those asshats!"

I turn and realized I raised my voice intensely.

"Jay, I… I'm sorry," she says, "I should have considered things more from your perspective. I just had looked at everything like a report and I- well now I understand the stress this has caused you."

We're quiet for a moment.

I say as I turn back, "I'm sorry I snapped, Mattie. It has been stressful… hell that's putting it lightly…"

She walks up and hugs me in an attempt at consolation. It's working. I embrace her back and for a moment the universe feels like it's standing still. I remember the many reasons I loved this woman. Her ability to calm my storm was unlike any other.

We break off and she asks, "Are you currently seeing anyone?"

I shake my head slowly, "Not since we parted ways."

"Yeah, me neither," she says, "I'm married to my ship now."

I chuckle, "I won't tell mine if you don't tell yours."

She nods in agreement and retreats to the bathroom. I see her personal holo-comp sitting on the desk, powered down. I contemplate for a minute whether or not I should access it to see if she sent the files to anyone. Did she really take that long to go through them? Is she stalling for time? I start to reach for it- no. At some point I have to be able to trust someone. And if I can't trust her then I might as well tunnel right to Sol and turn myself in.

I decide to walk towards the window and look out at the neutron star in the distance. It is beautiful; glowing a soft blue and not too bright to look at without filters. I almost want to just stay here.

As I start to turn away, something catches my eye. I look closer. Something is definitely there. I look around the window for touch control, activate the Digi-Nocs and zoom in on the area I see the object.

Sure enough, "Oh no…"

Chapter Fourteen: "I am more than just a miner."

(*Nathan*)I place my hand on Dev's face and she smiles, giggling slightly.

She asks, "Are we gonna bother sleeping any time soon?"

I answer, "Meh, why plan anything? It's our day off. I don't have anywhere to be, what about you?"

She smiles and half buries her face into the pillow. Finally things feel like they have calmed down to a point where I can retrieve my sanity, though I suddenly feel parched.

I start to get up and say, "I'm gonna get some water, do you need anything."

She half shakes her head.

As I begin to pour water into my unreasonably tiny glass, she asks, "Are you dead set on staying behind?"

I finish pouring and then stop, pondering a moment.

I slowly turn and say, "Let me guess... Donna asked you to say something."

Dev thinks for a second, "Well... she more or less asked me to consider our relationship or at least one we could have."

"So you want a relationship now?" I ask.

Dev explains, "I know you do."

"How?" I ask.

She tilts her head with a slight seduction on her face.

"I mean," I try to explain, "it had been a little while and-"

"Nate," she interrupts, "we get along well. There's no awkwardness between us right now and things come naturally. I understand you want to leave, but we could have something special. Wouldn't you rather see where it goes?"

I contemplate for a bit and then respond, "I… um… I do like you and yes it would be worth it I guess to stay around and see where things go, but I just feel like I'm being used on the ship."

"I know" she says, standing up and walking over to me. She embraces me and looks into my eyes as she says, "But we'd be together."

We start to kiss, but the room shakes violently for a few seconds, knocking us off balance.

"What was that!?" she exclaims.

I head over to the window and deactivate the shade revealing a Gerlak fleet illuminated by the neutron star. I see a bright orange light momentarily followed by the station shaking, but only a little less than before.

I turn and sternly say, "We gotta go."

Dev and I scramble to get our clothing back on. The room shakes a couple more times. I finish strapping on my boots and look out the window once again. The station's security forces fly after the fleet and into their death. Other ships begin to deploy, noticeably larger than the fighters.

I turn around and see Dev packing her bag up.

I say, "Leave it, we gotta go now!" and head for the door, flying it open as we leave.

We hurry down the hall as fast as we can. It's gonna take us a bit to get back to the shipyard since we're on the other side of the main section. We hurry around the outside of the Casino floor, we round to outside our hotel and into the main area, and as we start running towards the shipyard we're forced into a nearby resort as Gerlak storm towards us, guns blazing.

We take cover inside a restaurant.

"What do we do?" Dev asks frantically.

I try to think, "I… I don't know. Donna would know, but-"

I'm interrupted by laser fire as the mercenary security force clashes with the Gerlak. They are quickly forced to find cover as they don't know about the Gerlak weak points. I scream loudly, "Shoot at the thorax looking thing!"

One of the guards looks over at me, unsure of what I said. He then takes a hit to the shoulder and goes down before he's finished off with follow-up shots.

I grab Dev's hand and lead her towards the kitchen, staying low as we move. I bust through the door and look at the cook who is shaking in a corner.

"Is there another way out!?" I ask.

He looks around nervously, "Uh, out that way."

"Come on!" I say, "you're gonna die if you stay here!"

Dev and I head further back into the kitchen and proceed through another door into a low lit hallway with two options: one towards light and another towards another door. We start heading towards the more lit area, but stop as we see laser fire.

"Nope!" Dev says.

"Agreed," I say.

We enter through the other door which leads into another hotel lobby. I look around for any staff, but they appear to have fled. I look down the hall towards where we came from. That's obviously the wrong way to go so we head in the opposite direction. We proceed through an "employees only" entrance which takes us down another corridor and back out to the main area.

We look around and see Gerlak approaching from our left with a casino across the way. I see a large plant feature between us and the casino and a couple of mercenaries standing at the entrance.

I turn to Dev, "Our best bet is to run for that Casino. We'll make a run for the plants in the center. Hopefully those guys will see us and give us cover fire as we make it the rest of the way. You ready?"

She nods.

We get up and start running as fast as we can towards the middle. Lasers begin to wiz by us as we slide in behind the garden feature. The lasers continue to hammer our cover position. I look over and the mercenaries have taken cover in the entrance, but aren't doing anything to help us.

The laser fire feels like it's getting more intense as they seem to close in around us and more pieces of plaster shrapnel off the plant pot. Finally one of the mercs begins to lay down some cover fire. I immediately scramble to get up and run the rest of the distance to the casino.

The mercenary giving us cover fire goes down. As I slide into the casino entrance, I grab his gun. Dev slides in behind me with a laser barely grazing her hair. I help her up and we run into the casino.

"Get down!" the other mercenary yells.

We take cover behind a slot machine.

I yell, "Aim for the thorax looking thing! It's their weak point!"

"Got it!" he says and begins to lay down fire. I peek around and try to assist, but he clearly has a better vantage. I try hitting them in their weak point, but nothing seems to happen.

"They're not going down!" the merc screams irritably.

They must have learned their lesson at Keldon and reinforced their battle armor. I point my rifle at one of them and hold the trigger down. After about three seconds the armor appears to give out and it finally drops.

The merc screams, "We gotta fall back, we won't have enough-"

He's cut off taking a laser to the back and falls to the ground. His gun slides towards us. I hand mine to Dev and try to get his. He reaches out with his hand screaming loudly as if to reach out to me for help but he's suddenly snuffed out as another bolt clocks him in the side of the head, scorching him on impact.

I motion for Dev to follow me as we weave through the various gambling tables and machines, returning fire when we can, but also maintaining our cover. We're slowing them down, but eventually they will overtake us.

We dive in behind a bar which gives us a thick barrier for cover. I quickly am able to get a count: there's only about three coming after us.

I say, "I will distract them on this end of the bar. You try to concentrate on hitting them. There's only about three. We take them out, then we can keep making our way back to the ship."

Dev nods in agreement. I crawl over to the other end of the bar and begin to lay down fire. Dev pokes up and focuses on one. She hits one of the snake-mouths and the Gerlak screams in pain as it takes cover. Perfect. We can at least incapacitate them if only for a moment.

Even though I'm recklessly spraying energy, I make it a point to go for the mouths. I hit one and it goes down momentarily. The last one tries to take me out, but Dev finishes it off. The first one she downed pops up but she hits it in the other mouth. We focus on the last one which doesn't stand a chance.

I know it didn't happen this way, but I remember it as though it did. The first Gerlak recovers quicker than we thought and is able to get a shot off. I could have sworn I watched it all the way in slow motion, but in reality, I just knew where it was headed. By the time I turned my head, Dev finished falling to the floor, having let out only a quick, but snuffed out scream... I quickly get down next to her, but her face is scorched black, unrecognizable and smoldering... I instinctively place my fingers on her neck... she's gone.

In a trance-like daze I get up, point my gun at the struggling gerlak and fire until it stops screaming. I look around at the dead gerlak and realize that I'm now alone.

I take one last look at what's left of Dev, take a breath and murmur, "I'm sorry."

Making my way back towards the shipyard, I encounter no other gerlak right away. Then I round a corner in the main corridor and find myself pinned inside a small hole-in-the-wall type of shop. I hop behind the counter and find the shop owner dead. I look for another way out, but the door appears to be sealed. I guess this is where it ends for me. Oh well. I slump down and prepare for the inevitable.

There's some shouting and laser fire rattles off. Sounds like some more unprepared mercenaries fighting their way to their inevitable demise.

It stops and the station appears to go quiet. Guess my time is now coming. The question is, do I want to go out-

"Nate!" a familiar male voice shouts, "Nate, its Commander Keller! I saw you come in here for cover, are you still in here!?"

No fuckin way. I get up and sure enough, "Holy shit I never thought I would be so relieved to see you."

He motions at me to leave, "Come on, we gotta go while there is a break in the fighting."

I hop back over the desk and follow him out. He seems to be joined up with more mercenaries and some woman I've never met.

He asks, "Was it just you by yourself?"

I contemplate how to answer as we hurriedly down the corridor, "No... I was with Crewman Belkrest. There's no easy way to say, but she's gone."

"Alright." He acknowledges, "No one else?"

"No," you cold blooded asshole.

He explains, "These four gentleman have offered to get us back to our ships in exchange for rides off the station. Nate McNill, this is Captain Matilda Wrennor of the Constellation Destroyer Andromeda."

I acknowledge, "Hello."

Keller continues, "We need to get her back to her ship first. Without Andromeda, we don't have a way out of here. Believe it or not, the Traverse Drive was compromised, again."

"Awesome," I sarcastically say, then ask, "I don't suppose you ran into Donna or my buddy Tim did you?"

"Sergeant Kroeling?" Keller confirms, "I ordered her to defend the ship at the docks. She was already back aboard. I'm afraid I don't know about your friend."

So she must have gone back to the ship. Hopefully Tim stayed with her.

We come to one of the entrances of the shipyard and find ourselves in a massive firefight. We find cover and Keller and Wrennor figure out what to do.

Keller says, "Alright, we'll proceed in twos, except for myself, giving cover where we can. The important thing is that we get the Captain back to her ship. Then one of you can go with her while the rest get Nate and I back to my ship."

Wrennor shakes her head, "Jay, I appreciate the chivalry, but we both need to head for our respective vessels. I'll take you three and we can cover each other from a distance."

Keller explains, "Mattie, it's not that at all. I know this is the worst time so I'll keep it short: I never got over you. I don't think I ever will. If anything is gonna happen to anyone, it's gotta be me."

"Well I can't live without you either," Wrennor says, "so let's go with my plan, we all have a fair shot."

I intervene, "Let's just all go to whichever ship is closer, then we can shuttle whoever to whichever ship once we're safe."

"Valkyrie it is, then," Keller says standing up.

He looks around at the chaos as the mercenaries, other captains and crew attempt to fight off the never ending swarm of Gerlak.

Wrennor contacts her ship real quick and gives the order to depart ensuring them she will be safely out on Valkyrie. We all get up and after a deep breath join the frenzy as we make our way to our specific docking corridor. After taking out about five of them, we help a few other people get to their ships. Two of the mercs are taken out before we arrive at our ship's brow which is being guarded by Donna and a couple of other guys from the ship.

Keller starts asking if everyone is back on as the rest of us get on board the ship. I pass a few other crew members dressed in full tactical gear before getting into the ship itself. I arrive at a table setup just inside the airlock.

A Crewman asks, "I'm sorry, who are you?"

I reply, "Nathan McNill. I'm a civilian who's been mining for you guys since Keldon."

"Oh, sorry," he says, "guess I never saw you. Were you with anyone?"

I slowly nod and answer, "Yes."

"Who?" he asks.

"Crewman Belkrest," I answer.

"And where is she?" he asks.

I say, "Gone."

"Gone? What do you mean gone?" he presses.

I snap, "She got shot in the fuckin face! She's dead! And before you ask, no I didn't see anyone else… Is Tim M'Nar aboard? He's the other civilian I've been working with."

Another Crewman assisting him checks the roster.

Keller walks up, "Is everyone accounted for?"

"Uh, no sir," the Crewman interrogating me replies, "We're still missing several people."

Wrennor says, "Jay, we don't have time…"

Keller pauses for a second, unsure of what to do. His personal COMM goes off, "Keller," he answers… "Okay… yeah I agree… alright let's go."

He puts his COMM back in his pocket and orders, "Prepare to cast off. Gerlak fighters are moving on the shipyard."

The Crewman looking up Tim's status runs down the brow telling everyone that they were about to retract it and get back inside the ship. I stand back a bit and wait as everyone clears out. As they start to tear down their little setup, I ask again, "What's the status of Tim M'Nar?"

Donna answers, "He's on board, Nate. Follow me, we need to take our weapons to the armory."

As I walk with Donna, I don't have much to say.

She asks, "What's wrong?"

I stop. Reality starts to set in. A little bleary eyed I look at her and mutter, "Dev is gone…"

Donna grabs my gun and says, "I'll find you on the Crew's Mess."

The ship shakes and I stumble my way to the Crew's Mess. We shake again. Maybe if we're lucky we won't make it. I'm starting to realize after all I had been through, I really cared for Devorah. Maybe even had come to love her. She was right; things came easy between us, and we might have actually been together for a while and now we'll… *sniff* now we'll never know.

It looks like I made it to the Crew's Mess. My mind obviously elsewhere. I'm wishing there was more I could do.

"Wwaaahhhh…" I look up and see Tim stumbling in, "what's going on?"

I answer, "The Gerlak found us."

Tim suddenly becomes stone cold sober for a second, "Shit… well at least you made it back. Where's Dev? Probably doing something in engineering."

"No" I shake my head, "she's gone… as in dead."

Tim has no immediate response. Then he asks, "How are you holding up?"

I… "I don't know…" I can't compose my thoughts.

Tim sits down next to me and starts to ramble on about something. I guess his mother's passing years ago or something to try and relate. All I can do is think about what has just happened to me. And at the same time, I can't. I want to think about nothing. Right now, I want to be nothing... like Dev.

I get up in the middle of whatever Tim is saying and head for my rack. Maybe I can die comfortably...

(*Keller*)..."Andromeda's singularity is stabilized," Gravimetrics Crewman Neft reports.

I order the Helm, "Take us in."

The ship shakes considerably as we enter and then steadies into the expected rolls and sways. Mattie and I walk over to the aft of the bridge to confirm that Andromeda did in fact follow us in.

The ship is a little larger than ours and the bridge sits a bit lower. Instead of modules extending diagonally out of her sides, she has two very large rail guns mounted horizontally on the sides with six rounds each. That may not seem like much, but consider that one round would split my ship in half. The rail guns can also convert to energy based weapons, but it requires a massive power output and therefore a long recharge time. The energy weapons also aren't as effective as the projectiles, at least against hull. They may prove useful against the shielding.

Something catches Mattie's eye. She activates the digi-nocs on the transparent armor and zooms in just behind Andromeda's Port Quarter.

"Looks like one of them got in," she says.

I acknowledge, "When we resurface, order your ship to disable them. We've already got a fighter captured, but we can always use more parts."

"Parts for what?" Mattie asks.

I explain, "We've been attempting to adapt their energy shielding to be used by us. Granted it's not going as quickly as we had hoped-"

She cuts me off, "You've been stealing their tech? That's... isn't that a violation of something."

"What, exactly?" I ask.

Mattie can't think of an answer.

I continue, "There is nothing that says we can't because six weeks ago, we were the only sentient beings to exist in the universe. Before we continue with this ethics debate, I need to know where we are going."

Mattie says, "I ordered a two hour trip into the middle of nowhere. I figured that would be a good place a regroup. Away from any particular system."

"Sounds good," I say, "let's get down to my office."

"Concur," Mattie says.

We don't say much on the way down and almost lose our balance a couple of times from the rolls.

As we enter my office, I get ready to sit at my desk when Mattie asks, "Can we go into your room? This seems unnecessarily formal."

I nod and lead the way into my quarters. Mattie closes the door behind her and walks over to the kitchenette area while I sit down on my couch. She searches through my cabinets until she finds my stash of beverages. She pulls out a bottle of wine and two glasses.

She says while pouring, "I don't know about you, but I need a refreshment in order to clear my head and accept all of this."

"Oh I know the feeling," I say, "I think I killed three bottles of whiskey during our sub-light transit to Thretta."

She hands me a glass and sits down next to me, "So I have an idea on how to present this situation to the Commodore, but we should talk it over first."

I say, "Before we get into that I need a moment... I left members of my crew behind."

Sighing remorsefully Mattie adds, "As did I... but you saw what happened, they severed the shipyard corridors as we started to leave. If you hadn't given the order to cast off when you did, the entire airlock could have decompressed before retracting the brow."

"Yeah..." I reluctantly agree, "some of them just hit a little harder than others."

We sit silently for a moment. She knows me well enough that when I need a quiet moment, to just give it to me. I take a sip or two.

"Thanks, Mattie," I say.

She says, "Not a problem, Jay." She takes a sip form her glass and then says, "I see your preference of cheap wine hasn't changed."

I point out, "Cheaper to buy in bulk and some end up fermenting after a while. Okay, so now you've seen the Gerlak for yourself. How do we present this to the Commodore?"

"Well..." she begins, "I will be going alone. I have an established rapport with him. Plus, if the Gerlak have some sort of advanced tracking, one of us should be commanding our ship in case they arrive."

I take a concerned deep breath, "Okay... but you don't find it at all curious that they attacked Lantic Station?"

She says, "Unless they intercepted your communication, they must have been tracking you somehow."

"Right…" I acknowledge, "Or someone told Stellar Command where we were."

"Who would have said that?" she asks.

I stand up and say, "I don't know, Matilda, but it got me thinking. You took a while to review all the data I presented. Unless you actually read every single page and watched every single sensor clip I provided-"

"You think it was me," she interrupts.

I reiterate, "I've said it before, any time we have talked to Stellar Command, the Gerlak have somehow anticipated our moves. I wrote it off as coincidence at first, but then they intercepted us at Melyar. Now they come all the way through Republic Space to a Free Port far from Keldon or any of the other colonies they invaded. Why? What threat to them did Lantic Station pose?"

Mattie searches for an answer. She can't seem to find one, but she doesn't seem to be lying to me.

"Jay… I…" she thinks for a bit, "I agree that the situation seems convenient. But I didn't tell anyone. And my crew was instructed not to discuss our whereabouts on the Free Net. So unless someone slipped up or there was an informant on the station, it wasn't me."

I stand quietly for a moment, "Okay, but you can understand my suspicion."

She acknowledges understandingly, "Yes, I do. If you really think you should be there with me, then by all means, however, Adien is extremely particular and doesn't trust easily."

"I'll make that decision when we meet up with Sixth Fleet" I decide, "As for what to say, it might be best to present your personal experience first."

She nods, "I agree. If I open with the sensor data from Lantic Station, that should get his attention right away. I might not even need to soft play the possible conspiracy."

"Okay," I say, "In the meantime, I need to get my Traverse Drive working."

Mattie says, "We'll conduct repairs in dead space. When you feel your ship is ready, we'll meet up with Sixth Fleet."

I nod, "By the way, what was your excuse to go to Lantic Station anyway?"

She explains, "I kept it simple. Told Command my crew needed a break and to let loose a bit. Nothing more than that. When we resurface, I'll just tell them we sustained damage and are conducting repairs."

I shake my head, "Too risky. Keep your long range COMMs offline."

She reminds, "Eventually I will need to contact Sixth Fleet to find out where they are."

"Okay," I acknowledge, "but until then, we stay dark."

"Very well," she says.

My personal COMM goes off, "Keller," I say.

"**Jaysen,**" Sub-Commander says, "**I have the final accountability report.**"

I hesitate a reply momentarily, "Send it to my computer. I will read over it."

"**Understood,**" he says and closes the line.

I look down at my glass and contemplate a refill.

"What was that?" she asks.

I look over at Mattie, "Accountability roster is about to come in."

"Ah," she says and gets up to grab the wine.

I remote into my computer using my personal COMM unit and access the list. Mattie fills up my glass. Here we go...

...(*Nathan*)Finishing my pour I stare at my cup. I haven't felt this empty in a long time. Instead of fiery death, we ended up in a tunnel. Woo.

I sit down at the table where she was at that morning we surveyed Melyar. I stare at an empty seat in front of me. I look down at a table that is only occupied by my cup. I didn't think I was going to become attached to anyone on this ship and yet I did.

Lede Kamerov sits down in front of me. He's quiet at first. It's almost like we don't have to say anything at all.

Then he does, "I can't believe it, man. I mean I can say she wasn't really a fighter, but I don't want to."

I inform, "You'd be surprised. We actually took out two of them before she, uh... was shot."

"As I said," he says, "not much of a fighter."

I snap, "You know that's pretty fucking asinine to say right now. I get it, you wanted her, but she didn't feel the same. But rubbing in the fact that neither of us gets her now is-"

He interrupts while raising his voice, "I didn't mean it like that!"

I stop and we're quiet for a moment.

He starts to formulate thoughts, "I just... you're right: I did care about her and not totally opposed to being more than friends, but that was never our dynamic. You gotta remember, I worked with her for the last three years and to lose her like this it's..."

I digress, "We're in this together..."

He nods, "Yeah… yeah we are. So what are you gonna do now?"

This is the last thing I would want to do, but now the game has changed.

"I'm gonna join the crew," I say as I get up and leave, "I'll see you when I see you."

I drop off my mug and head up to the bridge. After asking the Deck Officer were Keller might be, I head back down and towards his office. I rap on the door and hear another door inside open followed by the one I'm standing in front of.

"Mr. McNill," Keller says, "what do you need?"

"Can we talk for a second?" I ask.

"Come on in," he says, walking towards his desk. Wrennor walks to the doorway leading into Keller's quarters. She's dressed down to her uniform shirt and pants.

Keller says, "You remember Captain Wrennor."

I nod, "Ma'am."

"What's on your mind, Nate?" he asks.

I take a second to compose my words, then I look directly at Keller, "I wanna join your crew."

"So you come up here to formally accept the offer you initially rejected?" he inquires.

I shake my head slowly, "No I want to do more than just mine. I wanna serve as a Navigator again."

"Like help with the watch?" he asks, "why?"

I explain, "Crewman Belkrest and I… we became close. Working closely together, one thing led to another and… well, maybe this is more of an impulse, but at the same time I know my talents can be better served alongside the crew, not just mining for you."

"I see," Keller nods, "So instead of sleeping late, only working when we're mining and getting free food, you want to be put into the watch rotation, given a job during Battlestations, work with one of the shops and have a work day?"

I nod again, "There's more that I could do here. I only got into mining because it was one of the few occupations that didn't dig too much into my past, but I never cared for the mining aspect of it. It was the travel; seeing the galaxy. Those were reasons I joined the Armada in the first place. I'll still help with the mining and if needs be, it will still be my primary responsibility, but I am more than just a miner."

"Yes, you are," he acknowledges, "I'll see if we can get you into the watch rotation, but you are correct: mining is your first priority. I understand it's not your favorite thing to do, but if you want to serve with my crew it's where I need you."

I nod reluctant, but acceptingly.

Keller asks, "Is there anything else?"

I contemplate for a second and then ask, "Actually there is. Do you actually give a shit about anyone on this ship?"

Wrennor busts in, "What? We were in the middle of going through the accountability roster of everyone he lost. Wh- where do you get this notion he doesn't?"

I try to answer, "Uh… aside from hanging me out to dry over three years ago, you seemed very disconnected when I told you about Crewman Belkrest."

Keller nods largely, "I… can understand how that may have seemed cold. And you're right, it was. In that moment I needed to focus on getting all of us to safety. But to insinuate…"

Keller appears to start breaking down. He lowers his head for a moment to compose himself. I hear him sniff and then he looks back up, somewhat somberly.

"I, uh... I failed you all those years ago," he says.

Fucking finally.

He continues, "But it's not because I didn't do anything to reverse the Admiral's decision. It's because I did."

I raise a brow wanting to know more.

Continuing, "I had an investigation launched using our people to get a second opinion. I didn't believe all of the facts that were presented either and things seemed more circumstantial. I can only speculate, but I definitely believe they were covering for someone else in the shop. Wernival used his influence to get Command to force me to stop the investigation, but what's odd is instead of threatening action against me, they offered me a promotion."

"What..." I gasp.

He nods affirmingly, "They were more interested in buying my silence, which indicated to me there was something to hide. Unfortunately, it will remain hidden. After I turned them down, I submitted a resignation since I had lost control of my ship. Instead they gave me Valkyrie and I chose to remain in."

Wrennor adds, "Just so you understand the impact, Jay and I had to decide years ago which of us was going to raise our son during his younger years while the other continued their career. His dream was to be an Admiral for the longest time until you inadvertently exposed him to the politics of the organization. It mattered more to him to keep influencing people on whatever ship he served, than trying to play politics to get ahead."

I nod slowly.

"Don't feel guilty," she says, "it wasn't your fault. Sometimes Jay can be a little too modest for his own good."

Keller states, "And you can be a little too forward with things. Point is Nate, yes, I do give a shit. I care about everyone who serves under me or has ever served under me," he holds up his COMM unit, "every loss is my loss. And they each affect me differently, yet the same. Yes, some of the names on this list didn't know me more than their Commander and I didn't know them more than just Crew, but others I have gotten to know well which makes losing them all that much harder. Crewman Belkrest in particular made it her mission to double check maintenance on the SLVRDOs after her husband was killed."

I stare off, processing everything I have just heard. My perception was way off.

Keller says, "Take the time you need to mourn. Right now we're going to regroup in dead space in an hour and conduct repairs. Andromeda will spare us parts for now so you can stand by on the mining. Actually we'll use your other talent of finding us a potential prospect in the event we need to fabricate more parts, but I'll find you when we're ready."

"Okay," I say standing up, "Guess I'll go wait."

Keller finishes, "One last thing, I'm sorry that this had to be what brought you around. And I'm sorry again that things had to go the way they did before. I can't reinstate you, but that doesn't make you any less of a member of my crew for now."

I nod, "Thank you... sir."

I leave Keller's office feeling a sense of purpose for once. Dev's death may be my driving force, but it beats wallowing in sadness the entire time. I head back to the Crew's Mess.

Donna comes up behind me, "Nate! I was wondering where you went. I came here earlier and Tim said you just walked off while he was talking to you."

"Yeah," I say, "I wasn't really listening to him anyway."

She asks, "Well do you want to talk to me?"

"No," I say, "I want to train for combat."

Chapter Fifteen: "You have to avenge yourself first."

(*Nathan*)*THUD!* My face hits the mat yet again. I get up, a little more dazed this time.

Donna asks, "Alright, what did you do wrong this time?"

I say, "Agree to do this in the first place. Seriously, Donna, what is the point of this? We don't know the gerlak vulnerabilities."

Donna reaches her hand out to help me up. I grab it again. It's just her and I using the sparring mats. Most of the rest of the crew are on their workday routine as we conduct repairs in dead space.

Donna explains, "Before we continue the rifle training, you need to get all your rage out. Whether you like it or not, you're distracted."

I say, "Distracted? I was trying to channel my anger."

"I know," she says, "but not everyone can do so effectively. Unfortunately for you, your anger distracts you. It is not your ally and you need to get rid of it."

I scoff out an answer, "Well, how am I supposed to do that if you keep kicking my ass?"

"That's the point," she states, "to see how much rage it takes before you finally figure out how to concentrate." She finishes taking a swing at me. This time I avoid it.

I try to throw a punch back, but miss. And again and again and again. I attempt a kick and yet again she's able to grab me and throw the rest of my momentum against me forcing me back to the ground.

I slam my closed fist on the mat, "This isn't fucking working!"

"No, I think it is," she finishes giving me a solid kick to my right thigh.

"Ahhhh!" I let out.

She goes in for another kick and gets me in the same spot.

"Come on, Nate, let it out," she says, shuffling to my left side and kicking my other thigh.

I attempt to find my anger, but it just turns into useless, shaky adrenaline. I attempt to get up but fall back to the ground. It's like my body is trying to shut down and now- tears? "Are you fucking kidding me?"

Donna squats down and explains, "You cannot use anger. For you it becomes fear that envelops you entirely. You can't control your adrenaline, and instead your body wants to shut down. You need to let go of your anger."

"HOW!?!" I shout.

"By figuring out what's causing your anger and facing it," she says.

Now my anger crying turns into sobbing as I try to face myself again. The last couple nights I've been falling asleep- well, I haven't really slept. In fact, I've spent so much time awake trying to think about Dev that I... I... "I couldn't save her, Donna..."

She sits down, criss-crossing her legs and says, "No, you couldn't. No one could. And you need to stop blaming yourself."

sniff "I... I think I loved her, Donna. As crazy as that sounds."

Donna says, "You spent the last few weeks working closely together and getting to know each other. There's nothing crazy about it. People for years have tried to put a time limit on things, but sometimes feelings just happen.

They take root and they grow. Did you know she felt the same about you?"

I kind of shrug, "I guess so… she wanted me to remain on board to see where our relationship might go."

Donna nods, "Even if she didn't get the chance to say it, she did."

I reveal, "It was just so sudden. One second we were taking out the Gerlak and then the next she… she was just gone."

"Sadly, I can relate," she says, "And you're doing the right thing wanting to avenge her death. But you need to avenge yourself first."

I sit up and try to compose my thoughts, "It's more than just her. It's everything else. The Gerlak have fucked up my life more than I did. I know, I know it's self-absorbed, I could be dead-"

Donna interrupts me holding up her hand, "Nate, yes, you could be dead, but we are alive and need to cope. So no, I don't think you're self-absorbed at all. Get all your thoughts out there. I know this has been hard. You were kicked out of this life and now you've been forced to serve it under someone you personally don't like very much."

I shake my head, "Yeah… and even that has changed…"

"How so?" she asks.

I explain, "Keller apparently tried to save my career. But as it turns out the people above him told him not to. And then they offered him a promotion, but he threatened to resign."

"So your perception has changed…" she says, "Wow… in small matter of hours your universe view has been shaken along with losing someone special to you. I can see how that adds to the distraction. Do you even know who you're angry at anymore?"

I shake my head, "No. The Admirals of the Armada, the Gerlak… the idiots on the Ex Del Seven… I just, right now I wanna focus on doing what I need to for the ship."

She nods, stands up and helps me back to my feet and says, "This time, try to focus and don't rely so much on your emotions."

I take my stance and get ready to spar, but the clock catches my eye.

"Oh shit," I say, "I gotta go. Sorry, but I have a meeting with the Flight Commander."

Understandingly, Donna nods and says, "Okay. I've got a sweep and clear drill scheduled for after lunch. Just find me then."

"Okay," I say as I turn to leave.

I quickly rush to my berthing area and hop in the shower. Hopefully this meeting goes well. By the time I more or less rip my way back into my work clothes, I have five minutes to get all the way to the starboard module.

I rush as quickly as I can down to the other end of the ship, board an empty lift and make it with thirty whole seconds to spare. Only problem is, the Flight Commander isn't in his office. He must be out on the hangar, then.

I look around until finally I spot the five foot nine slender gentlemen with slicked back hair in typical pilot fashion. He's wearing his jump suit as though he's gonna go out for a flight soon.

"Lieutenant Lester," I say.

He turns around, mildly irritated as though I have interrupted his day. He waves me over to come closer to him.

I begin, "So I think if I-"

He holds out his hand, "Look, I know if I didn't say it directly, you would keep asking, but here's the deal: I already have enough pilots and co-pilots. I'm aware you have done battle with the Gerlak and have been successful. That's impressive considering you didn't have that much prior flight experience."

He takes a breath and continues, "But these," he says pointing to one of the Outfighters sitting close by, "require specialized training. There is a three months long school just learning the basics of how it flies in space and in planetary atmosphere. There's a reason Officers are selected for the training as it requires full career dedication."

I point out, "Okay, but enlisted can learn to fly them too."

He acknowledges, "Yes, but that's after years of experience on other ships and months of hands on simulator training- the point is, I can't just stick you in a simulator for a few hours and let you fly on one of our ships during live training. I get it, you want to get out there and take some vengeance, but the answer is a flat 'no'. You can't just one day decide to hop in a fighter and become a hotshot pilot."

I lower my head, disappointed.

He says, "Look, there are some operations where if needed we man up the Outflyers and it's getting to the point where we are going to have to use them for combat. Talk to Crewman Kamerov, he's the one who runs the program."

"Okay," I say, "Thank you, sir."

Well that's disappointing. But I suppose combat in something is better than nothing. I head over to a communications terminal and contact the bridge.

"Crewman Fisp," a male voice says.

I ask, "Is Crewman Kamerov up there?"

He answers, "Negative. He's probably in the Port Hangar."

"Thanks," I say and I close the line.

It'll take me a few minutes to get there depending on the availability of lifts.

I step off the lift into the port hangar. Looking around, I see Tim working on the fabrication device along with some of the other engineers and even the Grav-specilists. They seem to be having an in-depth conversation with Commander Keller and Captain Wrennor.

I check some of the drop-ships being worked on, but no sign of Lede anywhere. Then I see him sitting in Miner Two. I walk over to him.

"Are you busy?" I ask.

He looks up, "Naw, man. What's up?"

I say, "Lieutenant Lester said you run the combat program for these things. I wanna join the team."

"Oh," he says, "yeah he mentioned something about needing some of these since we've lost a couple Outfighters. I suppose since you have some combat experience against the aliens I could officially make you an SLVRDO combat pilot. But shouldn't you be helping with fabrication?"

I shake my head, "I don't know anything about that. If we're not actively mining, I'm pretty much useless. I asked to be put in the watch rotation on the bridge, but I know I can be doing more."

Lede asks, "What's got you so eager to be helpful?"

I ponder momentarily. Then I speculate, "It seems in her death, Dev has given me a reason to fight."

"I see," Lede says, "well, we should run you through a couple of combat simulations before we officially put you on the roster."

Suddenly an idea, "What if we pulled the sensor data from when Dev and I fought them in the Melyar system?"

Lede nods, "That's actually not a bad idea... we should also get the data from the CMRO engagements as well. We can compile it into a new training program for the simulator. Especially since the other pilots are going to need it. I'll have to see if Sfed is available to help us," he finishes getting out of the ship.

"I'll start downloading the data," I say climbing in.

It takes a couple of minutes for me to go through the computer system and locate the files. I pause a second... some of this data will contain the black box, meaning I'll hear Dev's voice... I can do this.

Lede comes back and says, "Sfed says he can help at the top of the hour. That should give us enough time to get the sensor data from the Outfighters."

"You got a data-stick?" I ask.

He nods and pulls one out of his pocket. I download the data and as we head for the lift, Keller and I make eye contact momentarily and nod...

(*Keller*)...I return Nate's nod and then ask, "How long before we can test?"

Lieutenant Jerak answers, "I won't know until the capacitation fluxer is sealed. After that all we have to do is energize the dish, run at least five tests and then we should be good to tunnel. And again, I have to insist on conducting ALL the tests this time. I am very sure that it wasn't just the hit that compromised the Core Transference Chamber.

It was using the Drive without testing it the last time we repaired it."

"Okay," I say, "keep me updated."

I turn and Mattie and I both start to leave.

"I'm thinking at least another day," I say, "I know you don't like remaining off the Net, but we can't risk it just yet."

"I agree," she unexpectedly says, "I'm still trying to figure out how the Gerlak found you. So far there haven't been any signs of them following us yet."

I say, "I'm tempted to wait two days to rule out some advanced tracking."

"I understand," she says condescendingly, "but we need to get to the bottom of this. The entire Republic could be in danger."

"I'm well aware of what's at stake here," I say, "which is why we need to rule out advanced, sophisticated technology like 'super tracking'. But we'll see how long it takes us to get our ship repaired. It might take an extra day anyway when all is said and done."

"Guess we'll find out," she says.

Lieutenant Slaighter, the ENGCOM walks up to us and casually says, "Hey. I think I figured out a way to make the shielding work,"

"Oh?" I ask indicating I desire an explanation.

He explains, "Yeah, so I don't think we can sustain a bubble like they do," he says motioning for us to walk towards the direction he is pointing, "but I think we can set up small generators inside the ship that direct the energy into the armor directly like my guys have done with this piece here."

We walk up to a piece of armor that at first appears un-changed, but as I lean in closer, it appears to be faintly glowing a greenish brown color.

ENGCOM explains, "Yeah so I guess the reaction of energy into the armor seems to cause this glow. Here, throw this at it," he hands me a wrench.

I toss it, it makes an electrical shocking noise as it slightly bounces off, and then clanks on the deck.

"Nice," I compliment, "how does it work against lasers?"

ENGCOM is quiet for a second, "Well… that's what I would like permission to test. I don't know if it will be absorbed or bounce off, but I assume you want to know the reliability before I start installing generators throughout the ship."

I nod, "Yes. Rig up an enclosed testing range and then run it by me."

"Will do, Commander," he says.

Mattie and I start walking towards the lift.

She says, "If that shit actually works, I want it for my ship."

I say, "Absolutely. See why I wanted those gerlak ships disabled?"

"Yes," she acknowledges, "I'm not so sure about the ethics of stealing their tech-"

I interrupt, "Now you're starting to sound like Devlin."

She explains, "Right, well at the same time we need every advantage we can get, but in the meantime," changing the subject, "you should have dinner at my ship tonight. I think we're having Prime Rib."

I chuckle, "You know I prefer the real thing."

She states, "Yes. That's why I'm asking you over."

Oh, it has been a while since I had real beef, "That actually sounds good," I say accepting her invitation.

I head up to the bridge. My presence is announced and I allow the Deck Officer to retain command. I ask, "Still nothing?"

Lieutenant Esker informs, "Nothing, sir. We've continued scans and don't have any sign of Gerlak activity."

I confirm, "And no issues with the equipment?"

"No sir," she says.

Wow. We might actually get a breather for once. The bridge COMM goes off and Esker answers. She informs it's for me and I take the hand unit.

"Keller," I say.

A male voice says, **"Hey, it's Gregoru. I've run some tests on the alien and I think I was able to determine a see-oh-dee."**

"And?" I prompt after a few seconds of silence.

He says, **"It was our ee-em-pee missiles."**

"How do you... I'll be down for an explanation." I end the conversation and close the line.

As I'm leaving the bridge, Mattie asks, "Where to now?"

"Medical," I say.

After descending the stairs she further inquiries, "Is everything alright?"

I inform, "MEDCOM has informed me that he thinks the alien pilots were all fried by the EMP missiles."

"I'm interested to hear this explanation," she states.

"As am I," I say and we exchange no words until we make it to the medical bay located on level 4.

We enter the medical bay. It's lit with a soft blue glow. Aside from a front desk, it's basically the size of a small clinic, but with every inch of space utilized. It has five separate rooms; four for patients and one for surgery. It's staffed with Officers as Doctors and Nurses, the lower officer ranks being the nurses aspiring to one day become doctors.

We walk up to Gregoru, "Sub-Commander Gregoru Jackson, I'd like you to meet Captain Matilda Wrennor of the Constellation Destroyer Andromeda."

Gregoru nods and shakes her hand then says, "Follow me please."

We walk into one of the rooms pretty much littered with gerlak corpses.

"Forgive the mess, Jay," Gregoru says, "but I didn't want to pollute my other rooms with their stench."

"I don't smell anything," I say looking at Mattie who is glaring at me confused. "What?" I say, "he's the Medical Commander. He pretty much outranks me."

Gregoru reminds, "Only if you go nuts. Now try to bear with me. I ran some initial scans. I won't bore you with the specific details of the last twenty four plus hours, but as you can imagine, I initially didn't have a point of reference or didn't know where to begin. So I had to start with a simple dissection to learn their anatomy."

Mattie says, "When you got more bodies you were able to learn some things."

He confirmingly nods, "Correct, ma'am. I started noticing consistencies, but also some inconsistencies. However, one thing was true in all four of them: they fried from the electromagnetism. What specifically, I don't know. Without a live one, I can't exactly run tests so I took one of the arms and exposed it to electromagnetic radiation: it fried more. But keep in mind I was testing decaying tissue."

"I see," I say, "Is there anything else?"

"Aside from compiling some research papers," he says, "I can't think of anything tactical. Most of their vulnerable spots are in the thorax, but I've got nothing I think you'll care for at the moment. I do think ee-em-pee grenades should be issued to all deployment team personnel."

"Noted," I say and then ponder for a moment, then continue "I'm gonna find Sergeant Kroeling. I want you to tell her everything. She'll make the decision about the grenades."

"Sure thing, Jay," he says...

(*Donna*)...Everyone lines up in the gym with their practice rifles and fully strapped up with gear and armor. I look at all the familiar faces, but don't see Nate. Guess he had better obliga- the door flies open and Nate walks in with rifle, armor and gear.

"Sorry I'm late," he says, "I got caught up with something else, had lunch-"

I hold my hand up, "Just fall in, Mr. McNill."

"Aye, Sergeant," he says and slides next to Crewman Dayson in the third row.

I explain, "Today's training has changed. I spoke with Doctor Jackson over lunch and he believes he has found a vulnerability that we need to learn to exploit. Some of you know already, but I need to inform those that don't, the Gerlak have modified their thorax armor. It's now more resistant to our standard bolts. You hit them enough times and the armor will fail, but it takes a lot of energy spraying to do that that."

I look around to make sure everyone is still following along.

I hold up an object, "In my hand is an ee-em-pee grenade. We're going to try and manufacture more. Correct me if I'm wrong, but the standard Boarding Team kit only has two of these."

I look at everyone, most of whom are giving me nods.

"Right." I continue, "So the armory isn't exactly stocked full of them- I mean it is, but not in the quantities we now need, so that means learning to shoot charged bursts. The disadvantage to this is it takes three seconds to charge and then between two to four seconds for the diodes to cool off before conducting another charge. Those of you who know your math know that's five to seven seconds that you are vulnerable. Does anyone have any ideas as to how we might work around this?"

Putvel suggests, "We all take turns charging. Make sure everyone is charging at different times so there is no delays in fire rate."

"An excellent suggestion," I condescend, "If we were planning to kill our enemy by impressing them with our coordination. But there is a more practical and functional way. Any guesses?"

Crewman Regon, a Gunner says, "Shooter spotter?"

"Close," I say, "It's more like shooter covery. You will be paired off into teams. One will focus on making successfully charged hits while the other lays down cover fire so the enemy doesn't have a chance to steal the advantage. But to find out who is doing what," I stop talking hitting a button on a controller that dims the lights and projects a range on the bulkhead in front of everyone, "we're going to score everyone and whoever is most accurate will be practicing charge shots first."

Crewman Fepner, whose specialty is working on the engines asks, "Why aren't we just using our scores from the last time?"

I explain, "Because that was almost a month ago and we have had more people join since then. I'm sure others, including yourself would like to improve their score. If there are no other questions, everyone line up, sync your rifles to the range server and begin when ready."

The range really isn't as special as it sounds. It just projects silhouettes like a live fire range. Delta Larrodo and I worked painstakingly hard to get as correct to scale for the gerlak as we could.

Everyone cycles through once fairly quickly and when finished they return to their three lines. Delta Larrodo steps up, holding a pad, and starts pairing everyone off based on their score. Everyone gathers with their partner and starts setting their rifles for their designated roles. I notice Nate seems a little displeased he's designated for covery fire, but he shouldn't be surprised. He only decided yesterday to start training more intently.

We run a sweep and clear simulation through the forward portion of level three. Afterwards, we run a defensive dirll using teams of four covering down both ends of the passageway. Delta Larrodo and I also run a couple rounds. Yes, that's right, despite our experience we do in fact need to train against this enemy.

We do a final round utilizing the projection range that plots a target at different distances and even fires back. We get the final score and our egos take a second place bruise.

As expected, Nate and his squad mate were last. Didn't help Nate got picked off almost immediately.

As everyone leaves, I ask Nate to remain behind.

"How do you feel?" I ask.

"This isn't for me," he says.

I point out, "You do realize these guys have been training and have had live experience over the last few weeks, right?"

Nate protests, "I have live experience too. I made it through both times."

I say, "The first time was with me and the last time someone with you got killed-" dammit Donna, should have quit while you were ahead!

Nate instantly fumes anger but turns away.

He takes a huge sigh, "You're right... that's why this isn't for me."

"Nate, I didn't-" I try to fumble for words, "that was a cold way of putting it. But yes you did survive. One of those times was more or less on your own. My point, if I can make it without sounding fucked, is that you need practice. I can try to set aside time if needs be, but at the same time I've got a set schedule."

Nate informs, "I've got watch soon. And also, Lede and I started working on a training program for the SLVRDO in case we need to use them for combat. That's why I was late. And if we need to mine anything..."

I nod understandingly, "Just try to make one session a day. The training is more to help you survive if you get shot down again or whatever the circumstance. But I'm glad you are occupying yourself with other activities especially productive ones. I'm going to turn in for the night. You should go get your stuff stored back in the armory and find some food."

"Thanks, Donna," he says.

As he turns, I decide to grab him and we briefly embrace. He lets out a huge breath of air. We break our hug and I say, "Despite the circumstances, I'm glad you're here. I know we haven't hung out much. Would you be interested in a drink in the Delta Lounge in an hour?"

"Yes," he says and turns and leaves...

(*Keller*)...We land softly on the deck of the hangar on the Constellation Destroyer Andromeda. It's smaller than either of ours; probably due to the fact that it only has transport shuttles and not a compliment of fighters. Yes, you heard that correctly, no fighter craft. Constellation Cutters are built to maintain peace and function independently. Destroyers provide heavy weapons support with their massive Rail Guns, missiles and heavy laser battery. The ship is designed to be a giant fighter craft.

We walk through the decks, much sleeker and newer than my ship. Design aesthetic seems to be given more precedence on naval ships. We step into a lift. Indeed, Cutters are built for operational periods of eighty or more years, whereas the Navy gets new toys every twenty. Or at the very least they get heavy refits.

But I wouldn't have it any other way.

Mattie interrupts my thoughts as we step out of the lift and into the bridge, "And this is the bridge."

Oh... never mind. I guess I wouldn't mind having one of these.

A soft, female computer voice announces, "Captain on the Bridge."

"Okay, I want that," I say.

I take it all in for a minute. For three years these Destroyers have been in service and I haven't had the chance to see one. The bridge is loaded with holo-screens in just about every corner. There is actually a low level magenta lighting throughout and yet I can see the outside clearly.

Mattie correctly guesses, "You're wondering how we see. Come on."

She walks up to one of the windows with me behind.

I look closely, "It's a screen…"

She nods, "Yep. Cameras placed along the top project the image in, but…" she trails off pressing some buttons. The screen retracts below revealing transparent armor and the stars beyond. It's almost a seamless transition.

"…we can switch to real view at any time," she finishes saying.

I say, impressed, "That's pretty nice. Would certainly make bridge watch more lively."

She walks over to her chair, which is actually placed in the center of the bridge. It sits much lower than mine. She offers me the chance to sit down and I do. It's large and thick.

She explains, "I can take control of any system here at any time. Fire control, helm, communications, you name it. I can either use the holo pad or a set of control sticks will pop out. I can set these holo-displays to whatever I want."

I say, enviously, "Yeah I more or less have that."

She says, "Sure, but they aren't hologram."

"Alright, enough bridge envy," I say, "you promised me Prime Rib."

"Is that all you came over here for," she asks.

"At the moment, yes," I say.

We head back to the lift and ride it down a couple of decks, but then it starts to move sideways.

Mattie smirks knowing full well I didn't see that coming. We get off and we're next to her office; also bigger than mine. We head towards it, but a man in Navy Uniform pants and Andromeda T-shirt walks up to us.

He greets, "Captain, welcome home. I heard you had gotten back."

Mattie introduces, "Lieutenant Captain Quinn, this is Commander Jaysen Keller of the Constellation Cutter Valkyrie."

"Welcome," he says, shaking my hand. Then he asks Mattie, "So what is the latest?"

She starts to speak, but I explain, "My Grav Specialists will probably be starting tests soon. Depending on how long they last, or what they need to check we could be looking at another day."

Mattie asks, "Did you make contact with Sixth Fleet?"

He nods, "Yes, they gave us their intended positions for the next three days."

I ask, "Did they ask us for our position?"

He shakes his head, "They didn't seem interested in anything about us. I don't think they knew we were at Lantic Station."

"Very well," Mattie says, "If you don't mind notifying Gruff, I'll take dinner for two in my room."

"Sure thing Captain. Enjoy your stay, Commander." he says and heads into his office which is across the passage way.

Mattie's office is similar to the size of mine and Sub Commander's front entrance. She has a large, transparent bulkhead that she can opaque at any time for privacy. We walk passed her unnecessarily large desk and into her cabin. She has a massive living space with a large table.

She heads into her full blown kitchen. Why she gets a full sized kitchen, I don't know.

I sit down in the large L couch and say, "I can see there's no shortage of wasted space."

Mattie laughs, "Well a lot of our components are smaller. But yes I do prefer the cozy comfort of your place over this one."

She comes back in with a glass full of wine and hands it to me.

She catches my off look, "What's wrong?"

I take a breath, "I thought we were gonna wait until my ship was repaired before contacting Sixth Fleet."

"Oh," she says, "Well I figured it would be a good chance to test the conspiracy theory about Command being compromised."

I nod, "Okay, but we were ruling out tracking technology first, weren't we?"

She says, "I ruled that out after about twelve hours. Especially since we had captured their ships. If they weren't coming after their fighters then does that not rule out them tracking you through Traverse Tunnels?"

I ponder for a second, "That does make sense."

A doorbell-like noise goes off.

"Come in," Mattie orders.

The cook, Gruff, I assume comes in, "Captain, good evening," he says hovering a cart into the room, "I present to you a medium cooked Prime Rib with horseradish and a side of garlic mashed potatoes and asparagus."

He sets the plates at two of the seats then says, "I would make a drink suggestion, but it seems you have it figured out. I have the dessert now if you would like, I can put it in your fridge."

"Please," Mattie says, "and I must say this looks fantastic as always."

"Enjoy," he says and bows respectfully and leaves.

The fragrance reaches my nose, "Yes, I'm looking forward to this."

I sit down to the plate, stab my fork into the glorious slab of pink meat and stop myself momentarily before cutting into it. The moment of truth: it cuts in smoothly. It's real.

I take my first bite, untainted with sauce. The meat rests in my mouth, the sensation one of the best I have felt in a long time. I chew slowly as if it were to make the moment last forever.

"Good?" Mattie breaks my thought.

I shake my head, "How do you guys have fresh meat like this? Are your patrol schedules cut short?"

Mattie laughs, "No, unfortunately. It's our new preservation unit. It creates a vacuum inside the food storage compartments. There are some more sophisticated components, but it's essentially creating a zero environment around the food."

I finish another bite, "Ours is basically a freezer still. We'll probably get an upgrade on our next refit."

We focus on consuming the rest of our dinner. Mattie talks about some of the other impressive features of her ship, but I am too concerned with the food to care. I can't think of the last time I actually had real red meat.

We retire to another couch facing a bulkhead. Mattie pushes a button and it retracts revealing another transparent bulkhead with open space on the outside.

"They gave you guys real windows?" I enviously ask.

She says unzipping her uniform jacket, "Yes. And if I forget to put it up it automatically closes if we set Battlestations."

She goes into her room for a bit and comes back out wearing only a shirt and panties. She sits down and cuddles up next to me. I look at her and find myself lost in her gaze momentarily. I almost forget that I'm not in our apartment on Ricotta Colony. It's almost as if we haven't left, except we don't have the glow of the city illuminating the room.

"So you never moved on?" She asks.

"I tried," I answer looking back in my glass, "but I guess the ship was enough." I sigh, "Part of me wonders what could have been... maybe what should have been."

"Should we both have found new careers?" she asks.

"Maybe I should have," I say, "but it is what it is."

There are questions I want to ask, but I fear the answers. I didn't exactly stay loyal to her even though I had no obligation, but I wish I had. And I know that thinking she did is wishful, but I don't want to contemplate or even think that. Right now, I want to be husband and wife for the rest of the night, if not the rest of our lives.

My COMM goes off. I pull it out of my pocket, "Keller," I say.

"**Commander,**" a female voice says, "**I'm patching in Sub-Commander Devlin from your ship.**" There's a beep, "Keller," I say again.

"**Jaysen,**" a male voice says, "**our tests were more successful than anticipated. The Traverse Drive is back online.**"

"Excellent news," I say, "Let's go ahead and have Rest Routine for the crew tomorrow. Especially since the Lantic port call was a literal bust."

"**I agree,**" he says, "**If there's nothing else, I'll see you back in the morning?**"

I look at Mattie, "If I'm not back by tomorrow evening, come after me. The ship is yours tonight, Mike. Keller out."

I set my COMM down and say, "Tests were successful. We can tunnel again."

"Rest Routine, huh?" She asks raising a brow.

I say, "The crew more than deserves it. And I have things to say to you that… I should have said long ago."

Mattie looks down at her glass and nods slowly, "I… was initially angry, but I am also wondering if parting ways was the right thing to do."

I say, "I wasn't faithful… and I wish I had been. I tried so hard to move on- to focus. And after everything that went down with Nate, I ultimately questioned our decision. But was it worth it to you?"

She looks up slowly at me and says shaking her head, "No… I wasn't faithful either, but I never stopped loving you. I wanted to resign my commission permanently, but I thought we were doing the right thing for what we both wanted. I mean, I regret the infidelity- I mean technically we weren't married, but still…"

"We were still married in here," I indicate tapping on my heart.

She nods in agreement, "But I still love my ship. Command is… it's something else. Especially when we go on detached duty. Hell you must know what that's like. I almost envy you for your freedom despite flying around in that dinosaur."

I chuckle, then set my wine glass down on the table next to the couch. I then grab her hands, look into her eyes and say, "I think we could make this work. I think we can remain loyal to our ships and each other."

"I would love that," she says smiling, "But I think we need to contemplate it before we recommit."

I nod, "I agree. This could just be heat of the moment… but…"

"But…" she says.

I slide over to Mattie and press her lips to mine. She pulls me in closer and everything becomes as it should be.

Chapter Sixteen: "Matilda, what are you doing!?!"

(*Keller*)"How long has it been?" I ask.

Lieutenant Esker replies, "Almost an hour, sir."

Damn. I don't understand what is taking so long. Mattie should have contacted me to come over to the Carrier by now. It only took us six hours to meet up with Sixth fleet, a fleet comprised of Constellation Carrier Pyxis, Constellation Destroyers Musca and Hydrus. These Destroyers are a different class. They have a larger, single rail gun on the front of the ship with their Traverse Drive modules on their Starboard side that kind of stick out similar to our Port and Starboard Modules, but with no hangars and no port modules. Their overall size is also smaller than us and Andromeda; we are similar in size.

Yes, the carrier group seems small, but that is because the fleet's Battleship is probably in a dock somewhere for maintenance. The other advantage of the Bayer Class Destroyer is that it has more missile launchers.

I ponder in my chair. This feels like it's taking too long, but there is nothing I can do. I have to trust in Mattie's ability to convince the Commodore.

Pulling out my COMM unit, I try to contact Slaighter. There's no response.

"Lieutenant Esker," I order, "Have ENGCOM contact me."

She nods in acknowledgement, "Aye Commander."

A crewman announces over the PA to have ENGCOM contact me directly. I used to think it was a silly rule that people couldn't call me directly anytime they wanted, but after a day I realized it was necessary. I am not some dog on a digital leash to be at everyone's beck and call and more often than not, the Sub-Commander's role is to funnel the nonsense. I do my best to take care of my crew, howe- my personal COMM goes off. It's ENGCOM.

"Keller," I say.

"**Yo,**" he replies and says nothing more.

I ask, "How is the installation coming?"

He says, "**I got about one more to tie into the power grid. Every plate of armor should be protected, but I won't know until we fire it up.**"

"Okay," I say, "I don't want to rush you, but we may need it sooner than expected."

"**I understand,**" he says and hangs up.

After a mostly successful test, I ordered him to begin fitting the entire ship with the shielding enhancement. My most paranoid fears seem to be coming true. I originally wanted it for our next Gerlak encounter. I mean I still do, it's just… I might be using this to defend against a foe I don't want to have.

But even with enhanced armor, I don't think we would last against three destroyers and a carrier. I might not have a choice, but to have come this far only to surrender.

"Any changes?" I ask.

Esker shakes her head, "Nothing, sir. Everything is quiet."

I would wait below, but there is no room for error. I've got split second decisions that need to be made. The question is, can I really ask my crew to go to the extremes necessary to expose the truth. I guess I will find out. The seeping anxiety sure as fuck isn't helping.

I trust Mattie. I've never had reason not to. I think she will come through.

Kaight informs, "Commander, the Captain's shuttle is leaving Pyxis."

"I see…" I acknowledge. Odd. She was supposed to contact me when it was time to head over. Sounds like the meeting didn't go well.

My COMM unit goes off, "Keller," I say.

Sub-Commander Devlin calling from the secondary bridge says, **"What's going on? I thought you were supposed to go over to Pyxis."**

"I don't know," I say, "She hasn't contacted me yet, but it sounds like the meeting didn't go well."

"What are your orders?" He asks.

"Stand by," I say.

No I can't exactly make a decision when I don't know everything that is going on. Maybe she's bringing the Commodore to her ship as a middle ground. Or maybe she's heading back to her ship to be in command while she takes us into custody. Or maybe something has changed. I won't know until she contacts me.

I watch on the digi-nocs out the back view port as her shuttle arrives at her ship. Behind her sits the carrier along with Hydrus, and Musca is off their Starboard Quarter while we sit in the traditional position as picket ship. Though I pulled ahead a little for… reasons.

None of the other ships are moving yet. So who knows what's happening. I would like to know as I'm getting a little antsy. Do I need to act? Do I need to get under way? Spin up the Traverse Drive? What am I-

"Valkyrie. This is Andromeda, come in," we all hear Captain Wrennor over the COMM on our ship to ship frequency.

I pull out my COMM and activate the channel on my device patching me in directly, "This is Valkyrie," I say.

"**Commander Keller**," she says almost robotically, "**you are asked to stand down and await while your ship is taken into custody. You have been acting as a rogue vessel, endangering potential and sensitive peace with an alien race purporting lies and accusations while aggressively killing them when they tried to take you in peacefully at the direction of the Prime Minister of the United Constellation Republic. Do you understand?**"

I... I can't answer. What am I supposed to say? Or do? I'm but one little ship against four well-armed battle cruisers. But if Mattie is the one taking us in after talking to the Commodore... "I understand," I disappointedly say, "Valkyrie stands by to receive your envoy."

Mattie says, "**I will be taking command of your ship upon arrival. Make sure your crew is ready to accept my flag.**"

"They will be," I say.

Yep. I'm giving up. At this point I'll have my day in court. Assuming I make it to court. Am I a coward? Now it's about my crew. They would more than likely follow me to hell even if there was no coming back, but I refuse to lead them there.

"I know," I say turning to face everyone on the bridge, "But if we don't have Andromeda, we don't stand a chance. I don't think I'll get the opportunity to speak again and this isn't where I want to say my good-byes, but life rarely ever gives us our preferred opportunities. It has been my distinct honor to serve. But more importantly, do not forget to spread the truth. What you saw and experienced at Keldon, at Thretta, at Melyar and at Lantic Station cannot go untold. We know what these Gerlak really are. Now it's up to you to-"

I'm interrupted by Captain Wrennor speaking over the COMM, "**This is Andromeda, our port thruster is malfunctioning.**"

I walk back to the viewport I had set up and zoom it out. Andromeda starts to drift to the right slowly. They start to slow down as soon as they are facing Musca and open fire with their port rail gun, striking Musca in the center almost instantly splitting her in half.

"Battlestations." I order.

The alarm goes off.

Lieutenant Esker reports, "Most all stations are set. ENGCOM reports he's ready to activate the enhanced armor on your-"

"Do it," I interrupt. I order, "Helm, swing us around. Main and Dorsal guns stand by to fire."

"Aye, Commander" some Crewman and Officers say.

Over the external COMM we hear an angry male voice, "**Matilda, what the fuck are you doing!?**"

Mattie says, "**I don't know who you are, but you are NOT the Commodore Aiden that I knew. Jaysen, get the hell out of here. You were right: high levels of Constellation Command have been compromised. I don't know to what extent, but you need to survive.**"

I reply, "We can take them. I've got my armor enhancements online-"

There's a large, bright explosion. By the time my sight recovers, I see Andromeda drifting down. Looks like Hydrus landed a shot on her starboard railgun battery completely destroying it.

"**Get out of here, Jaysen!**" I hear Mattie struggling to say, "**The information you have... is too valuable to lose here!**"

"We're not-" I notice Hydrus fire off a projec- *BAM!* I'm knocked off balance as we take a hit. I regain and look around, "Damage!?" I frantically ask. Seeing what happened to Musca, I can only imagine how bad we've been hit, but I can't see anything from the bridge.

"DAMAGE REPORT!?" I ask more aggressively.

Crewman Nedre stutters an answer, "Uh, I… none reported so far…"

I look around the window and happen to see a mostly squished up projectile floating above the bridge, "Holy shit…" I express, "the enhanced armor held!"

I catch another mild flash out of the corner of my- *BAM!* we're hit again and knocked a little shifting us back and tilting us.

"Return fire!" I order, "Take out their main gun!"

Lieutenant Esker skips to carrying out my orders. The Main and Dorsal guns fire six rounds each along the main shaft and taking out the four compartments holding the projectiles. As the compartments crack open, large, bullet shaped objects spill out and into space.

"I'm detecting missile lock on!" A crewman shouts.

Esker orders, "All laser batteries, defensive stance, prepare for incoming projectiles! Main and Dorsal guns, prepare additional salvo targeting missile launchers."

"Negative!" I order, "We'll get behind them and take out their engines!"

ENGCOM stumbles on the bridge, "Commander! I got the enhanced armor working as you saw, but the engines are exposed at the exhaust ports. I couldn't protect them without shutting off the engines."

"Missiles incoming!" a Crewman shouts.

I watch out the starboard side as an array of missiles approaches the ship but all except two are stopped. The other two make impact with barely any noticeable effect.

I ask, "How long can the enhancements hold?"

ENGCOM shrugs, "I got the generators recording data, but I won't be able to make sense of it. We just did the initial tests with lasers. I don't know how they will hold-"

We're interrupted by Mattie yelling over the COMM, "**What are you waiting for Jaysen!? You disabled Hydrus's main cannon now get out of here!**"

I look out the viewport again and see Andromeda has maneuvered closer to the Carrier.

I pull up my personal COMM and connect it, "Mattie, what are you doing?"

"**Buying you time, Jay,**" she says, "**don't let it be in vain...**"

Andromeda's engines explode propelling her ship into the Carrier. There's a massive explosion followed by me irrationally yelling, "Mattie!!! MATTIE!!!!"

I'm stunned. I don't know what I'm supposed to do. She just... how could she? We start pulling away.

"Helm, what are you doing!?" I aggressively ask.

Helm starts to answer, but Kaight steps in, "All due respect sir, she did say we needed to run..."

I'm quiet for a second. I don't know what to say except, "Bring the Traverse Drive online."

"Already did," she says.

I nod, "Good job..." and look back out the aft as we start to turn away. Hydrus breaks off its attack and proceeds towards Carrier Pyxis and whatever is left of Andromeda.

The Navigator shouts, "We got fighters on the incoming!"

Sure enough a fighter squadron is fast approaching, probably going to enact vengeance for what my ex-wife just did to their home.

"Disabling fire only," I order.

They may be our adversary, but I don't want to kill any more humans than I already have. This already has turned reckless enough.

Delta Crewman Bostwik announces, "Singularity stabilized!"

"Take us in!" I order.

We rattle off a few lasers before we get pulled into the tunnel. Before the entrance closes, half of the fighters get through. Thankfully, all they can do is sit there for the ride.

I walk over to the Navigator, "Where are we going?" I ask.

Crewman Destun answers, "I just plotted a one hour trip into dead space. Seems to be our safest location."

I nod in approval, "Good." I walk over to the Crater and ask Lieutenant Ephrryn, "Are the fighters still ready for launch?"

He nods, "Yes, Commander."

I order, "Once we resurface, tell them to launch. Let them know they will be disabling Naval Fighters."

"Uh," he hesitates, "Aye Commander."

I walk back towards my chair, turn and face everyone.

I pull out my personal COMM, "Standby, going to address the crew," I push a button and activate the ship's PA system, "Good afternoon, Valkyrie Crewmates, this is the Commander… as most of you know, our meeting with

Sixth Fleet went about as badly as I could have expected, but was not prepared for… we'll have the sensor data compiled for those who want to review it, but we fired in self-defense. Captain Wrennor was supposed to convince Commodore Aiden, a Flag Officer, that we needed to enact Directive Seventeen to expose the truth about the Gerlak… I'm sure some of you read on the Free Net that no one but ourselves knows of their existence.

"Captain Wrennor chose to fire on the Navy after being ordered to take us into custody. She felt that Sixth Fleet was compromised and under the influence of those who seem to want us dead… yes… I believe there is a conspiracy and that our existence is thwarting whoever is trying to keep the Gerlak a secret. I don't want to speculate any further than I already have, but I have to ask you to trust me more than you have before.

"When we resurface, we will be engaging Naval fighters that followed us in. I intend to disable them and bring them aboard to explain our side of things. The more people we can bring to our cause, the better chance we'll have of getting justice for Keldon and our fallen Crewmates. Keep up the valiant work, everyone. Keller out."

Almost as if on cue, my COMM goes off, "Keller," I say.

"Jaysen it's Mike," Sub-Commander says, "so we're just telling them everything now?"

I point out, "We fired on a Naval vessel. Granted it was in self-defense, but that doesn't explain what led to us doing so. I need the Crew's trust and support, not just blind loyalty. Which reminds, are you still with me?"

He replies, "Oh absolutely. I just… I'm still trying to make sense of what just happened."

I explain, "Mattie thought she could convince Aiden, but insisted she spoke to him alone. Now I think that might have been a mistake."

"I disagree," he says, "He probably would have arrested you there. Then who knows what would have happened."

"Fuck..." I express taking a large sigh, "we should have planned for this. Instead she just..."

"She did what she had to," Mike says, "would you have done differently?"

I'm quiet for a moment. Then I say, "No. But that doesn't make losing her any easier."

"Do you need me to take command?" he offers.

I consider it momentarily, but, "No. I need to be strong for the crew. I can mourn later. Let's just get these Navy boys aboard safely."

"Alright," he acknowledges, "I'll alert Delta Larrodo to get his team together."

"Thank you," I say and close the line.

I hop in my chair and pull up the tray which has a couple of buttons. I hit one that lowers a screen above me and pull it down the rest of the way to eye level. A holographic keyboard illuminates on the surface of the attached tray.

I pull up the sensor data from our three sixty camera mounted on the top of the bridge. The quality of video is okay. It's meant for analyzing occurrences close to the ship. I plug in the desired time index and lock the playback on Andromeda smashing into Pyxis. What am I hoping to find here? Could she have survived? No. I'm being overly hopeful.

As expected, when I try to zoom in it's heavily pixelated. I can see the explosion and chunks of the two ships. I look at the footage from the cannons. Some of it is a little better. I guess I have to rebuild what happened with the holo system.

After about thirty minutes, the data is compiled. The imagery is projected from the screen just above my tray. I play the footage. Based off what the RADAR, SONAR and everything else recorded, Andromeda did break into many pieces. One of them, the bridge looked to remain intact.

"Maybe..." I whisper to myself. But then I realize even if she is alive she'll be executed. She might not even make it to trial.

Kaight breaks my thoughts, "Commander, ENGCOM is requesting to speak with you."

I nod and pull out my personal COMM. She connects the transmission.

"Go ahead, Jeff," I say.

"I think you might want to come down and look at this," he says.

"Indeed, I might," I say, "but can you give me more reason to leave the bridge?"

He explains, "Well, the enhancements did help prevent any major damage, but... the places where the large projectiles impacted, I mean I'm looking at one of them and the hull has depressed."

I, concerned, "How bad?"

"It's basically a giant dent," he says, "I'm not seeing any stress or strain, but if I had to guess, were we to get hit by larger projectiles in one spot enough times, it would breach."

I point out, "At least it stops one hit. Can you repair it?"

"I'll look into it and let you know. Bye." And he closes the line.

Okay, then.

Lieutenant Esker informs, "We're thirty seconds from resurfacing."

I nod and order, "Battlestations."

Again the alarm goes off, but we didn't really stand down so not much changes. However if we remain at BS for more than thirty minutes and nothing is happening, typically station leaders will allow the crew breaks from their station. The Crew is also authorized to relax to Alert Status without being prompted when we're in a tunnel.

Lieutenant Esker informs that all stations report battle ready.

Helm announces, "Resurfacing in, five... four... three... two..."

He's sort of interrupted by us taking one large gravimetric roll as we "drop" into normal space, successfully resurfacing.

"One," he finishes.

I order, "Swing around, stand by laser batteries. Launch fighters."

My order is acknowledged as I pull out my Personal COMM and connect to the HAD frequency. The Naval Fighters resurface and assume an attack formation with one of them in the lead and the other four on its four corners.

I speak into my COMM, "Navy pilots, this is Commander Keller of Valkyrie. Stand down, come aboard peacefully and let's discuss this unfortunate predicament we're in."

The lead ship, a female replies, "**By the authority of Commodore Aiden of Sixth Fleet, I order you to stand down, Keller. We will escort your ship back to the remains of Sixth Fleet where you will be properly relieved and face justice for your crimes.**"

A crewman reports, "Commander, they're hot and locked!"

"Alright the hard way it is," I say into the COMM and then close the line. I look at Kaight, "Disabling fire."

Maybe one or two missiles from the fighters gets launched before we light them up with EMP laser blasts. The CMROs follow up with one EMP projectile each for good measure. Adrift, the CMROs take them into tow and bring them to the starboard hangar.

I walk into the Crater and ask, "Did any kind of transmissions or transponder signals go out?"

Lieutenant Ephrryn informs, "My guys didn't report anything. We'll double check."

I acknowledgingly nod and head out of the Crater. As I leave, "Lieutenant Esker, stand down to Cruise Condition. Have Sub-Commander meet me in the Starboard Hangar, the bridge is yours."

"Aye, Commander," she acknowledges as I head into the ladder-stairs.

I step off the lift and into the catwalk heading back to the tower control room. I enter and a young male voice announces but also cracks, "Commander on de-eck!"

Oh hell it's the young nervous guy, "Carry on," I say.

"Aye, Commander," he says aloud.

Oh lordy. Anyway, I walk up to Delta Larrodo and Sergeant Kroeling, "Are you guys ready?"

They both nod.

I remind, "Remember, these guys are humans. We're trying to win them over. Hopefully they won't be too aggressive, but let's try to-" Sub-Commander enters and the nervous young crewman starts to say, "Sub-Comman-" I interrupt, "Shut up!"

"Ay- uh. Um." He mutters and turns back to his post.

I continue, "Let's try to make them feel welcome. If they try to do anything stupid then we'll stun and bind them. But I don't want them to feel like prisoners unless we have to. Is that clear?"

"Yes Commander," they both quietly acknowledge.

We watch as the last fighter is towed in and in a coordinated effort, the gravity is slowly brought back on resting all ships on the deck simultaneously. The hangar begins to recompress and the security detail heads to the lift to prepare to greet our new guests.

I take a breath and walk over to the Crewman and ask, "How long have you been in service?"

He answers, "Uh- I- uh bout six months."

"Okay," I say, "and did you forget that once you announce the most senior officer on deck you don't announce anyone else?"

"I um, yeah uh," he fumbles cringily, "it's just I'm, I guess I thought-"

"Alright, deep breath," I interrupt, "I'm sorry to have snapped, but you need to relax. You seem more intimidated than you were the last time we interacted. Why?"

He tries to answer, "I- um I guess I was just shaken up at Lantic Station. I don't know sir, this whole situation, just... I'm scared."

I nod, "I understand. These are scary times. But you're doing a good job and I need you to keep it up if not better. Focus less on formalities like announcing officers and more on just doing the best job you can at what you're assigned, alright?"

"Aye, Commander," he says.

I order, "Now put Larrodo's feed up on the screen so I can watch."

He softly smiles and nods and does as I ask.

The screen buzzes on and Larrodo is standing next to one of the fighters, having two of his men activate the manual release.

The cockpit opens and the pilot with hands raised says, "I surrender, I surrender, I'm unarmed!"

Larrodo orders, "Okay. Welcome to Constellation Cutter Valkyrie, just step out nice and slowly. One of my guys is going to make sure you're serious. Then come stand over here."

Sub-Commander says, "Taking your orders a little literally, eh."

"Yep," I say.

One of Larrodo's men, Dayson I think, says, "Delta! One of the others is opening."

Larrodo orders, "Sergeant, if you don't mind."

All the pilots get out mostly without issue except for the leader who is incredibly obstinate. I order Sub-Commander to go down and meet them and have them escorted to the Officer's Mess.

In the Officer's Mess I have some refreshments laid out, along with some pads detailing our reports. On the screen behind me I have some video files ready for viewing. Sub-Commander enters followed by the lead female pilot.

I stand up and extend my hand, "Welcome aboard. I'm Commander Jaysen Keller. I know this isn't an ideal situation, but I'm gonna ask for your patience."

"Cut the crap, Keller," she says, "you were relieved. If anything, Sub-Commander is the only authority I should recognize in this room, but even then your vessel is technically a pirate ship. I should just assume Command."

Mike steps in, "I can assure you that this crew, myself included, will sooner toss you out an airlock. This is a fucked situation all around, but you can either make it harder for yourself or you can sit down and be exposed to the truth."

"Whatever treason you have planned, we want no part in it," she says, "just go ahead and lock us up or kill us, whichever is more convenient for you."

One of the male pilots steps up, "Um, she doesn't speak for me."

The other three pilots share similar sentiment.

"Are you fucking kidding me?" she expresses, "Traitors, the lot of you!"

"Go fuck yourself," the other polits say in almost perfect unison.

"We've arranged special quarters for you to do just that," Mike's patience is worn, "Delta Larrodo, take her to confinement."

"Gladly," Larrodo half smiles.

I wait a few seconds, then address the more rational pilots, "Well, maybe she'll change her mind. Please, have a seat. In front of you are reports and accounts of what this ship has seen and experienced since the attack on Keldon colony a few weeks ago."

"What attack?" a different female pilot asks, "We were just told communications with the colony were lost."

"Well, Lieutenant…"

"Henan. Julie Henan, sir," she says.

"Well Lieutenant Henan," I begin, "there is a lot we have to discuss."

Sub-Commander and I trade off giving a breakdown of all the events we have experienced. It's exhausting. Especially when thoughts of lost crew come to mind. Fortunately no one seems to be questioning the authenticity of our info and video files which means we might have them on our side. But only by the time we reach the end will we know for sure.

By the end, everyone is still understandably a tad skeptical, but also intrigued.

"It's… a lot to take in, sir," one of the male pilots, Lieutenant Gibb expresses, "But… it's impossible to deny what you have presented. I don't want to believe it and yet…"

Sub-Commander says, "Believe us, we don't either. Yet here we are."

Lieutenant Henan asks, "Well what do you need from us?"

I explain, "I need you to convince your squad leader."

"She's not our squad leader," Gibb clarifies, "she was just the ranking pilot of our wing. We actually were told to fall back, but she pressed on and the rest of us followed. We couldn't just let her face you alone. Though maybe we should have…"

"I understand," I say, "never the less, we need all the help we can get. At this point, we are one ship against everyone else. Until we can figure out how to take our case before the Council of Nobles and enact Directive Seventeen, we need to know who we can trust. Right now, that starts with you. As outsiders, you could potentially help to influence others. Starting with Lieutenant Figg."

Everyone is quiet. Then Lieutenant Henan says, "It's a lot to think about, sir. We'll need to look over these files you've presented and go from there."

"I understand," I say, "we've prepared a room for you if you would like to get more settled in. We'll meet after evening chow and see if you all have made a decision." I look over at a Crewman who was selected to help the pilots to their quarters, "If you please."

She introduces herself and leads the pilots out of the Officer's Mess and to their quarters leaving Sub-Commander and I on our own.

Mike says, "Here we are once again."

"Square fuckin one," I note. "I don't know what to do at this point, Mike. We can't just fly to the capital; at least not without some more support. And for that we need more proof about higher levels of Command and the Republic being compromised."

Mike nods, "Yeah..." he ponders for a bit and then proposes, "What about the civilians and the Sergeant? How can they help us in this situation?"

"I don't really know," I say.

We try to come up with a solution: a plan on what to do next. "I could use some tea," I say, "But we didn't get nearly as much fresh water as I had hoped."

Sub-Commander nods in agreement and heads to a picture mounted on the inner facing bulkhead. He swings it open and behind it is a safe. He opens it and pulls out a bottle of Rare Amberglash Select.

"So the legend is true," I say.

He nods and pulls out two glasses, "Absolutely. But I don't feel like going up to our rooms and I think you need the good shit. And it beats drinking poop."

He hands me a glass and I take a sip. I usually like it on the rocks, but this blend is so smooth it doesn't need any ice.

"Perfect," I say, "how much did this run you?"

"I got a two for one special," he answers, "cousin of mine has some connections. Hooks me up with family discount during the holidays."

I half smile, "I'll be sure to send him a thank you card…"

We don't exchange much else between each other. We're trying to figure out our next move, waiting for the alcohol to slow our thoughts just enough. At least for me to stop thinking about Mattie, Crewman Belkrest- unfortunately I think the alcohol is forcing me to feel more.

"I've got it," Sub-Commander says slapping the table, "the civilians are dead. Or rather the Republic thinks they are dead, right? At Keldon?"

I nod slowly, "Yes… I guess that would be the case. Well until their accounts were tapped into at Lantic."

"Maybe," he says, "but we don't know for sure. I mean this whole galaxy, that station full of people, and you really think that they were specifically looking for two miners and a reserve Sergeant?"

"Yeah actually I do," I say, "but where are you going with this?"

He sits up, "What if we boarded a freighter? Came up with some bullshit infractions and seized the vessel, put a crew on it and took it to Earth to infiltrate Command Headquarters. We could find more evidence and then proceed with Directive Seventeen- hell maybe even bump to Directive Zulu Lima"

I nod, "It's a start, but how do we get into aitch que without flashing credentials? We'd practically have to break in. And while we might be able to slip in with the freighter, we can't get much further than that."

"Hmm…" Sub-Commander ponders, "What if I knew some people that could get in? I've got an old buddy who got out after eight years to keep a desk job as a civilian at aitch que."

"How high is his clearance?" I ask.

He explains, "I think high enough to find what we need. The question is, how do we make contact?"

"Directly," I say, "I think you should lead this team. Take the Sergeant and the miners to make it look convincing enough to get you to Earth. Contact your friend and see if he-"

"She," he corrects.

"If she can get you inside and on the Galnet," I say, "we'll wait for you to return and go from there."

"But first thing is first," he notes, "how do we find a mining vessel?"

I nod and contact the bridge using my personal COMM. I order Kaight to locate Mr. McNill and have him and the other civilian to meet in the Officer's Mess.

It only takes about fifteen minutes before Nate and his friend walk in.

"Would you like a drink?" I offer.

"Please," the other civilian says eagerly.

Nate nods. Sub-Commander gets up and pours them both a glass.

"Please, sit," I say, "we've got a lot to plan."

Nate begrudgingly expresses, "Are we mining something?"

I explain, "Not exactly. We need to commandeer a mining vessel. Nate, you're no stranger to conspiracy. We have reason to believe that high levels of government are working with the Gerlak. To what purpose exactly, we don't know. That's what we intend to find out. In order to do that we need to infiltrate Command aitch que. And in order to do that we need a vessel that can get us to Earth inconspicuously. That's where you both come in. We need to locate a mining vessel, board it and seize it for infractions."

Nate asks, "Are you planning to escort it to Earth?"

I answer, "No, Valkyrie must remain as far away from Sol as possible."

"I see," he says, "then we'll have to find one with a Traverse Drive... which is rare. Only freelance Captains use them because they're expensive."

"Freelance Captains?" Sub-Commander asks, "I thought all ships were registered through the guild."

The other civilian explains, "Well they are, but they pay a discounted fee since they don't use transport ships. They're also responsible for their own maintenance and don't have a vote in the Guild Union."

Sub-Commander inquires further, "Then what exactly are they paying for?"

"Mining and trading in Republic Space," Nate says, "The advantage is they can go wherever they want whenever they want and aren't limited to transport routes and running out to places at sub-light."

"How do we find one," I say asserting the conversation back on topic.

Nate takes a breath, "That is going to be tricky. We'll need to look at charts to figure out where one might be operating. It may require multiple trips on the Traverse Drive."

I nod, "That's fine. Once we have it, we'll need both of you on the crew to infiltrate aitch que and get Sub-Commander to Earth and back."

Nate agrees, "Okay. I would also like Crewman Kamerov on board as well. He's proven himself an effective combat pilot and if something goes wrong, I would like him at the wheel."

"Done," I say, "we'll figure out the specifics once we have the freighter under our control. I'll meet you on the bridge in ten minutes. Dismissed."

Nate nods and he and the other civilian leave.

I turn to Sub-Commander, "This is a long shot... unfortunately until a better plan comes up, it seems this is our only option."

Sub-Commander points out, "I mean, we could also surrender."

I shake my head, "Mattie gave her life for this. We have to figure out a different way. I wouldn't put it past the Prime Minister to order the Navy to destroy us on sight at this point."

"You think she's directly involved?" Sub-Commander asks.

I nod largely, "Peace envoys got me thinking that this is something she is trying to work towards her favor. The only problem is we jeopardize that with what we know. Do you think that people would be on board with a peace treaty if they saw what we have seen and experienced?"

Sub-Commander supposes, "Would it not be the preferred outcome?"

I take a breath, "Not without some form of recompense. Especially from those who have families on those colonies. But this speculation is nothing without more proof. Let's get some coffee and find us a freighter to steal."

"I don't know about you," he says, "but I'd rather mix it with whiskey… I'm not ready to stomach re-meds."

I nod, "Same."

Chapter Seventeen: "I got some T.E.A. you can put on in the back"

(*Nathan*)"Anything?" Keller asks.

Shaking my head for the sixth time I say, "No, sir."

Keller expresses his irritation with a loud grunt that half sounds like a mashup of two swears. Then he says, "We've been at this for twelve hours... let me know when the core is cooled off and we can get moving again."

A female Lieutenant, Esker I think, acknowledges his order and takes the bridge. I begin to pull up charts to plan our next tunnel.

She walks up to me, "Okay, what are we missing here?"

I shrug, "I'm literally guessing right now. Without ship positional data, we can't just find where a vessel is located. And we can only get that if we connect to the Gal-Net."

"Is any of that information available on the free net?" she asks.

I answer, "Probably. But I'm pretty sure we're out of range of any free net hub."

"I'm going to look into it," she says, "good luck on your next choice."

I begin looking for other places that were marked rich for minerals. I've checked areas with moons, asteroid fields, baron worlds- I look out the viewport at the planet in front of us. It has no atmosphere, but potentially has precious metals under the surface. A ship COULD be on the surface.

The Lieutenant comes back, most likely to see what our next course will be.

As she starts to open her mouth, I ask, "Can we drop to a lower orbit and conduct a more aggressive scan?"

She answers, "I don't see why not... but at closer range it will take longer to scan the entire surface. What are you thinking?"

"A ship might be down there," I say, "some mining vessels are configured for mining a planet's surface, especially freelance vessels. Only thing is they might be in a cavern or something. The further down you go in a planet, the more valuable the mineral finds... typically."

She says, "Okay, but that could take hours depending on how low we drop, though we could launch ships to scan different areas of the surface."

"I was thinking the same thing," I say nodding, "I think if we had six ships search along with the Cutter we should find a vessel or wrap up by the time we're ready to tunnel again."

"What about the other planets in the system?" the Lieutenant asks.

I answer shaking my head, "Nothing of value. Just a couple of gas giants. No moons in orbit of either."

"Okay..." she acknowledges, "I'll call the Commander."

I nod and resume cycling for a system. There's a chance she might take credit for the idea. Not that it matters to me. I will never wear a uniform again. I'll only have so many chances to get back at the Gerlak before I'll be removed from this ship and then forced back into mining.

Of course, I could look into joining a mercenary group. I'm sure once war officially starts the Republic will use whoever wants to fight. Hell maybe I'll join the Marines like Donna- wait... no. Well, maybe...

I finish plotting the next course and the Lieutenant walks up to me, "The Commander has signed off on your plan. He wants a brief in the next ten minutes in the briefing room."

I nod, "Aye, Lieutenant," and begin prepping.

I download the planet info onto a pad and take it down a couple of decks to set up for the briefing. Some of the CMRO pilots start to trickle in; a few holding coffee mugs. Everyone else comes in as I finish and get ready to present.

We wait a couple minutes and then Keller walks in, "Attention on deck," I announce.

As everyone starts to stand up, Keller mutters, "Carry on."

I look out at everyone and begin, "Commander Keller, Crewmates, welcome. Um... pretty straightforward brief. We'll just be," I being manipulating the holo image projected out to every one present of the planet, "conducting a quick recon of the planet. Basically we're just looking for an energy signature that indicates the presence of a mining vessel. Examples include signatures like this that your instruments will dispaly if one is detected. The Cutter will take a high orbit and search the north pole and the rest of us will search down from that and go closer to the planet's surface.

This planet has pretty much no atmosphere, I suspect that if there is a ship on the surface it will probably be hidden in a large cavern, so we'll be set to full invasive scanning."

One of the pilots raises their hand, "Won't that alert them we're here?"

"Most likely," I say, "but remember we're not chasing criminals. And we'll be able to catch them before they leave the system if they decide to get underway. If there are no other questions I think this pretty much explains it."

Keller stands up and faces the group, "If you find the ship, let everyone know and return to Valkyrie. We'll send in a boarding team to take the ship. Good hunting."

Everyone gets up and starts leaving.

I head out and catch up to Lede Kamerov, "Hey, man," I say, "I figured I'd ride with you."

"Alright," he says and we keep going.

We don't say much on the way to the hangar. We go through the standard procedures, ask permission to leave and get underway, heading towards the South Pole region, our assigned search area.

It's continually quiet except for the hum of the engines and the equipment.

"So, uh…" I begin, "how have you been dealing with the whole Dev thing?"

He's quiet a second before responding, "As I can, I guess. You?"

I say, "Just focusing on making it to vengeance, I suppose."

"I know what you mean," he says, "oh and I think I've got the new training program ready. It's not a hundred percent accurate to Gerlak flight patterns- at least compensating for changes, but I think it will work."

"So it still managed to integrate the adaptive learning program while still maintaining close to a hundred percent consistency?" I verify.

Lede chuckles, "I'd say it came out to seventy percent which should be good enough. Unfortunately no one on board is a game designer and I only took basic coding so I can only fine tune the code so much."

"I'll check it out after our next tunnel," I say.

There's an awkward pause. I guess Dev is a sore subject with him.

"You know, I've been wondering," I begin, "With all your knowledge of training programs and SLVRDO piloting, how come you're not a Mark Three Crewman yet?"

Lede is quiet for a moment again. He lets out a mostly noticeable groan, "Well... I guess you weren't in long enough to learn the truth about this organization, though I would think you of all people would know."

"Know what?" I inquire.

He explains, "That people aren't promoted based on skill and merit, but it's mostly political. If someone doesn't like you for whatever reason, you're not advancing."

"That's unethical," I point out.

"Yep," he acknowledges, "Coming into orbit and beginning descent."

"Bringing RADAR, SONAR sound and energy detectors online," I say. Then I continue, "So, hold on, you're saying you've been held back because a supervisor didn't like you?"

"Supervisors," he corrects, "and some of it is my own lack of trying I suppose, but it's hard to want to try when no one wants to give you a chance. I inherited the jobs I have now out of necessity of other crew members transferring."

I say, "Okay, but why did you let a few shitty supervisors slow you down?"

He explains, "Nate, I've been doing this shit for almost ten years. I'm not sure if I'm even going to stay in- but my point is if this organization was based on skill and experience, I would have been a Mark Three by now and probably pinning on Delta sometime this year at which point I would be the one choosing who gets screwed over."

"Then why do you keep doing this?" I ask.

"Money, I guess," he says, "hell, sometimes I don't even know. Look, man I like you and all, but do you mind if we just get this done for now?"

"I understand," I say.

I focus on my screens indicating what my instruments are finding. This whole planet is less exciting than a graveyard. But I get it. He's got grudges against his past much like I do. Maybe that's why we work well together. Or maybe we're just the two losers on the ship who have no one else, especially since the one girl who would hang out with us is dead.

Fuck do I miss her. And I'm sure Lede does too. Coffee just hasn't been the same in the mornings and probably won't be again. Granted, it's made of shit, but still, it seems I made myself so busy that I forgot to give myself time to sit and think and now here I am. I haven't let myself feel. But I don't want to feel this way right now, or ever. So I'll just focus on my sensors and hopefully locate a mining vessel.

Lede lets out an audible sigh, "Man… I'm really not doing well with Dev's passing…"

"Yeah me neither," I say, "but I'd rather not discuss it if it's all the same."

"You sure there was nothing to be done for her?" he asks.

I irritably sigh, "As I've said: she was shot in the face. The energy bolt probably fried her brain. I checked her pulse. She was gone."

"Man… I can't imagine," he expresses.

"Haunts me in my sleep," I say, "and in my awake-again, I really don't want to talk about this now."

"Well I mean you have to at some point, don't you?" he asks.

I contemplate, "I guess, but probably to a professional."

"Well it's not like we have a counselor on board," he points out, "and unfortunately, Dev isn't the first person I gave a shit about to die on me. You can try to distract yourself with work, but it only lasts so long. I prefer to drum at the sound of my own beat, too, so if you don't want to talk to me, fine. But you need to talk to someone soon."

"I'll get around to it," I say, "We're over halfway through our search. Still nothing."

"I mean do you really think something is here?" he asks.

We hear a muffled transmission, but I barely make out "Miner Two" which is us.

"Take us up," I say, "sounds like someone is trying to reach us."

Lede nods and tilts the ship upward to increase our altitude.

I pick up the handset and say, "Unit calling, this is Miner Two."

"**Miner Two, this is VAL-CON,**" a voice says, "**We've located an energy signature that indicates the presence of a mining vessel. We're recalling all our ships and putting together a team to board it.**"

I say into the mic, "Uh, did we confirm it is a mining vessel?"

They respond, "**Commander wants to confirm by sending the boarding team to investigate instead of risk** scaring them off. Get back to us as soon as you can, we're entering high orbit in the Northwest hemisphere."

"Understand all," I say and put the mic down.

Lede turns the ship towards the direction of where Valkyrie might be.

He then mutters, "Welp this was fun. Guess it's back to waiting around."

I remark, "Uh, you do know you're coming with us, right?"

He retorts, "Not until after the initial boarding. Unless they want to take our ship, that's the most participation I do in boardings."

"Yeah, I'll probably have to wait too," I suppose.

We don't say much else. We locate Valkryie and upon landing, Sergeant Kroeling and Delta Larrodo embark our ship from the back.

Donna immediately comes into the cockpit and informs, "You guys are taking us over there. Nate, you're going to be conducting the boarding with us since you'll know what to look for."

"Look for?" I confusingly advise, "Just make some discrepancies up."

Donna says, "Apparently you're better suited to do that."

"The boarding teams know what to look for," I point out.

Donna says, "Yes, they know problems when they see them. You know what to make into a problem. That's the difference. I got some T.E.A. you can put on in the back."

I shrug my head, slide the center console forward and head into the back of the ship. One of the Crewman, Putvel has the armor suit in the box. I turn around, undo my pants and start suiting the T.E.A. over my legs. The metal bonds uncomfortably tight to them.

As I get ready to pull it over my underwear, Putvel holds out a cup. I grab it, place it as comfortably as possible and resume pulling up the rest of the armor.

Putvel notes, "It's not a flight suit. You need to remove your shirt."

I nod, quickly remove it and finish pulling the armor over the rest of me. It bonds. Constricting in tightly.

"You get used to it," Putvel says and I head back into the cockpit clanking loudly on the deck as I walk.

I take my seat and Lede snorts amusingly. I feel more naked wearing this thing than if I were actually bare. But I've seen the protection these things provide, and the universal fit was no exaggeration. It's a bummer I'll never get to try one of these in battle.

We get permission to take off and head towards the location from which the energy signature was picked up.

Donna gives me a quick debrief, "Delta Larrodo is taking the lead on this since he knows the procedures for initiating a boarding. You and I will be working together to "find" discrepancies. Since I am unfamiliar with Armada boardings and you're just making things up, I think we'll work fine."

I nod acknowledgingly, "I get that everyone thinks I'm some kind of mining genius, but we should have brought Tim along. I really don't know much more than these guys for discrepancies."

"Whatever," Donna says, "You'll do fine."

Lede informs, "We're coming up on the position of the energy signature. I'm not picking up anything yet."

I start looking at the terrain data from the radar and 3D project it in front of me. I zoom around it and come across a large, unmapped opening.

"There," I say, "Proceed there. I think they may have shut down completely."

"Why?' Lede asks.

I postulatingly explain, "On the Ex Del Seven, we were trained to hide in the event of pirates. Considering we scanned for them and now we can't find them, they may be hiding thinking we're pirates."

Larrodo asks, "What if they left?"

I shake my head, "No we definitely would have seen them." I think for a second and then grab the handset, "Mining vessel, this is the Constellation Cutter Valkyrie boarding craft. We know you're in the area. Come out and if you have weapons, power them down."

I look at Lede and shrug, "I mean it's worth a shot."

Then we get a response on the COMM, "**Armada boarding vessel... we detected several of your signatures. Is that a new scanning procedure? You seemed intent to find us...**"

I hesitate for a second, then fumble out, "Uh, we were specifically looking for you. Our records indicate you haven't been boarded in a while."

"**I was boarded two months ago,**" the ship answers back, "**Do you even know who you're talking to?**"

Well he's got us there. I answer, "We're coming in. Please have your weapons powered down and prepare for boarding."

"**You come in here, and we will open fire,**" they reply sharply.

I answer with a little anger behind my tone, "Excuse me? I strongly advise against that."

"**What's my ship's designation?**" They ask.

I can't answer that not having their info in front of me. I look at Lede trying to figure out what to do next.

Larrodo points out, "We can use that to our advantage. If they shoot at us, we can seize their vessel with no issues."

Donna snaps, "Getting shot at sounds like an issue, Larrodo. Nate, can we just wait them out?"

I ponder Donna's question a bit, "I mean… we could be here for days depending on how long they intend to mine."

We look dumbfoundedly at each other figuring out what to do next.

Then we hear over the COMM, "**Mining vessel this is Commander Keller of the Constellation Cutter Valkyrie, registry number see dash see you two two one nine. My boarding vessel is going to approach your ship in the cavern. If you fire upon them, they will retreat back and I will send my fighter craft in to disable your weapons. Then I will send four boarding ships to seize your vessel, imprisoning you and your crew for attacking an Armada vessel. Am I understood captain?**"

There's silence as we await a reply. Then he responds, "**I would like to visually confirm your boarding craft. I have the specs pulled up on your SLVRDO and if it matches I will stand down and prepare for boarding.**"

"**I can agree to that,**" Keller says, "**my boarding craft will enter slowly and then stop for visual inspection on your command. Be warned again, I will take your ship if you fire on them.**"

"**I understand,**" the mining captain acknowledges.

VAL-CON comes over the working frequency to confirm we understand Keller's orders.

Larrodo maniacally laughs, "Looks like we're gonna risk getting shot at after all."

Donna replies with an annoying groan. Lede begins to pilot the ship into the cavern very slowly. We come down, relative to our perspective, in a slope and rounding into the inside of the planet. We see the mining vessel a few hundred meters from us parked "up" relative to us.

"**Alright, stop,**" the mining vessel captain orders, "**Orient yourself to us and turn ninety degrees to your right.**"

Lede rolls the ship and turns to the ship ninety degrees to the right. We sit still for a bit wondering if we're going to get shot at, especially since we're in prime target position. We could sustain a hit or three, but if they hit us in the engines, we would be screwed.

"**Alright,**" the captain comes over the COMM, "**I am heading to my starboard airlock. You have permission to dock there. Understand we are actively engaged in mining and are on a tight schedule so we'd like to make this as quick and painless as possible.**"

I grab the COMM unit and say, "We understand, captain."

Lede pilots the ship to the mining vessel's starboard side. This one is massive. Probably only a third smaller than Valkyrie. It has what looks like two drills and claws on its belly. It's specialized for ground mining, unlike the Ex Del Seven which was built for long range orbital mining. They probably have a processor and fabrication unit on board and probably just sell parts to ships they come across. I look around, but can't seem to find a traverse drive dish. Hopefully these guys are freelance, otherwise we'll be continuing our search.

Lede lines the back of the ship up and slowly backs it in. The hatch extends and we connect to it sealing the walkway to our door.

I sigh, "Here we go," and slide the center console up to get out.

The rest of the team, having stood up waits for Larrodo and Donna to take point. One of them hands me a rifle and I nod a thank you. The door opens and we walk into the walkway. It's not as stable as I thought it would be. The airlock door opens and we're greeted by the Captain and two of his crew.

Larrodo greets, "Captain?"

Begrudgingly, the mining Captain nods.

Larrodo continues, "I'm Delta Ranked Crewman Larrodo. This is Sergeant Kroeling and the rest of my team. We'll try to keep this quick."

"Please do," the Captain informs, "we're in the middle of operations so please try not to disrupt my workers too much. We're willing to cooperate, but I expect not to be delayed."

"I understand," Larrodo says, "We're going to begin having a look around."

Larrodo looks over at me.

I think for a second, "Uh, can we look at your credentials?"

The Captain, having anticipated this pulls out a booklet with his paperwork.

I say, "No we want to inspect, everything. Crew status, citizenship of workers- all of it."

Noticeably annoyed, the Captain takes a deep breath and then motions for us to follow him. The condition of this freighter is a little better than the Ex Del Seven was. Of course these are work vessels so the notion of ever expecting them to be pristine is just ridiculous. I mean keeping the thing clutter free is one thing, but it's going to get dirty. Weird how pulling in space rocks causes that.

We walk onto the bridge. Okay, this is a bit surprising. It's a lot cleaner than I was expecting and some of the display screens and work stations almost look more advanced than what's on the Valkyrie bridge. Rather, that could be the abundance of holo-monitors.

The Captain leads us to his office, which is attached to the bridge. Smart design, actually. It allows him to be available right away instead of having to come up from his cabin. The Armada should consider adding this feature.

He walks behind his desk, "Okay. Here's everything. What do you want to see?"

"Everything," I say, "we'll just look through things here."

I pick up a pad and hand it to Donna. As Donna starts to hand it to Larrodo, he says, "I'm going to inspect the facilities. Let me know what you find." He leaves the room.

I look back at the Captain who is not hiding his feelings. He clearly feels he shouldn't have to be going through this.

"I didn't catch your name," I say.

He mutters, "Trinn."

I ask, "Is that a first or last name?"

"For you," he irritably says, "my first name is Captain."

I pick up a pad and begin looking through it as though I know what I'm looking for. I mean I do know what I'm looking for, but if I don't find anything, I'll have to make something up.

Trinn slouches into his chair, staring me down as I try to focus on what I am looking at. I try to ignore him, but I have to resort to turning my back. Scrolling through this info, it's pretty useless so far. Not going to be able to pin him on mineral survey data.

I turn back and set the pad down, "So, which of these has your itinerary?"

He ponders a second then answers, "One of them."

I nod slowly, "Okay, Captain, we can let this go easy or hard. It's up to you, but if you help us get the information we're looking for, we'll be out of here a lot sooner.

He scoffs, "I've heard that before. It doesn't seem to accelerate anything except you'll get to go back to your drop ship and wait for everyone else to finish. Everything that you need is in this booklet," he says holding it up, "but you wanted to look at everything else so here we are. Find everything you think you need and then get the fuck off my ship."

I take a breath for a second and try to think of a response, "Uh… Captain I don't understand why the hostilities."

"Really?" he scoffs hard, "You board my ship after threatening to seize it after I dare contemplate defending myself. You come aboard and disrupt my operations, but you don't even know what ship this is. Otherwise you would have known that we were boarded a month ago. Right now the only difference between you and pirates are that what you're doing is sanctioned by the government."

"We're not here to steal anything," I say

"And yet you are stealing something," he quips, "my time."

"We'll get this finished as quickly as possible," I note.

Trinn rambles, "You know, maybe if you weren't so heavily armed, Captains like me wouldn't be so disgruntled. You claim to be ships of peaceable enforcement, yet you carry enough armaments to take out a fleet of pirate vessels."

"It's more for defensive," I point out, "Compared to the Navy, we're sailing light."

"Light," Trinn chuckles, "You have two sixty-four millimeter projectile cannons, eight laser batteries and a squadron of fighters. Yes I'm familiar with the Valkyrie Class. You know what I have to defend myself against pirates? A dorsal and a keel laser battery. And if I want more it's a rigorous, expensive process to get them. Missiles? Fuck no. Large projectile canons? Ha! So yeah, I feel a little imprisoned at the moment seeing as you're the ones with the considerably bigger guns."

I nod slowly and begin to rummage through some of the other pads on his desk. A title for one of them catches my eyes regarding contracts. I pick it up and begin to scan through it. Some of the places listed are systems I'm not even familiar with. What is actually odd is these sites seem to be exclusively given.

"Captain, Trinn," I ask, "What are these contracts? Since when does the guild give systems exclusively like this?"

He leans up and says, "Those aren't in effect yet."

"Okay…" I inquire further, "when will they be? And again, since when is the guild partitioning systems like this?"

He takes a breath, "The Guild is going away. Or at least will be in time. Del Areeba Corp has exclusive claim rights directly and is contracting them out to the freelance vessels like mine. I won't be paying my Guild Tax, just a small contract fee and percentage on my earnings."

I nod and look at the contract. This is very much irregular. The Guild was established to protect miners and vessels, well initially, but like all good intentions it became corrupt, though not as badly as a single corporation could with exclusive, "Government contracts? The Republic is dealing these out?" I ask.

The Captain nods, "Yeah. I guess you guys don't have your new regulations yet. You also won't be able to just board me at random. Inspections will only happen before and after mining deployments."

I scoff slightly, "Um... I can tell you..." trailing off I search for that specific agreement in the contract and sure enough, "Oh... yeah that's going to be provisional. It'll be gone within a year."

"So sure?" Trinn asks.

I nod, "Absolutely. This would just blow the door open for traffickers and smugglers. This is an incentive to get more people to abandon the Guild. Once the corporation has enough participants, we'll be boarding you at random again- but what's really bothering me here is that the government is directly handing out contracts to systems that haven't even been explored yet."

The Captain speculates, "Maybe they haven't been announced by Stellar Exploration."

I shake my head and turn the pad over to him, "There are over ten systems here that have been "discovered" in secret, systems with minerals that will make Del Areeba the richest mining corp in the whole fucking galaxy in a matter of months… now this doesn't seem oddly suspicious to you?"

The Captain looks at me, "Why? Should it? The guild is outdated and I'll make a shitload of that money for myself."

I realize I am analyzing this situation with information he doesn't know. Unsure of what to do, I try to figure out what to say. But I don't want to just bludgeon him with the truth. Especially not without our evidence.

"Give me a moment," I say and motion for Donna to talk with me privately.

"What?" she asks.

I say, "I think we need to tell him."

"What?" she asks again.

"Everything," I say.

"What? No! We don't have any proof with us on hand he'll think we're nuts! Just think of something to impound his ship on-" she's interrupted.

"I can hear you," he says, "and I know my rights, if I feel my ship is being improperly seized, I can either file a petition in court, or," he finishes brandishing a pistol and firing three shots at me.

I flinch harder than I would like to admit, but when I realize I'm unharmed I try to regain what's going on.

"DROP IT RIGHT NOW!" Donna orders.

The Captain, stunned, drops his pistol on his desk and raises his hands. I look at the scorch marks on my armor. I think that was a kill shot.

Trinn fumbles for words, "I uh… Well that didn't work."

Donna, placing Trinn in binders says, "Would defeat the purpose of wearing armor if it didn't work." She looks at me and says, "I think we have reason enough to seize his ship now, wouldn't you agree?"

I shake my head, "If someone was hijacking your restaurant, would you react any differently?"

Donna contemplates what I said and realizes I'm right.

She turns the Captain to face her and explains, "There is a lot more going on than you're going to accept. But I would like to take you back to our ship and give you a full, and detailed explanation of what's going on here."

The Captain rolls his eyes, "You act as though I have a choice."

"You do," she says as genuinely as possible.

Trinn sighs for a bit, "Fine. But I'm not going in binders. Not in front of my crew. Mainly because if they see that it'll cause a firefight."

Donna ponders for a bit. She starts to undo them and says, "You will walk in front of us. And if you try anything you may find yourself leaving in a body bag."

Trinn scoffs, "And? Anything happens to me, my crew is loyal."

"Then you're condemning them to die," Donna says, "I'm willing to be civil. But it's in your best interest if you are as well."

Trinn stares at Donna's unwavering determination, "Kay."

After informing Larrodo of our intentions, we escort Trinn through the halls of his ship. Some of the crewmembers stop and ask where he's going. He does his best to reassure them that he's going over to Valkyrie to speak to Commander Keller about something important skipper to skipper.

On the ride back, Trinn doesn't say anything. He mostly stares at us intently possibly seeing if we'll say anything.

I end up cracking, "Look if I told you right now, you wouldn't believe anything. Can you just trust us for now?"

Trinn replies with a glare. Yeah I should have known better. Maybe it's just personal arrogance, but I have a feeling he's going to change his opinion entirely.

After landing in the Port Hangar, we make our way to the Officer's Mess. Keller was informed we were coming back and ordered us to take him directly there. He again remains silent the entire way.

We enter the Officer's Mess and Commander Keller greets, "Captain Trinn. I am Jaysen Keller, Commander of this vessel. Welcome."

"Commander," he says respectfully, "I don't entirely feel welcome so you'll understand if I'm a little less than cooperative."

Keller nods, "It seems my personnel have found something that may correlate to something else larger going on. But before we get into that I need to know what you know about Keldon Colony- ah but first, can I interest you in a drink?" Keller finishes presenting his whiskey bottle and a couple of glasses.

"It's a little early for me," Trinn informs.

"Fair enough," Keller says, "So tell us what you know about Keldon."

Trinn shrugs, "Apparently some communications blackout? None of my crew have been affected by it."

"And the other colonies that went dark?" Keller asks.

Trinn shakes his head.

Keller takes a breath, "Okay... gonna have to ask that you take a seat. This may take a while."

As you might have guessed, we started showing him video and sensor clips of everything that has happened so far. And as expected he was quite skeptical. At first. As we went on, explaining everything that has happened, he seemed to become more and more convinced that we weren't fooling him.

Unexpectedly, though it should have been, came the sting of hearing Dev's voice and seeing her again in an edited portion of the ground mission on Thretta. And of course remembering what happened on Melyar and Lantic Station... no. Not now.

We finish the presentation with an explanation of why we were searching for Trinn and his ship.

Keller asks, "I know that's a lot to take in, but do you have any questions?"

Trinn doesn't say anything. He just sits quietly then struggles to say anything, but dramatically points at the whiskey bottle.

"Oh of course," Keller says grabbing the bottle and pouring a glass for Trinn.

The Captain takes it and downs it in less than thirty seconds. He motions for another pour only chugging half the pour before sitting back and momentarily collecting his thoughts.

Finally he says, "So... aliens are real. You guys have been on the run from them and now it seems like the Navy is after you? What have you dragged me into?"

I stand up and chime in, "Uh, actually, Captain I have reason to believe you were already a part of it- or rather you were about to be."

Trinn looks over at me and Keller says, "Explain."

I begin, "Let me know if I start to lose you. I was looking through this contract and discovered something alarming- something that connects a little too well with what we suspect is going on. So, the way things have been for the last seventy plus years; all mining within the Republic has been handled through the Guild. At its inception the Guild was purposed to protect ships and their crews. It was also designed to settle claim disputes among miners and get vessels that didn't have Traverse Drive Tunneling, which is a majority of the fleet, to potential prospects.

Well, as fees increased, captains started to have a hard time breaking even. They could share a prospect with another vessel and split the fees, but the guild prevented more than three ships working a site at a time. In comes corporate sponsorship. Now the ships were finally able to turn a bigger profit again while their corporation took care of the guild fees and claim distribution. The Guild moved into an oversight of claims and began to sponsor exploration vessels to seek out resources to mine.

These contracts circumvent the Guild entirely and award nine, unknown system claims to a single corporation. The government is essentially going without the Guild on this which means a single corporation will now set safety standards. Not only does this set a potentially bad precedent, but it's oddly suspicious as to why the government is suddenly circumventing the Guild and even more strange that nine new systems are about to be revealed. I can double check our maps, but I don't recall these systems previously existing on any chart before."

Keller nods, "That is an interesting find, but what is the connection here, exactly? What does the Republic stand to gain from this?"

I'm silent as I think of a reply. The entire room falls silent as everyone tries to come up with theories.

Keller asks, "Captain, was there any other information regarding these contracts?"

Trinn shakes his head, "Only thing was our new servicing contracts for maintenance and our Traverse Drive crew members. We were given the list of systems to choose which ones interested us the most."

I raise a brow and begin reading the contract more. I click on one of the systems. In it is detailed survey data, as if an explorer vessel had been sent out on an expedition.

"What is it, Nate?" the Commander asks.

I answer, "These planets have detailed survey data… Yet they haven't been officially charted. They include mineral readouts, atmospheric data, planet classes- how did they do this without the information being posted publicly? And to add to it, why?"

Keller asks Trinn, "Where is the maintenance in your contract going to be handled?"

Trinn answers, "I believe it's in the contract."

I nod and scroll through the pad to find it. I quickly read through and inform, "Looks like Mars."

Devlin, having quietly observed the entire time pipes up, "That's our mission. It'll be easier to infiltrate Mars than going to Earth. We'll break something on Trinn's vessel and head to Mars to use the contract. While there, we can infiltrate the offices to try and uncover more information."

"I'm sorry, what?" Trinn says.

Keller informs, "That is why we were trying to find you. Originally our plan was to commandeer your ship and take it to Earth, break into Stellar Command aitch que and find answers. But my crew chose to bring you aboard and

I've explained everything, so instead of coming up with some bullshit charge, I'd like to ask you to help us."

"Do I even have a choice?" Trinn cynically replies.

Keller nods and sits back down, "Absolutely. And I think you know the choice you have to make. You have seen the situation we're in so let me ask you, do you want to live in a world where you become a slave to a corporation while your government conspires with an alien race to gain more power and control over you? Or do you want to take a stand and fight for your freedom? I mean you became a freelance captain for a reason, didn't you? To be free."

Trinn snickers a little and ponders, "I'm just a miner, man. Just trying to make a living. I mean... sure I don't much care for you guys, but I prefer to keep to myself."

Keller persuades, "I'm not sure that's even going to be an option, Captain. Let's say you don't help us- let's say we all just give up and go along with this. You're talking about guild regulations going away. You're talking about working for a company that probably will own you not just on contracts, but will probably claim ownership of your vessel after all the maintenance- look I'm not sure of the particulars, but I know guild regulations and as much of a pain in the ass as they are, they protect you. This corporation won't. So if you want to go on as you are now, keeping to yourself that's your decision, but we need you to help us."

Trinn sighs, "I need to speak with my crew. I also need to tell them everything. We have a trust amongst us that needs to be maintained. But I need to tell them alone. Then I will let you know if we'll help willingly or not."

Keller rubs his chin and then nods, "Very well. We'll take you back and await your answer."

Trinn stands up and Donna escorts him back to the Port Hangar. I, being hungry remain on board and decide to wait for evening chow.

I head back to the armory, but then realize my clothing is on Miner Two so I head back to my bunk and get a different pair of green pants. Then I realize my boots are also on the dropship.

I drop off the belt and tell them I'll be borrowing the suit for a bit until my boots come back. The Crewman shows me how to strip the armor down to the waist and put it in "relaxed mode". The armor bunches up around the waist. Not super comfortable, but oh well.

Tonight's meal, vegetable protein burgers. Yum. I unknowingly attract attention as I sit down and clank loudly on the bench. Crewmembers look up momentarily, but return to their meals and nonsensical conversation. Me? I just try to eat. My one friend is out flying and will hopefully be back soon.

I clank around the decks aimlessly checking at the hangar only to find nothing that I am looking for. I head up to the bridge in search of answers. I'm informed that they are waiting until Trinn signals them to be picked up so he can be brought back to formulate a plan. So I'm stuck wearing the armor until then. I decide to head down to Keller's office. I knock on the door.

"Come in," he says.

I enter and then slump into the chair.

"How can I help you, Nate?" he asks.

I answer, "Well… my boots are on Miner Two so I'm stuck wearing this thing and until the good mining Captain agrees to come back."

"Oh…" Keller acknowledges, "And I suppose you came here to ask if I can recall the ship?"

"What? No," I say, "I was wondering if you had anything to drink to pass the time."

"You wanna get drunk before we plan our infiltration of Del Areeba?" Keller says raising a brow.

I ask, "Why? Do you think it'll take longer than four drinks?"

Keller ponders, "It's tempting, but I think tea would be better."

I sigh, "I mean… sure, but… I haven't taken my re-meds yet…"

Keller nods and gets up. He goes into his room and comes back with a pair of glasses and a bottle. He pours me a glass, we clink and I take a sip. Ooof. Amberglash.

"I'll be lucky to make it through one of these," I express.

"I've got wine if you'd prefer," Keller informs.

I shake my head, "Maybe later."

There's a silence of awkwardness.

I break it, "So… you thought Wernival was out to get me."

Keller half nods, "I suspected things weren't as they wanted me to see them. It was convincing, but not enough. I didn't suspect Wernival specifically, but why did you name him?"

I shrug, "I mean he was the leader of our shop. And I wasn't really friends with any of them. I got along with other people across other divisions. But I'll tell you now what I told you then, I did not betray the Republic."

"I know," Keller says, "which is why I allowed you on the bridge instead of confining you the whole voyage. And now I need to trust you more than before. We're sending you on the infiltration mission. But I have a specific assignment for you: I want you to make contact with my son. He's in the Stellar Army, specifically a Rover Mechanic."

I ask, "Are you wanting me to bring him back?"

He shakes his head slowly, "No. I want you to give him a data disc containing all of our sensor data, logs and an internal investigation that Sub-Commander and myself conducted. Make sure he understands that the information is dangerous."

I nod, "Okay... are you sure you trust him?"

Keller explains, "I have no other choice, unless you know anyone who can make sure our side of the story is told."

I ponder for a bit. I can't think of anyone I bothered to keep in touch with back home. But maybe I could leave the information with my mom. Then again I don't think she would know what to do with it.

I shake my head, "I'm afraid I don't know anyone who would be willing to take on such a task. But if you want, give me some copies. Maybe Tim knows someone."

"You intend to take Mr. M'Nar with you?" he asks.

I nod.

Keller shakes his head, "Not possible. We need him here to continue to assist with repairs."

His COMM goes off. He pulls it out and answers, "Keller... Very well," Keller acknowledges, "have him escorted to the briefing room as well as all the crew members who have been selected for the infiltration mission."

Keller, setting his empty glass down, "Trinn is on his way back. Let's get to it."

I make my way to the briefing room while Keller does the same, but takes a longer route. Probably pre-planning discussions. I, myself, stop on the Crew's Mess to grab a coffee. Despite the contamination I need something to wash down the whiskey.

I walk in, being one of the first and sit down in the second row. Everyone trickles in, the last person being the Commander, someone calls attention and deck and then Keller orders us to carry on.

Sub-Commander takes center stage and begins, "Greetings all. This will be our brief for infiltration. We had originally planned to go to aitch que on Earth but now with a new discovery we have chosen a slightly less dangerous mission. We will be infiltrating the Del Areeba Corporation on Mars."

He pauses for a second and then continues, "We're going to pretend- well rather cause a problem on Captain Trinn's mining vessel. The Captain is going to ask for an early use of his contract. Once the ship is moored up and undergoing maintenance, that is when we'll disembark. Once we're provided our temporary quarters, we go off on our assignments. Mr. McNill, Crewman Kamerov, you are both excused from the remainder of this brief. The less you know, the better."

I nod respectfully and Lede and I almost get up at the same time and leave the room.

Lede says, "I was told you were going to bring me up to speed as to what we've been assigned."

I explain to him what we will be doing and then we go to our berthing rooms to pack for the trip. Aside from a couple pairs of slacks and white shirts, I don't have much. Wish I had stopped at one of the shops on Lantic Station. I think I'll make time once on Mars.

Lede and I wait in Miner Two for Sub-Commander, Captain Trinn, his two crewmembers and our five other crew members embarking on the mission. After about twenty minutes, everyone else finally arrives and in about another ten minutes we're off to Trinn's ship.

We get settled in, pull up his mining equipment and get ready to tunnel for Sol.

Commander Keller comes in over the COMM, **"Mining Vessel Lambadda, this is Valkyrie Actual. I think I've stressed enough the importance of this mission. You are all capable of pulling this off without incident. Good luck and come home safe."**

Home... I'm actually heading home. Rather the home I grew up on... hmm... maybe this is where I get off. After completing the mission of course.

Chapter Eighteen: "...I'll be the one checking you into the brig. Have a nice day."

(*Nathan*)Upon resurfacing, the COMM comes alive with chatter. Trinn has three of his COMM units set to different channels; the HAD frequency, one for ship to ship and the standard traffic control frequency. One of his crew members turns off two of the radios.

Trinn orders Lede, "Bring us into high orbit."

I explain to those who don't know, "Traffic control is going to reach out to us and ask what's wrong. We're not scheduled to arrive today."

"Yep," Trinn confirms.

We wait as traffic control contacts other vessels in queue to enter the planet. Mars is a buzz with ships coming in from many different systems. It's become Sol's industrial hub and is the primary base for Stellar Command's repair facilities both on the surface and in orbit. It's where most of the Mining Vessel Transports are housed as well as the home of Ex Dell Corp, my old employer, well in a way.

Traffic Control comes over the COMM, "**Mining Vessel Lambadda this is traffic control. You're not a scheduled arrival. Explain your intentions.**"

Trinn grabs the COMM hand unit and speaks into it, "We had an accident on one of my two drills. I wanted to see if Del Areeba wants to give a demonstration of their upcoming repair contract."

"**Meet on frequency see-ex-ten,**" Traffic Control orders.

Trinn notes, "They've established frequencies. Guess this might actually work." He inputs the frequency into the radio and says, "Del Areeba this is mining vessel Lambadda, come in."

"**Lambadda,**" a voice replies, "**hear you loud and clear. What brings you to Mars today?**"

Trinn explains, "I have suffered a major casualty on one of my drills. My productivity will be severely impacted without it. I need it fixed as soon as possible and seeing as we're about to enter into contract, I figured this would be a good time to try out your maintenance compared to the usual guy I go to."

The response is sharp, "**I'm sorry, we can't help. Until the contract is in effect, you're on your own unless you want to pay servicing fees.**"

"Okay," Trinn acknowledges, "I'll just stick with my current maintenance shop. Oh and while I'm at it, I'll probably reconsider this contract, maybe talk with some of my fellow freelance captains about how you left me high and dry instead of taking the time to give a proper demonstration of your services. Now of course you could assume I'm just a nobody freelancer who knows maybe a couple other guys in the biz, but I could also be a well-known self-employed miner with connections throughout the entire Republic. If that's a gamble you want to take at this stage of your business ventures it would be foolish, albeit ballsy."

There's no response for a bit. Then someone comes back, "**Mining vessel Lambadda, stand by.**"

We wait for about ten minutes before Del Areeba says we can land at their repair facility. Traffic Control gives us a designated path and time to enter the Mars Atmosphere.

The next few steps are routine. We confirm we have permission to enter low orbit, then we confirm we can enter the atmosphere, then we follow our designated track to the Del Areeba buildings where finally we land at the repair facility. It is quite large; able to hold several large mining vessels: very industrial looking. Next to it is a larger, office building structure with green tinted windows.

Lede brings the ship into a hover then announces, "Above designated el zee. Extending landing struts."

We hear the loud clanking as the landing struts extend from the hull.

"Bringing her down," Lede announces.

He slowly lets up on the landing thrusters gracefully bringing the ship into the drydock. The ship shakes a bit as we softly rest on solid ground.

"Not bad, Guardian," Trinn compliments.

As soon as the ship is secure in the repair dock, we begin to disembark. One of the Del Areeba representatives talks with Trinn about repairs while another gathers the rest of us and Trinn's crew together and leads us to the guest quarters. Based on the damage we caused to Trinn's drill, we may be here a couple of days. Devlin begins to make small talk with the rep, asking questions, pretending to be interested in all of this. I look around at the facility. There are two other ships undergoing repairs, sparks falling from their hulls and onto the ground. Tim would love this shit. Me? I'm just ready to get this over with.

We're given our rooms. Lede and I get bunked together. The room is furnished with basic beds and desks, each with a computer. As we're laying out our pillow and sheets, there's a knock on the door. Lede answers and in walks Devlin.

He gets right to business, "Alright, at this point we're pretty much settled in. So let's get started on our assigned tasks. I'm just down the hall. I expect a status report at the end of each day. What is your plan for the day?"

We're silent momentarily, then I answer, "I guess we could head to the Army Mech facility and I can make contact with Keller's son."

Devlin nods, "Very well. Let me know how that goes. Oh, and make sure you look like you're trying to relax, but not too much. We may have to jet outta here at a moment's notice. Carry on," he finishes and leaves our room.

Lede asks, "So how much alcohol do you think is not too much for being relaxed?"

I answer, "We'll find out when we get back for the night. But I am looking forward to some fresh water first," I finish walking into the bathroom.

I take a small glass and pour into it water from the faucet. I don't care if it's filtered perfectly or not. It's better than piss water.

Lede says, "If you don't mind, hook me up with some."

I chug the rest of my water and pour myself another glass as well as get him one and bring it out.

He takes it and chugs it like it's the last water on Mars. I do the same.

We look at the glasses, empty and he says, "Nothing beats the pure shit."

"You mean no shit," I retort.

We both chuckle momentarily at my bad joke, then add more water to the glasses. After a couple more glasses of the best water I have had since Lantic, I finish setting up my bed. I then pack one of the pads containing all the information Keller wanted me to give to his son into the satchel. Lede and I head down to the main lobby of the office building that is also where our guest quarters are located. From there we discover that a tram runs through the facility and head to the terminal.

We board the tram bound for one of the main tram stations. It's pretty much brand new with the interior colored in an off white and the upholstery on the seats lacking food stains. Arriving at the main station we connect to another that takes us straight to the Mech facility. This one is significantly dirtier and obviously used. Seats adorned with years of food and beverage from soldiers commuting in for their work days, unable to stop for a proper meal.

Upon getting off, comes the confusing part, locating Keller's son. We wander a little until we come across a main desk.

The soldier looks up, "Can I help you?" he asks.

I answer, "Uh, yes, I'm looking for an old friend of mine: Jeffrey Wrennor."

He asks, "What division is he in?"

I shake my head, "I don't know. I work on a mining vessel and we just happened to be in town. Last time we spoke he said he was stationed here, but we've been busy living our respective lives and we haven't exactly spoken in a while."

"I understand," he asks, "you got eye-dee?"

I pull out an identification card and hand it to him.

"One minute," he says and begins to type away on his computer. After a few seconds he begins calling around on a COMM unit. After a couple of people he finally finds who I'm looking for.

"Corporal Wrennor?" he confirms. Then a second and a half later, "Yeah I have someone claiming to be an old friend of yours… according to the eye dee, Jaysen Keller… yeah… okay I'll let him know."

He disconnects the call and then informs, "He'll meet you in the lobby of the em forty-four facility. Just head down this hall and take a left. You'll head back outside, passed another building until you see the big sign. If you get lost, just come back here."

I take the ID card back and nod, "Thank you. And we're good to just walk around?"

He says, "Yeah. Main entrances and lobbies are open to the public. Try to penetrate them without escort or authorization and I'll be the one checking you into the brig. Have a nice day."

Walking in the direction we were told, Lede mentions, "Is it just me or does security seem lax for a place like this?"

I nod and respond, "They probably have-" I interrupt myself, having looked up and noticed a gatling turret suspended on the ceiling. I point up.

"Ah," Lede notices, "Projectile weapons… seems rather messy."

I suppose, "Considering laser weapons require energy, those can probably function in the event of an ee em pee. Their power source is probably also isolated to protect from such."

"Makes sense," Lede agrees.

We continue towards the M44 facility, noting the beautiful orange sky with red mountains on the horizon. I must say, it's giving me an unexpected nostalgic sensation being here. I mean, this is where I grew up. I guess I never expected to get back here for a while.

We enter the M44 lobby. It's much smaller than the first one we were in. The lobby host, probably another private, asks if we need help.

I answer, "No thanks, just waiting on a friend."

I watch, waiting for Jeff. I have an older photo of what he might look like. Apparently Keller didn't have any recent pictures. Apparently Matilda had some she never forwarded. I wouldn't describe Keller's relationship as estranged, but he did indicate that they haven't spoken in some time. When I asked, he didn't get more specific.

I see someone coming out who I think is him. This is it, the moment I either get it right or inadvertently blow my cover in a rather awkward situation.

"Jeff!" I say excitedly approaching the confused corporal, "How you been, man? Hell the last time I think we saw you was that Yosemite fishing trip with your father."

Jeff then replies, "Uh, oh yeah! Jaysen, you've changed a bit since then. Say how about we meet for some grub in like an hour at the Tavern Brew Burger just outside the food court. I got some things I need to finish up first then we can catch up."

I nod awkwardly, "Oh okay, yeah I think we can spare the time. Hey, bring it in, man."

We engage in a mostly awkward yet convincing embrace.

When done he says, "Alright, man. I'll see you there."

I smile and nod as he walks off then I turn and Lede walks along with me.

Lede notes, "And now we wait to see if he turns us in or comes through."

"Yet another round of Wait-n-see," I say.

We make our way back the way we came after asking where the food court was located. We find the Tavern Brew Burger. It's in its own structure. So far Jeff has picked a spot that is somewhat isolated, but also inconspicuous enough to not draw attention.

Lede and I go in and grab a table in a corner away from most of the other patrons. It's always interesting to see a restaurant chain decorated the same as any other, but with customers who are all wearing military uniforms. Thankfully, there are a couple of civilian contractors so we don't stick out.

Our waiter comes by and asks what we want.

"I'll do a water," I say.

Lede says, "I'll have an eye-pee-aeh."

My eyes widen.

"What?" he asks, "We're under some pressure, I need to come down."

I nod and then ask for the same as well as my water.

Lede asks while we're waiting, "Should we order food, or wait?"

"I mean if you're hungry," I say, "Or maybe we should just start with an appetizer. Or better yet, just enjoy our beer for now."

Lede smirks and nods in agreement.

We have about two rounds and are feeling… relaxed. Finally Jeff shows up in civilian attire.

I start to get up and acting all friendly, "Hey, my old buddie."

Jeff remains stoic and as he approaches he says, "You can cut the shit."

We sit back down now addressing each other as the strangers we know us to be.

Lede slides in next to me leaving Jeff a seat to himself.

He looks at us and then says, "Alright. You come in posing as a friend with my father's name and then talk about a trip he and I took together once many years ago. So I assume with that information you must be working for him or have some sort of cryptic message. What is it?"

We're silent a bit as we try to compose ourselves.

Lede remarks, "You're probably going to want to order a drink for this one."

I nod in agreement, "Definitely. What all have you been told about your dad?"

Jeff takes a breath, "Well… a lot of inconsistencies. First that his ship went missing after contact was lost at Keldon colony. Supposedly they were going to be declared dead, but then out of nowhere he attacked Lantic Station and then went rogue and destroyed an entire Navy fleet."

Lede chuckles, "Fucking wow."

"Yeah," Jeff continues, "That's a lot of destruction for one Constellation Cutter to commit. But let me guess, you're here to tell me it's all true."

I shake my head, "No, Jeff. We're here to tell you what is true. Most of what you have been told is total bullshit."

"Yeah, I know," he says, "I figured that was the case when he supposedly destroyed my mother's ship. My parents may have separated, but I know they still both loved each other or at least cared enough to not kill each other."

I take a breath, "There is a lot going on that even we don't know, but we need to tell you."

Jeff nods in agreement, "Close out your tabs. We'll resume this at my apartment."

Lede and I agree and close out our tickets using money sticks Keller gave us. We go on talking about nonsensical things like the latest Viktor Slenderman Movie of which Lede and I have to adlib our reactions since we haven't seen it yet. Not sure why I feel the need to be convincing to the clerk in the store. Oh yeah, we walked to the food supply store nearby to pick up some beverages for the evening. We pay and are on our way once again.

One close to twenty minute walk later, we're finally at his apartment building, a green structure with no notable features. It just seems efficient. The interior décor is as bland: grey walls, dark grey carpet and white bulbs illuminate the hallway.

Lede remarks, "A lot of thought was clearly put into this design."

I chuckle slightly while Jeff just scoffs. We come to his door. He enters his passcode and we all file in. After I close the door, it secures itself.

"Welcome," he says as lights begin to activate, "I know it's not the best house, but it's mine. So... where were we?"

Lede and I look at each other. "Aliens are real," I just come out and say, "we've been fighting- rather running from them since they attacked Keldon Station. I'm actually not a member..."

Jeff is understandably laughing, "Really? This is the best you could come up with? Seriously, who the fuck are you?"

I pull out the data disk, "Your father wanted me to give this to you. He said you would know what to do. Perhaps you should go look at it, we'll wait here, probably help ourselves to some of the alcohol. Trust me, you'll need it later."

Jeff rolls his eyes and takes the disk, "You know I have an authenticator. If this is fake, I'll know."

I nod in acknowledgment.

"Alright," he says, "If this is bullshit, I want you gone."

He walks into his room and closes the door.

Lede says, "Well this is off to a great start."

I go into the kitchen and try to find some whiskey glasses. I find one as well as one regular glass and a few plastic party cups. I grab some ice from the dispenser and pour Lede a drink in the glass and use the plastic for myself. I then sit down next to him at the breakfast bar.

Lede notes, "This could take a while. You should contact the Commander and let him know we'll be... late"

"Good idea," I say. I pull out my personal COMM unit and begin recording, "Good afternoon. We have made contact and are attempting to brief him now. This could take a while so don't wait up for us. Will notify you if anything else comes up."

I send the recorded message. He'll either send an acknowledgement of some sort or give us different orders.

"Cheers," I say smacking my plastic on his glass. We take a sip and the stare around quietly

Lede suspects, "Even though the authenticator won't find anything, I still feel like he's going to have doubts."

"Why is that?" I ask.

He explains chuckling slightly, "Cause sometimes I still do. Even after all we've been through, I still have a hard time accepting this is real."

He's not alone, "yeah I sometimes expect to wake up back on the Ex Del Seven mining." I take a large sigh, "but I won't. Tomorrow I'll wake either here or in Del

Areeba'a barracks, being one of the few people who has encountered these things-"

"On second thought, I'd rather not talk about it right now," Lede interrupts.

I nod, "Yeah…" and get up and head towards the back door.

The porch has room for maybe two chairs so I just stay inside and look out the sliding glass door at the red sky. Jeff's apartment is up about five floors, overlooking some of the surrounding city. The sun is beginning to set casting a dark red glow upon the red mountains. Some of the lights in the structures have already clicked on for the night.

My COMM unit goes off indicating a message. I check it with only a thumbs up. Guess the Commander is good with our intentions.

"Commander is good with our intentions," I inform.

"Cool," Lede says.

We continue to sip our beverages making small talk, but mostly staying quiet. We may not be on a port call, but this is a chance to get away from everything, even if just until Jeff is done reading what's on the data disk.

I sit down on his lounge chair and notice a controller on the small table. I pick it up and activate the holo-projector.

"Seems like a good time to see what is being said," I finish pulling up a 24 hour news channel. Well it's more news commentary, but whatever.

After sitting through the commentator's opinion regarding a land dispute on Luna, a news brief finally comes on. Most of it is just the usual: someone vaporized in Garden District here on Mars, celebrity nonsense, and the weather on Neptune. Finally we get what we have been wanting:

"And finally, the Office of the Prime Minister reports that soon communications with the far reaching colonies will be reestablished. Specific details as to why there was a communications blackout will also be given in a special State of the Republic address to be broadcast throughout the entire sector. Hopefully that will put an end to some of the ridiculous speculations that have been circulating the Net, I'm Beckam Glenderlin for..."

"Well that said absolutely nothing," I say.

Emerging from his room, Jeff says, "That's pretty much been every report since we lost contact... before we get into it, I need a fuckin drink."

Having already poured him one, Lede hands it over.

Jeff takes a large sip and then says, "So your disk cleared the authenticator. I haven't gone through all of it, but I have seen enough. What's our mission, then?"

I explain, "Yours is to disseminate the information. Your father said you might have a way to get it out and keep it from being suppressed."

Jeff answers, "Well yeah, I know people. But where is he? When is he getting here?"

I explain, "He's not. We came here on a mining vessel. The rest of our team is on another mission. Ours was to find you and give you the information so you could get the truth out there."

Jeff nods, "Okay. I can get it out there and then I think I should come with you. It won't be safe for me here if its discovered that I was given the information."

Shaking my head slowly I say, "Your father was insistent that you aren't brought into this more than we're asking."

Jeff becomes noticeably annoyed, "Figures. Couldn't be there for me when I grew up and would rather keep me out of the way."

Lede stands up, "Look, I'm not going to get into your relationship with your dad and honestly we really don't have the time-"

I interrupt, "So you want to go back to Del Areeba?"

Lede stops, "Fair point. Jeff, tell us about your dad. We got plenty of alcohol for a dysfunctional origin story."

Jeff walks over to the other breakfast bar stool, "I don't hate my dad. But there is a bit of a disconnect between us. Always has been. I mean growing up with him gone most of the time certainly made it hard and seeing him on extended port calls was always just fun and games." He takes another large sip, "Look, I know you guys work for my dad, but I don't know you both that well. He's given me my tasking, but I think it's best at this point if you both leave."

I mutter a sigh to myself and then say, "Okay. I'll give you my contact information should you want to reach out before we leave. We should be around for another day or two."

"I'll let you know," Jeff says and we leave.

Walking down the hall back towards the lift, Lede says, "I'm not quite ready to go back are you?"

I shake my head, "No I almost had a good buzz going. Let's find a bar."

We exit the complex in search of a nearby pub. Maybe some hole in the wall type place; nothing too fancy.

We find a billiard pub, again nothing special about the décor. Yeesh it's like no one has any creativity on or around the base.

Lede gets a local brew while I stick with the whiskey.

Looking at one of the laser-pool tables, Lede asks, "Go for a round or two?"

I nod.

"Cool," he says, "you rack."

That's fair. Lede runs his credstick provided as temp funds from the ship across the table which unlocks the controls. I push a button and the triangle forms then materializes holographic balls. Lede takes his aim and breaks. Nothing goes in.

"Open for business," he sighs.

He hasn't left me with much. As I pick a target I say, "You know, it's just occurred to me, I don't even know that much about you."

He responds, "Yeah there's a reason for that. Not really much to tell. And it's not like you've been talkative about your past. Not that I care."

"Well now seems as good a time as any," I say.

Lede retorts, "It's also a good time to play the game. You gonna shoot or not?"

Okay then. I take my shot, missing as I expected, putting a different ball in.

Getting ready to line up another shot, Lede scoffs, "Uh, was that intentional?"

"Well, no-"

"Then it's my go," Lede cuts off.

He sinks a solid on the other end of the table with a fast, straight shot. He shakes his fist in a minor victory expression and picks another target. He tries to bounce it off the bumper and into a corner pocket with no success. Guess I've met my match: someone who sucks as much as I.

Positioning myself, I get ready for a bit of a crazy shot. Guess I'm feeling brave. I sink the orange striped ball with some effort, but it plays off of one of Lede's balls. I get ready to take another shot.

"Are you not familiar with bar rules?" he asks.

I ponder momentarily, "I feel we just make them up as we go."

Lede smirks, "Yeah pretty much," and positions himself and takes a shot.

He finishes his beer and I my whiskey. I decide to cover the next round. I hand him the fresh glass and we clink.

"Cheers" we both say almost simultaneously.

Before he takes another shot, Lede says, "Eh fuck it. So what happened to ya?"

"Hmm?" I think for a second, "Oh. Well officially I committed espionage and gave information to pirates."

"And unofficially?" Lede asks.

I take a breath, "I'll just give you my side of things: I was framed by my supervisors and people I thought I could trust. Why? I don't know. I hope one day to find out, but right now I guess it doesn't matter."

Lede takes his shot, missing and then says, "It obviously matters to you. But that's quite the claim. I'm sure you don't want to, but-"

I interrupt, "I'll just tell you…" and I tell him as we finish out our game. By the time I finish my tale, we find ourselves sitting at a high bar table near where we were playing.

Lede nods, "Well that's quite the story."

I shrug, "That's all you have to say?"

He chuckles, "What am I supposed to say?"

"Well I told you my backstory, only fair you tell me yours," I say.

He chuckles even louder, "Bro, I already told you, there isn't much to tell. Just trying to make my own way in the universe."

I ask, "What about your family? Where you're from?"

"What about them?" he asks, "Why is it so important for you to know those things?"

"Helps me to get to know you better?" I suppose.

He points out, "Man, we've been working together for how long just fine. Is it really gonna make a difference?"

I ponder a moment, "No I guess not... any women in your life?"

"Nope." He answers sharply.

"Not even Dev?" I drunkenly ask.

He glares at me for a second then says, "Ah... so that's what you were working towards. No I wasn't actually romantically interested in her. We were good friends."

"Despite the tension?" I inquire.

Lede smirks, "There's always tension. That's just part of life. But no she and I worked well together. Occasionally hung out on port calls, but beyond that, no, we weren't ever romantically involved."

"Your choice or hers?" I confirm.

He chuckles, "It never came up. But I never tried anyway. I'm just not interested in relationships, man. I'm happy just going my own way."

"I see," I say, "So when you confronted me on the Crew's Mess after she died it was just because you were good friends?"

Laughing, Lede confirms, "No, Nate I wasn't jealous you banged Dev…" he collects himself, "I guess I have trouble expressing my intentions. I was in disbelief… hell I think I still am…"

"Yeah…" I say trailing off.

Lede gets up and heads to the bar. He comes back with a topped off drink for himself and two shot glasses.

"To Dev," he says and we clink our beverages.

Jamison. Ooof. There's silence between us broken only by the other patrons of the bar.

Then broken by me, "I really miss her…"

Lede nods in agreement, "Yeah… me too. She should be here with us enjoying drinks and playing with our sticks and balls."

I smirk and remark, "But if she were, what would we be crying over?"

Lede laughs, "Haha yeah. Wanna play another round?"

"Hell yeah I do," I say, starting to hold back some minor tears. Fuck feelings. They just get in the way, especially of good times.

"Hey wait a minute," I ask, "How did you know Dev and I… ya know."

He explains, "Was easy to figure out when she told me you both got a room at Lantic Station. Is it your turn to rack or mine?"

"Yours" I say, "I'm fresh out of beverage."

I head over to the bar for a refill. Man… I am starting to feel better. And to think I was going to ruin it over thinking about Dev… or maybe I need to. Nah.

I set my drink down, grab the pool que and get ready to put Lede in his place. I break sinking nothing. So far so good.

I end up losing that round and the subsequent round. I guess I don't have that... uh... I just don't get better with drinking. But we still have fun, discussing our theories with the Dimensional Man series and sharing our tastes in music, which is surprisingly similar.

Catching a glimpse of the clock and losing my balance momentarily I think it's time to turn in. We pay our tabs and make our way back to the tram station. It finally arrives, mostly empty and takes us back to our connection hub and finally back to the Del Areeba Barracks.

We stumble up to our room. Lede in front of the door seems to be standing still unsure of what to do.

"Whatisit?" I ask, "You okay, what's wrong?"

Lede snorts and turns his head, "Yo I forgot the combo to the room."

I ponder for a bit, "Uhh... it's uh..."

"Fuck!" He laughingly shouts.

"SHHHHH!!!!" I sharply say, "You'll wake Sub-Command Dick waffle. I think it's... Valkyrie's commission year."

I hear him punch in the number and it works. We fumble into the room and close the door. As I start to undress for sleep, we hear a loud rap on the door.

Lede whips his head over at me and stares. I roll my eyes as I am technically closer and walk over.

"Who is it?" I ask.

"Sub-Commander Dick waffle." Devlin says angrily.

Upon opening the door, a towering, angry Sub-Commander Devlin barges through.

Sternly loud, he says, "What the fuck is this!? It's almost four in the fucking morning! I thought you were staying with Keller's son for the night."

"Uhh," Lede drunkenly fumbles for words, "He, uh… he kicked us out."

"What!?" the Sub-Commander becomes anxiously concerned, but obviously still angry, "Why!? Did he turn you in?"

"Oh no," I take over, "He was just overwhelmed with the information we gave him and asked us to give us-er him some time. He'll hopefully call later today."

"And how long ago was that?" the Sub-Commander asks.

I try to think of a response that doesn't implicate us too much, but unfortunately the silence gives us away.

Sub-Commander speculates, "You went out drinking, didn't you?"

I decide to come out with it, "We had started at Jeff's place and when he asked us to leave we weren't ready to come back-"

"This isn't a fucking port call!" Devlin says sharply, "You were on thin ice to begin with, kid. If it were up to me, you would have spent this trip in the brig and wouldn't be here right now so give me one good fucking reason why I shouldn't use my mission authority to kick you out into the street right now!"

I try to think but can't. There's obviously no winning with him for me.

As I try to come up with a response, Lede says, "Why are you so harsh on him? Nate has done so much for our ship and crew when he has zero obligation to do so. So what if we went out drinking? This shit has been hard on all of us- so what if he decided to unwind a little? Our actual port call was cut sort and he and I don't have time to properly relax underway so what's the big deal?"

Devlin, not having expected Lede's response says, "Keep it down. We'll talk again later today at which point I'll have decided whether or not to keep you on mission."

He storms out gracefully slamming the door. I look at Lede who chuckles and then crawls into bed fully clothed. I begin to undo my pants and then remove my shirt and...

...I wake up with a bit of a headache. Looking at the time I see I've slept maybe five hours and I feel a little better than expected. That's what happens when you stick with the same drink all night... most times.

Lede is still passed out. I, however, am hungry. I get dressed quickly and head down to the main lobby. Attached is a breakfast buffet which I assume is also complimentary.

As I sit down with a plate full of scrambled eggs and sausage, Sub-Commander Devlin sits down across from me.

Handing me a pad he asks, "Can you make sense of any of this?"

"Good morning to you too, sir," I snarkilly say, taking the pad.

As I look through what he has brought me, he says, "Look... I know we haven't gotten along, but I suppose it was a little bit of an overreaction this morning."

I glare at him in return.

"Just let me know what you find," he says and gets up returning to his table, I assume.

I start to enjoy my breakfast but also start looking through the information. Afterwards I drop off my plate, find Sub-Commander and sit down at his table.

"It's more of the same," I say.

"What?" he asks.

I explain, "There's no new information here. We need to get access from higher ups in the company, assuming there is anything to actually be found."

He becomes confused, "If there is anything?"

I propose, "I mean, I wouldn't leave information, incriminating my company colluding with the government illegally to portion off exclusive mining claims just available anywhere, assuming I even kept it."

Devlin retorts, "They would keep the information on file. Contracts, at the very least, in case the administration renegs or pulls the deal so they could sue them and expose the deal to the general public."

I note, "Like HealCore did when healthcare adjustments were being drafted..."

"Exactly," he confirms, "but this is considerably bigger than that as you know. Have you heard from Keller's son yet?"

I shake my head.

The waiter brings Devlin's drink, orange in color but appears to be bubbly.

"Here's your mimosa, sir," she says setting it down.

I raise a brow.

He explains, "Crewman Kamerov was right, we need to relax a little."

"I'll take one of those," I say.

Devlin insists, "But just a little. You both were a little too inebriated to function in case we needed to bug out."

I nod, "Yeah I can agree with that, sir."

"Drop the formalities, please," he askingly orders.

"Okay," I acknowledge.

There's an awkward silence broken by the waitress serving my beverage.

I take a sip and then ask, "What exactly is this personal grudge you have against me?" I ask.

Devlin takes a bigger sip of his drink, "It's not personal. As far as I'm concerned, your presence is threat to the ship. You were discharged after being found guilty of espionage."

"I was never found guilty," I point out, "A verdict was never rendered because a court martial never ended up taking place."

"Look," Devlin says, "Keller trusts you so that is what it is. I don't and no amount of your side of the story is going to convince me otherwise. They don't just kick out people who did nothing wrong. At the very least you did something and that's all there is to it."

I clarify, "So you're prejudiced simply because the official story told you to be?"

"Okay," Devlin says, "Right now your usefulness outweighs your potential to harm the ship, but don't push your luck. See if anything comes up with Keller's son. If I need you for anything else I'll let you know. Beyond that, I don't care to know you and I never will. Leave me."

I nod and get up taking my drink with me. Fuck that guy. He's the typical career minded officer, programmed to be a good boy willing to do anything that gets him a promotion and please whoever is his designated master. That black and white thinking is what keeps people in line, never questioning the morality of the orders passed upon them. Perception is everything, but more importantly, perception is whatever he decides. You know what, I'm fucking glad I wasn't allowed to stay in. Seems it was for the better.

I return to my room waiting for Jeff to contact me. Lede eventually slogs out of bed and asks, "What are we doing today?"

"Nothing," I answer, "Just waiting for Jeff."

Lede nods, "Well I feel like shit, but I don't feel like staying here. Wanna get some lunch?"

"I suppose I could eat again," I say.

Lede showers quickly and I decide to do the same. After getting dressed we head out to the terminal. This time we head to Veranda. It's more like a cozy village, a little low key and relaxing. Like an ancient Thomas Kinkade painting, but with various red colored bluffs and cliffs in the backdrop and an orange sky.

We arrive at a fairly priced Italian restaurant. I inform Lede that we can drink, but should avoid getting drunk.

Lede acknowledges, "We'll just make sure we're sober when we get back this time," and laughs.

Meh. Might as well relax a bit more.

After lunch, we find another pub overlooking an artificial lake. It would be rather romantic if I were with Dev... but I guess my new friend will have to do.

We wait until the pool table is available, mostly sipping down light beer. I check my COMM unit regularly only to find nothing from anyone. Not even Jeff. Lede kicks my ass yet again in pool. Even more sober I still can't best him.

As the sun begins setting, I finally get a notification from Jeff saying he'll disseminate the information, but doesn't want to hear from me again. I inform Lede that our mission is done and that maybe this time we should turn in a little earlier.

We get back to our room without incident and pretty much pass out afterwards. Now we hang out until the other guys find what we need, to expose what's going on. Hopefully there is something to find.

Chapter Nineteen: "Time to go."

(*Nathan*)Rapping loudly, I awake to the sound of someone pounding on the door. Great. What did I do now? I slug out of bed, and upon opening the door am greeted by Captain Trinn.

"Time to go," he says.

"Wait, what?" I ask as he brushes passed and turns on the light.

"Up and at em, helmsman," he says, "time to see what you can do."

Lede groans loudly as he starts to roll around in the bed.

I ask, "What's going on?"

"No time. Get packed," Trinn orders rushing out of our room.

I grab my bag and start shoving everything I brought then I start putting on my pants and shirt. I finish packing the last of my things and the data disc copies catch my eyes. I decide to leave one behind. Maybe someone will find it. Clearly I missed an opportunity yesterday finding someone else to disseminate our info as well as pick up new clothing... dammit.

Strapping up my boots, Trinn pokes his head in the doorway, "Train is leaving the station." and starts leaving.

Lede says, "You don't think he'll actually-"

"Let's not stay and find out," I say picking up my bag and heading out into the hallway. Lede runs up behind me and slows down once at my pace.

"What is going on exactly?" he asks.

I shrug, "We'll find out on the ship."

Trinn's crewmembers and ours all gather in the lobby and then hurriedly out to the shipyard. We start moving at a light jog. It's too early for this shit. We round the corner into where the Lambadda is docked and start running to the main airlock on the port side of the ship.

As we're boarding, one of the dock workers comes out, "Captain Trinn! Captain Trinn, your ship isn't ready!"

"I don't care, we're leaving," Trinn says.

"Sir I have to insist you wait until repairs are-" he's cut off as Trinn brandishes a pistol, "Uh… okay if you insist."

Trinn smirks and then boards his ship. I pull out one of the data discs and hand it to him, "Here. It'll explain everything. Just make sure you look at it on a home system."

He takes it, unsure of what to do next.

Lede and I rush into the ship and onto the main bridge. Lede takes a seat at the main helm. I decide to sit next to him and begin the startup sequence. Trinn's helmsman arrives and I give him my seat.

Trinn, in his chair pulls up a screen.

"Mike, you there?" he asks.

"**Yes,**" the Sub-Commander says, "**Are you ready to receive?**"

"Send it," Trinn says.

"Send what?" I ask.

"**Transmitting now,**" a crewman on the other end of the communication says.

I look at Trinn dumfounded.

He explains, "Your Sub-Commander went with two of your crewmen posing as inspectors conducting a surprise security inspection. Unfortunately it went horribly wrong and we've had to go to plan bee."

"Plan bee?" I ask.

Devlin says over the COMM, "**I don't know how much longer we can hold out. You're probably not going to get all the data, are you recording this communication?**"

"I record all communication," Trinn says.

Lede informs, "Break-away thrusters are ready, but the shipyard is refusing to detatch its moorings."

"Oh well," Trinn orders, "take us up."

The ship begins to shake violently as we try to break away from the shipyard.

Trinn yells, "Ajax! Fire up the tee dee!"

Lede looks back at Trinn who orders, "Mind your stick!"

Lede continues to add more thrust as I stumble to a passenger chair located just behind him and to his left. I strap in. Outside we hear the shipyard clamps begin to break as we start pulling away. We smooth out and begin to ride a little easier.

Lede starts to pitch up and then Trinn orders, "Stay low! We're not going to make it out before we're intercepted by fighter craft."

Lede asks, "Then where are we going?"

"We're gonna tunnel," Trinn says.

"What?" Lede panics, "In the atmosphere-."

Sub-Commander yells over the COMM, "**Trinn! They're coming through the door! I don't know what information you're getting but we watched communications between officials of the Prime Minister's Office as well as meetings between the Del Arreba see ee oh and the Prime Minister herself about plans to give Del Areeba-**" he cuts out completely.

I suggest, "Why don't we go back for them! We can shoot out the window with-"

"Fighters on the incoming!" Trinn's crew member informs.

"Ajax, I need a tunnel!" Trinn says.

"Thirty seconds to spin up," Ajax says.

Trinn orders Lede, "Okay Guardian, let's see what you got. Keep em guessing for a bit. Gunner, hold off the fighters as best you can."

Lede maneuvers the ship towards uninhabited territory.

Looking at a map real quick I say, "44XR"

"Gotch ya, man" he says and turns the ship 44 degrees to the left then asks, "What do you have in mind?"

"Plenty of obstacles to use to our advantage," I say.

Lede thrusts the ship ahead full.

A crew member informs, "Got more fighters coming in! Looks like they've scrambled the entire defense force!"

"As expected," Trinn states surprisingly calm.

Lede sees a large canyon ahead and maneuvers towards it as the fighters close in. The gunner opens fire, trying his best, but unable to strike the trained and experienced fighter pilots.

Lede banks into a crevasse scraping the hull a bit as he does.

"Sorry," he mutters.

Trinn says, "Just don't smash into any cliff walls. My ship has thicker armor than most others, but it's not invincible to physics."

Ajax informs, "Tee dee hot and ready."

Trinn orders, "All stop. Pitch up sixty degrees."

Lede throttles into hover and then pitches the ship.

"Dig it!" Trinn orders.

The fighters quickly turn around, but it turns out to be a fatal mistake. As the singularity begins to form it starts to suck in dirt and small debris all around us, but the fighters are pulled into its backside and are completely obliterated.

The singularity itself appears unstable, bouncing around uncontrollably, but still growing. We start to feel a powerful pull forward which is strange since we're not yet moving... now we're moving into the tunnel.

We're pulled in and begin to be violently thrown around inside the tunnel. I look around expecting the ship to get ripped apart. I can only assume we're tumbling and getting pulled every which way by the gravimetric forces. My chair swivels and I look out the doorway into the passage to the rest of the ship and watch as it starts to twist and contort. I can't believe what I'm seeing. The sound stuns me as I am sure the bridge is about to be torn off any second.

Just as I'm sure we're about to die, Trinn orders, "Kill it!"

The tearing and sheering noises suddenly stop as we drift out into normal space.

Lede informs, "Thrusters are... amazingly intact."

Trinn unbuckles his seat and walks over to the doorway. He informs, "You're gonna have to stabilize manually... I'd say the ship has been twisted almost sixty degrees from front to back."

"How is that possible?" I ask, "Shouldn't we have been torn to pieces?"

Trinn says, "Your little Cutter would have torn apart, but my rig is a little more streamlined. As I mentioned, I also have thicker armor. Since I can't own any real fire power, I compensated by strengthening my defenses. That said, I may have pushed it too far. I'm gonna have to have her pulled apart piece by piece, my hull plating re-mended and aligned."

One of Trinn's crewman informs, "I think I've got our position calculated. Should I fire off the beacon?"

Trinn ponders a second, "Let's see what our status is. If we can't tunnel to the rendezvous point, then we'll have no choice. Just stand by for now. Have we got a full damage report?"

The crewman shakes his head, "Internal COMMS appear to be damaged."

Lede adds, "I just lost aft thrusters."

Looking at me, Trinn orders, "Head down to the Grav-Core. Get me a status update."

I nod and Trinn begins to task his other crew members to be runners. In times of communications blackout on board, runners are used to report updates from various stations. Only problem is, information flows only as fast as the runner.

I make my way to the Grav-Core, which happens to be located two levels below the bridge. The door appears to be sealed. I bang on it and a couple of seconds later it opens with dark colored smoke billowing out and the Grav-Crew members coughing.

"What happened?" I ask.

One crew member stumbles out, "Core overload," she says, "but it's under control. The smoke is just pieces of the core that have been pulverized."

Sure enough the room clears, revealing what I can describe best as a melted crater where the core should be. There's pretty much nothing left.

I ask, "Are you alright?"

All the crew members nod lightly. I look each of them over to make sure none of them have any major medical issues. As far as I can tell, none of them will bleed out. But I could be wrong.

I hurry back to the bridge and report to Trinn what happened.

"Fuck!" he expresses, clearly irritated. He walks over to the chart and ponders, "We should be far enough that Valkyrie will get the signal and get here before anyone else."

Lede suggests, "We should change the Beacon's Callsign."

"To what?' Trinn asks.

I say, "The Jeff Wrennor. That's Keller's son's name. He'll pick up on it faster than anyone else."

Trinn nods, "That's our best bet. Jem, set our callsign to that and put out an assistance request beacon. Emergency will attract unwanted attention."

The crew member nods. Trinn's other runners come back to report damage. There's a couple of injuries, but thankfully no deaths. Trinn leaves the bridge to inspect some of the damage himself.

Lede and I wait patiently since we would pretty much get in the way. Trinn comes back onto the bridge almost 20 minutes later. Before I can greet him, he looks towards his office where he storms off to. He's obviously not in a good mood. After he enters and closes his door, I get up and go after him to see how he is doing. I hit the buzzer on the door.

"What?" he asks.

I enter and close the door behind me, "I'm sorry," I say.

"Oh," he says, "Sorry doesn't fix my ship."

"Look, I'm just along for the ride," I confess, "I was actually a miner on the Ex Del Seven before I ended up on Valkyrie. They boarded us, terminated our voyage and I ended up on their ship out of necessity when the Gerlak attacked Keldon."

Trinn nods slowly, "So you're not even a member of the Armada."

I explain, "Long story short, I was framed for espionage and kicked out. But that doesn't mean I haven't faced sacrifice in all of this. I don't know what is going on, but I can tell you that with the information we have, it will all be worth all of this."

Trinn sighs, "I know. But this isn't just about my ship. It's my crew. That maneuver was reckless and so yes, I hope it's worth it. But what exactly is your motivation? Why did you volunteer for this mission?"

I explain, "I met someone on the Cutter and she was taken from me. Before that, these fuck ass aliens ruined my life and now it seems that people in our government are complicit in that."

"Is that confirmed in the information we stole?" Trinn asks.

"I'll start looking into it now," I say and I turn and leave.

I ask the communications crewmember if he can download the information Devlin sent to us- damn… it just hit me. The Sub-Commander and the two Crewmen he took with him are probably in chains now. Anyway, I get the information on a pad and take it to my seat. I begin to mull it over. A lot of it is more detailed information about agreements between Del Areeba and the Office of the Prime Minister. I notice that only about 60% of the

- 422 -

intended information was received by us, meaning the real damning evidence might not have made it.

There is a correspondence between the Interior Minister and the Del Areeba CEO explaining that nine new systems were going to be charted soon and proposing an agreement to give Del Areeba exclusive rights as long as Del Areeba only answered to the Office of the Prime Minister. Directly colluding with a corporation for mining rights is certainly obvious corruption, but I doubt it will win over public interest. Actually, it for sure won't, aside from the people who are against the Prime Minister and the entire Unitian Party.

I try to search keywords. Devlin had mentioned something about the Prime Minister being directly involved, but nothing seems to be pulling up. So it could be assumed that she isn't involved if at all.

I look for "gerlak" and "aliens" but nothing comes up. Looks like Del Areeba didn't know about them. Now it seems that the Gerlak might actually be a surprise foe. Could it be everything we thought was going on was wrong? Yes actually. Oh shit…

Contemplating how I'm going to spend my time in prison, my thoughts are interrupted by an alarm going off.

Lede mentions, "Singularity detected!"

The communications guy says over the PA, "Captain to the bridge."

Within seconds Trinn arrives on the bridge, "Are they coming through?"

"Seems like," Lede says.

The singularity is about twelve-hundred meters away from us. We wait hoping to confirm it's who we want it to be.

Lede reports initial readings, "It's a Constellation Cutter signature- wait… it's broadcasting…"

We all look out the viewport. It's definitely a Valkyrie Class. Then the ship info displays.

"Oh no…" I mutter and look at Trinn, "It's the Kara."

We hear over the COMM, "**Unknown mining vessel, this is Constellation Cutter Kara. Come in.**"

Trinn grabs a handset on his chair and sits down, "This is the Jeff Wrenner. How can we be of assistance?"

Kara comes back, "**First by identifying yourself. The Jeff Wrennor doesn't appear on the Guild Registry.**"

"We're a freelance vessel," Trinn responds.

"**Yeah we checked that list too,**" Kara retorts, "**so are you operating in Republic Space illegally?**"

Trinn thinks for a second, "We're a new vessel. We might not be on the registry yet."

"**I see,**" the Kara says, "**Well we'll have to check your papers when we come aboard. I also notice the damage on your ship is rather indicative of an unstable tunneling, which is interesting since we got a report of a mining vessel illegally tunneling out of Mars. So maybe we should start with my first question: who are you?**"

There's a silence on the bridge. This is it. This is where our journey comes to an end. Then behind the Kara, another singularity appears. We sit on the edge of our seats-well I do anticipating who it is and hoping it's- she comes though and sure enough

Lede shouts, "Its Valkyrie!"

Seconds later we hear Keller over the COMM, "**Constellation Cutter Kara this is Valkyrie. Stand down.**"

We watch as Valkyrie pulls behind Kara, guns poised at her engines. Best I can tell they're gonna go for disabling shots if needs be. Not that they'll return the courtesy.

The Kara comes back, "**Valkyrie... you've been marked as a rogue vessel. Not that I'm surprised, considering your guns are pointed at me. Do you plan to attack me like you did the naval vessels?**"

Keller responds, "**Commander Dougland, correct?**"

Kara says back, "**Yes.**"

Keller continues, "**Do you really think for a second we could take out an entire fleet?**"

There's silence for a bit before Kara, or rather her Commander, Dougland I assume says, "**I have to admit that is a bit unbelievable and yet it supposedly happened.**"

Keller says, "**Look, Dougland we can start shooting at each other, I can leave you adrift here disabled and be on my way with our mining vessel, or you can trust me Commander to Commander and come aboard my ship where I can explain to you everything that has happened to us so far. I could transmit all my information, but that's more impersonal for what I have to explain to you.**"

"**And how do I know I can trust you?**" Dougland asks.

A few seconds go by and Valkyrie's guns return to facing forward. They then start to maneuver alongside Kara in a more friendly posture. We eagerly await a response.

Finally Dougland says, "**Alright, Keller I'll prepare an envoy... though seeing as you've cut off long** range communications, I feel I don't have much of a choice..."

"**You'll understand why when you get here. See you soon, Keller out.**"

All of us on the Lambadda sigh relief.

Trinn goes out over the COMM, "Commander Keller, this is Captain Trinn. If you haven't noticed yet, my ship has been badly damaged and contorted. I require extensive repairs as soon as you can help make that happen."

"**I'll inform engineering,**" Keller says.

Lede and I sort of look at each other and then I ask, "Is there anything we can do to help?"

"I think you've done enough," Trinn says, "have you found the evidence you needed?"

I shake my head slowly, "The only thing we have is whatever was in Sub-Commander's transmission. I'll keep looking, but key words aren't even popping up."

Trinn becomes irritated and heads back to his office. I decide to follow him.

Hitting the buzzer again, "Come in," he says. He looks up at me as I close the door, "So... you mean to tell me that the sixty percent of data we secured is useless?"

I explain, "I mean it implicates the Office of the Prime Minister in blatant corruption and corporate favoritism, but..."

Trinn expectedly chuckles, "So you mean to tell me that I risked my crew and sacrificed my ship for petty politics."

I remain silent as I think of an answer, "It's starting to look that way... and I hate to say it, but it seems like the Gerlak were a random encounter."

Trinn's facial expression says, "You're fucking kidding" without having to say it.

I continue, "Based on the information, it seems that the Prime Minister might-"

The buzzer goes off.

Trinn says, "Come in."

The crew member Jem walks in, "Sorry to interrupt Captain, but Valkyrie is sending three vessels, two for assisting repairs, and the other to grab our Guardian passengers."

Trinn nods and Jem leaves. Trinn looks back at me, "Guess you had better get ready to go."

I nod slowly and turn and leave. His life is pretty much over. Hell most all of ours are. Do I want to board that transport and break the news to Keller, or walk out the other airlock? Nah. I'm not suicidal enough for that.

Lede, the rest of the Valkyrie Crewmates and myself climb aboard the transport ship. We don't say much on the ride back. I look out the viewport at the Lambadda. She's pretty badly contorted, but I don't think beyond repair. Trinn should be able to sell it for his legal fees.

My attention is grabbed by Lede as he slumps the pad into my lap after having mulled it over.

"Fuck..." he expresses, "I couldn't find anything either..."

I reply with an anxious sigh. Keller is not going to like the news.

The memory of my walk through the passageways back to the Officer's Mess is blurred by trying to figure out how I'm going to explain to Keller that we got nothing. Our entire journey hinged on this mission and we more or less failed. In my head I've been contemplating if the other 40% of data would really make all the difference. I mean, sure it's a big margin- we round the corner into the Officer's Mess.

Keller finishes, "And that's when I met with Captain Wrennor at Lantic Station. Ah, gentlemen. I'm bringing Commander Dougland here up to speed. Please sit if you don't mind."

We say nothing as we head towards the back, as most of the room is occupied by Dougland's envoy. I await my chance to speak, contemplating what I want to say as Keller rambles on about events I was already a part of.

Keller finishes, "Which brings us to the Lambadda mission, of which Sub-Commander Devlin who seems to be taking his time getting here-"

I interrupt, "Uh… I guess no one told you- he uh… didn't make it."

"What do you mean didn't make it?" Keller asks concernedly.

I explain, "He stayed behind to transmit data from the Del Areeba offices while we made our getaway- well he and two others. But there's a problem…"

Keller, obviously taken back by this asks, "Well what's the problem? Don't tell me the mission was a total failure."

I am silent as I try to figure out what to say, "Uh… well it may have been doomed to fail from the start. Lede and I were able to contact your son and get him the information, but… well what info we did steal from Del Areeba doesn't have anything damning."

Keller is quiet a second then inquires, "What data do you have?"

I walk up to him and hand him the pad, "It implicates the Office of the Prime Minister colluding with

Del Areeba for exclusive mining rights, but that's it. No mention of gerlak, no aliens, nothing."

Keller starts looking through the pad as Dougland notes, "Well collusion is hardly anything to sway public opinion over. Even if there is proof, Jackson will undoubtedly deny she was involved."

Silence takes the room as Keller tries to find anything that can back up his stance. He's sure there is something there.

I take no pride in having to say this, "Commander… I think we were wrong about this… I think the aliens were in fact a random arrival and I think the Prime Minister is in fact trying to work out a peace agreement…"

Keller looks right into my soul and shakes his head fastly, "No. It's all too convenient. How did the aliens anticipate our moves so accurately? I even have proof that Yelkin admitted to giving our position away to them."

I'm quiet a moment as I think of an answer but can only shrug, "Even then, they did say it was out of a show of good faith."

"More like cleaning up a loose end," Keller retorts then looks at Dougland, "Regardless, you've seen our footage. These things aren't peaceful, they're hostile in every encounter."

Dougland, a younger Commander who may actually be on the fast track to Admiral ponders, "Yes, but… your crewman makes a good point. Maybe it was the way you presented yourself that they felt threatened."

Keller becomes irritated and bends over supporting himself on the table, "Randall, I'm telling you they showed up at Keldon and immediately opened fire. And their tracking isn't that good, as we evaded them when we went dee ess ae and threw them off."

Dougland takes a breath then orders, "Kara personnel, give us the room please."

"Valkyrie Crewmen, the same," Keller orders.

I nod and leave the room, but where am I supposed to go...

(*Keller*)...The last of the Kara Crewmen closes the door behind them and Dougland and I are now able to speak freely.

Dougland says, "I don't doubt anything you have shown me. A lot of it is compelling and makes sense, but... I can take your information to the Armada Admiralty and try to get some answers, however like you have had to look after your crew, I must also think of mine- I mean conspiracy is a hell of a fuckin charge, Jaysen."

I take a deep breath, "It is, which is why I sent the mining vessel to get proof, but I'll need to sit down and read through all of this to be sure it was all for naught. I'd like to ask that you wait until I can confirm."

Dougland slowly shakes his head, "I already have to explain why the mining vessel 'Jeff Wrennor' turned out to be nothing of importance and then why it is I suddenly want to go to Armada aitch que."

I understandingly nod and grab the data disc and hand it to him. Then ask, "Is there a frequency I can reach you on if I find more information?"

He nods, "Yes, and I'll have it transmitted to you once I'm back on my ship. I wish there was more to be done here, Keller, but I gotta look after my own first. Would you do any differently in my place?"

I shake my head truthfully.

"I figured," he says and takes the data disc and leaves.

What really sucks is that if he were in my position he would be begging me to do more. I suppose the reason I am not is because I've already done this song and dance and it has gotten us nowhere.

I arrive on the bridge and take it upon my presence being announced. I head over to the port side saying nothing, only to stare out the viewport attempting to figure out what we do now.

Lieutenant Jefferson informs, "Commander Dougland's Outflyer has left, sir... I'm guessing things didn't go well."

I turn to him, "Nope... we've managed to get nowhere again. How are the repairs going on Captain Trinn's ship?"

He informs, "Well... we can fix the hull and structure, but it'll take a few days... his Grav-Core is... well it's gone."

"Damn..." I say, "Alright, we'll gather some funds from the ship's coffers to reimburse him and then send him on his way... Unless he wants an escort somewhere. Keep me informed on the continued repairs. I'm going to be looking this over," I finish, holding the pad.

I try to look for keywords but immediately nothing pops up. Guess I'm going to have to look it over word for word. By then Dougland will be long gone.

Lieutenant Jefferson shouts from the Communication and Information Crater, "Commander! We've picked up a transmission from the Office of the Prime Minister. It appears to be open sourced and uncoded. Looks like they're about to broadcast a live message. Do you want to see it?"

I exaggerate a large nod and order, "Play it throughout the ship!"

He nods and I turn my attention to the screen mounted above my chair. A clip of the Republic Anthem plays followed by someone saying, "Please stand by for an important message from the Prime Minister." This lasts for almost ten minutes until the screen changes and the address begins:

Ladies and gentleman, the Prime Minister for the United Constellation Republic. Good morning, good afternoon or good evening wherever you may be, across our great systems. I come to you in this way to speak on a matter that many have been curious about, but in the interests of intergalactic peace, have had to keep under wraps. We wanted to bring this information sooner, but peace is a delicate process.

Allow me to go back to a month and a half ago when we lost contact with three of our colonies. Initially we believed we were being invaded, but upon quickly making contact with our supposed invaders, we learned that we had actually encroached on grounds they consider Holy. Out of respect we chose to withdraw our military forces and begin discussions about a peaceful resolution.

Who are they? They are the Gerlak Sanctum. The question we have asked for thousands of years has been answered. We aren't alone. But let us not misunderstand their dedication to their religion as hostility. They are reasonable beings and we have been working towards a lasting peace between our peoples. Their systems belong to them, but in return they have shared nine new systems which contain resources which they have offered to us in the interest of friendship further enriching our great democracy. And the colonists of the worlds they annexed will be given full citizenship status under their leadership.

I know some of you are eager to contact your friends and families. I have to ask that you wait just a little bit longer. They have a very rare and special opportunity to learn the customs of the Gerlak culture firsthand and upon doing so, travel back to these systems will be reestablished. However this is a lengthy process and it takes time.

We are aware of the speculation surrounding what's happened and we are putting it to rest right now. Your friends and families on the colonies are safe. And let me be especially clear that the Gerlak are our friends. We are not at war and we will do everything we can to work together to improve each other and grow stronger together.

Hostile actions within the Republic are not tolerated, but consider this my mandate that they will be especially not tolerated towards our new friends. I am organizing a special task force with the express purpose of dealing with dissidents who mistreat our allies. This is not a threat. It is imperative that you understand how sensitive this process will be for years to come. In order to make peace possible and lasting I have asked the Chamber of Senate to pass temporary resolution in suspending Speech Immunity specifically towards the Gerlak Sanctum. That is the level of sacrifice necessary to secure peace. But no amount of sacrifice is too great and in this instance you're only surrendering a right temporarily instead of your lives permanently. It is not worth going to war when we can just be kind and respectful to each other to solidify a friendship.

More information about the Gerlak will start being composed and posted on the Gal-Net from official government sources. Other approved news sources will also have extensive information about their culture, customs and courtesies, and how we will communicate with them.

This is going to be a challenge for us all and I know a lot of you may be confused by this. I can assure you that speculation is unnecessary. We will inform you of everything completely and will do our best to answer everyone's questions accurately. Despite any information or so called "footage" of a so called "attack" on any of our colony worlds that may come up, I can tell you here with absolution that it is a xenophobic attempt to derail peace. Unless information comes from official sources, it is a fabrication and must be reported and then ignored.

This will take time. But I successfully united the two defecting factions. I will successfully bring our great nation and the Gerlak together with your help. Be good and be well.

As expected, she has to make it about herself at the end. Amazingly covered up what she needed to, except the destruction of Lantic Station, although that place sat just outside of Republic Space so she certainly wasn't obligated to.

Lieutenant Jefferson informs, "Sir! Commander Dougland is requesting to come back aboard."

I figured. I nod, "Have him escorted to my office once he's here."

Lieutenant Jefferson acknowledges my order and I hand him the bridge as I leave. Now the question remains: what do we do next? I'll have to turn to my pal Whiskey to help me think. Help us think. Commander Dougland and I have some hard things to figure out. But where do we even begin?

I arrive at my office and proceed straight through to my quarters. I go to my kitchen area and open the cabinet containing my remaining bottles of Amberglash. I move most of them out of the way to reveal the special reserve bottles. I take one and grab two scotch glasses and take them out to my desk. I set them down and pour them about half full. I sit down at my desk and contemplate what we'll discuss. I think I should just let him speak and go from there.

A few quiet minutes go by and there's a rap on my door.

"Come in," I invite.

Dougland comes in looking a bit more distraught than when he left. I point my hand to the glass and he grabs it before sitting down. He takes a large sip and then looks up at me.

He begins, "I don't know where to begin."

"Oh," I acknowledge, "you see, that's a problem because I don't know where to begin either."

We sit awkwardly silent for a few moments, sipping our respective drinks, attempting to fathom any sense. Well, I mean he's attempting to fathom sense I, more or less, already have. I guess it's just one of those situations where I didn't want to be right... again.

I state, "Initially I wanted to try and invoke Directive Seventeen, but I wanted more proof. At this point, however, I don't think any of the Directives will be recognized. She's directly working with the Gerlak, and she has pretty much secured public opinion."

Dougland nods taking another sip and upon finishing, "I uh.... I almost would rather go along with it for now, but that's playing the safe card and giving up leverage. You have all the proof we need. We know what those aliens are-"

I interruptingly shake my head, "She flat out disavowed us, or at least I assume so. My son must have uploaded the information already."

Dougland raises a brow, "General public opinion might be hers for now, but that is not guaranteed. We are technically an official source. Together, if we presented your information on a public forum, we could win support to demand an investigation of transparency."

"Okay," I acknowledge, "we divide enough public support and then what? Wait for an election cycle?"

Dougland is silent, formulating a response, then, "Well, I mean, the conspiracy nuts will start circulating everything, but we gotta move quick before she comes back with another address and outright names you as a rogue agent."

He's got a point there. I reply, "Alright, sure, but then what? We're basically banking on the Republic to sway, completely based on our information."

Dougland nods, "Yes, but we only need half the systems. We can also start going to other Captains and Admirals directly and explaining to them our side of things to persuade them to our side. If we get at least half of the Naval and Armada forces turned-"

"Then what?" I semi snap, "we try to compel her party in the senate to begin a Transparency Inquiry? Even if they do so it'll be for show and I'll still go to prison if not worse- I'm sorry, Randall I... I've just been through so much and I already tried playing politics with Mattie and now she's dead... I'm a simple Cutter Commander, man... I've already ended up deeper in this than I should have..."

It's quiet for a second as I try to regain my composure.

Dougland says, "The hardest part about this job... is never knowing what to do when we're clearly in over our heads... but we have to remember what we took an oath for. First and foremost to uphold the Articles and Directives of the Laws of Systems. Does that still mean anything to you?"

I contemplate a second and nod slowly.

He continues, "Same... we didn't take an oath to obey orders blindly and I know, compared to the might of the Stellar Navy, we're piss into the vacuum. Man I was ready to just leave you here, but the second that bullshit transmission finished playing I knew something much more sinister was going on. Now I won't pretend to know everything, but I know that a suspension of absolute rights is wrong, regardless of the intentions. You know what we have to do..."

I reply, "I... I actually think I do... but you don't just yet."

Dougland raises a brow.

I point out, "From a tactical perspective if the Gerlak felt they could win in all-out war, that's what we would be in right now. But instead they are entertaining the idea of peace talks, meaning they don't possess the capability to take us out head-on or at least they know it won't be a guaranteed victory."

Dougland nods and then speculates, "They must have thought they could at first, hence the initial attacks, but were quickly beaten back. However, we couldn't charge back at them; at least not immediately."

I affirm, "So that means on the battlefield we are pretty much equals. Enough advantages and disadvantages that balance out."

Dougland sounding defeated, "That means... we can't divide public opinion."

I nod slowly, "No... worst case scenario, we ignite a civil war, at which point the Gerlak come in and sweep us clean."

Dougland sets his empty glass on the desk and I refill it heavy. He takes it and then takes a quick sip.

He says, "We need to provoke the Gerlak into a conflict. The question is how?"

I look at him in a manner indicating I know the answer but don't want to say it. Judging by his expression, he knows too, but is also afraid to say.

I sigh bigly, "We need a nuke."

Dougland reluctantly nods in agreement and then adds, "We need several. And we need to find the homeworld of these bastards and hit it hard. If their society believes in some Divine Right then I'm pretty sure they're big on Divine Retribution... through themselves of course."

I nod, "Absolutely. So how do we go about giving them a reason? All nuclear facilities are pretty much impenetrable. In fact I'm pretty sure Armada Servicemembers aren't allowed in such facilities without an invitation."

"Correct," Dougland affirms, "Our best bet is going to be getting a Carrier."

I point out, "I already tried to recruit a battlegroup to my cause. It didn't go well."

Dougland nods, "Yeah I think we should see if those Navy pilots of yours can help and go from there."

"Help how?" I ask.

Dougland explains, "I can still safely get onto the Gal-Net. From there depending on what access the flyboys have, we can see if we can find a Carrier undergoing an extended maintenance. Hopefully at Nimitz shipyard. Most of the crews are typically rotated out since the periods of maintenance can be upwards of six months to a year."

I raise a brow, "How do you know this?"

Dougland answers, "My older brother served for a few years and was more or less my inspiration to join the Armada. His first assignment was a Carrier."

I inquire, "And the Carriers just keep their payloads on board?"

He explains, "Yes. Unless the maintenance is longer than a year, the ship should have a full complement of hot and ready nukes on board."

I nod slowly, "Okay, so we locate and commandeer a Carrier. After that we'll need to learn the location of the Gerlak homeworld…" I think for a second then snap my fingers, "The computer data! I'll have my guys see if they can determine a location."

Dougland nods and then all falls silent. Do we really want to do this? Is this the extreme we have been forced to go to?

Dougland shakes his head and then proposes, "How about instead we enact Directive Zulu Lima?"

I snort a scoff, "You really think anyone is going to accept that?"

Dougland points out, "If we were to present our findings as you suggested we could reason that the current government poses an imminent threat to the safety and security of the Republic and a temporary government must be installed to sort out the matter."

I counter, "And how would that not also risk a civil war?"

He ponders unable to come up with an answer.

I say, "Look... I don't want to do this either. But I would be turning my back on everything I took an oath to defend. And so would you. You reminded me just then that our oath doesn't mean shit if we don't uphold it. What we're going to do is extreme, yes. But unless there is another solution, our options are unfortunately limited."

Dougland appeals, "If the opportunity presents itself. I would rather we try to enact Directive Zulu Lima. We'll go with this plan for now, but if the Prime Minister is serious about peace she may be willing to step down and agree to an investigation under temporary leadership."

I nod in agreement, "Absolutely. If a less extreme route reveals itself we will heed to and take it. Until then, let's find us a Carrier," I say, setting my glass down and leaving my office.

Chapter Twenty: "All the way or not at all."

(*Donna*)I set my glass down after taking a sip of rum. With a pad in front of me I try to contemplate a fool proof battle plan to infiltrate the Nimitz shipyard. This is especially complicated, as I never once in my life thought I would have to fight against fellow service members. Don't get me wrong, as a Marine I found the prospect amusing initially, but these people are serving the Republic loyally as the rest of us. But they don't know what we know. They won't understand what it is we have to do. We're on the same side, but they won't know that. They'll see us as the enemy coming to steal a carrier and that's what I have to plan on.

I have thought about the political nonsense surrounding all of this and it's sickening. The fact that people were killed on Keldon Station, some of them my friends, will go without justice is maddening enough. But what I guess I can't understand is how Prime Minister Jackson is so damn blinded. Do they really believe these things are peaceful? I have seen them firsthand. They regard us as low and will most likely exterminate the colonists when it's convenient.

This is becoming a distraction. Keller is still my commanding officer and he has given me a very difficult task. Infiltrating the shipyard will be hard enough, but getting control of the carrier is an entirely different story. It's a new, triple deck carrier. Why is it back in the yards? Well, she's the first in class. According to the Navy Flyboys that means she'll have problems for the first year, or six, of her service, despite being promised to be fully functional upon commissioning... which I guess technically she was fully functioning for six months.

How does this benefit me? Well, one of the pilots was originally assigned to the Carrier Vidar. He claims the ship has minimal crew on board, but should be fully loaded since she was expected to reenter service early next year. But how is that a problem? Well, he gave me a rough schematic to go off of. And even then he never fully explored the vessel. So I have to plan on finding my way around which can be very time consuming.

I look at my glass. One more sip. I really should not pour another... so I won't.

My roommate, Delta Larrodo enters, "Hey how goes the battle plan?"

I answer, "Well I'm almost a whole glass in and no real plan to go on. I don't think we have the manpower to take the entire shipyard and then the Carrier."

Larrodo asks, "Why are we bothering with the shipyard? Why not just steal the ship directly?"

I explain, "According to the information, the magnetic moorings are controlled in the shipyard's main control center. The problem is we've got the shipyard staff and crews from other ships that may be docked there. Even with both deployment teams from both ships, we're extremely short... and not to mention, Kara's crew aren't as trained up as ours."

Larrodo looks over what I've attempted to put together.

He shakes his head, "This needs to be a collaborative effort. Too little crew to work with and too many moving parts."

I nod in agreement and contact the bridge, asking to get ahold of the Commander for me. Upon determining his location, Larrodo and I, with pad in hand, head out to Commander Keller's office.

Upon arrival I explain, "Sir, we just don't have the manpower to take both the shipyard and the Carrier."

Another gentleman present, Commander Dougland, I presume, clarifies, "Even with my deployment teams assisting?"

I shake my head, "Afraid not, sir. If the shipyard staff is there to watch over vessels with nuclear weapons, then their security teams will have outstanding numbers compared to both our teams. And not to mention your teams don't have my training so they'd be better off in a support capacity."

Dougland proposes, "Okay so we'll double down on training my men."

I shake my head. "Sir, all due respect, there just isn't enough time."

Keller asks, "Okay so what are our other options?"

Larrodo speaks up, "Well sir, I think we need to just go for the carrier directly. I don't know what to do about the magnetic moorings, but we should take the ship and not bother with the shipyard."

"How?' Keller asks, "This mission starts with the Sergeant's plan and then we build around that."

"We can't, sir." I say affirmatively, "We need to plan everything all at once."

Keller is quiet for a second and then pulls out his COMM. He orders the deck officer to contact Lieutenants Ephrryn, Dannis and Lester to meet in the briefing room.

He then says, "You both will meet with the el tees in the briefing room and come up with a plan. Then you will bring it to me and if it's good, I will sign off on it, but you will continue to keep this from the crew. Until we have a solid mission that shows we CAN pull this off, I can't exactly convince everyone why they're about to steal a carrier from their brothers and sisters in the Navy and then explain how in doing so they are still upholding their oaths. I understand this is going to take time, but I need you to work quickly. Dismissed."

We leave the room and stop by the Crew's Mess to fill up on coffee. I smell it. Thanks to Kara we reprovisioned our fresh water... it's never tasted so horribly good.

I think I'll just dive right in once we get to the briefing room. Hopefully all of us can figure out a plan- I mean I'm sure we will, but hopefully we can put it together in less than a day.

We walk into the briefing room. Larrodo secures the door behind us.

"Okay," I begin, "Keller wants us to come up with a plan of attack for stealing the Carrier Vidar at the Nimitz shipyard. He wants this as soon as possible."

Lieutenant Ephrryn says, "I thought you were supposed to make an infiltration plan and then build the rest around that."

Larrodo explains, "Sir, we just don't have the manpower to do that. We need to get on the carrier, separate it from the moorings and then tunnel out of the system."

Ehrryn speculates, "Ah... so we're gonna use our remaining Outflyers... I guess that explains why I'm here."

I point out, "The Kara also has some we should be able to use. I figured we'll brief our counterparts once Keller and I guess the Kara's Commander to authorize our plan."

"Alright so we board the carrier with Outflyers and then what?" Ephrryn asks.

I say, "We should probably figure out how we get the Outflyers to the Carrier. Do we know what the shipyard defenses are like?"

Everyone looks around sort of dumb founded.

"Right," I say and head over to the nearby internal COMMS panel.

I contact the bridge and ask them to have the Navy pilots head to the briefing room. Within minutes the names of some of the pilots are said and after some small talk amongst ourselves they finally arrive.

I begin, "Thank you for coming. We've been tasked with putting together the mission to steal a carrier. Before we continue, is this something either of you are willing to help with?"

The male looks at his fellow pilot and then says, "I'm very conflicted. I mean fighting the aliens is one thing, but our own people? I'm aware of the points Keller made, but… nah, I'm out on this one."

I nod understandingly and he leaves the room.

"And what about you, ma'am?" I ask the female pilot.

She answers, "I agree with Commander Keller. It's a shit situation, but those gerlak things are a threat. I also have family on Trista. So how can I be of help?"

"What can you tell us about the shipyard's defenses?" I ask.

She answers, "No mounted batteries that I know of. It's protected by destroyers and cruisers that rotate through the system. They'll either be close by or patrolling on the outskirts. Oh, and at least one Battleship is nearby at all times."

Lieutenant Dannis informs, "I've got an idea on how to grab their attention. We'll use our satellite to broadcast Valkyrie's transponder signal. That might be enough to pull all three of them."

Ephrryn points out, "It could also force them into a defensive posture of the shipyard making sending in boarding craft all the harder."

Everyone thinks for a second.

There's a knock on the door. Delta Larrodo opens it and Lieutenant Esker walks in.

I greet, "Ma'am."

'Sergeant," she acknowledges, "I just got off watch and figured that as acting second in command I should be present for this."

"Well, we're just planning it out," I clarify.

She nods, "I know. I wanna help. What have you got so far?"

I bring her up to speed.

She says, "Okay... Since Kara isn't on any watch lists yet, they'll be the ship we'll want to launch fighters and drop ships from. Valkyrie is going to have to keep the patrolling vessels busy..."

Ephrryn picks up where she left off, "What if we made it seem like Valkyrie was chasing Kara? Have them show up and ask for help. Then when Valkyrie resurfaces, say, all the way over here," he points to a spot on the system map about one hundred kilometers away from the shipyard, "then the fighters and drop ships will launch, once Kara is in range of the target. Sergeant Kroeling will lead the deployment teams to take control of the carrier and then we leave and regroup at our designated coordinates."

I point out, "That's too much time required. It's gonna take us at least ten minutes to figure out how to get to the bridge."

Larrodo asks, "Why? Why not just have your ship dock on the airlock that's closest to it?"

"Where does the rest of the team dock?" I ask.

"We'll we need to take the engine room at least," he points out.

"Okay," I say, "I will lead the rest of the ships that dock elsewhere. You will take the bridge since you can get there quickly. In fact I'll pretty much make sure that no one can retake the bridge from you by securing the rest of the ship."

Ephrryn realizes, "That still leaves too much time… you'll still have to break away from the shipyard."

Lieutenant Lester joins the conversation, "What if we took out the moorings? And what if we did it right away?"

Ephrryn clarifies, "You mean once the Outflyers dock you guys break off and take out the moorings? That would set the ship adrift and cause more chaos…"

Esker adds, "Good idea. That will save you guys from having to get the ship free."

I note, "We'll need to bring some Navigators and Grav-Specialists. Once we have control of the ship, we'll need someone to fly it."

Esker corrects, "Navigators, yes, but Kara will spin up the tunnel to take it through. You won't need Grav-Specialists."

Ephrryn recaps, "Okay… so we 'chase' Kara and while the ships are distracted, the fighters and drop ships deploy. Once the drop ships secure on the airlocks, the fighters will take out the moorings, forcing the Carrier off the shipyard and into a drift. Once we get the Carrier under control, or at least enough to move it, then we all three tunnel away to our meeting point. The only problem is… what do we do about the Battleship?"

No one has an answer until Lieutenant Henan gives hers, "There isn't a whole lot we can do to plan against it. If it gets into range of any of our ships then that's it. We're going to have to take our chances and hope we can successfully evade it."

Ephrryn asks, "Alright, so we want to just take our chances with the Battleship? Hope it's not too close to play?"

Lieutenant Dannis contributes, "I've got an idea: the Satellite transponder. We could have it broadcast a distress call far enough away to pull the battleship."

"How do we know it would be the one to respond?" Ephrryn arrogantly asks.

Dannis adds, "Better yet, we'll have it broadcast a pirate signal. That should be threatening enough to attract the biggest gun to respond."

Ephrryn raises a brow and concedes, "That might work… it would still take at least one of the ships out of play either way."

Esker suggests, "We should probably drift to that location. We don't want a singularity to be picked up by the shipyard's or the patrol ship's sensors. Did the Commander indicate any possibility of conducting reconnaissance?"

Larrodo and I slowly shake our head and he says, "It seems he wants to get in, take the carrier and get out. Recon could potentially mean getting caught."

Esker nods, "Seems we're banking a lot on chance, here."

I explain, "Ma'am, I know you're used to routine operations that mostly go according to plan. I know you're used to being in control of everything and being an overwhelming force when it comes to dealing with pirates, smugglers- whoever it was you would normally plan missions to apprehend.

"In this instance, we aren't the overwhelming force." I start to look at everyone, "This is something you all have to understand. We're the underdog in this op. There are factors we have control of and ones that we don't. Our advantage here is to take them off balance: surprise them. In the chaos, we'll remain focused and execute our plan."

Everyone nods, seemingly inspired by my confidence. Thankfully I am too, a little bit. Do I think this will work? I will make it work.

Larrodo and I complete our specifics on taking the carrier with the limited information we have regarding the layout. We discuss the plan one more time and then we ask Keller and Commander Dougland to join us.

After briefing them, and making a few minor tweaks to the overall mission plan, Keller asks us to prepare a brief in the main hangar, as most of both crews will be in attendance.

We get the holoprojectors set up and a control device uplinked so that each of us can explain visually what Commander Keller will be discussing.

After about two hours we get everyone gathered up around the stage. Lieutenant Esker informs the Commander that everyone is ready, and ten minutes later he arrives.

Keller takes a mic and begins, "Good evening, Valkyrie and Kara Crewmates... I know it's been a while and you've all been in the dark as to what's going on. But I and Commander Dougland didn't want to ask of you what we're about to without a mission planned out.

"By now all of you should have seen the Valkyrie logs and video files of everything that has happened so far. You should have also reviewed the Prime Minister's address that she sent out yesterday. You've seen our footage. You know what the Gerlak are capable of. What Commander Dougland and I realized is that they can't exterminate us in direct conflict. We also firmly believe they are using peace as a ruse to get us to lower our defenses and enslave us all from within.

"Sergeant Kroeling led a daring recon and rescue on their crashed scout ship on Thretta Five. I'll replay that conversation so you all understand where we're coming from."

Keller presses a button and a video plays of our conversation with the Gerlak:

"You swine! How dare thy disgrace our holy vessel!"

I respond, "Pretty sure it was already unclean when you brought the other human on board."

The alien says, *"I speak not of thy hideous presence, but of that which they slain. You deprived a noble servant of the"* the video skips briefly, but only I and probably a few others notice, *"Gerlak Sanctum."*

I continue, "My interaction with your species has consisted of hostile actions against my fellow humans and nothing more as far as we understand."

"That includes if we unarmed" the gerlak asks.

I continue again, "I didn't know and couldn't take that risk so I shot it- I mean them."

The Gerlak diatribes *"Ye race is a blight upon galaxy. In years to come we will extinguish ye aggressive and savage swine. Ye kills innocence out of fear. Ye will be easy prey*."

I sigh, "I can tell this is going to be a productive relationship. How do I reverse engineer your translation program?"

"*Ye is an inconvenience upon universe. Thy will be cleansed,*" the clip jumps ahead again, "*All ye needs to know is thy will be purged by Thee*."

There's a brief pause then we hear Agsnon say, "How many… very well, Sergeant! Six more have just entered the ship! Overwatch is asking for instructions."

"Tell her to try and slow them down," I order, then focus my attention back to the alien, "You clever mother fucker."

The Gerlak replies, "*I still meant every word.*" It continues, "*Your race is hideous, especially compared to some of the others we've wiped out*."

I clarify, "So you're not just a religious cult?"

The gerlak explains, "*I am a scientist, but I am also a patriot. We are the Supreme Race divinely blessed to purge swine such as yourself from the universe*."

"You sound awfully sure of yourselves," I note.

It replies, "*If it weren't true, how come we've never been beaten? How come every other scum we've conquered and eradicated hasn't been able to prevent their extinction?*"

The video pauses with the Gerlak in frame. Keller presses another button and the image changes to stills of all of our encounters with the Gerlak from both space and planetside.

Keller begins, "You know what we're up against. Yet we've been told by our Prime Minister that the Gerlak are interested in peace. You," Keller points to someone standing in the front row, "what is the first line of your Oath of Service?"

"I- uh," the poor Crewman fumbles, "to uphold the Articles of Freedom and Governance and to serve the citizens of the Republic."

Keller asks, "And do you remember the second line?"

"It's, um… to carry out all lawful orders directed to me by the Prime Minister and those that also follow from my superiors."

Keller reiterates, "To uphold the Articles and to carry out lawful orders."

Keller hits a button that replays the following from the Prime Minister's message, "In order to make peace possible and lasting, I have asked the Chamber of Senate to pass temporary resolution in suspending Speech Immunity, specifically towards the Gerlak Sanctum."

Keller continues, "She has directed the Senate to suspend Speech Immunity… The first Right of Freedom under the Articles is to be suspended. I want you to answer honestly, is this a lawful order to uphold such a resolution."

Some people start to mutter their answers and then an elongated "no" is heard in the hangar.

"What?" Keller asks.

"No!" the Crewmen say resoundingly through the hangar.

"No it isn't" Keller says, "The Prime Minister is willing to suspend the rights of the people in order to achieve her peace with aliens we know firsthand are NOT peaceful." He takes a deep breath, possibly contemplating his next words carefully.

"Unfortunately," he begins, "we can't just convince others of this fact. Yes, there are those who probably agree, but Prime Minister Jackson has made her party strong by securing peace and re-uniting the Republic. What's worse is that the Gerlak are equals on the battlefield. So I ask you all, what do you think a civil war might do?"

The Crewmembers look amongst each other and mutter some thoughts.

Keller says, "The Republic becomes divided, at which point the Gerlak swoop in and exterminate us with ease. So we either spark a civil war or we obey our Prime Minister and allow an alien race to exterminate us slowly from within."

Someone asks, "How do we know the Gerlak don't want peace?"

Keller answers, "Do I need to play the clip again? They make it clear."

A couple of Crewman shout from the back simultaneously, "Then what do we do!?"

Keller sort of smirks, "We attack them. We hit them where it hurts. Crewman Agsnon has worked tirelessly to determine the location of the Gerlak homeworld and he did." He hits a button and then displays the location of the Gerlak homeworld. He continues, "We need to provoke them into a conflict. So we're going to nuke their homeworld of Gerlath."

Most of the crewmembers become confused. Keller then shifts the briefing to our crazy plan we made to steal a carrier. Looking around, most seem to be skeptical. And why not? They're going to be expected to attack a naval facility, steal a carrier, then fly to the heart of the Gerlak Sanctum and nuke their home planet. Fuck. Hearing myself say it really puts the crazy into perspective.

Keller finishes the briefing, "I won't sugar coat this. It's extreme, and I'm asking more of you than you all probably initially signed up for. I could try and force your oaths, but I would rather you consciously accept this operation willingly."

The room is mostly silent.

Then someone breaks it, "Isn't there something we can enact to temporarily overthrow the Prime Minister?"

Keller acknowledges and sighs, "Yes... Directive Zulu Lima. That requires significant political and military support of which neither we have. Now... should an opportunity arise for a less extreme and more peaceful resolution, we will take it. Commander Dougland and I are not dead set on nuking the Gerlak. In fact we really don't want to do it. Unfortunately if we don't, the extinction of the human race will be entirely guaranteed."

I look around at everyone and they seem to be satisfied with that explanation.

Keller says, "I'm reminded of Cutter Gondul's motto, 'Anything and everything for the cause in which we believe' and I must say I do believe in this cause. The question is, do you?"

Esker yells loudly, "Valkyrie, sound off!"

All of the Valkyrie crewman shout aloud, "ALL THE WAY OR NOT AT ALL!!!"

Commander Dougland then orders, "Kara, sound off!"

And all of the Kara Crewman shout aloud, "For Freedom the price is never too high!"

The echoes of both crews sounding off their respective chants is awe inspiring even to me. I'd join in if I knew any of them. Thankfully it seems most everyone is willing to accept the mission.

Keller orders, "Lieutenant Esker, step forward, please."

She walks up to the Commander.

"All crews, attention to advancement," he orders.

Everyone snaps to posture up. I can only imagine what's going through Kaight's head. It sounds like she's about to be field promoted.

Keller begins, "Before we embark on the second phase of the mission, I will be transferring my command to the carrier, meaning someone will need to take full command of Valkyrie and a First Lieutenant isn't sufficient for that. I'm sure the Sub-Commander aboard Kara is a capable leader, however I'd feel better if you were led by someone we already know."

I think I can hear her sniffling. Understandable. She's about to get a huge career bump.

Keller promotes, "First Lieutenant Kaight Esker you are hereby field promoted to the rank of Sub-Commander in the Guardian Armada. You will continue your duties as already assigned aboard Constellation Cutter Valkyrie with the addition of assuming full command once Commander Keller assumes Command of Carrier Vidar. Do you understand your assignment, Sub-Commander?"

Kaight tearfully joyful responds, "Y... Yes Commander Keller!"

"Very good," Keller says and the hangar erupts in cheers.

I look over and see Keller handing Sub-Commander Esker her new rank insignia pin, three and a half shields. She doesn't hesitate in removing the First Lieutenant insignia marked by just three shields.

Keller then asks, "Sub-Commander would you like to address the crew?"

She nods and then holds out her hand indicating she needs a second to get herself straightened out.

Then she takes the mic, "Oh my... I just... okay, well I know I was acting Sub-Commander, but I guess it's official now. Anyway, um, I'll be taking complaints in the Sub-Commander's office from anyone who doesn't understand the mission or needs to express concerns directly. Otherwise it sounds like everyone is on board and ready to perform so let's just, um... oh I can't believe this is happening... let's uh execute the mission so I can make it to Commander and the rest of you can advance in your careers also, thanks."

She hands the mic back to Keller who then speaks into it, "Yes, but first, I need Lead Sergeant Donna Kroeling up here, please."

No fucking way. I hesitate a moment and then approach Keller.

He says, "Last one for now, I promise. Attention to advancement."

I... I snap to. This is actually happening. I never thought this would and I'm really surprised.

Keller promotes, "Lead Sergeant Kroeling, for your valiant effort in training the Valkyrie Crew in intense combat as well as preparing to lead a larger battalion into battle I am hereby promoting you to Command Sergeant. For those who don't know, that's a Superior Delta equivalent. You will continue with your duties assigned to Valkyrie as well as the daring mission to secure a Constellation Carrier and any continued assignments that require your specific skills and leadership. Command Sergeant, do you understand your assignment?"

I, uh, "Yes Commander Keller!"

"Very good," Keller says and the hangar erupts in cheering once again.

Keller then asks, "Command Sergeant, I'm sorry we don't carry Marine rank insignias aboard and well we don't have a uniform for you, except what we can spare, but would you like to address the crew?"

I nod and take the mic. I'm a little bleary eyed, but I also know we still have specifics that need to be figured out.

I begin, "Well this is unexpected, but I am grateful nonetheless. Anyway, we have a very tough assignment ahead of us. Storming a carrier we don't know much about is going to be no easy task, especially for those of you with me on the deployment team. But I've been with the Valkyrie Crew since Keldon and I'm confident in the Kara's crew members ability to pull this off with us. It's been my honor to serve with you all and see that the fighting spirit of Marines exists in all of you. Let's get to it, everyone!"

Everyone shouts and claps as I hand the mic back to Commander Keller.

He then says, "Alright, you heard Command Sergeant. We still have some specifics to hammer out. We'll begin tunneling for Nimitz Shipyard later tonight. Anticipate beginning the mission after morning chow. Crews break off into departments."

I still can't believe it. Lieutenant Es- er I mean Sub-Commander Esker wastes no time in heading out, probably to deal with crew members who don't want to participate directly in the mission. I'm not sure what we'll do with them, but I can sympathize with their hesitation. This is an extreme undertaking, yet necessary.

As everyone disperses, I meet with Larrodo and the deployment team leaders form Kara. It's pretty straightforward: Larrodo will be taking his team straight to the bridge and I'll lead everyone to the engine room on one of the carrier decks.

Larrado and I head back to our room to get some rest. By the morning we'll be eating and then on our way into battle.

It's hard to believe that I ranked up. I wish I had my uniform and insignia to go with it to help it feel more official. But I don't. However, I know my accomplishments on this ship caused me to deserve it. I climb into my rack mulling over the mission in my head, anticipating everything that could possibly go wrong and…

…I am woken up by Larrodo indicating it's time to head over to the Kara. I dress lightly, since I'll be wearing armor anyway. As luck would have it, Nate of all people is flying my drop ship… actually that makes sense as most of the regular Outflyer pilots are on my deployment team.

The trip lasts under five minutes and we pack into the Kara's port hangar tightly. We exit to find several cots set up for everyone. Though I'll need it, I doubt I'll be able to sleep at all. The cot accommodations aren't going to be so much the problem as will be the rolls while tunneling and then add to that the battle anticipation.

Nate asks, "So is there some special way I need to greet you now?"

I answer, "COMSARGE is fine if you want. But I won't get upset if you call me Donna."

He then asks, "Want me to set you up in here? Pilots and squad leaders get priority bedding."

"Are they more comfortable than those?" I ask.

He nods, "Considerably."

"Then yes, please." I respond.

He begins folding down some of the jump seats and then folds them in a way that forms a decent sized bed.

I say, "So… I'm sorry I didn't assign you to a deployment team."

He replies shaking his head, "Don't be. I know I'm not much of a fighter, at least by comparison. Plus I like flying and since you picked up most of the other pilots, I get to fly one on my own. Well I mean I have a gunner, but I'm pretty much running the show."

I nod, "That's a very mature attitude… hey so I realized we haven't spoken much since you got back. How was Mars?"

"It was good," he says, "despite being cut short, it was nice to get back to society for a minute. See how different the world is when you're out and about like we have been. But for now I would rather be here. I mean, the fresh water was hard to beat, but thankfully that isn't an issue now."

"Well that's good," I suppose, "what about being here makes it so preferential?"

He explains, "With everything that's happened recently including the Prime Minister's speech, I realized that my oath doesn't begin and end with my service. But it's also something every citizen should understand and take to heart. I mean we've seen the Gerlak firsthand. Are they capable of peace? I personally don't think so and this is reinforced by the fact that she is suspending Speech Immunity. She wants to control the narrative. But why?"

I shrug.

He continues, "Yeah I don't know either, but one thing is for sure nothing good ever is accomplished by suspending our freedoms and that alone is enough for me to see the Prime Minister for what she is: a domestic enemy."

I nod largely, "Yes, very much so. I'm not looking forward to going to war with our own people in a few hours, but I'm sure they would join us if they knew the truth."

He nods, "Yeah. I wish Keller would take the time, but I guess he and the Kara see oh have their reasons. We should probably rack out. Gonna be a fun filled day."

I nod and then lay down on the rack. I pull the blanket up and about ten minutes later the hangar lights dim, allowing for everyone to get some rest...

...I awake to the rolling of the ship. The gravimetric sheering also echoes much louder through the hangar. It almost sounds like we're coming apart. But what's really got me awake is the uneasy feeling I have. I know I've said it before, but these guys aren't our enemy. They've taken the same oaths that we have. They believe they are fighting the same good fight. We will have our weapons set to a low power subdue setting, but theirs won't be. To them we're the enemy and there's nothing we can do to change their minds of that.

I hear what faintly sounds like music and look back and see light coming from the main cockpit. I get up and walk in and see Nate listening to some soft piano tracks. It almost sounds like a cover of a classical song, "Nothing else Matters".

"Trouble sleeping?" I ask.

He replies startled, "Fu... yeah I can never sleep when we tunnel. You?"

"I guess the same," I say, "where did you get the coffee?"

He says, "It's in the bay just behind the gunner seat."

I go and help myself, grabbing a thick plastic mug. Makes sense, wouldn't want to risk shattering a good mug. I take note of the rest of the features. I guess I never noticed, but this thing seems to have a full on mini kitchen. Interesting.

I come in and Nate moves the center console forward inviting me to sit in the copilot's seat.

I take a sip and then ask, "Are you ready for this?"

He shrugs, "As ready as I'm gonna be."

"Yeah, me too," I nod, "So these drop ships come fully loaded, eh?"

"Yep," he says, "They can be used for extended reconnaissance. They can stay adrift or on a planet deployment for up to two weeks if needs be."

"Two weeks?" I gasp, "That sounds horrible!"

He nods in agreement, "At most a small ship would probably be adrift in an area for a few days, observing and listening for pirate vessels or stalking smugglers. It's considerably less conspicuous than using the entire cutter. Actually the long range ships we had when I was in were almost three times the size of this, but that also meant more problems so they scaled it back."

"And these ones double as fighter craft," I confirm.

"I mean… if they need to," he clarifies.

I chuckle and listen to the soft playing of the music as I sip my coffee.

I then ask, "How are you doing with everything else? Specifically with Dev's passing?"

He answers, "It helps to keep me going. I never really realized how much I loved her until she was gone."

I ask, "Making love at Lantic Station didn't indicate that?"

He retorts, "Well of course it did, but I was expecting to do that more often. To grow together. To come closer with time. I miss what could have been."

"So do I," I say, "you both seemed really happy even just working together."

"If we had made it back to the Cutter I would have stay-" he's interrupted by the Battlestations alarm going off.

Seconds after over the PA we hear, "**Set Battlestations throughout the ship. All deployment teams and fighters prepare for launch. All hands man...**" as it continues I start to head back to the bay of the drop ship along with Nate who immediately starts adjusting the racks back into the jump seats.

I remove my pants and shirt and then begin to put on my armor. I catch everyone else in the hangar springing from their cots and doing the same. I begin to help Nate get all the jump seats back out and the other members of my team assigned to this ship start to file in and strap in. I then head back to the cockpit and sit behind Nate who is already beginning the pre-flight check.

One of the lower ranked Kara Crewman comes in with a basket and hands me and everyone a breakfast burrito. I unwrap it and try to enjoy it as I inhale it. I then focus on the COMMS.

Nate's copilot, Crewman Freedl sets one of the COMM units to the HAD frequency and we wait patiently. The rolling stops and the sheering noises cease almost immediately.

A few seconds later, Commander Dougland freaks over the COMM, "**Nimitz shipyard! Nimitz shipyard,** this is Constellation Cutter Kara! We've just had a run-in with the Valkyrie! They're on their way here, recommend you activate whatever defenses you have before he gets here!"

The shipyard replies, "Uh... how do you know he's on his way here and more importantly, why?"

Dougland explains, "He first followed us from Ninvar system to the Rit nebula. He's acquired some kind of tracking technology that allows him to track a ship's tunnel. He even held our last one open and followed us in!"

"That seems unli- wait a second," the shipyard says, "Your singularity is uncollapsing..."

"That's gotta be him!" Dougland says.

The station is quiet a few moments then orders, "Alright, position yourself behind us. The Destroyers will take care of Valkyrie."

"Very good," Dougland says.

Then we hear the Kara Control Order, "All ships, stand by to deploy. Opening hangar doors now."

Nate hits a button and powers up the ship's engines. His copilot brings the turret controls online. I just sit and wait for him to get us to the carrier. Nate lifts the ship off the deck and points it out the door. The shipyard begins to come into view as Kara points her bow away allowing for maximum hangar deployment.

"Fighter's stand by..." Kara Control says. Then about five seconds later, "Fighters launch! Drop ships stand by..." here it comes... "Drop ships launch!"

Nate throttles the ship forward along with all the other Valkyrie boarding craft.

I look out my viewport and see Kara's fighters, our fighters and Kara's drop ships flying out of the starboard hangar. Nate focuses on getting us to the Carrier's second deck. It's a massive ship; the biggest ever built. It's not so much its length that's impressive, but the three modular decks that deploy from the main section. I would love to actually see this ship in a real battle. Unfortunately we're just going to throw its nukes at the Gerlak.

No opposing fire seems to be coming for us at the moment. It looks like the plan is working. I hear Keller try to appeal what's going on to no end. Maybe he should have just pretended to be a pirate.

I then see two large explosions on some of the larger moorings attached to the carrier. Looks like Kara took them out with her main batteries. The fighters fly ahead and begin cutting the remaining mooring with their lasers. Guess there's been a slight change in plan.

One of the fighters reports, "**The carrier is adrift! Hurry up and board it!**"

Kara Control reports, "**One of the Destroyers is breaking off and coming back this way. Deployment teams hurry.**"

Nate increases speed, pushing the little drop ship as fast as she'll go. He then slows down and begins searching for an air lock. He finds one and quickly lines up the back of the ship. We shake as we make contact. He pulls a toggle which extends a cover for both airlocks.

I saddle up and enter the bay section where my team is already cutting through the airlock. We get through the door in less than a minute and are met with no resistance. We pass through the other airlock and close it behind us.

I report, "Nate, everyone is out and the airlock is secured. You're good to detach!"

"Good luck, COMSARGE," he says and that's all I hear.

I order, "Alright let's make our way to the engine room. If we can, let's not incapacitate every crewman. We might be able to get one to help us."

We quickly comb down a couple corridors looking for any indications of where the engine room might be. So far we have encountered no one.

Then Larrodo reports, "**COMSARGE Kroeling this is Bridge Team. We've secured control of the bridge, but could use some assistance keeping it secure.**"

"Noted," I acknowledge, "Support Team Three, make your way to the bridge and assist Delta Larrodo."

"**On it COMSARGE**" they respond, "**But the only other airlock on the command module was located near the Traverse Drive at the bottom. It'll take a minute.**"

"Understood," I say, "Bridge Team can you locate schematics and direct us to the Two Deck's engine room?"

"**I'll see what I can find,**" Larrodo says.

Crewman Putvel informs, "COMSARGE, we gotta hurry. That Destroyer is apparently coming for us. Kara is staying away since they don't stand a chance..."

Larrodo reports, "**I'm still looking for schematics, but I think we can bring engines online here. Will let you know.**"

One of my team members asks, "So then what are we doing here?"

I explain, "Some of the crew might try to sabotage the engines. We're mainly here to make sure that doesn't happen."

Larrodo informs, "**We're trying to activate One Deck's engines, but it looks like you should be able to locate a main engine control room near the aft and in the center.**"

"Thanks," I say and just as we round the corner, we encounter resistance.

"Cover positions!" I order. I take cover in a corridor way and lay down some cover fire for my team. The engagement lasts less than a minute. My team takes no casualties as I knew they wouldn't.

I walk up and see one of the carrier's crew moving around. I kneel next to him and ask, "Can you take us to the engine control room?"

"Fuck you, traitor!" he replies.

I order one of my team members, "Bind tough guy here and make sure the rest of his buddies are down for the count." The rest of us keep moving.

We round another corridor into a passageway and are fired upon by one combatant. We return fire then I see a laser pistol get tossed in the air and land on the deck.

"Hold fire!" I order.

A scared, young crewman comes out with his hands up, "I surrender!" he says, "Please don't kill me!"

"Can you take us to the main engine control room?" I ask.

He nods timidly, "Y- yes…"

"Alright. Lower your weapons," I order.

As the young crewman leads us down the passageways, Larrodo informs, "**COMSARGE, we can't get One or Three Deck's engines to respond. Looks like you'll be controlling the ship from there. But hurry, that Destroyer is almost on top of us!**"

"I understand," I say.

We continue walking

The scared Navy Crewman asks, "What- what are you guys here for?"

I answer softly, "We'll gladly explain to you why we're here once we have control of the engine room. I know it doesn't seem like it, but we aren't here to hurt anyone. We just want control of the ship."

"Okay..." he says.

I ask, "Is there any resistance we can expect in the engine room?"

He timidly replies, "We have weapons set up throughout the ship in case of a situation like this... so uh... I mean probably."

"Let us know when we're close," I say.

He informs, "It's just down this passageway."

"Stay alert, everyone," I order.

We round the corner and sure enough are met with laser fire. Judging by the bolt intensity, I'd say it's mostly laser pistols. At a longer range this would be an advantage as they are less accurate than rifles. At this range, it doesn't make that much of a difference, except that it shouldn't pierce the armor.

I yell, "Putvel! I think these are all pistol bolts!"

"Concur!" he yells back.

I press a button which extends armor over my nose and mouth leaving only my eyes covered by transparent plating. As I get up I see Putvel doing the same thing. I rush in taking a couple hits on my torso. I see one target and down him quickly. Then I look over to my right and quickly take out another. The third and fourth targets go down as I approach, leaving only one other who appears to be stunned to see us standing.

She fumbles out words, "Y- you guys have armor!?! How did pirates get armor?!"

I answer, "We're not pirates. Can you bring the engines online?"

Before she answers, the ship shakes and is accompanied by a loud rumble.

Then Larrodo informs, "**COMSARGE, hate to get pushy, but that Destroyer is opening fire! I think they're enacting destruction protocol!**"

I add, "Now would be a good time. One of the Destroyers is firing on us!"

She replies, "Then we all die together!"

"And that's something you're willing to do?" I confirm.

"I- uh…" she fumbles, "Yes…"

I move into her glaring into her eyes and say, "No it isn't."

She shakes her head in agreement, "No yeah you're right." She hops up and starts to configure the controls. The other younger male Crewman comes over and starts to help.

The female asks, "You helped them?"

He replies, "I- uh… they had me surrounded."

She scoffs, "Yeah they do. Who are you people anyway?"

I explain, "We'll explain everything once we're to-" the ship shakes again, "if we get to safety I'll be happy to tell you everything personally."

She nods, "Okay… I've got the engines coming online… I can route control to the bridge unless you'd rather keep it here."

I ask over the COMM, "Delta Larrodo, are you ready to receive control of the engines?"

"About five minutes ago!" He says.

"Send control to the bridge," I order.

We suddenly come under fire. I reactivate my mask protection and then take cover. These guys definitely have higher density weapons. I order everyone to take cover and we engage the assaulting forces, mostly exchanging fire in a never ending stalemate. I look around for other corridors or entrances.

I order, "Putvel! Take two others and find a way around to flank them!"

Then I hear a familiar clinking sound.

I look down, "Grenade-" before we can properly react, the explosion goes off destroying the console and sending me and just about everyone else flying. I look around and start to recover. Two of my guys are still up shooting. The other two Navy Sailors appear to be injured badly, possibly dead. Alright. We'll play hard then.

I unhook a "stun" grenade from my belt and set it to maximum. These don't always work, meaning it could kill someone if the charge is too much for their body. Oh well.

I toss it and see the corridor light up bright blue for ten seconds. The opposing laser fire stops.

I get up, "Advance! MacAlta, attend to the wounded."

Putvel, myself and the rest of the team advance on the opposing forces. So far everyone seems to be down. Then Putvel takes a hit from one of them stumbling to get up. I fire back, stunning him. Everyone else seems incapacitated.

"Bind them up," I order.

I walk back into the control room.

MacAlta looks up and informs, "Two of them are dead. The other three are looking critical. Unless we can get them to a medical facility…"

I nod and walk back to the group of downed Navy Sailors.

One of them starts to groan as he looks up. I say, "You killed two of your own and unless you can help, the other three in there will die."

"The fuck do you care?" He asks.

I squat down and explain, "We're on the same team. And in time you'll understand that. But those people bleeding out in there are your shipmates. I would think you would want to help them. I don't know where the medical bay is and I need to secure the rest of the ship."

He just stares blankly.

"Fine," I say standing up, "their blood is on your hands. Especially since you're the ones who threw the grenade."

"I'll help…" he mutters.

I order, "Putvel, go ahead and get an escort put together-" the ship begins to shake violently. It almost feels like we're about to break apart. Then we start swaying as though we have entered a Traverse Tunnel.

Larrodo then goes out over the ship's PA, **"Attention crew of the Constellation Carrier Vidar. This is Delta Larrodo of the Constellation Cutter Valkyrie. We have seized control of your ship and are now tunneling to a secure location where we will begin prepping this ship for an urgent mission.**

I am asking those of you still actively resisting to throw down your arms. Let us explain to you why it is we had to steal your ship. You will see that we have done our best not to harm anyone. The reason is because we are on the same side. We will explain everything soon enough. For now, you need to trust us. Once you are given the explanation you will have the opportunity to join our fight or return to the Republic unharmed.

This is not an ideal situation for any of us, but it's not beyond each of us to work together and figure out what's best. That is all."

The other Navy guys, having heard the message, suddenly seem more cooperative and start helping the others towards the medical bay. Looks like this fight is over. Time to prepare for the next one.

Chapter Twenty-One: "Well... would you rather we didn't?"

(*Keller*)"Absolutely not," Trinn argues, "we're just as much in this fight."

"No you're not," I reaffirm, "We need someone to get the defectors back to the Republic. I appreciate that your ship has strong armor, but both cutters are still more useful to us."

"Then what about one of the carrier decks," he proposes.

I take a breath, "I'm sorry, Captain. But this is most likely a one way trip and I already promised the one-hundred twenty-two crewman who don't want to go that they would be safely returned."

"And then what happens to me?" he continues to argue, "They seize my ship, my new weapons-"

I interrupt, "Captain, the discussion is over!"

Sub-Commander Esker injects, "Commander, what if he dropped them off at an embassy in one of the other sub-factions? It would be a lot harder to capture him there."

I nod, "That would be acceptable. As long as they can safely return home. We'll finish rebuilding your Traverse Drive with the components from the carrier, but you're not joining the battlegroup. I am beyond grateful for your sacrifice, Captain Trinn, but if you want to help us, then I need you to deliver on my promise."

He reluctantly sighs, "Fine... the Lambadda will retreat to one of the sub-factions. We'll be fugitives, but I suppose we'll be alive."

"I'd consider a name change for your ship," I suggest, "Thank you."

He nods and then leaves.

I then turn to Esker, "What's the status of the nukes?"

She sighs, "Without launch codes, they're not going anywhere... we can try to move them to different launchers, but the problem is priming and activating the detonation sequence as well. Lieutenant Ephrryn is working with the cooperating Navy personnel to look into remote launching the carrier decks and positioning them where we need them then detonating them with timers."

I inquire, "We can rig the primers with a timer? How?"

She explains, "It will take some time, but Delta Miranda and her team are working on a way to bypass the codes. But the only way that can work is with a manual detonation. Well instead of sacrificing one of our own, we figured a time release system would be more practical."

I ask, "Can we not rig a remote system?"

She points out, "We probably could... but the possibility of signal interference was brought up. Even with a coded signal, it can still be interfered with."

"And remote piloting the decks would be secure?" I clarify.

She confirms, "In a way. We need to set the autopilot. Once you enter the coordinates, the decks will detach from the command module and position themselves. Then all we have to do is wait for the timers and then... boom."

"This sounds too easy," I say.

She explains, "Ephrryn is still coming up with the rest of the plan. But I wanted to see how you felt using the autopilot and timers."

"If it's the most secure way of getting it done," I say, "Then it sounds good to me. Figure out the rest of the plan and then brief me. Dismissed Sub-Commander."

She nods and then leaves my office. Now I'm alone. I look around the room as I will soon be transferred off and this could be the last time I see it. I have no doubts the mission will be successful. In fact it's straight forward. We pop into orbit of the Gerlak home world, deploy the carrier decks, they detonate and we tunnel out of there. Upon our return, however, I suspect I will be forced to resign and be thrown in prison if not worse.

I get up and leave my office. I head down to the hangar decks and observe the crews doing maintenance on the fighters. I then head to the engine rooms and look closely at the beating heart of the ship. Then I observe the fusion generators which are all functioning normally.

As I walk the decks of the ship, I feel overwhelmed with a bitter sweetness. This ship has been good to me and my crew. She's been modified into a warship and forced to fill a role she wasn't designed for, but she's held true. The crew has really come together to make her more than what she originally was designed for. I'll miss her. But she'll be in good hands.

I head up to the bridge and allow Lieutenant Jefferson to retain control. I notice Mr. McNill is currently on watch on the navigation table.

"Nate, my office, please," I order. I then focus attention on Jefferson, "Can you track down the other civilians and have them meet in my office now?"

He answers, "Yes, should I get a relief for Nate?"

I shake my head, "We're just sitting here adrift. I think you can manage without him."

As we make our way to my office, Nate asks, "Is everything okay, Commander?"

I reply, "Yeah I just need to sit down with you and all the civilians. If you don't mind, I'll explain when we gather everyone."

Walking into my office a few moments later, I realize we'll need more room.

"Leave the door open," I say, "and come with me."

I walk in and Nate just stands not sure where to go.

"Take the couch," I say.

I then go to my kitchenette and pull out my wine and my Amberglash reserve. I leave a few cups on the table and then ask Nate, "Thirsty?"

He asks, "What are my options?"

"Water, whiskey or wine," I answer.

He says, "Whiskey, please."

I pour two glasses and then walk over to Nate and give him one. An awkward silence takes over. I then ask, "So did you at least get to relax a little on Mars?"

He nods, "Got to enjoy some normal life. Would have liked a little more, but we had to get back here."

"Meh," I say, "I wouldn't have blamed you at all if you had stayed."

The other three civilians trickle in and I ask the last one to close the door. I offer them beverages and pour and serve each request accordingly. I then raise my glass, "First off I wanted to say thank you. You all have done a tremendous job in making our survival possible. So cheers."

We all take a sip.

I continue, "But I cannot ask you to continue on with us. There's a good chance we aren't returning from this one, and you all deserve to live. Captain Trinn will be taking his mining vessel back to civilized space. I want all of you packed up and on it."

The engineer guy, I can't remember his name, says, "Are ya sure, sir? I can be of help in the engine room."

"We have more than enough personnel," I say, "And we have no further requirement to mine minerals for materials. Your work here is done," turning my attention to the civilian cooks, "And you both... words cannot describe how grateful I am to have had you."

"It was our pleasure, sir," the female accepts.

"I can only ask for one final meal before we depart," I say, "Feel free to whip up whatever you want. It should be a big feast."

The female replies, "We'll have something special planned."

"And Nate... you've done more than I could have asked for. Thank you."

He nods, but says nothing. We chat a little bit about what they're gonna do next. The cooks want to open a restaurant using their back pay. Tim wants to start his own mining company. Nate is mostly quiet. I think I can expect we'll have another chat after the other civilians leave.

We all finish about two rounds each and then they head out. Nate of course stays behind. I say, "If you want to have another round I'll top you off and you can keep the glass for the evening. But I'm not arguing with you on this. Your service is appreciated, but no longer required."

Nate finishes his last sip, "No, Keller. Fuck you, I'm staying."

Taken back a bit, I reply, "The fuck you are! You're not Active anymore. You have zero obligation and I'm not putting you in harm's way."

"And what am I supposed to go back to?" he asks, "I'm a fugitive at this point. I'm in this till the end. I may no longer officially serve, but I took an oath the same as you and I have a duty to see it through."

"You can do it in other ways," I say, "You have a life ahead of you-"

"And your younger crewmembers don't?" he interruptingly retorts.

I point out, "They signed the dotted line and raised their hand. You did too, but we got rid of you- no, I am not arguing this. Do not force me to have you escorted off."

He shakes his head, "You're unbelievable... you know I was starting to believe that story you made up about wanting to help me when I got kicked out, but now... now I see my suspicions were correct. You just needed to use me until I was no longer of any use to you."

I nod, "Yes... that's correct. Whatever you need to believe."

"Why?" he asks.

"I don't have to explain myself to you," I say, "this is my ship and I want you off."

He sets his glass down and then crosses his arms, "Then you're going to have to force me off. I'm not running from this fight and it's not fair for you to make me."

I shake my head, "You don't understand, Nate. If I could do this mission by myself I would not hesitate to do so, but I can at least make sure that some people survive."

"Then send one of your crew members in my place," he says.

"Some already have," I inform, "I afforded the opportunity for those who didn't want to go into battle that they didn't have to. Some took the offer, but I still have enough people to make the mission happen. You aren't needed."

Nate reaffirms, "I don't care if I'm needed or not. I lost things because of the Gerlak. I lost people I cared about too. I want to hit them back just as much as you and everyone else who is going to make that happen. I wanna be there when the nukes go off so I can watch as they burn and wither into space dust. So yeah, I'm in it for my own satisfaction too. If you don't want me, I don't care. I'm staying."

Maybe I am being unfair. It seems I only want him safe for my own selfish reasons. I have completely overlooked his feelings so that I can feel justified in thinking I'm doing him a favor by trying to save his life, yet it's his to throw away if he wants. My self-righteous indignation be damned.

I surrender, "Okay... I completely understand now. Just to make sure you understand we most likely will not come back from this."

Nate reminds, "I won't get another opportunity. I'm black listed from ever serving again- hell I don't think the Stellar Marines will take me. But here, this mission vital to humanity's survival, this is something I can participate in first hand. And if it's the only thing and we don't make it, then so be it. The truth is already being disseminated. There's no sense in me retreating."

"Fine," I say, "I'll make sure you get an assignment. Dismissed."

"Thank you, Commander," he says, "I apologize for cursing at you."

"Don't worry about it," I say, "I understand this is important to you and you didn't do so in front of anyone else. I forgive you. Get some rest."

He turns and leaves. He really has come a long way in just under a month. Hell my whole crew has. I hate that we've lost people along the way. There is no harder thing as a Commander than having to let go of those who served honorably under you. Especially the ones you got to know personally.

There's a knock on my office door. "Come in," I order.

Sub-Commander Esker walks in and looks around. She pokes her head into the doorway to my room.

"Come on in, Kaight," I say.

She closes the door behind her then explains, "So, we- my team- rather the crew is burnt out on planning. There are more variables and unknowns and with the complication with the nukes I think we should start with fresh heads in the morning."

"I agree," I say, "We're drifting in dead space so for the moment we have time on our side. But I don't want to wait longer than three days."

She nods, "I'll inform the crew."

She pulls out her personal COMM and calls up Ephrryn to inform him they'll continue planning tomorrow. I haven't decided whether or not to grant Rest Routine. We still have a lot of preparation work to do.

Esker finishes her call and then asks moving towards the booze, "Um, could I get some?"

"Absolutely," I answer.

She grabs the wine and pours herself a glass.

"May I?" she asks pointing to a spot next to me on the couch.

I nod. Then I ask, "So... have you gotten used to the new rank and responsibility?"

She says, "It's still sinking in… I just hope we live long enough to keep it."

I say, "Well… if we're going to use timers and auto pilot, then we'll put minimal crew on the carrier. Like so minimal I just want a bridge team."

Esker informs, "There's an airlock under the bridge. We could have a drop ship staged there in case you need to abandon the carrier for whatever reason. Valkyrie has the enhanced armor so I think we'll make it. But I'm worried about Kara… I'm sorry sir, can we discuss something else?"

"Of course," I say.

There's an awkward silence. She just stares at me. Then looks away.

"What's on your mind?" I ask.

She doesn't say anything and sets her glass down. Then she lunges onto me and presses her lips against mine most unexpectedly. We kiss for a good ten seconds and she finishes biting lightly on my lower lip.

I say, "Um… you do know I can't promote you any higher, right?"

She giggles, "I know… it's not that, I just… we might not make it so… why not?"

"I understand and more or less agree," I say, "but why me? You do know I'm close to fifteen years older than you, right?"

"So?" she says, "I've seen the way you look at me sometimes."

I pull back, "Well, for one, I'm a man. For two I think you mistook my admiration and respect for your ability to learn and adapt to command."

"I- um…" she says, "I guess you didn't see me looking back. I know you didn't promote me to do this, but... I mean... along with not being attracted to the other Lieutenants, well it also wouldn't be appropriate to sleep with my subordinates now would it?"

"This is inappropriate," I point out.

"Well... would you rather we didn't?" she asks.

I look into her eyes. She's not trying to get any favors from me so I know she's genuine. I clasp both my hands on her face and pull her towards me. But then I stop and release her and look down. I explain, "I'm sorry... but even after Matilda and I split it... I couldn't do... this. On the one hand, yes, I'd very much like to lead you back into my bed and forget about everything especially since we may die soon. But I can't. Even though Mattie is gone, I just..."

I catch her nodding out of the corner of my eye, "I understand... I don't want to, but I do... If you change your mind, well," she says getting up, "I guess you probably won't. Goodnight, Commander."

"Goodnight," I reply. I finish my drink and stare at the bulkhead. Man I wish I had a window. I miss my wife and also wish she were here with us. Since we have the time, maybe we will take the morning off. I really don't want to function anymore...

(*Nathan*)...I head back to the Crew's Mess feeling a little bad about arguing with Keller... well not so much the arguing, but the way I argued. I belong in this fight as much as everyone else. I can't blame Tim for agreeing to leave, though. I hope I- oh, in fact there he is sipping some evening tea.

I sit down next to him, "So... gonna steal my idea and prospects?"

He chuckles, "I thought we were going to do it together?"

I shake my head, "Not at first... I convinced Keller to let me stay. I got stake in this fight and this is probably my only time I get to hit these bastards for killing Dev."

Tim nods, "Alright... well I'll get the company started and you come find me when you come back. And you will be coming back."

"I have no intention of dying," I say.

Donna comes up behind us and says, "Well that's good. I just wish we were taking them head on. All I'll be doing is sitting on board Valkyrie waiting in case we get boarded."

"Which hopefully won't be an issue," I say, "I think the plan is to get in, nuke and get out. It's a suicide run, but without the suicide."

"A blitz" Donna clarifies.

I nod, "Yes... oh and I guess you don't know, Tim and your friends will be leaving us before we go into battle."

"I know," she says," I brought it up to Sub-Commander Esker. They shouldn't have to be in the fight if they don't want to."

I inform, "Well... he didn't give us a choice. He wanted me to leave with them. I insisted otherwise."

"Yeah..." she says, "I understand why he would want that, but he probably didn't realize how much you have to lose."

I raise a brow and suspect, "I don't suppose you recommended I leave..."

She shakes her head, "No. I wanted you to stay, remember? Keller's guilt for failing you the first time probably influenced his thinking."

She has a point. I then ask Donna, "So what are you going to do after the mission?"

She says somewhat condescendingly, "Probably join up with my old Marine Unit and wait for my next assignment which hopefully will include kicking more gerlak ass."

Tim says, "More? You're gonna nuke their home world and you'll still be hungry for more?"

"Marines are always hungry," Donna says, "especially me after all we've been through. Plus Nate won't be able to help so I gotta get some extras for him."

I nod, "Appreciate it. I would consider joining if it were an option."

Donna says, "You might be able to get a waiver, especially in times of war. You'll have to go through training though."

Tim reminds, "Or you can come get rich with me."

I look at Donna, "I'll look into it if I'm still hungry. Nuking the home world might not satiate you, but maybe it'll satisfy my appetite."

"Fair enough," Donna says.

It's silent for a moment then I point out, "You know… a couple of months ago we had no idea we weren't alone in the universe. And already we're going to nuke the home world of aliens we don't really know that well."

Donna says, "We know them well enough. We know them better than everyone else in the Republic."

I nod in agreement, "Yeah we do."

Tim rubs his shoulder, "Still hasn't quite felt the same."

Donna says, "They're gonna feel a lot worse soon."

"If they even get the chance to feel anything at all," I note.

Tim asks, "So, Donna, are you wanting a war?"

She answers slowly, "No... I would have rather they came in peace and I shared meals with them in my restaurant. But they didn't. Instead they killed my bartender and stripped my livelihood away. In my time in service, I combatted rebels and pirates. I knew the ones who surrendered and those who wanted to keep fighting... these aliens want war. So you're damn right I'm gonna give it to them."

I confused, ask, "You fought the other factions? And pirates? When?"

Donna takes a breath and reveals, "The Armada was the poster child. In the foregrounds of what the media was told, you guys were there to make it seem like the Three-War was less than it seemed: that it was radical cells within the factions who were acting out."

Tim nods in agreement, "Yeah I read that on the Gal-Net somewhere. That the Marines, Army and Navy were deployed to support the Armada but really were supposedly doing most of the fighting. I found it rather entertaining fiction."

I add, "Yeah, how were you able to engage without a War Declaration?"

Donna explains, "Because we were told they were terrorists. We were told the same story you were, that they were radicals. Truth is we were sent in to bring the factions to heel. And we did."

"How?" I ask.

"In ways we shouldn't have. Ways that forced me to question why I became a Marine. That was why I got out. I don't sleep at night with a guilty conscience because I knew we were lied to. Manipulated."

I point out, "But when Keller re-activated you, you seemed so eager to pick up a rifle and fight."

"Because I was," she says, "for once it seemed I was going to fight for the right reasons. Or so I thought. Then the Prime Minister came out with her message. Right then I knew it was all bullshit. It was the same bullshit she spewed on reunification."

I question, "But if any of what you said is true, how come no one said anything."

Tim realizes, "People have said something… several somethings. But they've either been censored or worse."

Donna nods, "When I saw how quickly people were silenced in one form or another I realized there was nothing I could say. People would have written me off as crazy. I would have been deemed insane and possibly cut off from society. So I went to the farthest reaches of the Republic to start a new life as far away as possible only to find myself in yet another cover-up."

I ask, "Why tell all of this now?"

Donna sighs bigly, "Because, Nate realistically what do you think our chances of survival really are?"

Tim answers for me, "They're very good as long as you keep thinking positive. Don't you be talking all doom and gloom you guys will be fine. I'd go into battle with you, but I feel I'd just get in the way. However you guys know what you'll be doing. And as far as I'm concerned, you're the best at it. And this crew… well y'all are an impressive bunch."

Lede says walking up behind him, "Thanks, I appreciate that." He finishes his sentence sitting down. Then continues, "And I also agree with your optimistic approach. We're coming out of this alive."

I nod, "Yeah."

Donna is quiet for a second and then says, "Alright. For morale sake I'd say we'll make it."

Lede asks, "So what was that you were saying about the Three-War?"

Donna retorts, "Well knowing we're going to survive now, I'm not sure I want to talk about it."

"Okay," Lede gives up, "probably nothing I haven't heard already."

Donna asks, "And what all have you heard?"

Lede answers, "Quite a lot. You should have considered telling your story on the Under-Net."

I scoff, "The Under-Net? Yeah cause everything posted there is true…"

Rolling his eyes Lede says, "Never heard that one before… but hey if you're incapable of sifting through the truth and the bullshit to figure out which is which, that's your problem. I don't believe everything I read on the Under-Net, but I know it's not all fake."

"Yes and I'm sure the universe is really a giant black hole," I remark.

Donna notes, "Nate… just because some theories are crack pot doesn't mean all of them are. You're in the middle of a conspiracy right now. Are you saying you don't believe it?"

I answer, "Well of course I believe it I can see it. There's a difference between theories and hard cold facts."

Donna says, "Okay, but when we tell people our story would you rather they believe you or chalk it up to crack pot?"

"Um…" I say. Well she's got a point there.

Tim interrupts, "Look, this may be our last evening together. Can we not have it end in pointless debate? Nate is obviously set in his thinking. So is Lede. Can we not just enjoy ourselves?"

We all fall quiet trying to think of what to discuss. It seems arguing with each other made for a distraction from the fact we're about to nuke the Gerlak soon. I look at everyone and we all kind of fall uneasy.

Then Keller comes over the PA, "**Good evening Valkyrie Crewmates, this is the Commander. In an effort to make sure we are prepared for our mission, I have decided to grant Rest Routine for the morning portion of tomorrow. For those of you doing mission planning, get some rest tonight and enjoy sleeping in. Right now there is no rush since we're hanging out in dead space.**

Once we can tackle this issue with fresh heads, we'll plan a time for transit and attack. I don't want to set a specific deadline, however anticipate moving out in the next three days at the latest. Enjoy your down time. Keller out."

Donna orders, "Delta Lounge. Now."

We all get up and follow her down one level. We enter the lounge and see a couple of other Deltas hanging out.

Donna says, "Hope you don't mind, gentlemen, but I figured since my friends and I aren't directly involved with mission planning we'd come and relax properly."

They both gleefully say, "Yeah come on in! We're just about to put Star Treader Four on."

We all find a place to sit and Donna gets all of us refreshments. We watch the film, laughing and making jokes, forgetting about what's coming. I also forgot how much I loved the Star Treader series. Its optimistic outlook on humanity's future is always refreshing from the doom and gloom that feels like reality. Of course, Star Treader Four gets a little too optimistic, borderline cheesy for my liking.

After the movie ends I... uh realize I guess... shit I lost count. I think six maybe? But Donna and Tim seemed to have left. And Lede is passed out sitting up. The other two Deltas left... I think. Best I be stumbling on back to my rack I suppose...

...ow my head... what ha- oh right. I awake to realize I may have had more than I should have. Whatever, we were having a good time. I stumble up to the Crew's Mess. The smell of fresh eggs, sausage and bacon is heavenly. Most of the deck is empty. Makes sense, most of the crew wants to catch up on sleep. I should too, but I'm hung over.

I sit down and soon am joined by Tim, who has the same discomfort as I.

I ask, "I noticed you and Donna were gone."

"Yep," he says.

"Wanna talk about it?" I ask.

"Nothing to say," he answers.

Odd. Maybe they did just go to their respective cabins and I just didn't notice. I take in a fork load of eggs. The sensation feels like it cures me almost instantly. Obviously it doesn't but it helps.

Tim and I exchange no words as we finish our meals. I return to my rack and make the best of the remainder of Rest Routine. Just before it ends I head up to the bridge to take the watch.

My passdown is more of the same. Dead adrift in space with Kara off our port side and Vidar sitting on our Starboard with the Lambadda behind us. I'll be spending the next four hours staring out the viewports and making sure we haven't moved.

Keller comes up to the bridge and allows the Deck Officer, currently Lieutenant Ephrryn to retain it. He seems considerably more chipper than normal. In fact he's never chipper. What exactly is going on?

He comes up to me, "Nate, how was your Rest Routine?" he asks gleefully.

"Uh, fine," I answer, "Are you okay?"

"Oh I'm great," he answers, "but I just want to make sure of something," he says a little more seriously, "are you sure you want to stay on for this mission?"

"Yes," I answer sharply.

"Don't hesitate to change your mind," he says. He then heads towards the ladder to leave. Lieutenant- er I mean Sub-Commander Esker comes onto the bridge. They glance at each other momentarily and go about their business, but... Esker seems more cold and stern than she was yesterday.

I overhear Sub-Commander, "I figured since you're on watch we could work on the plan up here. I mean it's convenient we have a chart that's not being used."

They both walk over to me.

"Sub-Commander," I acknowledge.

She orders, "Can you pull up the Gerlak home world location relative to ours?"

I nod and zoom out the chart and fit the planet and our position on opposite edges of the display.

Ephrryn notes, "I really would like to do a scout mission. We really should see what we're up against."

Sub-Commander informs, "I tried to convince the Commander last night. He does make valid points that we don't have many resources to spare. And if the mission fails, we'll lose people and could potentially give up our position, if our people are captured."

"I don't agree" he says, "but I guess we should anticipate the worst. I'd say two or three of those large capital ships we encountered at Keldon will be in orbit. Probably a dozen or so of their destroyer equivalent."

Esker points out, "Seriously? That seems excessive. I mean yes there's a fleet no more than thirty minutes from Sol, but we don't have orbital protection at times of war."

Ehrryn concedes, "Yeah maybe not that bad. But we should anticipate being out gunned heavily."

Esker explains, "Well I've already figured we'll have Kara form the first tunnel. Valkyrie will take the lead since we have the enhanced armor, followed by Vidar."

Ehrryn nods, "We should resurface as close to the planet as possible. The timers should already be set and ticking as well. We'll have the carrier separate its three decks sending them to these population centers where they'll detonate. Once they blow, everyone will regroup and Valkyrie will tunnel us out."

Esker notes, "We'll also have an SLVRDO docked at the bridge airlock in case they need to escape."

I ask, "Has anyone been picked for that job?"

"No," the Sub-Commander answers, "but if you want to go you won't just be flying the ship."

Ehrryn adds, "You'll also be setting the timers off. We're sending in a small crew which means you'll need to get familiar with the carrier."

"Okay," I say, "how long of a transit will we have?"

Esker says, "I was just about to ask you the same question."

"Ah," I acknowledge and reduce the 3D map back into 2D form on the table.

I run some lines, but realize there are some stars in the way.

"This is going to take a minute," I inform.

After figuring out a course that safely navigates the stars and double checking for black holes, I inform, "We're looking at thirteen hour transit time."

They both acknowledge with a nod and walk back over. I return the map to its 3D projection.

"Okay so we're sitting here at the edge of Republic Space," Esker says, "taking this track will get us there in thirteen hours so... I mean if the timers for the primers are ready, I'd say we have a plan. Get in. Get out. Go home."

Ephrryn states, "I'll check in with Delta Miranda's team and get back to you, Sub-Commander."

"Sounds good," Esker acknowledges, "I'll brief the Commander on what we have so far..."

(*Keller*)...I look up after there's a light knock on my door.

"Come in," I order.

Sub-Commander Esker walks in, "Kaight," I greet, "did you and Ephrryn put together a plan so quickly?"

Esker explains, "Yes, actually. Nothing much has changed, really. We're still on the get in and get out plan."

I stroke my chin, "Hmm... it just sounds too simple."

Esker makes the point, "Well, with so many unknowns there really just isn't much we can plan... Ephrryn brought up conducting a scout mission again."

I shake my head slowly, "No. I hate the idea of going in blind, but..." I pause for a bit. Inadvertently staring at Kaight.

She asks, "What is it?"

I shake my head, "I was just thinking, what if we make a final plea with the Prime Minister?"

"How do you mean?" she asks.

"I mean," I begin, "if we talk to her office directly. And we broadcast the conversation."

"You mean to trap her into saying something?" she clarifies.

I muse, "Well... not specifically. I promised if there was an alternate way we could go we'd take it. Since we have our plan ready, before we go, I want to plead with the Prime Minister. Give her the chance to right her wrongs in this and tell the truth about the Gerlak. We'll have the conversation transmitted on open net."

"We should also record it," Kaight suggests, "And then send the recording and copies of it with Trinn and the defecting crewmembers... is defector the right word?"

I clarify, "It's just a technical description. They're defecting from us back to the Republic. Otherwise, I agree... we'll broadcast it openly and have recordings made and disseminated. What's the status of the timers for the primers?"

She answers, "Ephrryn is looking into it and said he'd get back to me."

"Okay," I acknowledge, "When you check in with him, have Crewman Agsnon come to my office. I need to speak with him."

She nods. And then stands there quietly.

I ask, "Is there something else?"

"It's just," she begins, "I'm sorry to bring this up now, but... I really wish you had reconsidered last night..."

I sigh and explain, "It would have been nothing more than physical. Kaight, I still love Mattie. Even though she's gone, I always loved her. Even when we were no longer together I felt that we were.

"But at some point, don't you need to move on?" she asks.

I scoff, "Sure… but it takes a little longer than a week and a half. In another life, I wouldn't hesitate. But we live in this life. It wouldn't be fair to you to indulge myself. Even though we might not make it, I'm also going to prison after this mission if we do come out of it alive."

Kaight, noticeably disappointed, turns and leaves saying nothing more. I'm flattered. I really am. And I know how she feels being turned down. It would be convenient if feelings could be reconciled with logic. But that has never been the case. You can put feelings aside, but eventually you need to face them. And the emptiness I know I would feel after laying with Kaight would make my current feelings much worse. I'd feel more hallow and that's the last thing I need especially now.

My thoughts are interrupted by a rap on my door.

"Come in," I order.

The door opens and Crewman Agsnon walks in, "You asked for me, sir?"

I answer, "Yes, how are the timers coming along?"

He answers, "As best as I've been able to observe, we've almost got it figured out. But it's not really my area of expertise."

"Well I have an assignment that just might be," I say, "I want to contact the Office of the Prime Minister but I don't want our signal to be traced. I figured the best way to go about that would be the Free Net."

Agsnon hesitates a reply, "I mean… yes it would be easier to reject tracking protocols, but we also run the risk of our signal being intercepted."

I nod, "That's fine. I don't want a secure connection. In fact, I want it broadcast openly. I also intend to record the conversation. Oh, and I also need a video connection."

His eyes widen.

"I know, I'm asking the impossible," I acknowledge, "but if anyone on this ship can do it, it's you."

He slightly nods in agreement, "I mean I'll definitely see what I can do. In fact would it be fine for me to head over to the carrier? They might have a more powerful transmitter."

I nod, "Granted. Let me know when it's ready."

"Aye Commander," he says and leaves.

I slump down into my chair contemplating what to say to the Prime Minister. I'm false hoping myself into thinking she'll actually bend. But it's worth a try. It's never been a secret that I never liked Valyree Jackson. However, my personal feelings are irrelevant.

Noticing the time, I decide to head to the galley for some noon time grub. Standing in line, I notice how everyone is remaining mostly upbeat. Or maybe they're just putting on their happy faces in front of me. I banter small talk with my junior officers in the Officer's Mess. They seem ready to take on this mission, but also feel we'll all make it home.

Ephrryn walks in with a tray of food and says, "Oh, Commander, um... so we've got one of the timers ready, but I would like to conduct a test."

I raise a brow as he sits down, "how?"

He explains, "I would like to load a single nuke on a drop ship, take it out a few million kilometers, set the timer, unload it and then wait to see if it blows."

I nod, "Good idea. Get a crew together and we'll brief in my office when it's ready."

"Aye Commander," he acknowledges.

I get up and leave. A half hour later, Ephrryn does as I ask and we hammer out the specifics of our test. This also seems simple and straightforward. Perhaps an omen of our mission to come.

On the bridge forty-five minutes after the briefing, we all wait as the SLVRDO travels far out to a safe distance.

We hear over the COMM, "**Safe distance reached. Depressurizing bay.**" And then a few minutes later, "**bay depressurized. Starting timer for fifteen minutes... offloading package.**"

Ephrryn, standing next to my chair reassures, "They will have more than enough time to beat out the blast."

I clarify, "Beat out the blast or they'll be out of range before it goes off?"

"Oh, the last one, sir," he says.

I nod. We wait in quiet anticipation for a flash out in the distance. We watch the timer on our end as it seems to tick down slowly. Not sure what else we'll try if this doesn't work. Guess we'll deal with that when the time comes.

We watch the clock. Some of the crew start to sound off, "Ten... nine... eight..."

"Quiet, please!" I order.

The bridge falls silent. I look at the clock and after the last two seconds I look out the viewport. Nothing happens. I look back up and the timer reads zero... I look back out and ask, "Was there a sync-" I'm interrupted by a bright flash out in the distance.

Esker informs, "Everything detonated on time, sir. We just didn't see it right away due to the distance."

"Right of course," I acknowledge, "I'll be in my office."

As I start to descend the bridge Esker informs, "Commander, Crewman Agsnon is saying he has a transmission set up and ready for you. But needs to discuss the particulars."

I half smile. Then I turn around and head into the Crater. I speak with Agsnon as he explains it's an open frequency and that it may take some time for them to answer us if they even do at all.

I sit down in my chair and pull the monitor mounted above it down to eye level.

Esker informs, "You're broadcasting, Commander."

I begin, "Attention Prime Minister Jackson. This is Commander Keller of the Constellation Cutter Valkyrie. As you know, I am more or less responsible for the theft of the Nuclear Carrier Vidar. What I intend to use it for is simple: we have found the Gerlak home world and will be taking the carrier there and raining down hell upon them. You have not been truthful with us about who they are. We have seen them first hand. Keldon was not a misunderstanding, and they were responsible for the destruction of the free port Lantic Station.

"What we are doing is extreme, but you have forced our hands. Peace efforts with a hostile alien race should be something that we as a whole agree to and not something you arbitrarily decide and then force people to accept. We might not have rushed to going to this extreme if you hadn't rushed to suspending our freedoms. You are not above the law and in this instance you have put our personal freedoms below your agenda. You are in direct violation of the Oath of Service and that is why we must do this.

You will have two hours to respond before we carry out our mission. We'll be standing by on this frequency. If you don't contact us back, then we go to war ourselves."

I lift the monitor up and we sit and wait. I stay on the bridge. This is something I need to respond to immediately if she decides to reply, and part of me is really hoping she does.

The first hour goes by with no response. I'm getting less hopeful. I look over at the Crater to see Ephrryn conversing with the COMMs Crewmen.

He then looks up and says, "Commander... the Prime Minister is responding."

I nod replying, "Bring her on this frequency and begin recording."

I pull the monitor down and Prime Minister Jackson buzzes on screen.

She smugly greets, "Commander Keller... I don't think you and I have been acquainted."

I shake my head in agreement, "No, Madam Pri-Min we have not."

She gets right to it, "Well, I'll tell you right now, I do not negotiate with terrorists."

"Then why did you respond?" I sharply ask.

She says, "To extend the olive branch and give you the opportunity to surrender. Unconditionally. Your crimes are numerous, but you will bare them alone. Your crew will be forgiven, despite following your unlawful orders. I am aware you have control of Carrier Vidar, but I know you can't use the nuclear weapons without the launch codes."

"I beg your pardon, Madam Pri-Min, but we found a way to bypass your codes and activate the primers. We actually completed a test with them over an hour ago," I inform.

She scoffs, "You're bluffing."

I look over, "Prepare the Traverse Drive-"

"Wait," she cuts me off almost panicked, "are you seriously going to commit nuclear terrorism over vast misconceptions?"

"These are rather coincidental misconceptions, Madam Pri-Min," I reply, remaining as calm as I can, "I know you have seen some, if not all of the information of our exploits thus far. I know you have tried to eliminate us since we escaped the attack on Keldon- look, our actions can be prevented if you tell the people the truth."

"What truth is that?" she asks, "Rather what version of your truth do you think is being left out."

"Everything, Madam Pri-Min," I say, "the fact that the Gerlak are hostile. The fact that your office was engaging in secret mining contracts directly with Del Areeba Consortium. Tell people why they can't talk to their families on the other colonies. And more importantly, tell them the truth about the Three-War."

She scoffs smugly, "All this is speculation. Your so-called evidence is made up, Keller. As far as everyone is concerned, you're a terrorist and everything you say is meant to subvert the stability of the Republic. This is your last chance to surrender."

I smile and point out, "You were smart to not publically name me an enemy. You did the right thing by not acknowledging us in your grand speech the other day. But now you're getting desperate. As your plan crumbles, you're becoming unstable-"

"How dare you!" she interrupts, "Who do you think you are!? I am the Prime Minister of the United

Constellation Republic! I am your Chief Officer and I order you to surrender now!"

"No, Madam Pri-Min," I reply more sternly, "I hereby enact Directive Zulu Lima. Based on the evidence we have, your rule is in conflict with the Articles of Freedom and Governance and a provisional-"

She forces out a big laugh as if to discourage me, "And who is going to enforce it?"

I answer seriously, "Everyone who believes in the Oath of Service and the Articles of Freedom-"

She scoffs some more, "Oh Keller… if you only realized by now that the Oath is just words and the Articles a piece of paper. They have no real meaning or power especially for terrorists like you."

"If fighting for my life and the lives of my crew is terrorism," I say, "Then I guess I am. You have one last chance to tell the truth and then step down with dignity."

"Keller, surrender now. You are condemning your crew and forsaking the Republic," she grandstands, "I hereby relieve you of command and order your-"

"As you wish, Madam Pri-Min," I look over to Ephrryn and knife over my neck with my hand indicating for him to cut the transmission.

I ponder quietly for a few minutes.

Esker informs, "Sir, most of the defectors have come forward and have changed their minds."

"Center of the bridge, please," I order.

I raise my hand above my forehead, rendering a salute, "Sub-Commander Esker, I hereby relinquish command of Valkyrie to you."

She stutters, "I- uh, why?"

I explain, "I'm taking official command of Vidar. It's go time."

"Oh," she says, "Then, um, I assume Command. Did you want to go over the particulars first?"

"Yes, briefing room," I order.

I leave the bridge, possibly for the last time.

Chapter Twenty-Two: "An acceptable risk for now."

(*Nathan*)I can only wonder what's going through Keller's mind. I know mine is all over the place. It's a simple plan, but that doesn't mean we'll get a simple outcome, especially considering all I've been through already.

Keller wasn't too thrilled with me being assigned to the carrier crew. Oh well. I have spent the last few hours familiarizing myself with the ship. I have been assigned to the Two Deck nuke. I'll make sure the timer is ticking, when told, and then run back to the bridge. We'll separate the carrier decks, send them on their way, watch them explode and then tunnel out.

I sit, snacking on my ration pack, going over the plan in my head, reminding myself of what I need to do. This isn't exactly the last supper I had planned. Guess I'll have to survive and the promise of a good meal seems reason enough to do so. We rushed out rather quickly after Keller's chat with the Prime Minister. That went about as well as any of us could expect. I was really looking forward to that Prime Rib and lobster though. Meatball ration packs don't quite prepare a man to face his demise.

And that's the big question isn't it... will we make it. I think our chances are good. I think we've got the personnel and capability to pull this off. We'll make it. Just wish Keller felt the same.

Keller orders, "Alright everyone, gather up!"

The other twelve of us gather around him on the bridge.

He begins, "We're about twenty minutes from resurfacing. Before you go to your assigned bombs I just wanted to reiterate the importance of staying focused. The threat of death looms over us all the time. The only difference is when you can see it. Pay no attention to it. Just stay focused on what you are doing and we'll have a make-up last meal on the other side of this. It has been my honor serving with you all and it will be my honor to continue to do so. Get to your posts and wait for the order to start your timers."

We all nod and proceed to the elevators. The ride down to the second deck connector is quiet. There isn't much to be said among us. Especially since I don't know these guys.

We make our way to the middle of the hull. In case the Gerlak try to intercept, we hope this ship will hold long enough until detonation.

The tech crew member begins to configure the timer. He has the other crewman check his work, then both of them explain that it's hooked in. We wait listening only to the howling of the tunnel outside.

One of the Crewmen, Pran sounding a bit down asks, "Do you guys really think we'll make it?"

I take a breath, "Well… half the battle is believing we can. If you begin to doubt yourself and focus on death, you're more likely to get it."

He retorts, "Yes, but… even if you do everything in your power it doesn't mean you will survive."

I shake my head, "Nope… unfortunately. When Crewman Belkrest was killed I wasn't sure if I was going to make it either, but I knew giving up would ensure that. The fight isn't over until it's over."

Pran says, "I'm just trying to be rational."

The other Crewman, an electrical engineer named Blasso says, "There's nothing to rationalize, man. You can't rationalize death until it happens. Otherwise, you're just worrying about something that hasn't happened yet. Focus on living. That's what I do."

He nods.

A few seconds of silence pass and then I add, "It is much easier said than done."

Blasso agrees, "Oh absolutely. As the Commander pointed out, the threat is looming all the time. It just depends how much attention you care to pay it and sometimes the less you do the better."

Pran says, "I guess I just didn't see myself getting to this point. I mean I thought it would just be interior defense and saving lives, not all out warfare, being in the Armada."

I chuckle slightly, "I know how you feel. I started out in the Armada, then got kicked out. Then I was a miner and now... now I guess I'm a nuclear terrorist. Been an interesting month."

"Are we all terrorists?" Pran asks.

Blasso answers with a question, "Do you feel like a terrorist?"

Pran is quiet as he contemplates his answer.

I say, "I'm sorry, I should clarify, the Prime Minister has labeled us as terrorists. But I don't actually think we are. Does your Oath of Service mean anything to you?"

Pran nods.

Blasso adds, "I think a lot of us," he pauses taking a breath, "myself included, take that oath for granted. We never consider the fact that it may require us to go to extremes we shouldn't have to, but must."

Then we're interrupted by the COMM, "**Start your timers and get back up here.**"

Pran clicks the switch and the clock begins ticking. We head back to the lift and ride all the way back to the bridge. Keller confirms each deck is set to separate and proceed. It'll be a few minutes before we can plot coordinates. The navigation system has been loaded with the Gerlak info, but we still need to confirm by scanning the stars, once out of the tunnel. Then we can separate the decks and send them on their way.

After about five quietly tense minutes, the helmsman informs, "Ten seconds to resurface at Gerlath…"

We all eagerly look out the viewport, unsure of what to expect. We planned on resurfacing pretty close, so this could get interesting if we get caught in the planet's gravitational pull.

"Three… two… one…" the helmsman informs.

Valkyrie resurfaces ahead of us and then we gracefully come out of the tunnel. The planet is a greenish-blue color with no moons in orbit. Seeing this place fills me with a sense of anger as we prepare to enact some vengeance, finally. There appear to be light green clouds in the atmosphere, and from what I can tell, and remember from the holo image, one singular large continent surrounded by a body of liquid. For the moment there doesn't appear to be any defenses. The planet is alone. Innocent looking. It's hard to believe this is where the hostile Gerlak originate from.

Keller goes out over the COMM, "All ships, ahead full. We're preparing the decks for sepera-"

He stops, stunned momentarily with the rest of us, at the sight of a huge ship coming from behind the planet. It looks like one of the large vessels that attacked Keldon. No, it's probably much bigger. We haven't seen one like this. It's got to be over a thousand meters long with the smooth and jagged prongs on both the front and the back of it. In formation with it looks to be about three vessels, comparable in size to Valkyrie and Kara.

We hear over the COMM, "**Vidar, this is Valkyrie, looks like a Capital Ship fleet was waiting for us in orbit. This one is much larger than the one that attacked Keldon.**"

Before Keller can respond, we're hit with a large beam. A small chunk of the forward portion of the One Deck breaks off floating away in front of us.

Keller orders over the COMM, "We need to draw fire from at least two of the decks. We're going to separate Two and Three for now and use One as a missile against the Capital Ship. Valkyrie, you will help keep their fire drawn. Kara, escort the other two decks into the planet's atmosphere."

Everyone responds with their acknowledgement.

Then one of the helmsman reports, "Sir, One Deck isn't responding to separation commands. I'm attempting to figure out a work around."

Keller says, "Fine, we'll just steer it while remaining attached. If needs be, we'll set it on a collision course and escape on the drop ship."

Lede, assigned to Three Deck team, "What about the possible radio interference? I thought the point of the autopilot was so we could get them to their targets without any issues."

Keller explains, "An acceptable risk for now."

Crewman Pran, Blasso, and I walk over to the helm controls for the Two Deck. I must note, it's an interesting concept, controlling all three decks from a safe distance on one single bridge. Here's hoping we can maintain control the entire way through.

Pran asks, "Anyone know how to remote fly a carrier?"

I shrug, "Guess we'll figure it out."

I hop in the helm seat and begin searching the controls. I pull up the separation command and press the button.

A computer voice says, "**Two Deck separation initiated.**" And then a few seconds later, "**Three Deck separation initiated.**"

Keller orders, "Be aware of where you're flying and don't crash into each other."

"Aye Commander," I acknowledge.

Blasso discovers, "Looks like there are two modes for remote piloting: conventional radio transmission or what appears to be a line of sight dish."

Pran notices a display with the Command Module schematics, "That's what those must be on the top and bottom. We can send a signal directly to it possibly punching through interference."

One of the Navy crewmembers who accompanied the entire team for oversight confirms, "Yes! Are you guys figuring out your controls?"

"So far!" I answer, "Will the line of sight dish still work in the atmosphere?"

There's silence as he hesitates a response, "I, uh... I don't know. The purpose of the carrier is to fight in space."

"Guess we'll find out," I state.

I send a command to steer the ship in a direction towards the planet. After a few seconds it does.

We hear over the COMM, "**Fighters on the incoming!**"

Keller orders, "Launch fighters! Try to hold defensive patterns!" he then directs his attention to us,

"Power up whatever weapons this thing has. Free to engage."

The Navy Crewman informs, "Uh, just defensive batteries, but Aye Captain- er Commander, free to engage… also, I'm remote launching all fighters."

Keller asks, "What?"

The Navy Crewman informs, "There were at least forty-two fighters in total that are still in the decks. Obviously we didn't have any pilots to fly them and well… Navy Fighters are more complicated than CMROS. BUT I can activate them and fly them remotely. They won't be as effective in defensive auto mode as when I'm controlling a couple at time."

Keller asks, "Can any of the others here be of assistance in flying them?"

He shakes his head, "No. Even remote piloting is complicated."

"Very well," Keller accepts, annoyed.

Pran sits down in the seat next to me and locates the laser battery turret controls.

The lead helm of the command module informs, "Sir, it looks like some of the enemy fighters and one of their destroyer equivalent vessels is heading towards the other two decks."

Keller goes out on the COMM, "Kara, looks like you got one of their ships following. Can you draw them off?"

Dougland replies, **"We'll see what we can do."**

Keller looks over at the Navy Crewman, "Get all the fighters to protect the other two decks."

"I'd like to have at least ten take defensive posture around us," he replies.

"Acceptable," Keller says.

The bridge suddenly lights up bright orange and we shake violently for a second. We look around each other trying to figure out if we were hit directly or not.

Keller asks, "Were we hit or not?"

The Navy crewmember explains, "The armor is thicker on the Command Module. But I don't know how many more of those hits we can take."

Esker comes over the COMM, "**I saw where that weapon emanated from. I can move in to take it out.**"

Keller replies, "Negative! We're going to move above them. Stay out of that thing's sight."

I remind, "Even though that ship is much bigger, they have been shown to be more maneuverable even in space, sir."

Keller ponders a second, "Valkyrie, order your squadron with the Navy Fighters to take out their weapon."

"**Understood, Fleet Commander,**" they acknowledge, "**But I'm going to follow them. They have lots more fighter craft than we do and we've managed to use our defensive batteries to help take them out.**"

Keller says, "Alright… I trust you, acting Commander."

The Navy Crewman informs, "I'm going to take three of them and help out. I'll watch how the defensive squadrons are doing closely and switch over if needs be."

Keller nods in acknowledgement.

Locally at my console a computer voice says, "Impact sustained."

I fumble out, "Oh, uh… looks like I've been hit."

Blasso jumps on another console and manipulates a camera to see that sure enough the Gerlak ship has moved in range of my carrier deck.

Keller orders, "Kara, protect the carriers!"

In a panic we hear, "**The fighters are swarming us like flies on shit! We're trying to force them off, but it's not going so well. Our dorsal gun has been destroyed!**"

Keller considers his next play. Then he orders us, "Drop into the atmosphere now," then says into the COMM, "The decks are dropping into the atmosphere. Follow them. That might take care of the fighters for a few minutes."

"**Good idea,**" Dougland acknowledges.

Keller orders the Navy Crewman to pilot the ships protecting the carrier and to help out the Kara. He does as he's asked.

Focusing on what I'm doing, I point the ship in a way that will get it down quicker. Heat indicators start to go off meaning that we've hit the atmosphere. I pitch the deck up so it goes in on its keel. I watch the speedometer and apply the braking thruster every so often so that I don't end up in freefall.

Our ship shakes indicating we've been hit again. Out of the corner of my eye, I see another chunk floating away. Guess they targeted the deck again. Keller directs a response while I and my team remain focused on our task. Two Deck breaks atmosphere and arrives above a large body of liquid. I don't know for sure if it's water. Could be acid or something similar. Or maybe their water is just naturally green. Honestly, I don't give two shits. I'm ready to make these fuckers burn.

Kara reports, "**We're moving in closer to the Carrier Decks. Can they provide assistance with the fighters?**"

Keller looks over at us and we nod. He looks over at the Three Deck team and they nod.

The Navy Crewman says, "On it!"

He then says into the COMM, "Affirmative."

Blasso asks, "Are there other turret controls?"

"Check your sidebar," Pran suggests.

"Ah, got em," he says and from what I can see he starts shooting.

On my monitor I see a population center directly ahead.

"Target in sight!" I inform.

Keller looks at the clock. We have five minutes before we have to evacuate the module assuming we can't get the One Deck to separate.

The One Deck team informs, "Commander, we still can't get the One Deck to separate!"

"Noted," he acknowledges then orders, "Two and Three teams, I want you on the drop ship once your decks are in place."

"Aye, Commander," we acknowledge.

For a few moments, things seem to be going smoothly. Rather as smoothly as they can. I try to remain focused on flying my deck while Blasso and Pran try to take care of the fighters. Everyone else seems focused, but I can't look around long enough to be sure.

Blasso and Pran aggressively try to hold off fighters and give Kara as much support as possible. A squadron of fighters then breaks off from attacking Kara and begins to strafe the Two Deck.

I tell Blasso and Pran, "Guys, I need cover. I got fighters on me."

"I see them," Blasso acknowledges, "They're hitting my guns!"

"Mine too!" Pran adds.

Another group breaks off of Kara and begins to strafe along the side towards the engines.

Then my console informs, "Propulsion failure!"

I start to panic, "Uh… I'm losing engines!"

Keller goes out on the COMM, "Kara, Two Deck is losing engines! What's going on?"

"There's too many fighters!" They reply panicked, **"We're going to have to retreat!"**

Keller says, "Negative! Stay with the carriers!"

"I've already sustained too many hull breaches!" Dougland snaps, **"I told you we should have given my ship full armor!"**

Keller says, "There wasn't time or resources for all your plating!"

My console informs, "Hit sustained. Engine failure, altitude dropping."

"I'm going down!" I say, "Attempting to compensate with emergency thrusters."

Blasso informs, "Looks like the last hit came from-"

He's interrupted as we shake violently in the Command Module, taking another major hit from the capital ship. This time an even bigger chunk floats up and collides with the bridge testing the Navy Crewman's claim that the Command Module is in fact heavily armored. Thankfully his claim holds.

The Navy Crewman informs, "I'm now down to twelve fighters. Guess I just provided extra targets…"

Keller recomposes himself and then orders, "Dougland, I need you to make sure that Three Deck makes it to their destination. Otherwise we'll be mission failed. The future of the human race depends on the effectiveness of this strike."

There's no response for a minute then Dougland says, **"We'll make sure it gets there…"**

Blasso says, "Commander, recommend they take out the destroyer vessel! The last hit to Two Deck engines came from them!"

Keller nods then orders, "Kara, take out the destroyer vessel."

"**Gladly,**" he acknowledges.

We then hear over the COMM, "**This is Valkyrie, the large weapon has been taken out!**"

A few of us cheer. Finally a little good news.

I sit at my console and helplessly watch as Two Deck falls from the sky. The other two give as much help with the remaining laser batteries as they can but give up once we're out of range. The Carrier Deck hits the water. We're out of the fight.

Keller asks, "How much further to the population center?"

"Three minutes," the Three Deck helmsman says.

He looks back at the clocks. The One Deck timer reads zero and also displays, "disconnected"

Keller notes, "There's no way it's signal interference. One Crew, go check it, now!"

"Aye Commander," they acknowledge.

He then looks at us and orders, "Get to the drop ship. Three Crew and I will be right behind you."

We acknowledge his order and proceed to the ladder which leads us below and to the airlock. I sit in the main pilot seat and prepare the ship for takeoff. We can't see most of it since we're on the back side of the bridge superstructure. Some Gerlak fighters fly by pursued by Outfighters and are quickly shot and obliterated by defensive batteries.

We hear over the COMM, "**This is Valkyrie, one of the Destroyer type ships has been destroyed, but our enhanced armor is starting to fail.**"

Keller comes back, "**Valkyrie, fall back. I'm setting the carrier to ram the capital ship. The nuke will hopefully take care of them.**"

Blasso notes, "Five minutes until Two and Three decks detonate."

"Then we should be leaving now," I note.

Three Crew enters the drop ship, "Commander has ordered our departure. The Navy guy said they'll be able to get out on escape pods," Lede informs.

"Escape pods," I scoff, "Will they get clear in time?"

"Keller's orders were clear," Lede reiterates.

I sigh, "Very well."

I make sure the doors are locked and sealed then detach from the carrier. Lede activates the turret controls and we soon find ourselves in a dog fight. It seems like they have an endless supply of fighters. Lede starts to hit them and I try to make evasive maneuvers. A squadron of fighters comes to assist and gets the Gerlak off us. We then fall back towards Valkyrie which is moving away from the battle in a starboard broadside drift.

Blasso informs, "Detonation should be happening… now."

I look out the port side and sure enough there are two bright flashes followed by two big explosions. I cut the engines and turn the ship to face the explosions while still moving away. Even though ours didn't make it, knowing we helped get the third one to its destination is good enough. From all the way up here I could swear I could hear the screaming of Gerlak as they're vaporized into nothing. Short of their extinction, I don't think Dev will ever be properly avenged. But this this starts to put a smile-

Another explosion catches my eye. I look over and the carrier, or what's left of it has smashed into the Gerlak capital ship.

I scramble, grabbing the COMM unit, "Commander Keller! Tell me you got out on a pod! Keller-"

There's an even bigger explosion forcing us to look away. The One Deck nuke has been detonated... I... what... I don't know what to do...

Sitting in stunned silence we look at each other, trying to figure out what to do.

Then Valkyrie comes over the COMM, "**All ships, recall recall. All hangars are open, dock and prepare for immediate tunneling.**"

I shake my head and start to steer the ship. From what I can tell maybe about seven total fighters of the combined force of about thirty from Kara's compliment and the Navy fighters that joined us are returning.

Over the COMM we hear Sub-Commander Esker, "**Not to rush you, but we have detected more Gerlak ships. Kara, we need you to get up here so we can tunnel out!**"

There's no response right away.

Then in a somber tone, "**Our engines don't have the power to make breakaway speed. All our fighters have been destroyed. I have no choice but to inflict as much more damage as I can while I'm still flying. Get out of here, Valkyrie.**"

Esker replies, "**What about a propulsion blast?**"

Dougland replies, "**Even if we make breakaway speed, you would have to return. We downed their destroyer and are heading to another population center** where I'll empty my shells and then find an adequate target to crash into. Get your ship and crew to safety, Esker!"

Esker begins to say something, but my attention is on setting down safely. We land in the starboard hangar module. I power down the ship as the last of the fighters land. The doors begin to close and as soon as they secure I open the pilot airlock door and get out. There's hardly any ships here when compared to the vast space of the hangar.

Lede and I sort of wander aimlessly unsure of what to do. The ship begins shaking and I realize we've entered the tunnel. We made it. We live to see tomorrow. Unfortunately many others do not.

I don't remember much else except realizing that I'm staring at my slab of meat for evening chow wondering what I'm supposed to do with it. Most everyone else is rather quiet. The tone on the ship is rather somber, when we should be celebrating.

But what is there to celebrate? Keller is dead. Our Crewmates on Kara are also dead. And more immediately concerning is we don't know what awaits us on the other side.

Then Acting Commander Esker comes over the COMM, **"Good evening Valkyrie, this is ACTCOM Esker... I wanted to congratulate you all on a job very well done. Right now we are tunneling to the closest Republic Port where we will learn what happens next. I don't have any answers, but I want to reiterate that you all did very well and that we did what was necessary for the preservation of the human race. You all have done extremely well and should be commended. Rest Routine** is granted for the remainder of our journey and I am opening my door for any of you who need to talk.

Lieutenant Ephrryn has also been selected as my second in command. He will be in the Sub-Commander's Office also taking questions. Rest easy for now and have a good evening. You've earned it. That is all."

Everyone returns to their quiet murmuring and chewing. No cheers, no partying: no real celebration. Just this overcooked, synthetic steak.

Lede breaks my thoughts, "Why don't I feel like celebrating?"

Without looking at him, I shrug, "I don't know... is it possible the cost was too high?"

Lede responds with silence.

Pran and Blasso, who have also sat with us, provide no response either. We and pretty much the rest of the crew are just stuck looking around wondering what we're supposed to feel and what exactly is supposed to happen next.

I look up and see Donna and pretty much all the other Delta Crewmen entering the Crew's Mess. Each of them appear to be holding bottles. They all sit down at different tables. Donna predictably sits down at mine.

She asks, "Anyone thirsty for some real drinks?"

Everyone nods with mostly muttering yeses and we each finish whatever was in our drink cups. She pours each of them rather full. Without hesitation, I take two large gulps. The burning sensation alleviates the knot in my stomach for a few seconds.

Donna then says. "I know it's hard... losing Commander Keller, the Kara and all the other crew members who didn't make it. So here's to them," she finishes raising a glass.

I sort of half raise mine and then take two large gulps again.

She notices, "You seem pretty thirsty there Nate. Is this affecting you that much?"

I begin, "We keep telling ourselves that we did the right thing…"

I pause too long and she intercedes, "That's because we did-"

I interuptingly snap, "Then why doesn't it feel right!?"

Most everyone else nearby in the Crew's Mess turns their heads towards me.

I take another quick sip of courage and continue, "We should be celebrating, right? We're the big fuckin heroes who just saved humanity aren't we? Well why doesn't it feel that way? Why are we all quiet and sad? Is it because deep down maybe this mission really did push us too far? That maybe we should have sought a more peaceful solution in the end? I mean if we're doing the right thing, why do I feel like the bad guy?"

Donna stands up and very calmly yet sternly addresses, "Because what is right doesn't always feel like it's supposed to. We should be celebrating with the rest of our crew mates… but we're not. We're running away torn and tattered. And what's worse is it's not over for us. We're going to have to lick our wounds and then get back out on the battlefield.

If you aren't in the mood to be happy and sing drinking songs, that's fine. I get it. I've been here before. But we all saw what these bastards can do. They took something and someone away from each of us! And no, no amount of revenge will bring the ones we lost back, but it sure as hell helps.

We have plenty of alcohol for the return trip. Drink up and relax this evening if needs be. But don't think for a second that their sacrifices and ours will go in vain."

She's quiet for a seconds then continues, "You know, I've said something similar before and I'll say it again, each of you really has proven yourselves to be outstanding Guardians. The Armada doesn't deserve you-hell the Republic doesn't deserve you. I guess what I'm trying to say is that along with the crewmen we lost, I'm going to miss all of you as well."

Someone else shouts back, "We'll miss you too COMSARGE!"

She smiles, "That means a lot," she raises her glass again, "here's to our friends again."

As she sits back down I take my tray and my drink cup to the dish drop off and then head towards where my bunk is located.

About halfway down the passageway I hear Donna yell, "Nate! Hold on a second."

I turn and wait for her to catch up.

She approaches and asks, "What's really bothering you?"

I reply, "For once I was actually straight forward. I just... I feel empty inside. And I don't know what to do about it. I think sleep is the best answer for now."

She nods, "Look, I don't know what the immediate future holds, but as I said, I would like to try and remain in contact."

I answer, "We'll figure that out later."

She motions to try and hug me but I pull back.

She asks, "What?"

I explain, "You couldn't let me finish... You had to inject your perspective on things before I said my piece. Just like on Lantic when you had to make sure that Tim knew I was leaving. It's like if things don't fit into your world view, you gotta go out of your way to make them."

Donna is silent for a moment.

I finish, "Those people may be in agreement with you, and that's fine. In fact they could use the illusion right now. Me? It shattered years ago. This whole thing was a mistake."

"You're wrong, Nate," she retorts-

I snap, "See!? Here we go again with the Universe according to Donna!"

She raises her hands up and says, "I mean... yes. If you don't feel it was then that's what you need to deal with. If you want to go talk about it more then let's do so. Or you can speak with Esker. You really shouldn't bottle this up inside."

"I'll see you when I see you, COMSARGE," I say and I storm off. I guess I'll just head to bed. Part of me wants to drink myself into oblivion, but I don't like to consume alcohol when I'm angry. It became a negative coping mechanism during my discharge and I promised my mother I would never use it as a crutch like that again... but this circumstance is making it hard. Hence why racking out is the answer.

Chapter Twenty-Three: "How hard can it be to clear your name?"

(*Nathan*)We arrived back to the Republic to open arms and cheers. Celebrations were held in our honor as the realization of the Gerlak being a threatening evil force took hold of everyone. Prime Minister Jackson realized the major error she was making and resigned as well as every member of her staff. A provisional Prime Minister was selected to replace her for now and we are united like never before and marching our way into war. My record was wiped clean and I was allowed to reenlist in the Armada. And now we get to steam in a battlegroup to fight the Gerlak firsthand.

Yeah... that's what I wish was happening. Sitting in shackles outside the Mars Military House of Court main courtroom, I feel like I suspected this would be my fate. I feel like I was in denial the entire time and that I should have bailed when I had the chance.

Not only am I looking at prison if not death, but my service record was in fact reversed so that I could be reactivated and tried in Military Court. The last few months have only gotten more depressing especially for me since I have been stuck in limbo.

We arrived at outpost Berlinia after our nuclear strike on the Gerlak home world went horribly right, and soon after, the ship was taken into custody. Sub-Commander Esker was relieved, the entire crew imprisoned in their berthing or staterooms and the ship was staffed up with an armed guard security detail for our transit to Mars.

The Prime Minister demanded that we were all made examples of. She made sure that publicly we were labeled terrorists and would be treated as such. Terrorists don't have rights in the Republic, and what's worse is there are no provisions that protect anyone from being declared a terrorist. This became a hot button issue during the Three War when Jackson labeled all defecting factions as such to justify her use of full military force against them: the difference being that back then she wasn't as public with the term to make it appear as though she was negotiating peace. Regarding myself and the crew of the Valkyrie, she used the term so liberally, it started to lose its meaning.

They began with Sub-Commander Devlin and made us specifically watch the proceedings in our holding cells. He was handed down a sentence that is only humane by the technicality that he'll still be alive. For failing to stop Keller and relieve him of command, he was ordered to five hundred years in a brain vat. His brain will be disconnected from the rest of his body. With no eyes, ears or any senses he will sit in liquid on life support alone with his thoughts. I can only imagine what kind of hell that will be. The science says that after so many years the brain activity resorts to minimal to none, but they don't declare them dead. There's no way of knowing whether or not they actually die or if the conscious mind just collapses into a void in of itself and just awaits its release from the brain.

Whoever developed such a torture deserves to die a thousand such deaths. I never liked Devlin personally for obvious reasons, but I would never wish such a horrendous demise. In fact when I heard that was his sentence, the remorse for him was almost enough to move me to tears. In fact, I think as I lay in my cell one evening thinking about what that must be like, I did let a few out...

Sub-Commander Jackson, the chief medical officer almost met the same fate. He was accused of "failing to diagnose Keller insane", but managed to hold his line with evidence that Keller's mental state was fine. When the judge realized he wasn't going to get him on anything medically, he had to send his case to a lower court. He probably got the better deal, being demoted and then permanently assigned to a military prison hospital. He'll basically be on house arrest at his assignment for the foreseeable future.

Sub-Commander Esker was another hard one to watch. She wasn't demoted, at least not right away. The judge decreed that since her rank was granted by a terrorist it didn't count. So she was never recognized as being advanced. As such she was "tried" as a First Lieutenant thus allowing for a lower level of Court's Martial of which this judge also presided over. She was demoted to Sub-Crewman, the lowest rank in the Armada and sentenced to fifty years in solitary with no possibility of appeal. She tried so hard to fight back tears and keep her composure, but even I in her spot would have probably acted no differently.

Donna's new rank was also not recognized, but her counsel advised her to play the "dumb Marine just following orders" card. Under any other circumstances I might have lost respect for her taking a coward's way out in the hopes of a lighter sentence, but I honestly don't blame her and might consider doing the same. She was sentenced to eighty years in a work detail: location to be determined.

Lieutenant Ephrryn and the remaining Lieutenants were all demoted to Sub-Crewmen and sentenced to forty year work details. After fifteen years they will have the opportunity to prove themselves rehabilitated and possibly appeal or commute their sentences.

The Mk III, Delta and Superior Delta Crewmen were given a similar sentence except they only got thirty years instead of forty. And the remaining Crewmen Mk II and below were put on probation and forbidden from reenlisting in any branch ever again.

Then it comes down to me. The special case. There's been debate about whether or not I'm to be tried as a civilian or military. As a civilian I can't be handed a death sentence unless I can be proven to be a terrorist. At least as a Republic citizen I have that minor protection. But as a military service member, well… then I'm eligible. My past history of my espionage accusation has been a huge motivator in trying to push the maximum punishment through. I'm at the point where I just want to get this over with. I'm not afraid to die unless it's in a vat crushed by my own thoughts.

The guardsman walks up to me, "It's time."

I nod and stand up. I've been shackled from my wrists to my ankles; a restraint typically used for mastermind criminals, so it seems a little excessive… then again they have branded me as a nuclear terrorist.

The guards lead me into the room. I stare straight ahead as the audience of spectators seems mostly to glare at me, possibly in disgust. Thankfully they have to restrain themselves.

"Traitor!" One of them yells, but is quickly muffled and then escorted out, I assume. I stop next to my lawyer, an attorney whom I have been told has been hired by my father. He's a slender, older looking man with glasses. As far as lawyers go, he seems like the type who has a losing streak of cases.

"Mr. McNill," he greets extending a hand, "Tom Reginold, I'm the attorney your father hired to help represent you."

The guard jumps between us, "No shaking the hands of the prisoner!"

Tom cocks a brow and looks over at him, "Excuse me, am I to understand that my client has been proven guilty already?"

The guard snaps, "You know he is."

"Actually, I'm here to prove that he isn't," he says, "now unless you want a violation of rights suit against you, I suggest you change your attitude and respect my client's rights."

The guard glares at him in a failed attempt at intimidation. Maybe I have a shot after all.

Tom continues, "Why don't you make yourself useful and unshackle him?"

"The order is-" he begins, but is quickly interrupted.

"The order is wrong. Unless he's had a history that requires this, I suggest you unbind him now. You're making my case for full acquittal rather easy."

The Guard retorts, "He was accused of espionage-"

"Exactly, accused," Tom interrupts, "Not handed a verdict. On this alone I can make a motion for acquittal due to cruel and unusual treatment of the suspect."

The guard snarls, but does as he's told. I conventionally rub my wrists as though they were put on too tightly. And then shake Tom's hand.

We sit down and he begins, "This should be a formality. They're going to establish the proceedings then we'll be granted a day of recess at which point we can converse privately. Say nothing. I will handle the talking. I know it seems bleak considering what has happened to everyone else already, but you need to have hope if we're going to win."

I nod trying to give confidence. Then ask, "Why not just motion for acquittal? I've been living on prison rations and shackled like this since day one."

Tom sighs under his breath, "I'm afraid the likelihood of that working is very… slim. But the guard doesn't want to risk his job so I can leverage it to our advantage, but nothing more than that."

I face forward, irritated. More fuckin politics.

Ten quiet minutes pass by.

Another guard then says, "All rise for the honorable Judge Phanberg presiding."

We stand up and dressed in black robes that have been the traditional garments for centuries walks in an arrogant looking gentleman in his forties. Handpicked by the Prime Minister herself to pass down sentences on all of us so called traitors, Judge Tinnial Phanberg. His military service background? None. As I said before, we're here to be made examples of.

Phanberg begins, "Mr. McNill… you were put back into active service so you could be tried here. For the sake of the record let's go ahead and begin reading the litany of crimes you stand accused of."

"Objection," Tom states.

"What?" Phanberg asks directly stern.

Tom stands up, "I was briefed that this was going to be a formality hearing. The rules would be established for the proceedings and then a twenty-four hour recess for me to confer with my client."

"Well I'm sorry you were mistold." Phanberg brushes off, "Alright, Mr. McNill-"

Tom interrupts, "I'm sorry Your Honor, but it seems like you're jumping right into sentencing."

Phanberg nods, "Yes I am. Speak out of term again and I'll throw you out on contempt of court."

Tom, brazenly states, "No that would be very bad for you, judge. You see, public opinion is very divided on this issue and you are publicly trampling on my client's rights. Already he was brought in here shackled as though he had already been sentenced. Then the guard wouldn't allow me a proper greeting. I have a solid case already for suspect cruelty."

Fuming, the judge says, "This is not a civilian court! He is a member of the-"

Tom interrupts holding out his hand and pulling out a pad, "Actually your honor under the Code of Service, Nathan McNill cannot be legally reactivated except for time of war when the situation deems it necessary, but even then he's restricted to serving under planetary militia only and in a defensive civilian capacity." He hands the pad to the guard who hands it to the judge, "It's all laid out in his service record. So unless we proceed on civilian rules, I motion for complete acquittal."

The judge overlooks the pad for a second then sighs irritation, "Given these circumstances I am forced to deny Mr. McNill's so called "reactivation" and move for civilian court proceedings. A formal prosecutor will be established and present the evidence. The defense will be granted time to counter the prosecution's claims of the accused crimes."

Before the judge can bang his gavel, Tom adds, "I also request my client be given planetary autonomy. You know, to overlook the shackle thing."

Phanberg glares at Tom and then says, "Very well, Nate McNill will have planetary autonomy to move about

Mars, however any attempts to leave will result in immediate confinement and charges will be added." He finishes and bangs his gavel.

The guard gives us the "all rise" command and after he leaves Tom looks at me, "Let's get you into some appropriate clothing. We have too much to discuss and no time."

I ask, "How much is my father paying you?"

Tom says, "We have more important things. Let's go."

We leave through a special entrance to avoid media attention. Tom's vehicle is waiting for us, a self-driving sports car. Not super conspicuous, but I guess not so obvious.

He says, "I don't know what they have told you in there, but a lot of people are rooting for you. The Prime Minister has been wanting to give an appearance that she has public opinion on her side, but she does not. We might have a chance to get you out of this."

I acknowledge, "Okay, but how? The evidence against me is pretty cut and dry."

"It may be so," he says, "but this whole thing has been wrong from the get go. Unfortunately the Prime Minister does seem to have support from military commanders for now hence why she got her little show. You are an exception to that given your circumstance. But I need you to first tell me everything."

"What do you mean?" I clarify.

He explains, "I mean everything that led you to getting involved to now. I need your side of things before we discuss anything else."

I ponder a second then ask, "Do you have access to the UnderNet?"

"Would be a pretty shitty lawyer if I didn't," he says.

I say, "Good... cause that's probably the only place that can verify everything I am about to tell you."

Since he was familiar with my discharge, I was able to skip ahead to the Ex Del Seven and everything that happened on Keldon. For the remainder of the car ride and about an hour or two after getting to his dwelling, I recount my entire tale. After repeating everything, maybe I did make the right choice after all. Tom asked questions when he wanted clarification about things he knew and then got on the UnderNet to locate the Valkyrie files we had left behind.

I finish by saying, "And then we nuked them and that's why I'm now here."

Tom says, "Okay... so it seems the accusation is that you participated willingly. Is there any way you can convince them you were a prisoner aboard the Valkyrie?"

I become a tad irritated, "I'd rather not."

Tom points out, "Nate... their sentencing has been done. Tarnishing them or Keller will change nothing except your own fate."

I say, "I... I realize that, but still. Won't that tarnish public opinion?"

"Are you wanting a civil war?" he asks, "Because I thought nuking the Gerlak was supposed to prevent that."

I say, "Yes it was... and I'm glad more or less that it worked, but... fuck man... I went through so much and I know I'll never see them again, but..." my thoughts trail off and I try to think of what to do. "There's got to be a better way," I say.

Tom concedes, "There is... it might not get the results we want, though."

"Let's hear it anyway," I say.

Tom explains, "We could say that you were convinced that everything you were doing was right only to learn later that you were lied to. Influenced to do the wrong thing. That you didn't know any better until it was too late."

I shake my head, "That still tarnishes Keller's legacy."

Tom reiterates, "Keller is dead. And unless you want to be too, you're going to have to make some hard choices. I mean you came this far, how hard can it be to clear your name?"

I pause for a second then say, "My father must be paying you some damn good money for you to care this much."

"You and your father haven't spoken much have you?" he asks.

"No not since he cheated on my mother," I answer, "but I guess this isn't the time to get into that."

Tom shakes his head, "No. We need to form a defense. You could use this opportunity to spread the truth, but that would defeat the purpose of your original mission. The Republic is at least united against the Gerlak right now and that needs to stay that way. You guys were right, a civil war will annihilate us. We need to put the Gerlak at bay first."

I reluctantly nod.

He continues, "The public is rooting for you. That's why we need an acquittal. Otherwise we risk things plunging into a civil war."

"Seriously, what is your motivation here?" I ask.

He establishes, "Because I care about my livelihood and being annihilated by the Gerlak will interfere with that.

Yes, I do have my own interests at stake, not just your father's money which is actually at half my going rate. I have been following the conspiracy theories. As much as I'd rather turn this into a show trial to expose the truth and depose Jackson, we're going to have to forgo that for now and fight the system another day. I don't like it, but it's what's necessary."

I nod and then ask, "Okay... do you have anything to drink."

He shakes his head, "Not for you. If your case was one hundred percent locked in and you were going away to some hole in the universe, I would gladly afford you the opportunity to get sloshed. Probably even pay for an evening in the red light sector. But we have to build a defense and keep you a free man. Thus, we'll need your wit about you."

I sigh and then we begin discussing our plan. I reluctantly agree to testify that I was forced into the Valkyrie's rogue mission. Tom eventually convinced me that it would be a greater chance of full acquittal if I go that route instead of trying to sell out just Keller. I hate the idea of selling out the crew like this to save myself. One of them even became my friend. But their sentencing has been handed down. Nothing I can say will overturn any of that.

As the late hours draw near, Tom shows me to the guest quarters. Before turning in, he says he won't lock away his liquor, but emphasizes the need for me to remain sober. I lay in bed unsure of how to relax myself to sleep. At this point, being hungover might be comparable to sleep deprivation. But then again, no I must try and get some rest.

Of course, now every thought of what's happened continues to race through my mind and now I question whether or not I can hang my conscience and go into the courtroom an honorless scumbag out to save his own skin.

Yet that's how I was before all of this happened. Then the thing that changed that was losing Dev… Yeesh, did I really commit nuclear terrorism because of a woman? No. I did it because I reflected on my Oath of Service and did what I felt I had to… what we all felt we had to… I sure hope I don't get the vat. It seems when my thoughts are alone I get extra existential.

I turn over, thinking of the memory of Devorah. Even on the run from the Gerlak, things seemed to make more sense. I really wish she was here now. But even then she wouldn't be. She'd be on probation probably on some other planet. And I'd probably never see her again anyway. Well that thought is also depressing enough to induce tears…

…The smell of bacon and eggs has me popping out of bed. Finally some real food. I throw on some of the clothing Tom had set aside for me and walk back out into the kitchen.

"Oh good, you're up," he greets and asks, "how did you sleep?"

"Meh," I respond, "I could use a couple more hours."

He nods understandingly, "Unfortunately we don't have the time. We need to go over the process for today's proceedings."

He fixes up a plate and sets it down in front of me. Then he grabs a pad and eats his food directly from the dishes he used to cook it.

He then begins, "Alright so the prosecution is going to make their opening statement then I'll make your rebuttal. I don't anticipate them calling any witnesses aside from the statements given from the guards that you were in fact on board Valkyrie.

We'll then move on to you taking the stand at which point you tell them what?"

I then finish swallowing and answer, "That I was forced to work for the crew against my will. That Keller held a grudge against me for my espionage accusation and thought I should have been thrown in prison if I didn't help him, I would be treated like a prisoner aboard."

"What else?" he presses.

"Oh right, I had to work for my food and berthing." I answer.

He nods and continues, "You were treated like an outcast. Forced to go on dangerous missions you wanted no part of and the reason you didn't leave on Mars, pending that information even comes up, was because Keller had a kill order from his second in command who kept a close eye on you."

I nod, "Yeah that sounds about right..."

"I'm sorry, come again?" he asks.

I sigh briefly, "Yes that is correct."

"I can't emphasize enough the importance of making affirmative answers," he says, "if you give the prosecution ANY indication of doubt in your testimony they will tear into you until you either crack or they can get an inconsistency on record. If they can get your testimony thrown out, then that's it."

I nod understandingly. We rehearse my upcoming song and dance for the next two hours. Then he instructs me to get ready. It was hard to imagine that I could be taking my final shower, at least not surrounded by other prisoners. The ride over was more rehearsal until my testimony came off rock solid. Before exiting his car we go over everything one final time. Tom's emotions are harder to read when he's not performing on the courtroom floor, but I feel he has confidence in me.

We sit in the courtroom awaiting the judge. People are full of whispers, but are reminded many times they need to remain silent while in the room. The guard from yesterday gives the "all rise" and announces Judge Phanberg. He sits down followed by everyone else.

The judge begins, "Before official opening statements begin, defense, are you calling any additional witnesses besides the accused?"

Tom responds, "Not at this time, Your Honor."

"Prosecution, do you have any witnesses besides from the accused and witness statements confirming the accused was on the Cutter Valkyrie when she was taken into custody?"

"Uh, no Your Honor," the prosecutor says.

Phanberg says, "Defense, you have the floor."

Tom gets up and motions for me to do the same. The guard leads me to the witness stand.

He instructs, "Raise your right hand for the Oath of Testimony."

I do so.

He asks, "I, state your full name."

"I, Nathan Grol McNill," I say.

The guard continues, "Do solemnly swear that I will accurately and truthfully give an account of all events."

I repeat the phrase.

He continues, "So help me preferred deity of choice or lack thereof."

"So help me lack thereof," I say.

"Be seated," the guard instructs.

I sit. Tom approaches the stand.

He asks, "About when were you brought aboard the Constellation Cutter Valkyrie?"

I answer, "During the attack on Keldon Station."

"And how were you brought aboard?" he asks.

I answer, "Forcibly. I tried to retreat to the Mining Freighter Ex Del Seven of which I was a crew member, but I was forced aboard the Cutter."

"Describe how you were 'forced,'" he instructs.

I say, "It was more or less the heat of the moment. I think initially they were just trying to save me. It wasn't until they learned who I was…" I pause contemplating whether or not I want to do this. I continue, "It wasn't until they learned who I was that I became a servant on the ship."

"A servant?" Tom clarifies, "You mean like a slave?"

I answer, "I was forced to mine resources for the ship in order to earn my food and bed each day so yes I would say that it was forced labor."

Tom asks, "And did Commander Keller promise you any compensation in the form of currency?"

I'm quiet initially.

"Mr. McNill?" Tom prompts.

I begrudgingly respond, "No. He made very clear that I was lucky to be alive and that if I didn't want to sleep in space, I would work to help him repair his ship."

"So you were also a prisoner?" Tom asks.

I clarify, "Not exactly. I could move about the ship and wasn't under guard, but if I didn't do my duties, I would either be put into the brig or executed under… war terms."

Tom nods, "I see. And did he treat the crew with this kind of cruelty?"

I hesitate a moment then shake my head and answer, "No... just me. Cause of who I was."

Tom asks, "And when you heard about the nuclear strike what did you do?"

I shrug, "There was nothing I could do. It was either brig or airlock if I didn't go along with it. I looked for an opportunity, but it never came. And everyone on the crew..." oh man... I really don't want to say this.

Tom coaxes, "Everyone on the crew what?"

I sigh, "Everyone on the crew was... loyal to Keller to the end."

"Interesting," Tom notes, "so the crew was fine with how you were treated?"

I reply, taking a breath as I do and remembering my time on the Gondul for reference, "Honestly... no one cared. I was just some outcast. A scapegoat. I didn't belong and so I had no one. And no one was going to turn on Keller."

Tom nods and then turns and walks passed the prosecution table, "Your witness."

The persecutor gets up and walks towards me. He asks, "What were you doing on Mars?"

Oh shit. Well good thing Tom thought of this contingency, but here is where I break ranks. If I can, I'd rather keep Keller's son clear of all of this, yet for now I remain silent.

He presses, "One of the workers at the Del Areeba shipyard identified you having been there. Why were you there?"

I take a breath, "Keller wanted to exploit the fact that I was presumed dead on the Ex Del Seven to infiltrate Mars."

"Why?" The prosecutor asks directly.

I explain, "He believed Del Areeba had information to support his theory."

"And did you believe his theory?" the prosecutor presses.

I shrug my shoulders, "Honestly I was too focused on trying to survive through it all to have an opinion. Right now I feel like I'm just trading one prison for another. I don't care about any of the political ramifications. Never have." I just about lose my cool, "You wanna know what I believe? That I was wrongfully imprisoned on a ship I didn't want to be on in the first place. That I was caught up in some bullshit when all I wanted to do was mine rocks and get on with my life. I'm not some criminal mastermind who had this grand plan of sabotaging the Republic. I'm just a guy who was trying to make it in the universe like every other schlep and instead I got caught up in all this… stuff."

I take a breath and catch Tom staring intently at me. Guess I've gone too far down the rabbit hole.

The prosecutor says, "Okay… so you have no feelings towards Prime Minister Jackson or her administration one way or another?"

I shake my head, "I… will be truthful I don't care. I don't care about her. I don't care about what she's been trying to do, none of it matters to me. I've just been trying to get on with my life. I get that she's upset about Keller interfering with her peace effort, but I had nothing to do with that and I was completely powerless to stop it."

The Prosecutor then asks, "Okay then why didn't you try to escape when you were on Mars?"

I explain, "Keller had a kill order placed on me. Devlin was to kill me should I try to escape or contact anyone. In fact he kept me on a tight leash."

"So you never left his sight?" the Prosecutor specifies.

I shake my head, "No."

"Except when he was caught at Del Areeba Headquarters and you weren't there?" He asks.

"I, uh…" I struggle, "I was shuffled back on the freighter, it was early in the morning I don't remember much except being put on and Devlin wasn't here."

The prosecutor asks, "Okay and what ended up happening with the freighter?"

"They escaped," I inform.

"How?" he asks.

I answer, "I don't know. A few crewmembers defected and helped them escape. By that time I was already back in Valkyrie's custody."

"And you didn't try to escape with them?" he clarifies.

I answer, "No. No one from Valkyrie left. It was people who we captured from the Carrier and I think some from the Kara who chose not to be radicalized."

"But you weren't radicalized either?" the Prosecutor presses.

"No." I reaffirm, "I was a prisoner."

The prosecutor is quiet as he contemplates what to ask next.

The judge breaks the awkward silence, "Prosecution is there anything else you need from the witness?"

He looks over at him and shakes his head, "Nothing further, Your Honor."

"Mr. McNill, be seated," Phanberg orders.

I get up and sit back down in my seat.

The judge begins, "Well, then... it appears in light of this testimony I am forced to consider these new facts. Initially it was assumed because of your espionage accusation that you were obviously complicit in everything. However, it was not brought to my attention until yesterday that you were in fact never formally convicted. So not only does that mean I have to recognize your civilian rights, I need to consider the fact that you don't technically have a criminal history as well..."

The prosecutors, having exchanged mostly inaudible whispers stop and the one interrogating me speaks up, "Uh, Your Honor, we'd like to request another recess."

Phanberg asks, "For how long and what purpose?"

He explains, "To verify the claims and also I think it best your honor to consider the facts overnight so... twenty-two hours."

The Judge nods, "Very well. Twenty-Two hour recess, Mr. McNill's planetary autonomy remains in effect," he finishes banging his gavel.

Tom and I leave the same discreet way we arrived. We get into his car and he plugs in a destination.

After a few quiet moments he begins, "You did fine. You spoke a bit more than you should have, but... I think we'll be okay."

I ask, "What if they decide to call in one of the crew members?"

Tom raises a brow, "The Crew members loyal to Keller? That would be a matter of 'he said she said'. Unless they have recordings… it's a long shot for the prosecution. I also doubt any of them want to cooperate. Were you close with anyone on board?"

I ponder a moment, "Um… There was one girl… but she died at Lantic Station. My buddy Lede Kamerov and I were close, but other than him and the Marine, no. I wasn't close to anyone else."

"Good," Tom expresses, "I highly doubt that they'll get those two to cooperate and even if they do, again it's your word against theirs. Without documented proof or audio or video evidence… no at this point you're pretty much free and clear."

"I hope you're right…" I sigh.

I watch the passing lights as the car drives us along to our destination. I don't feel good about any of this. I feel like I betrayed the only friends I had left in the universe, but I guess there is no helping them now either way. Tomorrow I should get my verdict and sentencing. I'm actually relieved it will be over quicker instead of drawing it out into a full civilian proceeding which would have meant a jury, more downtime and yeah- the civilian proceeding under military tribunal may have worked in my favor after all.

The car stops and I look up and notice we're not at Tom's home.

He says, "I don't think there is much more to be done so as far as I'm concerned, you've earned this."

He starts to get out and as I do I realize he's taken us to a bar. It doesn't look like much, a nice hole in the wall type of place. We walk in and sure enough it's quiet and dark with a couple people who look like they pretty much live here if they're not at work or wherever they sleep.

We sit down at a table at the end of the establishment in a dark corner. He pulls out a menu and hands it to me and takes one for himself.

He states, "This is a nice out of the way place I like to come to from time to time. They mostly do fried food, but I think it's best we keep you on the down low."

I nod, "I agree... plus poppers sound delicious anyway."

"Indeed they are," Tom informs.

The bartender walks up to us, a woman in her early to mid-thirties. For a second I'm reminded of Donna, but this person looks like she's only been in the bar business and not in the battlefield. I order a local brew, and when it hits my lips the sensation is... refreshing. In a way I feel a weight lifted as the beer courses into my stomach and the alcohol into my veins.

The poppers are about what I expected, but still preferred to the prison rations. I guess when Tom said they are delicious he meant for fried food. It seems the food on the Valkyrie was better than I realized.

I start my second round of beer and then ask Tom, "So... you think this is it?"

He nods, "I am very confident that their last kangaroo bounced before your trial. This has been dragged out longer than it should have."

I ask, "How many military proceedings have you participated in?"

He responds, "This was only my fourth. I'm mainly a civilian lawyer."

"How did my dad find you?" I ask.

He takes a breath and ponders his response. He looks at me intently, "Your father was specific about us not talking about him. When you're acquitted, he wants me to contact him and has asked that I mediate a conversation between you two."

I nod slowly and exaggeratingly as if I figured it all out, "So he found a way to twist my arm into feeling obligated into speaking to him."

Tom sighs, "Look, you're a grown ass adult so once you get your freedom you can do as you please. I understand if your father is a sore subject and I'm not going to force you to do anything. Just consider everything before you decide."

I don't want to think about this. On the eve of my acquittal my father has to somehow inject himself into my thoughts. Guess it's time to drink him away.

Chapter Twenty-Four: "We've made it this far. We'll keep going."

(*Nathan*)I wake up with a bit more of a headache than I would prefer. I guess that's to be expected. It has been a couple of months since my last binge. I slug out of bed, shower and put on the suit that Tom had fitted for me.

We don't say much on the ride over. Hopefully we get this over with soon. I start to realize I have a lot to figure out. What I'm going to do with my life. Who I'm gonna work for- hell how am I supposed to get ahold of Tim? I'll probably have to talk things out with my father... as much as I'd rather not, he does have the means to help me get back on track.

We head into the courtroom for the final time through the same entrance. We get settled in our seat and wait almost thirty minutes. The prosecution shuffles in and gets seated and five minutes later Phanberg enters. We reseat and things are rather quiet. I notice one of the prosecutors nod and Phanberg nod back.

Phanberg looks over at us and asks, "Does the defense have any further statements to make?"

Tom stands up and says, "No, Your Honor. We'd like to motion for full acquittal based on my client's testimony yesterday which has not been disputed."

The prosecutor stands, "Your Honor, we do have disputed testimony we'd like to submit for review."

Tom asks, "What is the source?"

The prosecutor says, "Some of the Valkyrie crew members have come forward claiming that Mr. McNill's statements were blatantly false."

Tom clarifies, "The crew members who were loyal to Keller? That sounds like an obvious conflict of interest.

Not to mention, without video evidence it's their word against his."

The prosecutor is silent for a second, "Um... well..."

The judge sighs and asks, "Does the prosecution have video or audio evidence supporting these witness accounts?"

"Not at this time," the prosecutor says, "but we do have two witnesses not involved with the terrorist nuclear strike to bring forth who will shed new light pertaining to Mr. McNill's service record and intentions."

Taken off guard, my stomach knots.

The Judge responds almost as if he knew what the persecutor was about to say, "Oh? And this would affect my decision on acquittal?"

"Very much, Your Honor," the prosecutor says, "We would like to motion for this evidence to be presented in the form of testimony by both Superior Delta Crewman Justin Wernival and Delta Crewman Dashun Fenz."

"Objection," Tom states in an almost panic, "The court already decided to proceed with civilian proceedings and this is testimony from people not involved in the incident."

"Overruled, counselor," the Judge almost smirks, "that decision to try on civilian rules was made before this new evidence was rendered available to the court. As Judge, I have a duty to hear and consider it. You will have the opportunity to cross examine. Prosecutor, bring forth your first witness."

I look over my shoulder and through the doors comes one of the men responsible for ruining my life in the first place. He doesn't look at me. He keeps a stern face as he struts in full dress uniform at his "towering" five foot, eleven inches. He approaches the stand, takes the Oath of Testimony and sits down. He glances over at me momentarily and then focuses at the prosecutor.

The prosecutor begins, "Superior Wernival you served with Nathan McNill aboard the Gondul correct?"

He nods, "Yes that is correct."

"And you were there for his accusation of committing espionage?" he clarifies.

Tom interrupts, "Objection, where is this going? What is the relevance?"

Phanberg, irritated, "Well if you gave the man a chance to speak. Overruled."

The prosecutor says, "Alright the defense has a point, you served with then Crewman McNill when he was accused of espionage. That accusation never saw a Court's Martial and he was discharged with no benefits and no ability to reenlist. Can you walk us through real quick what brought about that accusation in the first place?"

"At that time," he begins, "Nate was thought to have been sending sensitive info to an informant of a pirate faction we were trying to capture in the act of smuggling resources." He takes a breath, "What had actually happened was one of my other crew members was sleeping with that informant on our port calls and inadvertently sharing sensitive information."

The courtroom gasps. I fucking knew it. I knew he was covering for someone, but why now is he telling the truth?

The prosecutor asks, "And why then did you make false statements and pin the blame on Crewman McNill?"

Wernival takes a breath and answers, "Well… at that time I was the shop supervisor and had a very difficult decision to make. You see, Crewman Fenz was above the cut to advance to Delta Crewman. This would have been a beneficial pay increase to his family for his wife and kids... but more importantly... his wife is the daughter of Admiral Yelkin and an espionage charge against the son in law of an Admiral would have been very bad pee arr and brought unnecessary hardship and discredit against the Armada... so I formed a cover for Fenz and had to pick a fall guy."

The prosecutor asks, "Why did you initially pick Mr. McNill?"

He confesses, "Because he was young. He could take a hit like that and come out of it the other side with the rest of his life to find a new career. Delta Fenz had served over ten years and was halfway to retirement and as I said the public embarrassment... it just wasn't worth it. Fenz and I have had to bear the guilt all these years... I don't think I've slept well since." He finishes, clearly lying about his sentiment.

The prosecutor confirms, "And you made this decision on your own?"

"I... um," he fumbles indicating he's not being completely truthful, "Fenz came to me directly and confessed the affair. He then, uh, begged me for my help and expressed how uh, sorry he was, but emphasized that we needed to do something. So I, um... that is when I made the call to pin blame on McNill."

It is taking everything in my power to not snap. I am visibly fuming at this revelation, but am confused as to why he's confessing. What is the play here?

The prosecutor finally asks my question, "And why are you coming forward with this?"

"Well... um..." he begins fumbling his words, "It's just, I've been watching this whole proceeding and when I saw that McNill was getting a civilian trial whereas, uh, everyone else involved in the nuclear strike was tried in military proceedings, I knew that, uh, the, uh, truth needed to come out so that, um, proper justice and sentencing could be, uh, rendered."

Un. Fucking. Real. I sit shocked, unsure what I'm supposed to feel. He seriously went out of his way just to make sure I get punished.

The prosecutor asks, "Did you see Mr. McNill's testimony?"

Wernival nods, "Yes I did."

The prosecutor asks, "And what can you tell us about Mr. McNill when you served with him?"

He replies, "He loved the Armada. He was very ambitious to succeed in his career. But when the initial accusation took place I could tell he felt betrayed."

I lose containment and snap, "Felt betrayed? You mother fucker, I was betrayed! By you!"

Phanberg doesn't hesitate to bang his gavel and shout, "Another outburst like that and you and your counsel will be thrown out of this courtroom along with yesterday's testimony! Am I understood?"

I mostly mutter, "Yes, Your Honor."

The prosecutor prompts, "You were saying, Delta Wernival?"

Wernival continues, "As I had mentioned, Nate was quite passionate about the Armada and felt he was wronged. It is my firm belief that if… he were in a position to do so he would not hesitate to take vengeance and so I am absolutely certain he was in fact radicalized by Keller."

"Objection, supposition," Tom says.

Phanberg rolls his eyes, "Overruled."

"No further questions," the prosecutor says, "your witness, defense."

Tom clears his throat then approaches, sizing up Wernival as he closes in. He then asks, "Why is McNill's punishment so important to you?"

Wernival answers, "I took an oath to protect the Republic."

Tom presses, "Okay? But why are you going out of your way to do this? What is your motive?"

Irritated he responds, "I just told you I took an oath to protect the Republic."

"But what does that mean to you?" Tom asks.

The prosecutor says, "Objection, irrelevant."

"Sustained," Phanberg says.

Tom begins, "Your Honor, I must appeal here. The relevancy being that motive needs to be established in order to determine legitimacy of testimony."

Phanberg scoffs, "Legitimacy of testimony?"

"Yes, Your Honor," Tom explains, "I'm trying to determine if justice is his intention or if he's holding a personal grudge and taking advantage of the justice system to fulfill it."

Wernival asks, "Your Honor, may I speak?"

Phanberg nods.

"Counselor, I am insulted," Wernival begins, "Insulted at the very notion. I am a patriot doing my duty. If that is not good enough for you, I don't know what else you expect me to say, but to insinuate that I would do such a thing, hell if it was my courtroom I'd have you thrown out for acting dishonorably."

Tom looks over at him and slow claps condescendingly, "Well done… but if you knew anything you would know you can't be evicted for something so ridiculous. What are you hiding?"

Wernival reiterates, "I told you I am doing my patriotic duty."

"That is an ambiguous statement," Tom says, "Who are you now covering for?"

The prosecutor stands up, "Objection. Your Honor the witness is not on trial and the defense is way out of line."

Phanberg says, "Defense, unless you can come up with relevance in your next question, I'm gonna have to ask the witness to stand down."

"So is this what it's come to?" Tom begins, "I can't properly cross examine and do my job to defend my client-"

Phanberg bangs his gavel, "That's enough defense. Delta Wernival, you are released."

Tom sits down, taking a major sigh as he does so. This "trial" is a fuckin joke. I mostly zone out as Fenz testifies via video transmission, repeating pretty much everything that Wernival claimed and playing up the fact that he supposedly felt bad about it. Bullshit. These two carried on just fine after the fact. Fenz fucked up literally and to hide the embarrassment from his wife Wernival went to bat for him. They could have easily kept everything behind closed doors, but because I was more or less an outcast, because I was not in their little club, they ruined my life to save his mistake.

Fenz catches my full attention when he says, "I've lived with this lie for too long and should have been truthful from the start. As such I am resigning my position… and reluctantly will submit myself to a Court's Martial for my actions."

The prosecutor finishes, "Thank you for your testimony, Delta Fenz. Your Honor, it appears that Mr.

McNill's discharge was wrongful and as such his service status should be reconsidered."

The judge nods, "Indeed. This sheds new light on the situation altogether."

Tom looks at me, but I continue to stare ahead blankly. I thought for sure I was free and clear of my past yet here it came back to kill me. There's more to Wernival's statements, but Tom already tried to find answers. He shakes his head when asked to cross examine Fenz knowing full well it would be a waste.

The Judge states, "Well Mr. McNill considering this change in circumstance I'm going to reverse my decision to try on civilian rules and proceed to sentencing."

Tom stands up, "Your Honor, I must insist that Mr. McNill be given final opportunity to make one last statement."

"Fine," Phanberg says.

I get up for whatever reason and return to the witness stand. I take the Oath of Testimony yet again.

Tom begins, "Mr. McNill, I need you to answer truthfully. Did you love serving in the Armada before your discharge?"

I take a second to consider my response. Then I say, "Yes... at that time I did."

"And did you feel betrayed with everything that had happened?" Tom asks.

"I did," I answer, "however... the Armada wasn't the end all be all... I knew a week or so after the fact that I could move on with my life and I did."

Tom clarifies, "You became a miner."

"Yes," I answer.

"Okay," Tom says, "We're gonna go over this one last time. Regarding your time on the Valkyrie, were you paid or promised compensation for your services aboard?"

I answer, "No."

Tom says, "Very well. Your Honor, if you'll note that semantics aside, my client was never compensated for his work aboard ship, thus rendering him a forced labor servant regardless of whether or not his service is reinstated. I would also like to point out that if he is reinstated, he will be required to receive back pay."

"Noted," Phanberg says irritated, "Does the prosecution have any questions?"

The prosecutor shakes his head, "No, Your Honor."

The Judge says, "You may be seated Mr. McNill."

I leave walking over to my seat and slumping into it.

The judge takes a breath, "Your testimony from yesterday compels me to consider a lighter sentence. But full acquittal is definitely off the table. You took the Oath of Service and in my view, whether on Active Duty or not, you failed to uphold your Oath by making no effort to stop the nuclear strike. Your defense attorney is correct, however that to reinstate you will mean proper compensation. But the problem is that means the same, acting in a civilian capacity… two hour recess. Remain present." he finishes banging his gavel.

Tom takes a huge sigh and then looks over at me. He says, "That outburst did not help anything."

"I know I just…" I try to formulate thoughts. But what is there to think about. I have said all I can and I can only hope it will pay off. But now that I can be tried as Active. Well… the longest two hours off my life passes with catching whispers of people in attendance. Fuck, I could use more alcohol. Hell at this point I wish I had some for breakfast. Then again that could have made my reaction to Wernival's confession all that much worse.

Phanberg returns about ten minutes later than he had stated. He gets seated and then begins, "This has certainly been an unprecedented proceeding all around. It certainly leaves me with a decision to make that could impact future proceedings and whether or not justice remains the strong arm that has kept the Republic intact.

I reconsidered full acquittal... but that just isn't an option at all. Whether or not we know the level of your participation in the nuclear terrorism, at the end of the day you didn't stop any of it nor make any effort to do so. I'm aware of the implication that it could have cost you your life, had you resisted and would have made no difference, but still... you did nothing. So, you don't get off easy. Death would be extreme, however, so I have considered a sentence that is fair. Rise for sentencing."

Tom and I do as the judge instructs.

"Nathan McNill, I hereby sentence you to thirty years on work detail with the opportunity to appeal at fifteen years served, depending on your conduct. Sentence to be rendered immediately. Guards take the prisoner into custody and have him transferred immediately." He finishes banging his gavel and gets up and leaves.

Tom begins, "I'm going to file an appeal. This isn't over. Your capacity was similar to the junior crewmen and they all got off with probation..."

I lose focus on what he's saying and as I start to be cuffed with my arms behind my back, it certainly has a feeling of finality. I guess I'm happy I won't rot in a brain vat, but then again, I was looking forward to getting on with my life.

I get taken through the press lines with reporters futilely shouting questions as if I have time to even think about what they want to know. Whatever, it's not like it's going to change anything at this point.

I'm taken swiftly to a processing facility where I'm stripped bare in front of everyone, given a physical examination, and then forced to wear a light gray standard issue prison jumpsuit. I give them retina scans and fingerprints. I'm shackled back up and taken to a transport vessel. Without windows, I have no idea where I'm going.

This seems almost as bad as a brain vat. A low-lit cargo vessel with scratches and damaged seats. Seems others couldn't keep calm during the ride. I, myself, am not so much remaining calm as just sitting, knowing that if I do try to damage anything it'll just make my situation all the worse. A peep hole opens and one of the guards looks at me. I glance over for a second then just look forward and stare some more. I'm actually kind of grateful they're leaving me alone. I have nothing more to say. I can only go over in my mind everything that has happened.

We shake for a second then the back door opens out into a large room, after four hours of transit. It's filled with other prisoners standing around aimlessly.

The guard orders from the peep slide, "Come on over."

I get up and he un-shackles me from the safety behind his door. Then he orders, "Out."

I recognize one of the Valkyrie Crewmen who says, "Didn't realize we treated you so badly."

I realize everyone here is from the Valkyrie and they promptly start to shun me.

"Nate..." a familiar voice says. I turn and, unbelievably, it's Donna.

"What are you doing here!?" I ask.

She explains, "As best I can tell, they've separated the crew into various work assignments. But I'm unfamiliar with these types of work details."

"Have you figured out who all is here?" I ask.

She shakes her head, "It looks like they have randomized everyone, Officers and Crewman. There doesn't seem to be a specific grouping. We were all in a holding facility until your trial concluded."

I nod, "I take it you saw my testimony?"

She nods slowly, "We all did... I take it your lawyer told you to sell everyone out?"

I sigh and nod, "I didn't want to, but the goal was full acquittal. Instead I get sentenced to a work detail with everyone I've alienated."

Donna says, "In time, they'll get over it."

A loud buzzer sound goes off for four seconds, grabbing everyone's attention.

Then a voice comes over the PA, "**Welcome disgraced crewmembers of the Constellation Cutter Valkyrie. I am your warden. You have all been assigned to work details and will be bunched up with other prisoners who have been moved in with you aboard Prison Barge Seven Five Zero.**

"**Every morning the guards will come aboard, wake you up and escort you to your work assignment. You will be mining and processing resources for the Republic. By hand.**

"**Escape is impossible. The barge is pushed by two tugs that can detach at any time a serious threat exists. Even if you find a way out, you will only find open space. We will be tunneling to our first work assignment. I suggest you find a cell and a place to sleep**

as we will be working right away upon arrival. Speak to you then."

A large door opens up and we all file into a larger open area where the other prisoners, not from Valkyrie, start to gather in. There's a wide range of them, probably pirates or murderers or who knows. Either way I don't expect to last long. Maybe the brain vat was a preferred fate. At least I could day dream in peace.

We walk into the center slowly. I stay close to Donna who tries to stay with the other Valkyrie Crew members, but they seem to be banding together and away from us. I see some of the other prisoners starting to group up as we try to make our way towards the cell blocks. Everyone is sizing each other up and I'm just trying to remain alert to see who throws the first punch.

"I don't understand," I say, "why put us all in together? Why not keep us separated and in our own groups?"

Donna theorizes, "I think… I think this is how they intend to silence us permanently. If they kept us all on the same work detail we would be able to band together. This will not only keep us disorganized, these guys might try to kill us."

"Which leaves less witnesses," another woman speaks up.

I turn around to see, "Captain Wrennor!? But… how!?"

She gives a discouraged nod and explains, "My bridge module sealed and left us adrift. We were recovered within a few hours and thrown in the brig. I explained why I did what I did and refused to go along with their preferred narrative of Keller somehow taking out our fleet. Our 'trial' was closed-door and went faster than any other I had seen."

"Ma'am," Donna greets, "Ours was about the same, except we were all made public examples of.. I'm surprised they didn't have you executed."

Wrennor shrugs, "I suppose it would have drawn too much attention to have a Destroyer Captain and her crew executed, considering we all have families. Instead they just threw us into the work detail. These guys haven't seemed as interested in me or my other crew members. They've definitely established their hierarchy, but I can tell you that as Armada personnel, these people will most likely be out for blood."

"That's why they've grouped us all together," Donna speculates, "If we're killed by other prisoners it'll look less suspicious."

We look over and notice the other Valkyrie Crewmembers have distanced themselves from us.

Wrennor asks, "Did you guys say something to offend them?"

Donna explains, "I mean him more than me."

Wrennor says, "I see. Well you can stay with us, then. We've got some cell blocks. But I just want to know one thing: was it worth it?"

"Yes," Donna answers.

I look at Wrennor and slowly shake my head, "I don't agree. The Republic hasn't committed to all-out war. Just minor skirmishes on the border systems."

Wrennor lowers her head.

Donna objects, "Just because all-out war hasn't occurred yet doesn't mean it won't happen. Most of the people, from what I can tell, are seeing the Gerlak for what they are. I can assure you, ma'am, it was worth it."

I'm not gonna debate this right now. I've got bigger problems, like figuring out how I'm going to survive prison. Wrennor and two of her former crew members lead us to the cell block they have more or less claimed. Along the way I look intently at the prisoners. They mostly seem to have left us alone since we grouped up with the disgraced Navy personnel, which means their focus is going to be the other Valkyrie crew members, most of whom are older and probably won't last long. Hell, I doubt I'll last long.

We round the corner into the cell that Wrennor and her people have annexed.

"It's not much, but it's ours," she says.

We look around at the dark, dirty cell. "There's no beds," I note.

Wrennor explains, "Only about half of the cells have them and they're all claimed."

"So we sleep on the floor?" I confirm.

Wrennor explains, "We make do with what bedding we have. Most of the time everyone is exhausted from mining operations so we don't often get harassed. Meals are twice a day and probably the only thing here that's orderly, along with work. Otherwise during non-working hours we're pretty much on our own..."

Her voice trails off as she continues explaining and I begin to contemplate everything that has occurred to bring me here. What would have happened if I hadn't gotten discharged? Where would I be in all this mess? I begin to sit down in the corner of the cell. Wrennor stops talking and I think she asks if I'm okay. Donna walks up to me and kneels down. She doesn't say anything as I stare blankly ahead trying not to lose my composure. I know I initially feared the vat, but now I am fearing for my life. I want to lay down and sleep this nightmare away, but I can't.

Donna looks over at me, "Hey. We'll get through this, Nate. We've made it this far. We'll keep going."

I take a deep breath, "You, at least are still friends with the crew. I've got no one."

"You've got me, and the Navy guys," Donna says.

I close my eyes. I try to rationalize why I am here, but I can't. Having to face my dad sounds like a better fate than where I am now. I just... I can't do this. I don't want to be here!

"Nate..." Donna whispers, "I won't lie, this is going to be hard. Harder than anything you've been through. Harder than everything I have been through."

"It isn't fair!" I reply harshly soft.

She shakes her head, "No. It isn't. And it's not going to be any time soon. But if you want to get even, then you first need to survive this."

I nod slowly. She's right. If I die here then, Wernival, Phanberg, Fenz... they all win. And Dev, she dies for nothing. I know I can do this. I just don't want to. One day at a time. I will survive. And I will get even.

THAT IS ALL